THE DRAGON OF GOD

PRAISE FOR *The Dragon of God*

"Your next find—a book you will push onto family and friends, one that captures a profound idea about the world that you want to share."

—CHUCK MCFADDEN, veteran AP writer and author of *Trailblazer: A Biography of Jerry Brown*

"Suspenseful, clever, witty dialogue, even romance, are woven into a thoughtful discourse on religion and terrorism. American thoroughbred writing with John Grisham, Robin Cook, Dan Brown–style pacing."

—JERRY KONG, IT application integration consultant

"This story hits a home run with me. An impactfully convincing work that, with sensitivity and balance, answers all those suppressed questions everyone has about religion and the plausibility problems of the Bible."

—DAVID FLOWER, pharmacist

"This is a brilliant idea, to bring readers through a serious theological discussion as the protagonists seek both the resolution to a murder and the outcome of an unlikely romantic interest."

—HARWOOD HOOVER JR., PhD, professor emeritus at Aquinas College

"This may jolt skeptics and believers alike. It's a mystery, a personal search, and a romance. Get ready!"

—JO MELE, former director of the Emeritus College at Diablo Valley College

THE DRAGON OF GOD

---

a novel

Earl Thor

Gray Owl Press
Pleasant Hill, CA

Gray Owl Press
Pleasant Hill, CA 94523

Library of Congress Cataloging-in-Publication Data
Name: Thor, Earl
Title: The dragon of god / Earl Thor
Description: Pleasant Hill, CA : Gray Owl Press, 2019. | Includes bibliographical references.
Identifiers: LCCN 2018960989 | ISBN: 9781732892606
Subjects: LCSH: Faith and reason—Christianity. | Heaven—Christianity. | Thought and thinking—Religious aspects—Christianity | Religion and science. | Near-death experiences—Religious aspects—Christianity. | Reincarnation—Christianity. | Fundamentalism—United States.

ISBN: 978-1-7328926-0-6
eISBN: 978-1-7328926-1-3

Printed in the United States of America

10 9 8 7 6 5 4 3 2 1

FOR MY WIFE,

OUR SON AND DAUGHTER,

AND OUR GRANDSONS

LIST OF CHARACTERS
(in order of appearance)

Oscar Johnson, Victoria's father
Bill Miner, assistant professor of religion, UC Berkeley
Brad Russell, department dean
Jessica Morris, Mono County 911 operator
Victoria Johnson, Pleasant Hill, CA, Oscar's daughter
Jacob Jones, search-and-rescue (SAR) team leader
Tim Lane, Martinez, CA
Barbara Lane, Tim's wife
Noah Lane, their five-year-old son
Peter Shreve, Mono County sheriff's inspector
Roy Milford, senior pastor
Marc Drexel, associate pastor
Angie, Victoria's best friend
Alex Browne, reporter, *San Francisco Chronicle*
Connor, young boy on airplane
Sherry Bowers, Overland Park, KS, police captain
Dale Kent, Overland Park, detective
Larry Smith, Overland Park
Virginia Baldwin, Larry's mother-in-law
Mandy Frankel, Ballard, WA
Chester Parks, pastor, Waynesville, MO
Sam Jordan, Kansas City, FBI Special Agent-in-Charge
Matt Collins, FBI agent
George Toscone, FBI agent
Daniel Reynolds, FBI negotiator
Liz Robinson, C-130 pilot
Janie Hughes, Buhl, ID
Ginette Ojha, MD, UCSF heart surgeon
Felix Kingsley, MD, UCSF psychiatrist

"The question of life after death is the most important question of existence." —Plato

1

Oscar Johnson
Sierra Nevada, CA
Day 1, 12:30 PM

Hiking alone in the Sierra Nevada always came with risks. Oscar Johnson knew this well, and while the protests from his daughter were never enough to dissuade him from doing one of the things he loved, the sixty-seven-year-old had consented to take trails that had cell phone reception at occasional points. He figured this was enough of a concession to safety. Besides, his doctor had said hikes would strengthen his heart.

The early-afternoon sun filtered through branches of lodgepole pine and white fir overhead. Johnson climbed a series of switchbacks that led to his favorite destination, Devil's Fall. The spectacular viewpoint overlooked a precipitous fifteen-hundred-foot drop-off to the valley below. He always exercised caution when he approached such beautiful yet dangerous spots. Johnson removed his backpack, eased himself into a prone position, and crawled forward to the edge.

As he took in the grandeur of the vista before him, he heard footsteps approach from behind. Johnson drew back and came to his feet. A young redheaded man dressed in hunting clothes and armed with a rifle moved toward him with a sense of urgency.

"There's been an accident," the man said. "My phone's dead. Can I use yours?"

"It's in my backpack," Johnson said as he reached for it. "Sorry to hear that. How serious?" He handed the man his phone.

The man didn't answer as he appeared to scroll through the contact list for a name.

Johnson, uneasy, edged closer. "What are you doing?"

"I'll explain in a minute." The man typed a text message, then handed the phone back.

Johnson looked at the message that had just been sent. His apprehension turned to shock. "What!"

As Johnson looked up in disbelief, the man abruptly thrust his rifle butt forward, striking the stunned hiker in the chest. The impact knocked him backward to the ground, perilously close to the edge. Bewildered, Johnson sucked in breaths of air and staggered to his feet. By instinct he grabbed the assailant's wrist and twisted hard to deflect another strike.

For a moment, the two men struggled, chest to chest, until the rifle discharged, sending a shot in a wild direction. With a forceful pivot, Johnson wrestled the man to the ground, landing on top of him. With all the strength he could summon, Johnson drove his right fist down, scoring a hard punch.

But Johnson soon realized he was not a match for this man many years his junior. The man rammed a knee into Johnson's groin and doubled him over. Coming to his feet, the man shifted his stance and gripped the rifle by the barrel. "Devil's Fall. Perfect justice," he said as he swung the weapon like a batter aiming at a fastball.

The blow struck Johnson square in the chest, sending him careening over the edge of the cliff, plummeting toward the valley below.

2

Bill Miner
UC Berkeley
12:35 PM

I sipped a cup of Peet's coffee in my office after a lecture on textual criticism. I felt solemn, but it wasn't due to the subject matter. I was worried I could lose a position many would have given their right arm to have.

A tap on the door interrupted my troublesome thoughts. Brad Russell, dean of religious studies, popped in. "How are you coming on your book, Bill?" He paused and waited for a response. When none came, he said, "You know the tenure review meeting is in a few weeks. What will I tell them?"

"Brad! I'm working on it. All right?"

"Well, you don't have to take that tone," he said. "Look, I'm on your side." Russell plopped down in a chair and leaned forward with a steady gaze. "My hands are tied until you finish that book. I want to see you get tenure."

I drained the last dregs of coffee from my cup and looked into the eyes of the man who had hired me after I'd resigned from church ministry, the man who had mentored me.

"I don't mean to be testy," I said. "This situation has me irritable."

The looming tenure clock wasn't just a distraction from teaching. It threatened to end my career at Berkeley.

"Brad, why do people do bad things, sometimes unspeakable things, in the name of religion? Why do people who might otherwise be good surrender their own moral judgment to others and commit acts that violate their own conscience?"

"Hey," Russell said, "I *understand* the theme of your book. Those questions have taken on urgency. Homeland Security isn't just worried about ISIS. We've got religious fundamentalists of our own making. Church shootings, abortion clinic attacks, committed in the name of righteousness. But Bill, *you've* got a deadline."

"I know, I know. I've got my theoretical model, but I want to include the perpetrator's point of view. It's hard to reach these guys because they end up dead in a police shootout or by suicide."

"Look, Bill. I admire your integrity. You want to be balanced and comprehensive, but you've picked a tough one here." Russell eyed the Lone Ranger bobblehead that sat on my desk. "Maybe you should ask your masked friend if he'll loan you one of his silver bullets."

The Lone Ranger. My childhood hero. A man who symbolized integrity, the fight for moral justice in the Old West. Where was the moral justice in the tenure process? A race against an artificial deadline—publish or perish. Sure, I could take an easier route—produce a thematic overview of important religious traditions—but the world needs another such compilation like it needs global warming. On the other hand, my previous research on religious cults had proved useful to the FBI for better understanding groups on the fringe. This book would go further—to identify when religious beliefs become evil.

I glanced out the window as the ring of the Campanile bells reverberated across campus. It had never sounded more ominous.

"I better scoot," Russell said. He came to his feet.

I returned his silent stare.

He pointed a finger at the thin hair on his head. "See what you do to me? You bright guys, midthirties, future ahead of you—full of independent attitude and unwilling to listen."

I released a sigh of exasperation.

Russell tilted his head toward the ceiling tiles. "There's still time to switch topics," he said, "avert a disaster." He directed his gaze back to me. "It wouldn't take long to compile the data to analyze contemporary trends in America's religious landscape. That would sound more promising to the committee members and I might be able to buy you some additional time."

His words weighed on me. I knew he was trying to save my hide, not wanting a member of his department to be sacrificed like a goat on the altar of the Board of Regents.

"I couldn't ask for a better boss," I said. "Thank you. But I'd rather go down swinging than give up what motivates me and switch to another subject."

Russell shook his head. "Yeah, well, you know I'm rooting for you. Just try to understand what *motivates* the tenure review committee." As he reached the door, he said, "Being an academic administrator is like trying to push a wheelbarrow full of frogs while keeping them from jumping out."

3

Jessica Morris
Bridgeport, CA
12:40 PM

Jessica Morris, the 911 dispatcher in Bridgeport, California, grabbed the phone for her first call on the emergency line in two days.

"Thank heavens I've reached you. I'm panicked out of my mind. It's about my father, Oscar Johnson. He was hiking to Devil's Fall and he's in trouble."

"What's your name, ma'am?"

"Victoria Johnson. I'm his daughter."

"What makes you think your father's in trouble?"

"He sent me a text . . . a message that sounded . . . suicidal."

"When did you get this?"

"Ten minutes ago."

"What specifically did it say?"

"He wrote: 'Nothing to live for. I can't go on. Love, Dad.' We talked this morning! He'd never . . ."

Jessica leaned forward in her chair, tense. She drew in a breath and reminded herself she'd been picked for this job because she was comfortable talking to people in various emotional states. Most of her emergency calls were for injured or lost hikers, missing skiers, or sick campers. Seldom for a suicide. The rare, tragic instances she knew about had left family members in total shock. She was probably dealing with such a case now.

"We'll send out a search team," Jessica said. "I'll need a description of your father, so we know who we're looking for."

She asked his height, weight, hair, clothing, whether he wore glasses, and the car he drove.

"I'm at a conference in Phoenix."

"OK, sit tight. I'll keep you posted."

"I can't just sit," Victoria said. "I had to jump through hoops to reach you. I'm heading for the airport to come there."

Jessica gave Victoria her location and after they hung up she dialed Jacob Jones.

"I've got a missing hiker for you," Jessica said. She gave the details to the leader of the search-and-rescue team—ground-pounding, volunteers with the expertise of professionals, trained in technical rescue in all the environments in the Sierra. "I hope this will be a rescue and not a recovery operation, Jacob, but I've got an uneasy feeling. The message he sent his daughter sounds short, sweet, and final."

"We can be at the trailhead in about sixty minutes," Jacob said.

Jessica's emergency line flashed again. "Got another call. Thanks, Jacob, and good luck." Quiet for days, then boom.

"Sheriff's Department, what's your emergency?" she answered.

"My buddy and I are out hiking. We were staring up at Devil's Fall and thinking about climbing it someday."

"Sir, do you have an emergency?"

"No. Well, listen. As we looked up, we saw something brown and blue fall from the top. We thought maybe a BASE jumper. We watched, but no chute opened. Instead the body just fell the whole way down. I thought, *Holy crap!* With my binoculars, I saw another person up there, arms stretched out like Moses or something."

"How long ago?"

"Maybe fifteen minutes."

Jessica logged the caller's contact information, then phoned Jacob again.

"About that Devil's Fall hiker, someone just phoned who saw a person fall from there," she said. "I'll request a CHP helicopter be dispatched to the meadow below. The caller saw someone else up there, so be on the lookout for any hiker who may have seen Johnson."

Jessica hung up and punched in the number for the CHP dispatcher. Her heartbeat quickened.

4

Jacob Jones
Bridgeport
1:00 PM

Jacob Jones loaded his gear and drove to a rendezvous point to pick up his team. They piled into his jeep and headed north on US 395. As they drove, he briefed Kayla Maine and Steve Moore.

"I've never had a case like this," Jacob said. He felt tightness in his face. "The hiker sent his daughter a good-bye text . . . then jumped." He tapped his fingers on the wheel. "People just don't travel to scenic places in the Sierra Nevada to do themselves in."

Kayla pinched her lips. "The difficulty and pressure of everyday life," she said.

Steve gestured to a car ahead with a bumper sticker that read: I'D RATHER BE FISHING.

"There'd be a lot less stress in the world if more people followed that guy's advice."

"I can picture brookies, rainbows, and cutthroats," Kayla said. She squinted as if to visualize herself on the shaded bank of a mountain stream.

The afternoon sun highlighted the western slopes as they drove through a broad valley. Jacob felt an agitated emptiness in his stomach—a sensation he often got with the commencement of a search. The outcome of this mission appeared already determined. Maybe what he felt was just sadness.

They reached the trailhead at one forty-five. The only car in the pull off was a brown Toyota. Jacob touched the hood to see if the engine was still warm, did a visual search through the windows, checked the doors, and pulled up on the trunk to see if it was unlatched. He made a note of the license plate number. "Steve, phone Jessica and ask her to run the plates, then call for a wrecker."

The team grabbed their gear and headed up the trail under a fairy-tale blue sky and light breeze—a contrast to the gloom Jacob felt inside.

After hiking about three-quarters of an hour, they had encountered no one.

Jacob's phone rang.

"It's Jessica. CHP found the body at the base. Wallet and driver's license confirm that it's Oscar Johnson. But there's something else. Where are you now?"

"About twenty minutes from the overlook," Jacob said.

"OK, listen. Sheriff's deputies have talked with those two hikers in the meadow who saw Johnson fall. What they saw raises questions. The sheriff wants you to check the area for anything out of the ordinary."

Jacob disconnected the call and briefed his team members.

Steve's eyes widened. "This just got interesting."

It was 2:50 when the team reached Devil's Fall. The temperature had dropped a few degrees. They surveyed the ground area from the perimeter of the overlook, then moved closer. Steve took photographs of the scene. No sign of a suicide note. A backpack lay thirty feet back from the edge. Jacob slipped on a pair of gloves and inspected it—binoculars, sunscreen, canteen, and a lunch.

Kayla approached the edge of the vertical drop-off. "We had thundershowers last night," she said. "This area's been roughed up since then." She studied the area, then eased down onto her knees. "Here's something."

"Let me grab a plastic bag," Jacob said.

Kayla lifted the object with a gloved hand. "It looks like a medical ID bracelet. Has a broken link."

Steve photographed it. "The engravings don't look medical," he said.

Jacob phoned Jessica. "We've got photos: Johnson's backpack and a metal bracelet. We're ready to head back."

"See anything suspicious?" she asked.

"One thing bothers me," Jacob said. "There may have been a scuffle." He fingered the tube of SPF 30. "And why would a man who was about to take his own life be worried about sunburn?"

5

Redheaded Man
Sonora Pass, CA
3:30 PM

The redheaded man stopped at a pull off on CA 108 near Sonora Pass. He gazed at a vista of granite beds and valleys rich with western white pine, the thin air crisp in the late afternoon. At over ninety-six hundred feet, the highway had climbed almost two miles into the sky. He allowed himself to think he was that much closer to God.

He stepped out of his car and punched a number on his cell.

The party he reached offered no greeting, only a question: "Were you successful?"

"Yes."

"Excellent," the party replied. "The Lord's eyes are upon you and he is pleased. But you must continue quickly. There is no time to waste."

The redheaded man hung up and walked to the edge of the pull off. A Clark's nutcracker sounded a loud, guttural kraaaa, then swooped from his perch among the weather-beaten pines toward the valley. The man bowed his head and prayed he'd remain true to the trust that had been placed in him. How could he not render unquestioned obedience to one who spoke for God? He was humbled and honored to have been chosen.

The soreness in his ribs didn't bother him as much as the loss of his treasured bracelet—badge and symbol of his mission. He was not superstitious. He would persevere. God was on his side.

He returned to his car and sat for a few moments as he contemplated a task he dreaded. He squeezed the bridge of his nose. He needed to make a difficult disclosure.

He turned the key in the ignition, eased back onto the highway, and headed west, toward home.

6

Bill Miner
Berkeley, CA
7:00 PM

It was early evening, and instead of my normal practice of grading student papers, I paced around my small Berkeley home like a restless hound. Cup of herbal tea that was supposed to calm me in hand, I followed a circular path out of habit, through my Victorian kitchen, into the dining area, then the study, the living room, and back to the kitchen. Colleagues have described my place as a collection of curiosities, like a German *Kunstkammer*. The walls were covered with religious art: a stained-glass panel depicting Hannah in the temple from the church of Sainte-Chapelle, a mosaic from Jerusalem's Church of the Holy Sepulchre, an etching of a biblical shepherd searching for a lost sheep. I felt like that sheep. Where would I turn if forced to leave Berkeley?

The sound of my cell phone jarred whatever was left of my concentration. The screen showed a name I didn't recognize.

"This is Inspector Peter Shreve, Mono County Sheriff's Department. May I speak to Professor Miner?"

"You've got him."

"Professor, I heard you speak on cults at a conference in Sacramento last year. We had a fatality earlier today—"

"What? Someone I know?"

"Doubtful. A man named Oscar Johnson. We're trying to sort out what happened, and the reason I called you is that we found a metal bracelet with engravings that look like they could be religious symbols. We can't make sense of it and thought maybe you could help."

I'd been contacted before, usually by eccentrics who wanted to report their personal conversations with the Blessed Mary or tell me about an image of Jesus on a Frito-Lay. A motorist once sent a photo of clouds parting above the highway after a storm, convinced it was a spiritual message. But I'd never gotten a call from the police.

"Can you describe the engravings?" I asked.

"Two Christian crosses. Between them are hieroglyphic-like symbols. I think you'd have to see them. It may be nothing, but I'd like to send a photo. I remember you talked about mystic symbols at the conference. They're cryptic like that."

I reflected a moment. Hard to turn away someone who had *remembered* something I'd said at one of those talks.

"OK. You have my email?"

"It's on your card from the conference."

I hung up and had barely swallowed a sip of herbal blossom whatever when my phone buzzed. The attachment to Shreve's email sat me down in a chair. I stared at the symbols between two crosses on the bracelet.

†ᛞᛟᚷ†

A check of a reference book confirmed my hunch. I called the inspector. He answered on the first ring.

"Those symbols are letters of the runic alphabet," I said.

"The *what* alphabet?"

"Did you see the *Lord of the Rings* movies?"

"My kids did," Shreve said.

"Runes are letters of an ancient Anglo-Saxon alphabet dating back to around AD 400. J. R. R. Tolkien used a variation in his books."

"My young sons might get excited about that, Professor—hobbits and the like. But what does it mean?"

"In Norse mythology, the runic alphabet is said to have a divine origin. The word 'rune' itself can be taken to mean 'secret,' something hidden. Some cults revel in that kind of symbolism. I'll check the transliteration of those letters to see if they spell anything in English while I've got you on the phone. Hang on a minute. OK, the first symbol is . . . the letter *d*," I said. "The second symbol . . . is the letter *o*. And the third is *g*."

"So that's what the bracelet spells?" Shreve said. " 'Dog'?" His tone was half-incredulous, half-frustrated.

"Sorry, Inspector, I don't know what to tell you. In *Breakfast at Tiffany's*, Audrey Hepburn named her cat Cat."

I wished him good luck, disconnected the call, and sat back in my chair. *D-O-G* . . . Curious that someone would have enough creativity to employ the runic alphabet but so little imagination to come up with a name for their pet. I circled again through the house, stopped in the kitchen for another tea bag, and discovered I was out—sort of the way the whole day had gone.

I rummaged around in the cabinets and spied a box of Dragon-of-Guilin oolong buried behind soup cans and spaghetti sauce. I pulled it out and, for a moment, stared at the artwork on the front—a Chinese dragon, fearsome symbol of great power. A feeling nagged at me. I *had* seen those letters before, in a very different context. The hairs on my arm stood up.

I went for my phone.

"Inspector," I said, "I don't think your bracelet refers to a canine. I think *D-O-G* stands for 'Dragon of God.' "

7

Tim Lane
Martinez, CA
7:00 PM

Tim Lane pulled into the driveway of his home in Martinez, California, steering to the left of his son's tricycle. Lane sat motionless, absorbed in thought, until his wife appeared on the front porch.

"Hi, honey," she called. "How was the hunting trip?"

Lane went up the walkway, greeted her with a kiss, and held her close in a loving embrace, nuzzling her soft brown hair. To him, she was the symbol of beauty and innocence and human goodness.

Their five-year-old bolted out the door behind his mom. "Did you see any bears, Daddy?"

"No, but I saw a porcupine." He lifted the boy in his arms and gently tossed him upward. Noah's happy squeals always delighted Lane.

The patchy fog of evening had turned the sky of the Bay Area suburb to dark navy by the time they made their way into the kitchen. The aroma of cookies, warm from the oven, infused the air.

His wife dished up a cookie for Noah and poured him a glass of milk. "Daddy's home in time to read you a story," she said. "After your cookie, brush your teeth, and get into your pajamas.

"So how was the trip?" she asked again after Noah had gone down the hall.

Lane removed a pile of Thomas the Tank Engine books from a chair and sat down at the table.

"You're either tired or troubled," she said. "And you've got some sunburn. A college degree and two years as a military intelligence officer . . . and you forget to wear your hat?" She shook her head. "My dear brainy husband who doesn't remember how easily redheads burn. You want some coffee? Are you hungry?"

"Coffee sounds fine, Barbara."

His wife could always read his moods, and he knew he couldn't keep anything back for much longer. But he didn't want to burden her with any of the responsibility. He lapsed into small talk as his mind searched for the difficult words that still eluded him.

Noah came back down the hallway, a blanket in one hand, a Dr. Seuss book in the other, a smudge of toothpaste on his chin.

"OK," Lane said. "Go hop in bed, and I'll be right there." He pushed away from the table and smiled affectionately at his wife. "The Sierra are beautiful and inspirational, but nothing tops the sight of you . . . or that little towhead of ours."

"What story did you pick?" Lane asked as he sat down on the bed.

Noah held out Dr. Seuss's *The Lorax*, slid under the covers, and beamed with anticipation.

Lane tried to make a different voice for each of the characters he read—an imaginative challenge for a Seuss book, but Noah's amusement always validated the effort. Lane read for several minutes, paused when he came to a passage, then read it slowly:

> UNLESS someone like you cares a whole awful lot, nothing is going to get better. It's not.

Lane gazed into his son's face, so filled with young innocence. Soon blankets and Thomas the Tank Engine would give way to Oakland A's heroes and girlfriends.

"What do you think that means?" Lane asked.

"That you should protect things, or they won't get better," Noah said.

"That's right. But what if it's very difficult?"

Noah nodded solemnly. "You have to do it anyway."

Lane ran a hand through the boy's hair. This was a favorite story, which they'd read many times. Nevertheless, Lane knew the answer was a child's effort to please a parent.

"I think it's time for your prayers," Lane said.

Lane stayed with Noah until he fell asleep. What he wouldn't do for the love of this little boy.

Lane returned to the kitchen, refilled his coffee, and sat back down at the table. "Anything happen while I was gone?" he asked.

"Not much. The Smiths started their new deck. The regular doom and gloom in the news. That's all."

Tim Lane agonized over the doom and gloom more than most around him. He felt a vast emptiness, a frightening loneliness and loss of control.

"I wish I were savvier when it comes to politics, honey," he said. "Maybe I'd run for public office again."

Barbara pulled out a chair and sat down across from him. "You vowed you'd never do that again." She looked at him squarely in the eyes. "Not after the raw deal you got from that school board."

"That was before we had Noah," Lane said. "Here he is, about to start kindergarten. California schools are no different than those back East. They continue going in the wrong direction. Courts block God from the classroom, but they won't block abortions. How does that make any sense?" He rubbed the back of his neck. "You *know* how it gets to me. They won't even let schools teach the Ten Commandments, but they're happy to teach evolution." He pressed his lips together. "Gay marriage? What'll the Supreme Court legalize next? Polygamy?" He brought his fist down on the table, jarring his coffee mug. "America has lost its *bearings*. We're on a pell-mell course that will destroy the nation we love."

"We live in a broken world," she said. "You know that."

"I tried to work within the system," Lane said. "Strive to improve our schools, and all you get is ridicule and mockery." He sipped his coffee. "Education and social welfare should be handed over to the churches."

"Tim, you just got back from a trip that was supposed to *relieve* your stress, not heighten it."

He leaned his head back and closed his eyes for a moment. "You and Noah are everything to me. I'm a better man because of you. And our church has taught me not just the importance of serving the Lord but that my purpose is to protect you, to secure a future for our son. What kind of world will Noah inherit when our government's bent on shutting out faith?"

"Small is the gate and narrow the road," she said.

"But I'm tired of standing by . . . feeling hopeless."

"You're a good Christian. You take it seriously."

"Barbara, do you remember the sermon a few weeks ago? The one where our pastor said God wants us to step forward and be counted?"

She nodded, reached over, and squeezed his hand.

"He told us all that's necessary for evil to triumph is for good men to do nothing," Lane said, "that it's time for the brave and strong to step over the line, out of their comfort zone, and act like disciples of Christ. I felt like our pastor was talking to me. My soul hung on every word." He paused. "Remember when I talked with him after the service? He reminded us that a satanic attack is under way and Christ wants somebody, somebody like David in the Valley of Elah with five smooth stones."

Lane searched for words, trying out different ones in his head. *Nothing is going to get better. It's not.* "Honey . . . I decided I can be silent no more. These times demand it . . . our future depends on it . . . you and Noah deserve it . . . and above all, I know God is watching. Our pastor said red-blooded men must be willing to take a stand, and I want to do that."

He took a deep breath, his gut full of apprehension. He had to tell her now, or never.

"The Lord has told me how," he said.

"You're a godly man, Tim." Her gentle smile brimmed with admiration. "What do you think the Lord has in mind for you?"

"I haven't said anything to you because it involves . . . actions you won't approve of."

"Don't be silly," she said. "Why wouldn't I approve of something God wanted you to do?"

Lane leaned across the table and forced himself to look into his wife's eyes. "A messenger has come to me with a holy undertaking. He told me the Lord has recognized my faithfulness . . . has rewarded my devotion with an opportunity to serve him." His heart raced. "To serve him as a lion of the Almighty. To serve him as a Dragon of God."

Lane saw wariness replace the smile on his wife's face. Her eyes squinted.

"Dragon of God? What are you talking about?" Barbara sat straight up. "What do you mean?"

"I mean . . . take measures to stop certain individuals who are enemies of the Lord."

She pulled back. "You're not talking about harming anyone, are you?"

Lane was silent. He fidgeted with his coffee cup, turning it around and around. Now he avoided her eyes. The wall clock pounded in his ears.

"What if it were God's will?" he asked at last.

Barbara stiffened and rose to her feet. "You can't be serious!"

Her voice was full of alarm. He felt her eyes search his face.

Lane said nothing. He had dreaded this moment. He knew she abhorred all forms of violence.

"Talk to me!" she shouted. "What's happened to you? You know that's wrong! *God* has said that's wrong. How could the Bible be clearer?"

He turned his face back to her. "Jesus also says: 'Bring my enemies before me and slay them.' "

His wife collapsed back in her chair, stunned, fearful.

"I know the Bible *too*!" she said. "I know it foretells of a great struggle prior to Christ's return. Our church says we live in such times. I know good Christians should not hide their lamp under a basket. But, *Tim*! Is *this* what you think it means to shine your lamp? My own husband, the father of our precious son, speaks of breaking God's most important commandment?"

"Barbara, this is the most difficult decision I've ever faced. Jesus said: 'Do not think that I have come to bring peace to the earth. I have not come to bring peace, but a sword.' "

Her voice began to tremble. "This isn't the man I married. *Who* has told you to do this?"

"An angel of the Lord."

Her shoulders dropped, and she let out an uncontrollable sob.

He spoke softly. "Please trust me . . . *please*."

Her face became small.

Lane stood and moved behind his wife, who was now slumped in her chair. He put his arms around her. She pulled away.

"I have to be gone a few more days," he said. "I just wanted to see you . . . to try and explain." He kissed the back of her neck. She recoiled.

"Tim, this is wrong!" Her voice choked. "*Please*, let's *talk* about this."

His ribs ached. "Remember what Mordecai told Esther," he said. "If you remain silent at this time, relief and deliverance will arise from another place and you will perish."

This was not how Lane wanted to leave.

"I love you and our son very much," he said.

As he backed out of the driveway, the image of his wife's tears haunted him.

8

Car Rental Agent
Seattle-Tacoma International Airport
11:45 PM

It was fifteen minutes until her shift was over when a man entered the rental car facility at Sea-Tac Airport. The young female agent was tired but nevertheless pleased that her last customer of the day would be easy on her eyes—in his midthirties, well built, with thick red hair and a ginger-tinged five-o'clock shadow. In her opinion, the idea of male attractiveness involving dark hair was overrated. Maybe it was the Prince Harry effect that made her feel this way.

She flashed her best smile. "Welcome to Hertz."

The man requested a car for two days and asked about the driving time to Ballard. "It's about twenty miles due north," she told him. "This time of night, you're thirty-five minutes away if you take I-5." The man handed back the forms he had signed.

"Thank you, Mr. Lane. Take the elevator to level four. There'll be an attendant. Select any car you like, and have a great trip."

Her eyes followed him as he left the office. *Now, there goes a man who looks like he's out to make a difference in the world*, she thought.

9

Bill Miner
I-580 Freeway, Bay Area, CA
Day 2, 7:00 AM

Was this the break I needed? Adrenalin dumped into my bloodstream. Implications raced through my mind. The only thing not in motion was the southbound traffic as I edged my ancient Volvo through the early-morning congestion on my way to the Sierra. My leaf blower had more horsepower than that old buggy, which was in desperate need of a tune-up. I hoped it could handle the elevation climb ahead. I switched on the local sports-talk radio station as if the boisterous chatter of A's fans would goose traffic along. Callers bantered over the reasons for their team's current downturn. After a few minutes, I turned the radio off and returned to thoughts of my own slump.

What if fate had handed me a solution—the piece necessary to complete my book? The previous night's conversation with Inspector Peter Shreve had left me tantalized. Mysterious religious overtones surrounding a suspicious death? Not your everyday, garden-variety drama. My pragmatic side told me this whole exercise could be a big diversion of energy, a fool's errand, a waste of critical time. My imaginative side whispered, *But what if?*

I had come across the phrase "Dragon of God" on a website a few years earlier. The catchphrase was the war cry of a group that wanted to abolish the separation of church and state and mandate Christianity as the nation's religion. Nothing had ever come of their effort, and I'd encountered no references to them since then. Could the bracelet have been a sign of some new incarnation? Or could it have just been someone's idea of a funky designation? Someone who relished mystic symbols or slogans that intimidate.

Once past Livermore, traffic began to move. I glanced at the time and called my department's administrative assistant.

"We got the message you left last night," she said. "Dean Russell told me he'd cover your classes if we can't find a sub."

"Give him my sincere thanks," I said. "I've also got an appointment at eleven this morning with a couple of grad students to discuss subjects for their dissertations."

"I'll post a note on your office door. Dean Russell said to ask you if you plan to swing by Angels Camp on the way." She muffled a giggle. "The frog-jumping contest. He intends to put money on you if you are."

"Tell him I appreciate the confidence."

"Seriously, good luck," she said. "Drive safe, and enjoy the scenery."

I hung up and checked my GPS. Four hours to Bridgeport.

Traffic had slowed again. It took an hour and a quarter more to reach Escalon, a small agricultural town surrounded by fertile farmland and known for walnut processing. I would need to make up some time. I slowed to twenty-five going down Jackson Avenue and happened to notice an elderly pedestrian in a crosswalk crossing a side street. The man took a few more steps and then collapsed to one knee.

I pulled to the curb, jumped out of the car, and hurried to his side. "Sir, are you OK? Can I give you some help?"

"I'm all right," the man said. He appeared to be in his eighties and sounded a little shaky. I helped him to his feet.

"Thank you, young man."

He didn't seem lost or disoriented, just fatigued. "Where do you need to go?" I asked.

"My home is over on Second Street."

"Why don't I drop you off?"

"That's mighty kind," he said. I steadied him and held his arm as we walked to my car. A couple of minutes later his appreciative wife met us at the door. Then I was on my way again.

I'll get there when I get there, I thought.

10

Bill Miner
Bridgeport
12:30 PM

I arrived at my destination: a town situated in the middle of a valley at sixty-four-hundred-foot elevation. Bridgeport is surrounded by open grazing land and ringed by national forests. In this community with a population of fewer than six hundred, I had no trouble locating the Sheriff's Office, a block off Main Street.

The receptionist led me down a narrow hallway to Inspector Peter Shreve's office. Shreve paused in his conversation with a woman who stood next to him.

I was taken aback. She was a flood of beauty. Almost as tall as Shreve, her height in perfect proportion to a striking figure.

Shreve introduced me to Victoria Johnson, and I learned she was the daughter of the man who had died the day before.

An unexpected wave of shyness left me speechless for a moment.

"I'm so sorry for your loss," I managed to say.

"Thank you." Her voice was soft, vulnerable. She dabbed at her eyes. "Inspector Shreve told me you might be able to help." She swallowed and then held still in expectation. "I do hope you can."

She had me with that look. I was there for my book, but now I had a second reason: I wanted to help her.

"Ms. Johnson flew up from Phoenix late yesterday," Shreve said. "She's identified her father." He motioned to a small round conference table in his office. "Have a seat, and we'll go over what we know at this point."

I pulled out a chair for Ms. Johnson and took a seat next to her. She sat with her arms crossed, her hands clasping her elbows, probably to hold herself together.

"Ms. Johnson is certain her father didn't commit suicide," Shreve said.

She turned toward me. The loveliest brown eyes I had ever seen belied the immense grief I knew she must have felt.

"If you're looking for doubts, there aren't any," she said. "That text message was not sent by my father. He never signed, 'Dad.' In all his notes—since I was a little girl—it was 'Papa.' Always."

I nodded. She had my rapt attention, although I had to remind myself to concentrate on what she was saying.

"Can you think of anyone who would have wanted to hurt him?" Shreve asked.

Her eyes stared vacantly at the conference table. "It's inconceivable to me. He was gentle, kind, considerate to everyone." She looked up at Shreve. "Inspector, this was not a man with enemies."

"Do you know his whereabouts in the twenty-four hours before his death?"

"He just drove up here the day before."

"Active on social media?"

"No. He was fairly novice with computers, but comfortable with email."

"Did he have a girlfriend?"

She shook her head.

"Had he been under any stress?" Shreve asked.

Her answers seemed conclusive to me, but apparently, Shreve wanted to explore every possibility. This sun-tanned man with a large moustache and intelligent, dark eyes was all business.

"No stress I was aware of," she said. "He wasn't the type for mood swings, nor was he depressed. We'd see each other every week or two and talk on the phone between then."

Shreve turned his head toward me. "Ms. Johnson is positive the bracelet didn't belong to her father," he said. "From the interpretation of those symbols you gave me on the phone, I can't imagine it would. So here's what we have. We found signs of a struggle at Devil's Fall. We have a witness on the valley floor who saw a person at the overlook after Mr. Johnson's fall. And, of course, the bracelet. The coroner's autopsy may give us more to go on."

Shreve's demeanor was alert and confident. "Professor Miner, what can you tell us about the possibility of cult involvement?"

"I can't find any current reference to 'Dragon of God,' but some cults are tiny. They start out passionate about their religious views built around a single charismatic figure. Most dwindle away to nothing, but not all. Christianity was a cult once."

Ms. Johnson drew back with a startled expression. I regretted the comparison I'd often used in the classroom.

"Let me clarify that," I said. "I didn't mean anything derogatory. 'Cult' comes from the Latin word for 'to care' and 'to worship.' It may take a long time for a new religious movement to gain acceptance, if it ever does."

She nodded cautiously.

"Ironically," I said, "if a cult becomes accepted into the mainstream, it loses its radical fervor and develops into a more organized and integrated body in the community. It becomes a church."

Her body language told me I'd touched a sensitive area.

I paused. "The problem is that many groups have appeared and disappeared over the years. And what you worry about are the self-appointed messiahs who emerge during periods of social or political turbulence."

Shreve tightened his jaw. "As we have today," he said. "Immigration, gun control, abortion."

"Exactly," I said. "A time ripe for new religious movements to flourish."

"Do you think the bracelet indicates some group has resurfaced?" Ms. Johnson asked.

"Possibly," I said. "What puzzles me is that it's rare for a cult to send members out to target a specific individual. Leaders are known to become corrupted by their power and turn abusive. But it's their own followers they abuse."

"People should see through these false prophets," she said.

"Except they're dazzled by 'expository talks.' If they question the leader, they're accused of calling God a liar. It's very effective intimidation."

"Most are just con men," Shreve said.

"Except these leaders often believe their own stuff," I said. "There are many intelligent Americans who are attracted by a charismatic pastor who promises 'serious religion.' You can identify the charlatans by their refusal to tolerate any opposition. They preach it is a sin to question."

Shreve looked impatient. "Interesting, but where does this leave us?" he asked.

I felt a quiver of nerves and shifted in my chair. I wished I had a brilliant insight. "I'm at a loss right now. Maybe with more research?"

Shreve winced and pressed his hands to his temples. "Let's get back to the bracelet," he said. "If it belonged to the other person who was seen at Devil's Fall, he must somehow identify with this 'Dragon of God,' a group you say never espoused violence. Yet we have a suspicious death of a man who had no enemies. What would explain that?"

Shreve came to his feet. "I want to inspect the site. You're welcome to join me," he said.

11

Bill Miner
Bridgeport
1:15 PM

I was alone with Victoria Johnson in the break room while we waited for Shreve to complete some arrangements before he would take us up to Devil's Fall.

"Would you like some coffee, Ms. Johnson?"

"Tea if they have it. Thank you, and please call me Victoria."

"If you'll call me Bill."

We sat down at a small Formica table with chrome legs. The vinyl fabric chairs looked as if they were from a 1940s diner. Victoria had been understandably quiet. Her eyes showed redness, a sadness I wished I could soothe. I stirred my coffee as I tried to think of the right words to say.

"You must have been very close," I said.

She nodded. "I can't imagine who would want to do this," she said. "He was a dear man, to everyone."

"Is your mother still living?"

"No. She died when I was very young. Papa raised me. He was the kind of father any girl would want. He'd listen. The kind of father that would get you out of the woods when you got lost."

The white light of the California afternoon filtered through the half-open miniblinds. Victoria looked toward the window with a remote gaze. A glisten of tears came to her eyes.

"Anything I could have done for Papa, I would've. But what I wanted most . . ." Her voice quavered, and I felt the pain in her words.

"You fell short in some way?"

"I failed to get Papa to accept Christ."

I eased back in my chair. "How do you mean?"

"As a person of faith, you know what I'm talking about." Her eyes checked mine as if to seek acknowledgment. "He wasn't saved. Papa won't see the kingdom of heaven. I've lost him for eternity."

"I understand." I was stirred that her tears were not just for her personal pain but also for what she believed to be her father's fate. It was not the first time I'd seen a saved Christian anguish over the possible damnation of one they loved who had failed to see the Way. But this was such a personal outpouring to someone she'd just met. Did she think of me as clergy?

"I want to clarify something. I'm not a pastor," I said.

"I know. You're a professor of the Bible. And that means we share faith that God will guide us to find the person responsible for my father's death."

I realized I had a lot to explain.

"You sound like you have strong faith," I said. "How did you and your father end up so far apart spiritually?"

"We weren't in the beginning. It happened later, in adulthood." Victoria stared at the table for a few moments. "I was the one who changed. Papa brought me up the way he was raised, left it to me to make up my own mind on religious matters. Like most kids, I was much more interested in other things besides church. But Papa stressed education because he regretted he had not gone on to college. He worked hard all his life as a longshoreman. He limited my television and required me to turn in a book report every week." She paused as if to reflect on those times. "I discovered I liked science."

I again felt surprised that Victoria was so quick to confide in me.

"I attended San José State. To help with expenses, I waited tables at a popular restaurant in Sunnyvale. That's where I first got turned on to a career in high tech, by the young Silicon Valley crowd that would come in. They intrigued me with stories of their projects in software, artificial intelligence, and genetic engineering. I was fascinated by the complex puzzles they solved. A professor encouraged me to pursue neuroscience."

"That's an arduous major," I said.

"Papa always said I got my determination from my mother and my stubbornness from *him*."

She gave me a faint smile, and I sensed she was a person of strong resolution, stubborn, maybe, but kind and intelligent.

"After graduate studies, I got engaged to my college sweetheart and then landed my dream job at Genentech. It was a tough job market, and I wanted to prove myself, so I worked long hours. The field was exciting, and my company strove to push back the boundaries of knowledge. I was already a religious skeptic, and my research reinforced the notion that no scientist could believe in God."

"Something must have changed," I said.

She nodded. "A personal crisis." She looked away and paused for a few seconds. "My career thrived, but my personal life deteriorated. Long work hours took their toll. My fiancé got tired of phone calls about another late night at the office. He broke our engagement and a brief time later married someone else." She took a sip of tea. "It was like a tree fell on me. I would have crawled over broken glass to get him back. Papa offered a shoulder to cry on, but I knew he hadn't been too crazy about my fiancé in the first place."

"Like a good father—there to catch you, regardless," I said.

"Always. But he figured the purpose of life was to learn from your choices, develop a trust in your instincts."

Her eyes met mine. I nodded as she continued.

"One day," she said, "my best friend, aware of the anguish I'd been through, asked me what I believed about God. Her astute question was a jolt. She was evangelical and very well grounded. I wasn't at all sure what *I* believed anymore."

I was touched by Victoria's openness.

"The turning point came when she invited me to her church. I found support groups that became lifelines. Their compassion pulled me out of despair, and I began to heal." She gripped her elbows. "For God to get my attention, I had to be walloped over the head." Her lips pressed together with a hint of a self-aware smile. "One of the drawbacks of stubbornness."

"Stubbornness also correlates with the admirable trait of tenacity," I said.

"Thanks for the charitable spin."

The wrinkles on her forehead relaxed.

"That was ten years ago," she said. "The church was like a guiding star that gave me a known horizon. I learned to experience God as an intimate friend. I regained balance, bought a home in Pleasant Hill, and progressed in my career. I've followed Jesus ever since."

I sat back in my chair a bit overwhelmed. Victoria had just bared her soul to me. I knew more about this beautiful woman after less than twenty minutes than I did about people I'd worked with for years. But I was uncomfortable with what she assumed about my religious beliefs—that I shared her expectation God would "guide us."

"Both of our lives have been shaped by the church," I said, "but I don't want you to labor under a false supposition. I'm not a believer."

Victoria looked at me with a frown. "I beg your pardon?"

"I don't believe in a God that answers prayers or intervenes in the world to relieve suffering," I said.

A sudden reflex brought her upright in her chair. "I thought you were a professor of religion."

"I am." A knot began to tighten in my stomach.

"You teach something you don't believe?" She stared openly.

"The courses I teach aren't devotional. I don't teach my students that the Bible is the inspired word of God. Berkeley isn't a Bible college. I teach the Bible as historical literature, and I try to help my students understand what the authors are saying rather than teach them to accept as truth any particular set of beliefs about Jesus, heaven, or salvation."

She sat back, quiet a moment, as if to process.

"Whether one is Catholic, Protestant, Jewish, or agnostic," I said, "the Bible is the most influential piece of literature in Western civilization. The foundation of our heritage. To understand what it means is one of the most important pursuits one can have."

She leaned toward me. "So if you're not a man of faith, what made you want to become a teacher of religion?"

"I once was a man of faith."

"*Once?*" Victoria said, eyes widened.

The question hung in the air as Inspector Shreve appeared at the door.

"Let's go," he said.

12

Tim Lane
Ballard, Seattle, WA
1:30 PM

Tim Lane sat huddled in his rental car while a cool rain fell outside. He was parked on a street in Ballard, which appeared to be an older middle-class residential neighborhood, twenty minutes northwest of downtown Seattle. The rain tapped the car's roof and transformed the windshield into a semitranslucent veil. The homes along this block were blurry blobs. Occasional gusts blew in from Puget Sound. Moisture condensed on his door window even though he had rolled it down a crack. He rubbed some of the film away and took another look across the street. The house he had under surveillance was tiny—a single-story stucco with a few trees and woodland shrubs in its front yard.

He shifted his position time and again. There was no sign of activity. No one had come or gone. He would have to speed things up.

He reached for his phone, searched "florist," and viewed the names of shops nearby. His eyes focused on "Angel of Redemption Flowers." *How ironic*, he thought, *a redemptive bouquet for a person who has no chance in hell of absolution.*

Lane returned thirty minutes later and knocked on the front door of the stucco home. A woman in her midtwenties answered and broke into the broad smile he'd anticipated. "Floral delivery for Mandy Frankel," Lane announced.

"Oh, how beautiful! She'll be thrilled when she sees these."

"She must have a secret admirer," Lane said. "The sender didn't want to give his name."

"Oh, interesting," the young woman said, her smile now a coy grin. "She should be home from work soon. With a day that started at 2 AM, this surprise will pick her up. Thank you so much."

Lane turned, then pivoted back. "And I thought *I* had to get up early for the Flower Market." He smiled softly and bit his bottom lip. "What does she do that gets her up at that hour?"

"She's a baker who makes the best muffins in Seattle."

"Those hours must be hard on a family," he said.

"It's just us two housemates. I have the night shift as a nurse. It works."

"Enjoy the flowers," Lane said. He headed back to his car, dodging puddles on the way. There was a spring in his step. He knew what to do.

13

Bill Miner
US Route 395, CA
2:00 PM

"The trail your father took," Shreve said as he glanced to the passenger seat, "it's a few miles north of Sonora Junction, the other side of Devil's Gate Pass."

"Yes, I'm familiar with this area," Victoria said. "He brought me here from the time I was a little girl."

I sat in the back seat of Shreve's Ford Explorer as we drove northwest out of Bridgeport. Shreve gripped the wheel like a vise, and his intent eyes, visible in the rearview mirror, resembled those of a hound on point. The afternoon sun lighted the face of the Sierra Nevada and turned the mighty pines a brilliant green as we zigzagged along the windy road. I had never inspected a crime scene, and my anticipation was tempered by increased nervousness. What would I be able to contribute?

"There were no hits when we searched 'Dragon of God' in our crime databases," Shreve said. "There were no discernable fingerprints on the bracelet, and your father's cell phone was too shattered to reveal any."

My anxiety went up another click. We were coming up empty.

"How often did you see your father these past six or eight months?" Shreve asked.

She stared out the window as if remembering earlier, happier trips to the area. "I would make it a point to see him every week or two."

Even from the depths of sadness, she spoke with poise and dignity.

We passed a Honda Pilot with camping gear strapped to the roof and a girl in the back seat, face to the window, full of wonder. Perhaps a young Victoria experiencing her baptism in the beauty of the mountains. I realized my thoughts were more on Victoria than on the issues related to her father.

"Did you notice any changes in him?" I heard Shreve ask. "Anything he seemed worried about?"

She shook her head. "He'd been worried about an operation. The change came after his surgery."

"What kind of surgery?" Shreve asked.

"Coronary artery bypass."

"And you said he changed?"

"Yes, all positive. He greeted each day more relaxed, at peace with himself. Less troubled by things that at one time might have unsettled him."

She looked out the window. I could feel her despondency—her father's new lease on life cut short in, of all places, his revered mountains.

"Did your father ever associate with any religious group that could be considered on the fringe?" Shreve asked.

"Never. I couldn't get him to go to church with *me*. The one exception was a few weeks ago when I took him to meet my pastor. Religion was the only subject we ever argued about."

"Any close friends that might have had unusual religious associations?"

She shrugged. "I can't imagine. Papa had plenty of friends—fishing buddies, neighbors—but no one on the religious fringe."

"How about relatives?" Shreve asked.

"I have an aunt back East. My uncle was killed in an automobile accident recently. Aunt Laura is still recuperating."

"Is it possible your father might have confided in them? Something he wouldn't have told you?"

"I doubt it." Her expression seemed confident. "I saw my aunt when I flew out for the funeral services for Uncle Oliver. Papa was still in the hospital. I spent some time with her, and our conversations were all about family memories."

It seemed to me Shreve had explored every conceivable association but hadn't asked about Oscar Johnson's own apparent indifference to religion. "Did your father ever express to anyone that he considered religion unimportant?" I asked. "Someone who might have taken offense?"

Victoria was quiet a moment, then shook her head. "It's strange to even imagine my father would express religious opinions to others. He didn't like to discuss religion or politics. *I* would have had to bring it up. But when he and I talked about religion after his operation . . . it upset me." Her tone became wary. "To answer your question, my father wasn't the type to proselytize to anyone."

I'd hit a nerve. "What upset you?" I asked.

Silence. Victoria had gone from unreserved to guarded.

"That's between Papa, my pastor, and me," she said after a moment. Her words were measured. "I'm not comfortable with discussing that just now . . . after what you told me earlier about your own beliefs."

A few minutes later we turned into a dirt pull off next to a small sign that read, BEAVER CREEK TRAILHEAD.

14

Bill Miner
Beaver Creek Trail, CA
2:45 PM

Victoria and I walked side by side following Shreve up a ridgeline of mixed conifers on the trail to Devil's Fall. Fragrance arose from the pine needles beneath our footsteps. The air was pleasant, warm, and mountain clean. Victoria, in tan slacks, seemed to glide without effort. The sun caught golden highlights in her shoulder-length hair as her legs propelled her up the trail. I trudged—a reminder to make time for workouts.

"Did you ever camp when you were a kid?" she asked.

"No. My dad complained he could never get campground reservations, thought it ridiculous you had to sign up on a wait list to sleep under a tree."

She chuckled. "Mine liked to fish, so we came up here often." We'd walked a few minutes when Victoria stopped and turned to me. "Can I ask you a personal question?" she said.

Her tone had a slight edge, and I sensed what might come. I nodded but was glad Shreve was far enough ahead to be out of earshot.

"When you see beauty around you like this," she said, her arms out, palms open, "how in heaven's name can you not believe in God?"

I shoved my hands in my pockets. I hated to be on the defensive with someone I wanted to impress. "The short answer is because there's so much suffering in the world." I sensed Victoria might come back with a strong response. She did.

"I hope you give your students a better answer than that," she said. "You know God doesn't *want* us to suffer."

Even in her rebuke, Victoria's voice conveyed an underlying concern and thoughtfulness.

"We create our own misery," she said, "through our sins, our inconsiderate actions, our selfish behaviors. Besides, why would you go into religion if you felt that way?"

My gut tensed. I'd been through this narrative many times with friends and colleagues, so why did this feel so awkward?

We came to a level section. I huffed and puffed and motioned for a breather.

"A stiff climb, isn't it?" Victoria said, sympathetically.

"I bought a treadmill," I said. "This is a reminder I need to use it for something other than to hang laundry on."

She gave me a half smile, but the look in her eyes told me she wasn't about to let me evade her question. At least the pause allowed a little more separation from Shreve.

"When it comes to religion," I said, "you and I had similar experiences in the way we were raised."

"Tell me more."

"My parents left it to me to make up my own mind. Mom used to tell people she belonged to the 'Church of Saint Mattress.' Some would chuckle. A few thought she was serious and asked where it was located. Nevertheless, my folks offered to take me to any church I wanted. But as a boy who was active in sports and school life, I was happy to pass on Sunday school."

"I can relate to that."

"Like your experience, my drama was yet to come," I said. "When I was about ten years old, I asked my dad what happens when we die. My dad knew everything, so when he told me he didn't know, I was frightened out of my wits."

"So, it was that fear that led you to faith?" she asked as we continued up the trail again.

"As a matter of fact, I was led to faith," I said, "but not until college. I was a senior when my residence hall roommate hit me with a powerful explanation for my restlessness. He said it was because I didn't have Christ in my heart. He insisted that if I would ask Jesus into my life, I would experience the Lord's presence, power, and wisdom."

"That didn't make sense to you?" she asked.

"Oh, but it *did.* My roommate quoted the Bible with great enthusiasm. It was contagious, and he convinced me. I attended his church, prayed for Jesus to come into my heart, and received baptism. If Jesus was 'the truth, the way, and the life,' I wanted to be among the souls who would be saved."

She stopped. Her eyes searched my face as if waiting for the other shoe to drop. "And?" she asked.

"I'd fallen hard. I became certain that everything in the Bible was inspired by God, and I couldn't imagine any purpose in life more important than to understand the Lord's very words."

"What went wrong?" Victoria asked. "How did you fall off the tracks?"

A Steller's jay in the tree above issued a harsh squawk as if to accentuate her questions.

"I didn't. Not then. In fact, I decided I wanted to do more than just commit to leading a good life as a serious, sincere evangelical Christian. I changed my career aspirations and enrolled in Fuller Theological Seminary in Pasadena. I followed that with a PhD at the University of Chicago Divinity School."

Victoria looked more bewildered. "How would that not cement your faith?"

"At first it did. I was active in local churches and, when I graduated, was asked by one of them to serve as an interim pastor while they looked for a full-time person."

"You were a *pastor*?"

"For the better part of a year and a half, I preached on Sundays, visited sick parishioners—the usual duties of a pastor—in my community."

"It didn't suit you?"

"It wasn't that." My chest registered a dull pang. "As I preached in the pulpit on those Sundays, I realized I'd been losing my faith. It'd been a slow, cumulative process that accelerated more the longer I studied the Bible."

We paused at a view spot and gazed at a valley rimmed by granite peaks. Victoria looked at me with a gentle sadness, as though she viewed my soul as lost on one of those craggy mountainsides.

"It's beyond me to understand how you couldn't see God's truth after all that study," she said.

"I came to see quite the contrary. Rather than God's inspired word to humankind, I saw the Bible was full of contradictions. There were errors, even deliberate falsehoods."

Her face filled with dismay.

"Add to that," I continued, "the immeasurable suffering in the world. I felt disillusionment and hopelessness. I couldn't explain to myself how a God of love would allow such misery."

"I think you've lost sight of the forest for the trees," Victoria said. "Suffering may be necessary for spiritual growth."

"Maybe, but I don't think so. In any case, I could no longer preach or even continue as a pastor."

"So you traded your pulpit for a lectern."

I nodded. "My passion has now shifted to the world of academia, where I find great interest in studying how religion leads some people to altruism and others to malevolence."

The trail dipped and rose again past a vista of rocky bluffs on the other side of the valley. We paused for a breather near a clump of Indian paintbrush.

"Isn't it possible," Victoria asked, "that you're so close to your own subject you don't see the real reason people suffer? God has given us free will," she said, "to love and obey his laws, but also to disobey. That's where suffering comes from—the criminals, government corruption, the Holocaust!" Her eyes narrowed. "You must see that."

I drew in a deep breath, in part due to the eight-thousand-foot elevation, in part due to my weariness after the years of the free will explanation. "You know," I said, "the free will argument isn't prominent among the Bible's numerous, and often contradictory, explanations for why people suffer."

"I know the Bible well enough to know it's conspicuous throughout."

"Free will can explain *some* of the problems," I said. "Like when a hostile force invades a country—pillages the capital, rapes the women, slaughters the children, puts fellow members of its faith to the sword, and destroys libraries, precious relics, and art treasures."

Victoria nodded. "Exactly," she said. "Everyone agrees Islamic extremists must be stopped."

"I was referring to the Fourth Crusade in 1204 when Catholic knights sacked Constantinople."

"*Oh*," she said and winced. "That too was a heinous act of hypocrisy and abuse of power."

"And a good example of the free will you say is to blame for unspeakable atrocities today and throughout history," I said. "But how do you explain a famine in India that takes the lives of millions? Who chose not to obey God's laws that caused it *not* to rain? Or caused *too much* rain—hurricanes that put cities under water? How do you explain the million and a half deaths each year of kids under five from pneumonia and diarrhea? What did those mere children do wrong? Or the Black Death in the 1300s that killed over a hundred million vulnerable people, believers and nonbelievers alike?"

She looked perplexed for a moment but regained her bearing. "Yes, people suffer from natural disasters. But we're involved in an evolutionary process. The core of the Earth is still the same temperature as the surface of the *sun*. Our planet hasn't stabilized. It's a volatile place. Tectonic plates shift. Weather is unpredictable. Living cells divide, and chromosomes mutate, sometimes with unexpected and horrible consequences."

"*Of course*, our environment can be dangerous," I said, "but why doesn't God intervene to prevent suffering today like he did in biblical times? God blocked free will *then*. He destroyed the Egyptian army at the Red Sea, an army who's commander had *chosen* to keep the Israelites enslaved. And God intervened when he told Joshua how to collapse the walls of Jericho, whose inhabitants had *chosen* to resist Joshua's army. God intervened when he raised Jesus from the dead, to override the freely chosen decision to execute him."

Victoria stopped and turned to me with a sincere expression. "Have you considered that you may have overthought this? The Bible isn't an explanation for everything. Faith is part mystery. It's a mystical union with Christ that we may not fully comprehend.

Who are we to question when God should intervene? He works in mysterious ways."

"So does meningitis."

She chuckled. "We're talking about a moral compass," she said, "not a disease. If you submit *everything* to reason, you miss religion's spiritual truths."

I tilted my head toward her. "But if you submit *nothing* to reason, religion becomes absurd and ridiculous."

She gave a soft kick to a pinecone on the trail. "Keep in mind that people seek meaning in life," she said. Her tone turned philosophical. "Government, science, the business economies of our liberal Western democracy . . . they can't provide that. Science tells us how, but not *why*. It can't answer the questions we all ask ourselves: Who am I? Why am I here?" She peered into my face. "The consequence is that people today have an abundance of choice but a scarcity of meaning. Christianity *provides* that. That's why I value the church."

I nodded. "The search for meaning—that's something we do share."

Victoria resumed her smooth strides up the trail while I lingered a moment. I liked her thoughtful analysis of difficult subjects. I hastened to catch up.

Twenty minutes later, we reached the overlook at Devil's Fall. The scene exacted wonder from me—the remarkable beauty of a vast Sierra panorama. It would be just the opposite for Victoria—this was the place where her father had spent his last moments.

With slow, reverent steps, she edged toward the clearing, resolute in the face of tragedy. The world had just taken the most important person in her life, yet she was a fortress of self-control, bearing emotional pain with uncommon courage.

"There are four classic crime scene contaminators," the inspector said, "weather, suspects, souvenir collectors, and relatives of the victim."

I placed my hands behind me.

Shreve gave a wry smile. "Police personnel are also some of the worse contaminators."

He began to survey the area. His head turned in increments as he looked across the scene like a cinematographer in search of the best angle. He approached the first of a dozen lodgepole pines at the perimeter of the clearing and studied each tree trunk from the ground level to a height of seven or eight feet. After a minute, he would move to the next. He saw our curious looks. "Hope for some luck," he said.

Halfway around the periphery, he focused his attention on the bark of one tree. He took a photograph, removed a tool kit from his daypack, and dug into the trunk with a sharp probe. After a few moments, he removed a small object, slipped it into a plastic bag, and walked back to us.

"The coroner found some powder marks on your father's shirt," he said. "But no gunshot wound." He held up the bag. "This may be our bullet."

Victoria and I glanced at each other. I raised my eyebrows in an expression of hopefulness.

"The mark left on the tree is fresh," Shreve said. "The wood isn't darkened or scarred. No sign of a shell casing. The search-and-rescue team didn't find one either. Could have been picked up." He slipped the bag into his daypack. "This bullet is a key. Now we have to discover the lock it goes to."

Victoria looked upward into a cloudless cerulean sky, as if to appeal for an answer. "Who would do this?"

The only response was a soft breeze, a peaceful serenity. A sharp contrast to events the day before.

"I miss him," she said, her eyes moist with unshed tears. "I've such an ache inside. I'll not only miss his love but his advice. He once told me the person I must never try to fool, in any circumstance, is myself."

The lump in her throat was unmistakable.

"Maybe that's the case now," she said, "that I shouldn't even think I have the wherewithal to find the person responsible for his death." Emotion welled up in her voice. "I don't know how it will happen, but I will not let up until I do."

The degree of her reverence for her father was matched by the magnitude of her determination. We took one last look, then headed back down the trail.

15

Bill Miner
Bridgeport
7:00 PM

Rhino's Bar and Grille in Bridgeport was the kind of restaurant that would draw your attention by the size of the crowd that packed the place. I seated myself in a booth and waited for Victoria. Vests and hats festooned with fishing flies appeared to be the required dress for half the assemblage. The balance was rounded out by hikers in khaki shirts and dirt bikers in multicolored motorcycle pants. A big-screen TV was tuned to an A's game.

I'd just ordered a Sierra Nevada Pale Ale on tap when Victoria came in, spotted my booth, and slid in across from me. "I could use a glass of wine after today," she said.

I signaled the waitress.

"Chardonnay, please," Victoria said.

"You look nice," I said to Victoria. Her face was accented by a silk shoulder scarf with pale blue butterflies and a simple black blouse.

"Thank you. You clean up well too," she said with a soft smile.

Her wine arrived along with menus. A burst of raucous laughter rippled across the room from the bar. I asked the waitress if we could move to the adjacent dining room where it was a little quieter.

"Do you have any idea where we go from here?" Victoria asked as we seated ourselves at a corner table.

"I guess we wait for the forensics," I said.

She ran her finger around the rim of her glass and took a sip. "I can't imagine who would want to kill my father." Her eyes drifted around the room as if in search of a suspect among the men in hunting garb. "Maybe there wasn't a motive. Maybe it was just random violence. I mean, how could he have been targeted? Who could have even known he'd planned this trip other than me?"

She gazed toward me as if to coax out an explanation. I was helpless to relieve her ache.

"We know it wasn't arbitrary," I said. "The text message was specific and deliberate."

"I know. I just remember what you said, that cults don't murder people who aren't involved."

"I'm not sure what we're up against." My throat tightened, and I swallowed. "And I've not been much help to you."

"You came all the way here, and I appreciate that," she said.

"To be honest, I had another motive. I hoped to gain some material for a book with a deadline that's looming."

"What are you writing about?"

"Why good people do bad things in the name of religion."

"The world has seen a lot of that in recent years," she said.

"Indeed." I opened my menu. "Are you hungry?"

"I haven't felt much like eating since I arrived."

"You should have something," I said.

The waitress swung by, and Victoria ordered a cup of soup and a salad. I opted for a cheeseburger with fries.

"Tell me some more about your father," I said.

"I could talk to him about anything. He'd listen, sometimes make a comment, ask a question, then let me figure out the right thing to do."

"A good sounding board. We need more parents like that."

She nodded. "There was an occasional nudge at the right times, like when I began to date. He would tell me: don't do anything you'd be embarrassed about if you ran into that person again later in life." Victoria wagged her finger for emphasis.

"A dad with wisdom," I said, "but I gather your talks weren't always harmonious. This afternoon in the car, you said you were troubled by a subject you and he had discussed."

The hesitant look in her eyes told me she was judging whether to trust me.

"The trouble emerged from his operation," Victoria said. "Papa feared surgery, afraid he would die under the knife despite my assurances that open-heart surgery was an established, routine procedure. He worried because of guilt about what he'd done many years ago." She paused. "He'd killed someone."

My eyes widened. She held up her hand as if to prevent me from making an incorrect assumption.

"Papa was an infantry soldier in Vietnam. Self-condemnation always haunted him. He feared there would be consequences one day. Like in a country-western song, Papa didn't believe in heaven but was scared to death of hell."

Guilt, I thought. It can reach out from the church even when you don't belong.

"The army hadn't been anywhere on his radar when, after high school, he hitchhiked from Saint Louis to San Francisco and shared a cheap apartment in Haight-Ashbury. He used to tell me he thought he'd fallen right into the good times. That is, until Uncle Sam surprised him with a draft notice and sent him off to Southeast Asia."

Victoria's eyes had a distant, melancholy glaze.

"Papa's squad was on patrol along the banks of the Mekong Delta when they saw the enemy come down the river in a small boat. He heaved a grenade, and the explosion threw a Vietcong soldier up in the air. Papa had seen some deaths but had never been directly responsible. I sensed the memory always stayed with him, but he never wanted to talk about it."

"I'm moved by his remorse," I said. "With a war that received so much public rebuke, more people should hear *those* kinds of stories."

The waitress arrived with our food. The healthy appearance of Victoria's selection was a crisp contrast to my cheddar-dripping burger. "I confess," I said. "Sometimes I tell myself the calories printed on the menu are points and I want to win."

Victoria smiled. "Your funny side is a welcome antidote at a difficult time," she said. "Papa had a wonderful sense of humor too. He did so many positive things, yet that one incident in Vietnam haunted him."

"Hmm. Ask Bill Buckner," I said.

"Is he the baseball player remembered for the error?"

I nodded. "An easy ground ball went through his legs. Cost the Boston Red Sox the World Series. Poor guy. Despite a batting title and an all-star game to his credit, his sister told me he never got over that one mistake. I used to work with her."

"You're a baseball fan? Do you have his bobblehead?" I saw the hint of a grin.

"No, not his." Our conversation had digressed from the somberness of the day. A needed respite.

"I do have one," I said. "Don't laugh. The bobblehead I keep on my desk is the Lone Ranger."

16

Victoria Johnson
Bridgeport
7:30 PM

Had she heard him say, "The Lone Ranger"? He seemed intelligent, thoughtful, and mature, this good-looking man across from her with hazel-blue eyes and a full head of walnut-brown hair. She had noticed the absence of a wedding ring. "The Lone Ranger?" she repeated. "I'm trying to draw the picture here. An educated man abandons his belief in God, chooses instead a masked man on a white horse?" She let a half grin slip out as she sensed his attempt to gauge the amount of teasing in her question. "Is that right?"

Bill held up his beer glass as in a toast. "He never shoots to kill, lets the law dispense justice, and never hangs around to take any credit." He paused. "Nonviolence, fairness, humility. I figured one could have worse values."

She saw sincerity in his face and was surprised by the sudden warmth she felt toward him. "I think my papa would've liked you."

"I'll bet it would have been mutual," Bill said.

"Papa believed that taking human life was deplorable, even if it was a wartime enemy," Victoria said. "That's the reason he dreaded his operation. He imagined that if he died in surgery, hell was ready to gobble him up. Ironically, somebody would experience hell all right, but it wouldn't be the patient. It would be the surgical team."

Bill cocked his head to the side. "Why was that?"

"The evening I drove him to the hospital the fog in the Mission District was bad—'heavy as an old army blanket,' Papa described it. He worried it was an omen. I checked him in at San Francisco

General at seven PM. Surgery would be at nine the next morning. I waited until his preoperative tests were completed and kissed him good night, with assurances I'd be there throughout his surgery. I promised to keep Aunt Laura and Uncle Oliver updated."

Victoria took a sip of wine. She had second thoughts. Should she disclose the details of her father's operation to someone who wasn't a believer? She decided to trust her instincts.

"The next morning in surgery, things started off just fine," she said. "The preliminary surgical procedures had been completed, and the surgeon began to connect a cardiopulmonary bypass pump. That's when Papa's heart stopped. The surgeon yelled, 'Christ! He's arrested!' He shouted to a nurse in a yellow top to get a drug from a surgical cart."

"Wait a minute," Bill interrupted. "How'd you know what was going on?"

"I'll tell you in a second." She knew Bill would pick up on the significance. That was what worried her. There was the sound of glasses clinking in the background, and laughter from the patrons at the bar spilled into the dining area.

"The nurse grabbed a bottle, filled a hypodermic needle, and hurried back to the surgeon. Just as he was about to inject the drug, he looked at the bottle in the nurse's hand. 'No!' he shouted and raced to a cabinet. He almost knocked the nurse over in the process. He shouted, 'That could have killed him!' He searched the cabinet for the right bottle, returned with it, and injected atropine into Papa's heart. His vital signs remained flat. Frantic, the surgeon performed open-chest cardiac massage on Papa's heart. At last, blips. His heart began to beat. His vital signs began to stabilize."

"I hadn't realized there had been such complications," Bill said. "That's a pretty impressive eyewitness report. Don't tell me you were there in the operating room?"

"Of course not. The description is from Papa himself. He had a near-death experience and witnessed the entire scene. And if you find that a shocker, you haven't heard anything yet."

17

Victoria Johnson
Bridgeport
7:45 PM

"Papa's heart stopped," she went on. "In the middle of surgery, while he was under heavy anesthetics, yet he saw and heard every detail."

Bill gave a long, soft whistle. "What do your biotech colleagues think of this?" he asked.

"My company has studied near-death experiences. I'm familiar with the research but never expected to encounter one in my own family."

"I can imagine," Bill said.

"It was two months ago. I sat at the hospital bedside of the precious parent I'd almost lost. When Papa began to describe his near-death experience, I told him to wait a second. I fished my phone out of my purse and recorded our conversation."

She opened her voice-recorder app and selected the audio file. "Wait till you hear this." She hit PLAY.

Bill rested his arms on the table and leaned forward to listen.

PAPA — I lifted right out of my body. I floated up to the corner of the ceiling and looked down at frantic doctors working on a body lying on the table. . . . The body was me, Victoria!

VICTORIA — Easy, Papa. I can tell you're excited. A minute ago your eyes were drowsy. Now they sparkle. I'm listening to every word, and you're giving me goose bumps.

PAPA I could see and hear everything . . . kind of hovered there for a time, and then I felt my body pulled right up through the ceiling, then the roof. There I was, floating above the hospital looking around at the city skyline and the bay. Traffic on the James Lick was at a standstill near Hospital Curve, and I could see the reason—an accident. I heard the sirens as an ambulance and a police car fought their way through the congestion. A teenager was trapped in one car, and a woman was on the pavement. She looked in her early thirties, and for an instant I feared it could be you—a parent never ceases to worry about things like that. I continued to drift around in the air, and then something red on the hospital roof caught my eye—a Cardinals baseball cap.

VICTORIA This is amazing.

PAPA Without warning, I began to accelerate upward. The city fell away, then the earth. I traveled through darkness, I don't know how far or how long. In the distance, I saw a white light of dazzling brightness. I should have been terrified, but I wasn't . . . sort of the opposite. As I came closer to it, I felt an acceptance . . . warm and caring. I seemed to have arrived at some place, but I had no idea where. Three figures approached. They didn't have physical form, but I *knew* them . . my parents and my brother! What a joy. It was like I'd come home.

VICTORIA Your face has the most color it's had since you were admitted.

PAPA I hear a beeping sound.

VICTORIA That's the cardiac monitor. . . . Your pulse rate's up. Calm down a bit, Papa, but I want to hear more.

PAPA This light began to speak to me, Victoria. Not regular words, but with thoughts. It asked me, what had I done with my life to contribute to the betterment of humanity? I thought, *Oh no. This is it. This is my judgment.* Instead, I started to see pictures, one after the other, a movie of my life, like a movie camera had always been on. Time was like a series of blinks. Scenes flashed in front of me. Everything . . . with all the emotions, the good times, the bad. Many I'd long forgotten.

VICTORIA I'm breathless, Papa. The light? A life review?

PAPA It wasn't like a motion picture in a theater. I was in it, reliving my entire life. But this time from a unique perspective—from the other person's point of view. Victoria, you know how we all go through life with plans and intentions and maybe we settle for just being a law-abiding citizen? Turns out that what's of greater significance is how we *treat* each other. Manners may be more important than laws! Like when you're in traffic, and the driver ahead of you doesn't notice the signal's changed, and you get annoyed and lay on the horn. Trivial things like that matter, because manners have both the power to infuriate and to comfort. When I blamed others for my mistakes or my shortcomings—I now experienced how it affected the other person. I felt the sting they felt at the time. The Golden Rule . . . it's more than I'd ever realized. The light read my mind and told me the Golden Rule isn't just a moral edict. It's the way things *work*.

VICTORIA Papa! That's Jesus's message too—just as you treated the least of my brothers, you treated me. All this time I've been trying to get you to accept Jesus, and this is what it took . . . you almost *dying*. Maybe this is a blessing after all. You've made my hopes soar.

PAPA Well, then I said, "Could I ask a question?" And the light said yes, anything I liked. So I asked if Jesus was divine.

VICTORIA Whoa. OK. . . . And?

PAPA It said, "Of course Jesus is divine. Just as you are."

VICTORIA Just as *you* are? You must have misheard.

PAPA Yeah, well, I figured the light didn't understand me. So, I said, "Excuse me. . . . What I meant was . . . was Jesus the Son of God?" And the light said . . . "*All* souls are sons and daughters of God."

VICTORIA Huh?

PAPA I asked, "But wasn't he born of the Virgin Mary, rose from the dead . . . that kind of thing? And the light answered that Mary and Joseph conceived Jesus in the normal way.

VICTORIA Papa, don't tease like this.

PAPA I'm not. That's what it said. And it told me Jesus rose from the dead all right . . . but that everyone does.

VICTORIA A moment ago, you had me euphoric. Now you come up with this silliness.

PAPA I see you're flustered. I didn't know what to make of it either. So, I asked how come that was such a far cry from what they teach in chur—

VICTORIA Papa! It's not just a far cry. It's utter nonsense!

PAPA The light said the Gospels were written in a mood of euphoria and acclamation. Jesus was perfection, and the Trinity could be understood as a metaphor.

VICTORIA Ohhh, Papa.

PAPA Don't be upset with me.

VICTORIA I'm not upset with *you*, Papa. I let my hopes run wild for a moment there. I'm just . . . frustrated.

PAPA It didn't seem so unreasonable to me. Do you want to hear any more?

VICTORIA Of course.

PAPA I asked what people were supposed to believe. What about Adam and Eve? The light said the writers of Genesis wanted to assert their faith in God, not give a literal account of how the world was formed. That's left to scientists.

VICTORIA I'm OK with evolution, Papa. . . . This other stuff . . . You and I are right back at square one. . . . We need to have a serious talk when you're recovered.

PAPA There was something else. I asked if everybody ended up in this place. The light said everyone did, that there weren't any exceptions. I asked if that included murderers and rapists?

It said yes.

I asked, "Even terrorists?"

It said yes.

VICTORIA It's not that way, Papa. There're bad people . . . and they'll be judged.

PAPA I know that's what the church says . . . but that's not what the light said. It said no one is inherently evil.

VICTORIA Papa, that's not true. There's evil in this world.

PAPA Well, I didn't get the impression there were any free passes, because the light said *everyone* was accountable for their own conduct. If a person savagely wronged others, it was their *own soul* they injured. Injury that would require significant effort to heal and repair.

VICTORIA Oh, Papa . . . what will it take for you to understand? . . . You can't heal without Jesus.

PAPA Victoria, that's true for you but not for me. Anyway, the light told me it wasn't my time. I had to return. Then heaven just spit me back out.

18

Bill Miner
Bridgeport
8:30 PM

"It was an emotional whiplash," Victoria said as she turned off the recording and put her phone back in her purse. "I'd gone from a moment of exhilaration—that Papa might believe in Jesus—to a crushing letdown when he drifted into religious rubbish. I was numb."

I had no problem with the part about the divinity of Jesus, most of which was consistent with biblical scholarship of the last hundred years. My problem was that her father had gotten those responses from "*a light*." The racket of dishes and glassware being cleared from the table next to us mirrored the jangled thoughts in my head. How was it that a man who had shunned religion, had been nowhere near a church since his youth, could conjure up such an insightful dialogue about theology?

"I kept waiting for Papa to say this was all a joke."

No wonder Victoria had been hesitant to tell me about this—something so contrary to her evangelical faith, to someone who was no longer a believer. It could have been her wine that had made her tell me. It would have been nice to think it was a sign of her increased trust in me. But maybe that thought was my beer talking.

"It was very real to him," she said after a few moments. "But I know there has to be some explanation. Maybe anesthesia does play a role."

"Does anyone else know about this?" I asked.

"Papa told his surgeon, Dr. Lee. I was there. Papa told him that he had seen the whole thing—described the emergency in the operating room when his heart stopped."

I could picture the shock on the surgeon's face.

"Dr. Lee said that it would be out of the question that Papa could have seen what was happening, impossible. Papa was under deep anesthesia, had no cardiac electrical activity. Papa replied, 'Well, I saw how angry you got when that nurse handed you the wrong bottle of medicine.' When the doctor asked how he knew about the nurse, Papa said he saw her in the hallway when they transferred him, recognized her yellow top. The doctor kept frowning and asked if Papa had heard all this from someone on the medical staff. Papa said he hadn't talked to any of the other nurses or doctors. At that point, Dr. Lee looked uneasy. He eyed Papa, then me. He didn't know what to say."

Victoria pressed her fingers to her forehead as if still trying to sort out where to draw the line between that which she could believe and that which distressed her too much.

"Dr. Lee said this was new to him," she said. "Colleagues had talked about cases like this but attributed them to drug-induced hallucinations."

I looked down at my beer glass and didn't say anything, but I knew my reaction would've been like the surgeon's.

"Dr. Lee admitted Papa was correct about what had happened," Victoria said, "but said he was at a loss to understand."

Ditto, I thought. A twinge in my gut told me something would turn up to account for all this, some scientific explanation.

"The doctor asked him if he remembered anything else about the surgery. Papa told him about floating above the roof, seeing the red cap, and the traffic accident. He described talking with the light and the surprise of seeing his brother. He didn't mention his conversations about Jesus. I think because I was present, and he knew how upset it'd make me."

Our waitress stopped by our table.

"Just the check, please," I said.

We sat quietly for a few moments. I wondered if I could handle such a loss with her strength. Times like this I missed a strong faith to draw on.

"Did the surgeon ever buy your father's story?" I asked.

"Dr. Lee told Papa that hallucinations, whether caused by oxygen deprivation, drugs, or blood loss, tended to fade with time. He said he'd be interested to see if they remained vivid in the days ahead when he saw him for follow-up visits. Papa asked if someone could look for the cap in the meantime. The doctor chuckled and said he would ask building maintenance to be on the lookout. Papa answered with his unflappable grin that it was a Saint Louis Cardinals cap, but he hadn't gotten the size."

"I'll bet the surgeon thought he would eat the cap if they found it," I said. "I would have."

Victoria turned serious. "When Papa and I were alone, I said, listen: No one goes to heaven and receives forgiveness of sins without accepting Jesus Christ as their savior. There's no such thing as cut-rate grace. I said his story that everybody ends up in heaven . . . that's not the way it happens. I gave him a kiss on his forehead and said I'd be back later that evening.

"I drove out of the hospital parking lot and headed to the office, thankful but shaken. I clicked on KCBS to hear the news and weather. My mind was still thinking about how close I'd come to losing him when a newscast jarred me: There *was* an accident on the James Lick Freeway that morning. A thirty-four-year-old woman was critically injured when her car was sideswiped by another vehicle. Bill . . . nine thirty AM!"

I felt my eyes grow large. "The accident your father witnessed." I stiffened and sat straight up. "While he was flatlined." My thoughts scrambled to understand.

19

Bill Miner
Bridgeport
8:50 PM

"There's more icing on this preposterous cake," Victoria said. "Dr. Lee, to humor Papa—or maybe to disprove his story—requested the head of maintenance to look for the baseball cap. I guess maintenance wasn't thrilled and griped that it wasn't enough with all the calls about patients complaining their rooms were too hot or too cold. Now they were supposed to be a lost and found. The supervisor sent one of his workers to inspect the roof ventilation fans, telling him to look around while he was up there for a stupid cap."

Don't tell me, I thought.

"The maintenance guy said he walked out on the roof, inspected the fans, and strolled around the perimeter. Saw nothing. There are two five-story wings joined in the middle in an H shape. He patrolled the roof. Nothing. He was about to call it quits when sure enough there it was—wedged in a corner, invisible from any angle except from above—impossible to have been seen from a hospital window."

I shook my head. "Has anything like this been recorded before?"

"There've been many remarkable near-death accounts," Victoria said, "but few have been verifiable."

"What was the reaction of the hospital staff?"

"Incredulous, of course. I was there during evening visiting hours when the surgeon walked in with the Cardinals cap and stared at Papa. 'I have to ask myself,' Dr. Lee said, 'what is the probability that a sixty-seven-year-old man, in this hospital for the first time, under anesthesia, experiencing the cessation of all vital signs, is able to see a baseball cap, out of sight of his physical location, and identify its specific features? Well, it's not bloody likely. And your astounding observations during the surgery? Inexplicable.' "

I felt an uneasy twinge down my spine. Not just inexplicable, downright spooky. In contrast, the merriment of the bar crowd in the next room seemed to be just heating up, and I leaned closer to hear over the noise that had escalated.

"And I was about to receive yet another shock," Victoria said. "I got a phone call from a friend of my relatives in New Jersey. She told me Aunt Laura and Uncle Oliver had been in a car accident on their way home. It had been the night before Papa's surgery. Aunt Laura was in the hospital, injured but expected to recover. Uncle Oliver had died at the scene. I was heartsick, and then it hit me. My uncle had died just twelve hours before Papa had his surgery. And in his near-death experience, Papa *saw* him."

Victoria sat back and sighed.

"That's four verifiable events," I said.

She nodded. "Four things Papa could not have known about: the nurse who grabbed the wrong drug in the operating room, the traffic accident on the James Lick, the baseball cap on the roof, and that his brother, whom he saw in the near-death experience, had died the night before."

We sat a few moments in silence. If Victoria's father had been right about *those* things, the implication that what he'd been told about Jesus was also true was clear.

"It's been a difficult two days, and right now I need to find my bed," Victoria said.

We left the boisterous crowd and walked back to the motel.

"Thanks for dinner," she said when we reached her door.

"Sleep tight," I said, then steered my way down the walk to my room.

I should've been fighting to keep my eyes open by then, but what Victoria had described about her father had me wide awake. I grabbed a jacket, went back outside, and strolled around the block. The mountain air was chilly, the sky cloudless with a spectacular backdrop of stars, a crescent moon like something out of a Chiura Obata painting.

Astrologers would love what Victoria had told me that night. Was it a paranormal tale from the realm of the metaphysical, tarot-reading, spiritualist crowd that frequented New Age bookstores on Telegraph Avenue? Had her father lapsed back into a fog from his Haight-Ashbury years? That idea didn't fit with her description of him. Quite the opposite. A down-to-earth, caring, thoughtful father who sounded very rational.

But then how did you explain his description of events he couldn't have known about? My head spun with questions and my own personal doubts about whether I could be of any help in this investigation.

I made another lap around the block.

Then you add something unexpected: an intelligent woman who had captivated me with her grace. At thirty-five years of age, I'd dated a fair amount, even thought I'd been in love a time or two, but never deeply enough to establish a permanent relationship. This felt different.

Personal feelings aside, I knew I needed to focus on her father's death. That meant I should get some sleep if I was going to have any semblance of wits in the morning. I made one more lap around the block and strolled back to my room at the Silver Maple.

20

Mandy Frankel
Ballard
Day 3, 2:15 AM

The rain in the Ballard neighborhood of Seattle had stopped by the time Mandy Frankel stepped out onto her front porch. A cool moonlight flooded the front yard, etching it with shifting shadows from trees and shrubs. She reached into her purse for car keys, switched off the light, and closed the front door. She pulled her jacket a little tighter against the chill and started toward the car.

She had taken but a few steps when she saw movement near the large sycamore by the side of the house. She stopped, gripped by sudden alarm. The motion was not a branch swaying from the faint breeze. A man's figure stepped from the darkness. Mandy's heart pounded. Her throat tightened, unable to scream.

The last thing she heard was her name.

The last thing she saw was the knife.

21

Bill Miner
Bridgeport
7:00 AM

I was already awake, staring at the ceiling, when my alarm chimed. Thoughts swarmed in my head like gnats. Was I anywhere closer to my goal? Instead of providing the opportunity to complete my book, this crazy turn of events had become anything but that: a murder, by all appearances, of a good, decent man; a plea for help from his devoted daughter; a dearth of clues; a want of motive. But it boiled down to this: I was there to assist law enforcement. That had to be my number one priority. Material to complete my book—second. Dean Russell might argue I had gotten sidetracked, but since I hadn't advanced on either objective, I supposed it didn't matter. I scrambled out of bed, went into the bathroom, and stared in the mirror. Worry reflected at me. I showered, dressed, and met Victoria in the motel breakfast room. One glance at her raised my spirits. We made small talk over cereal and muffins.

After breakfast, we walked the two blocks to Inspector Shreve's office.

"We entered the bullet into NIBIN, the National Integrated Ballistics Information Network," Shreve said. "Results just came back." His voice was deadpan and emotionless. "There was no match to existing records."

I frowned. "Does that mean what I think it means?"

Shreve nodded.

I felt a sinking in my gut as the inspector explained.

"Agencies all over the nation use this system to acquire digital images of the markings made on fired cartridge casings and bullets recovered from crime scenes. They compare those images against earlier entries electronically."

Victoria's eyes met mine, her lips pressed tight.

"If a high-confidence candidate for a match should surface," Shreve said, "firearms examiners compare the original evidence with a microscope for confirmation. In our case, no match means that the weapon fired at Devil's Fall has no link to any prior crime."

I slumped back in my chair. So much for the lucky lead.

"So, what do we do?" Victoria asked.

"It's possible the firearm could be still outstanding. All information on this case will go into a regional information-sharing network. Something may turn up." Shreve's face softened in empathy. "I'm afraid there's nothing further I can do at this point. I assure you this case will remain open, and I'll keep you informed."

Victoria gave me a questioning look as if she hoped I would have some sudden flash of insight. I had zero. We left Shreve's office with stony expressions. My thoughts turned to the trip back home.

"How did you get here?" I asked, as we walked back to the motel.

"I flew into Reno, then Uber."

I gave a nonchalant shrug. "Pleasant Hill's on the way to Berkeley."

"Thank you. That'd be nice."

"Let's get our things," I said.

We checked out of our motel rooms and thirty minutes later were headed north on 395 for the five-hour trip home. We drove awhile without talking. I felt dispirited—we'd hit a dead end.

"Yesterday you told me there had been some changes in your father after his surgery," I said.

"Yes, but even his recovery was not without drama. There was the publicity."

"What publicity?"

"The article in the newspaper." She crossed her arms and grimaced. "Dr. Lee had discussed Papa's case with some of the other doctors. There's an organization that collects information on people who've had near-death experiences, and the hospital arranged for someone to talk to Papa. A newspaper reporter got wind of it and finagled his way in to see him. The next thing I know there's a story in the *Chronicle*: 'Man Witnesses Traffic Accident While under Anesthesia.' " I could hear the exasperation in her voice.

"So, it went public?" I chuckled the way you do when something is uncomfortable rather than funny. "That must've embarrassed you."

"I was mortified. And Papa knew I was. That's the only reason he agreed to go with me to talk with the pastor at my church. Papa told Pastor Roy the whole thing, complete with the part about Jesus."

"Good luck with that," I blurted before I could edit my words.

"Well, you're right. Pastor Roy remained stiff, with a downturned mouth, the entire time. I hadn't expected him to react like that. He insisted that Papa had experienced the work of Satan, scolded him that all angels were not of heaven, and said if my father had read Scripture, he would have known Satan is able to disguise himself as an angel of light."

Victoria clicked her tongue.

"My pastor reminded Papa that the Bible says whoever is not with Jesus is against him."

We passed a slow-moving eighteen-wheeler with a load of cattle. The smell drifting into the car reminded me of what I'd come to think of pastors who favored that verse. The thought, more than the aroma, left a sour tang in my throat.

"Pastor Marc, our associate pastor, had joined us earlier," Victoria said. "He had also seen the newspaper article and took a real interest in what Papa had to say. Pastor Marc is younger, doesn't come across as critical and judgmental. On the other hand, Pastor Roy didn't want to hear any more unless Papa recanted his statements to the reporter."

"What was your father's reaction?" I noticed I was gripping the wheel tightly.

"I thought Papa might have flared up, but he just listened. So I prayed he would take it seriously. I mean, Pastor Roy was harsh, but he did have a point, don't you think?"

I looked at the mountain scenery that streamed by and reminded myself it wasn't that long ago I too had been a man of the cloth. "The thing about the 'whoever is not with me' verse your pastor referred to is that Jesus used similar words in three of the Gospels."

Victoria nodded. "It bears repeating," she said.

I slowed for an RV ahead of us, then passed it. "But in two of those three Gospels, it doesn't repeat. It contradicts."

22

Bill Miner
California Highway 108 at Sonora Junction
10:30 AM

Victoria cocked her head to the side. "What do you mean, 'contradicts'?"

"In Matthew, Jesus says, 'Whoever is not with me is against me,' the version your pastor referenced. But in both Luke and Mark, Jesus says, 'Whoever is not against you is for you.' "

She hiked an eyebrow and gave me a cautious look.

"Two of the three versions say that if a person isn't *against* Jesus, they're *for* him," I said. "Bothers me when I hear pastors quote the minority opinion." I shrugged. "Did your father ever say he was against Jesus?"

"No, of course not. The point is you must accept Jesus as your savior. That's fundamental and I wanted Papa to do that."

"I just think your pastor's judgment of your father was unfair," I said. "I'm no longer a believer, so my interpretation of your father's experience is going to be a lot different from your pastor's, and from yours."

"I appreciate that. What is the interpretation of someone who no longer believes in God?"

I became ill at ease, hesitant to provoke an argument. "I suspect that what your father experienced was real to him just as I'm convinced that the apostle Paul believed he saw a vision of Jesus on the road to Damascus. That doesn't mean I believe Paul saw Jesus, just that it was real to Paul."

"Well, Papa's illusion was very real to him," Victoria said. She sat quietly for a minute. "My pastor is fond of saying that the devil's greatest trick, among Satan's other deceptions, is to persuade us that he doesn't exist. Maybe Papa was tricked."

"The devil's greatest trick?" I said. "That's not from the Bible. That came from the nineteenth-century French poet Charles Baudelaire. I don't believe in the devil, but if I did, I think Satan would be craftier than that."

"*Craftier?* You don't think Satan is the very essence of devious?"

"If the devil wished to create chaos in the world, turmoil to disrupt God's plans, all he would need to do is plant the seed of belief in each religion that *their* doctrine is the sole truth."

"But, Bill . . . you fail to appreciate that there's a war going on out there. The devil wants to turn you away from Christ, and if you don't think Satan exists, then you won't engage seriously in the fight."

"War? It seems more like a circular firing squad to me. Sincere human beings of one faith assaulting sincere human beings of another."

"I was speaking figuratively," she said. "Most armed conflicts have nothing to do with religion. Some of my colleagues point to the Crusades, Northern Ireland, and 9/11 as evidence that religion is the cause of most wars. But that's not true. Only seven percent of all conflicts throughout recorded history have been due to religion."

I nodded. I was familiar with that research, and Victoria was right.

"Most war is about territorial conquest and political disputes," she continued. "Two world wars, Korea, and Vietnam—the highest number of war causalities in any century in human history, and *none* were about religion."

"But there *is* a connection," I said. "The vicious competition between faiths is like a nasty sibling rivalry."

"I see that, but look at the positives: Christianity works to *build* communities of faith. It guides those communities. It nurtures marriage. It nurtures families."

"Perhaps, but we digress. Let's get back to your father."

She emitted a sigh. "I don't know how to explain what Papa said about the Bible, about Jesus," she said.

"You don't think he made it up, do you?" I asked.

"No. He wouldn't lie to me *or* himself. How could he have made it up? It's like he described a supernatural intervention"—she threw her hands up—"except that's ridiculous."

"Intervention? Who knows?" I said. "Think of all the miracles, the timely revelations that occurred just when civilization seemed most in need: Moses received the Ten Commandments; Jesus's birth, death, and resurrection; Muhammad obtained the Koran; Buddha found enlightenment."

Victoria gave me a quizzical look, as if to gauge whether I was serious.

"Well, just suppose your father's experience was a new manifestation of divine involvement," I said. "Don't you think the world could use a lift about now? That was a grand message your father got from his near-death experience: that everyone ends up in heaven, that in the meantime we should think about how we treat other people, practice the Golden Rule."

"You're talking like my father was some kind of *prophet*."

"What he said was pretty appealing."

"Papa wasn't even a *believer*."

"Neither was Paul until he had an epiphany."

She blew out an exasperated breath.

"A prophet? OK, maybe not," I said. "It just struck me that he brought back a vision of love and mercy without all the dogma. That kind of stuff often generates new religious movements."

"Those new religious movements are foolish—people taken in by some false prophet with a quirky reinterpretation of the Bible, people deceived by some self-righteous manipulator who says, 'Listen to me' when they should just pay attention to Scripture."

I smiled inside. She stuck to her guns. I admired that.

"Excuse me," I said. "Isn't that exactly what Jesus said? 'You have heard that it was said . . . but *I* say to you . . .'?"

Victoria crossed her arms. "Point well taken," she said.

"Indeed, Jesus made stunning *reinterpretations* of Scripture," I said. "And when Christianity came on the scene two thousand years ago, *it* was the new kid on the block."

"Please," she said. "I'd rather not do this all the way home."

"I'll take that into consideration."

A half smile slipped onto her lips.

23

Tim Lane
Seattle-Tacoma International Airport
10:40 AM

Tim Lane boarded his flight through Sea-Tac gate thirty-seven. His conscience disquieted him. Mandy Frankel had been young, but there were boundaries. He reminded himself that his job was not for the timid or weak. The Messenger had said this was a task for one who was willing to step over the line and out of his comfort zone. One who showed himself by his actions to be a true disciple of Christ. People like that would lay hold of the kingdom. Murder may be wrong, the Messenger had reasoned, but Lane's actions would be sanctified by the coming destruction of nonbelievers by the righteous fury of Christ at the End Times.

Lane settled into an aisle seat next to a boy with Harry Potter glasses. Lane judged the lad to be about six years old, a front tooth still coming in. "I have a son about your age. His name is Noah."

"My name's Connor," the boy replied. "I'm going to Kansas City to see Grandma and Grandpa." He gestured toward the window seat. "This is my mom."

The woman smiled and nodded.

"You have a charming and well-mannered son," Lane said. He buckled his seat belt as the flight attendant began routine safety instructions.

After a few minutes, Connor retrieved a book from his backpack. The large, colorful pictures caught Lane's attention, and his stomach tensed when he recognized the subject matter. He brushed back a curl of red hair from his forehead as if to sweep away memories of frustration and humiliation that had risen in him like agitated hornets. He closed his eyes and thought how he might approach the topic that absorbed his young seatmate.

"I see you like dinosaurs, Connor," Lane said. "What book do you have there?"

The youth's eyes brightened. "*Little Kids First Big Book of Dinosaurs*. It's by National Geographic. This is archaeopteryx," Connor said as he tilted the page for Lane to see.

"That your favorite?"

"Not my favorite, just interesting because it had feathers. It was a link between dinosaurs and birds. My favorite is this one here, triceratops."

Lane nodded and glanced over at Connor's mother. She had a book in her lap but appeared to have dozed off. Lane focused on her son.

"Do you believe in the Bible, Connor?"

"Uh-huh. Mrs. Withe reads us stories in Sunday school."

"Good, I'm glad you believe. Not everybody does. Let me ask you a question: Does your book say dinosaurs lived millions of years ago?"

"Two hundred and thirty million years ago," Connor said without hesitation. "But then they all died. Well, they didn't completely die, because we have birds, and birds came from the dinosaurs." He tilted his head back against the seat with an expression of satisfaction like a child who knew he had given the right answer when called on by his teacher.

"But, Connor, how do you fit dinosaurs into the Bible? That they existed millions of years before man—how do you fit that claim into the Bible?"

Connor became quiet, his face confused.

Lane leaned toward the boy. "The answer is very easy. You can't. You can't fit scientists' interpretation of dinosaurs into the Bible."

Connor's head flinched back slightly.

"Books like that tell people birds are living dinosaurs. You're being brainwashed. Reptiles have scales. Birds have feathers. Feathers are nothing like scales. You need to think."

Connor's head tilted forward, and his glasses edged down his nose.

"I'll bet they say birds evolved from dinosaurs to be able to fly," Lane said.

Connor hesitated and pushed his glasses back. "Sort of," he said. "It says archaeopteryx was a dinosaur *and* a bird, and then birds evolved."

"So, Connor, if they were *already* birds, they didn't need to learn how to fly. Did a dinosaur say to himself, 'You know, it'd be a lot faster to get around if I didn't have to walk everywhere? I think I'll fly'? If it were that easy to solve the problem, human beings would have been flying a long time ago. So is it believable?"

A flight attendant arrived at their aisle with peanuts and drinks. Lane got a ginger ale, and Connor got a chocolate milk.

"Look at how different birds and dinosaurs are from one another," Lane said. He kept his tone quiet and matter-of-fact. "Dinosaurs had solid bones like we do. Birds have hollow bones. Did you know that?"

"No," Connor said.

"There are many differences. Birds have a different breathing system than dinosaurs. In birds, air flows into their lungs in one direction. This way the air is always fresh and has more oxygen. Birds *need* more oxygen because flying takes so much energy."

Lane saw the boy's eyes grow large.

"Dinosaur lungs were like ours," he continued. "They had a two-way system. Air went in, turned around, and came back out the same way. Fresh air was mixed with old air that had already been in the lungs. Not as efficient."

The boy pulled the book close to his chest.

"If birds came from dinosaurs," Lane said, "how did they change a two-way system like dinosaurs have into a one-way system like birds have . . . and do it instantaneously? Because if you miss more than a few breaths . . . you're dead!"

Connor blinked, startled.

"So the idea that dinosaurs changed into birds is impossible."

The boy pulled himself upright in his seat. "But have you heard about the fossils?" he asked.

Lane smiled. Sitting upright with such an earnest expression made Connor look like a young Daniel Radcliffe.

"Of course," Lane said. "Dinosaur fossils are simply the result of Noah's flood. The mistake scientists make is their assumptions are not biblical."

"They don't believe in the Bible?" Connor asked.

"It doesn't sound like they do, does it?"

A static-punctuated voice from the captain announced the plane's cruising altitude, the estimated arrival time in Kansas City, and the plane's current location over southern Idaho. When the pilot tipped the wings to adjust course, Lane caught a brief glimpse of the Snake River. Idaho would be his final stop on the way back.

He turned his attention again to the boy. "Here's another thing, Connor. Scientists found evidence of cancer in the bones of dinosaurs . . . who they say existed sixty-five million years before man. Think about it. If cancer existed, then when God created man and said everything was good, he was including cancer? Can you imagine God saying cancer is good?"

Connor shook his head. "But then when did the dinosaurs come?"

Lane noticed a woman across the aisle with a frown on her face lean closer to listen. He lowered his voice. "That's easy," he whispered. "It wasn't millions of years ago. The Bible says they were created on day six. The word 'dinosaur' doesn't appear there, but neither does 'giraffe,' 'cat,' or 'kangaroo,' but I know they were all created on day six. You know why? Because God said that's when he made all the land animals. People *saw* dinosaurs."

Lane's softer voice seemed to heighten a sense of drama in the boy's eyes.

"Have you ever read stories about dragons?"

Connor nodded.

"Then you know many countries have legends about them. They're not just in Harry Potter. Maybe they weren't legends after all. Maybe they were real. Maybe they were describing dinosaurs. American Indians drew pictures of wild animals like eagles and bears. Did you know they also drew pictures of dinosaurs?"

Lane saw he had the boy spellbound.

"Here's something for you to think about," Lane said. He leaned closer again and stared into Connor's eyes. "How did they make such accurate drawings of dinosaurs if they never saw one?

Did you know there's a famous picture of a dinosaur engraved on a rock wall in Utah?"

Connor shook his head.

"The world wasn't created eons ago. The Bible tells us it's less than ten thousand years old. That proves dinosaurs and humans were here at the same time."

"I would love to see a live dinosaur," Connor said.

"Who knows?" Lane said. "Some believe they may still exist in the deepest interiors of countries like Africa."

He saw an expression of wonder on the young boy's face.

"But in the meantime, keep one thing in mind. Your thinking needs to start with the Word of God, because the Bible is giving you the truth."

Lane crossed his arms and leaned back in his seat. Maybe he'd planted a seed.

24

Bill Miner
California Highway 108
11:00 AM

Victoria and I drove by Leavitt Meadows and continued the steep climb to Sonora Pass at ninety-six hundred feet. My vintage Volvo made low-pitched complaints until I shifted into a lower gear.

"So, your pastor concluded your father had been seduced by Satan," I said. "With such a warm, compassionate reception, I can't imagine why your father shunned church."

"Do not sit in the seat of mockers," Victoria said, admonishing me for my sarcasm.

I shifted in my seat. "Psalm 1," I acknowledged.

What was I thinking? Instead of something that would help find her father's killer, something that would impress Victoria, I seemed to come up only with remarks that irritated her.

I paused a moment, then said, "Victoria, I don't know if you were expecting me to come in and solve this like Sherlock Holmes, but it's obvious that's not going to happen. I worry whether I'll be of any help at all."

"Don't feel that way," she said. "I'm venting my despair on you."

"Tell me some more about your father," I said. "What happened after he came home from the hospital? The more feel I have for him, the better I may get at this."

She was quiet a minute, as if focusing her memory. In the rearview mirror, I monitored an impatient driver who was halfway up my tail pipe.

"My main concentration was on his recovery," Victoria said. "He seemed more relaxed, with a renewed appreciation for life. More grateful. I'd even like to say, in a sense, more spiritual, but I couldn't get him to equate that with the church. My pastor's remarks didn't help. Papa said something interesting. He insisted that the place his near-death experience had taken him—the other side—was truer, more genuine, more real, than his existence on earth. It was his present life that seemed surreal by comparison."

This *highway* was surreal. I dropped my speed to navigate the crazy hairpin turns and steep elevation changes.

"Papa's recovery exceeded everyone's expectations," Victoria continued. "He resumed full activity, looked better than ever, became more outgoing. He befriended a neighbor he used to call the grumpiest man in the block, volunteered for Meals on Wheels, did a lot of reading, resumed his hiking. He became somewhat unflappable. You know what he told me after his home was burglarized?"

"Saved him a trip to Goodwill?"

"Exactly. He said the things taken were immaterial, and maybe the thief needed them more than he did."

"Unselfish attitude."

"Papa was always charitable. Now he became even more so. I still harped about the church. I told him I believed it all came down to Jesus, that he is God's only begotten son, that he gives my life meaning and purpose, and he could do the same for him. I said I would give anything for Papa to know the real Jesus and I would die for that. And what did Papa say? He said he *did* die, and he *did* learn about Jesus." She sighed.

Once again, Victoria had shared something intensely personal. From the moment we had met, I'd been attracted by her physical appearance. But there was so much more: her sincerity, openness, and loyalty. In addition, there was the sheer intrigue of the situation. Just what *was* this near-death episode that had had a powerful effect on her father?

I skirted a turn and slowed as we came upon a great gray wolf standing on a rise near the highway shoulder.

"Oh, look how handsome," Victoria said. "The wolf has always been a symbol of both good and evil, the mysterious versus the demonic. I can sense fire in those eyes."

In a blink the creature was gone, vanished into the forest.

"I think of them as predators," I said, "but your interpretation raises the question of whether your father had any associations that concerned you—anyone who might prey on a senior citizen."

"No one I was aware of other than an occasional salesman. I made him promise to check with me before he signed any contracts. But if you're asking who might do him harm?" She shook her head. "I can't even imagine."

"OK, let's consider what we know," I said. "It wasn't a random act. The text message was deliberate and sent to you before your father was killed. So the person who did that, the probable owner of the bracelet, must have known your father would hike *that* trail on *that* particular day." I glanced over. "Who would know that?"

"It would have to be a friend or neighbor," Victoria said, "because I didn't mention it to anyone. Whenever he planned a trip, he'd always let me know the details. I insisted on that agreement, so I wouldn't worry.

"We should be to the Bay Area by three o'clock. If you like, we could meet at your father's house tomorrow . . . talk to some neighbors."

I wanted to be helpful, but to be honest, I didn't want our acquaintanceship to end when we reached Pleasant Hill.

"That's very considerate," Victoria said. "Thank you."

I felt the warmth of her appreciation without taking my eyes off the road.

25

Victoria Johnson
Pleasant Hill, CA
3:30 PM

Victoria had been home for thirty minutes when she answered her front door and was enveloped in the arms of Angie.

Tears Victoria had bottled up spilled forth, uncontrolled, as she embraced her best friend.

"I held it in," Victoria sobbed, "until I saw you." She buried her head in Angie's shoulder. "I miss . . . Papa." Victoria's lips quivered. Each word felt heavy with the weight of eternity.

"I wish I knew what to say," Angie said.

"Nothing," Victoria murmured. "Our friendship means not having to say anything. Just your being here is enough."

The two moved into the living room and dropped onto the couch next to each other. "He always taught me to be strong," Victoria said. Her voice cracked as she cried softly. "I'm broken."

"You are one of the strongest women I know," Angie said, her eyes tender and full of empathy. "This would bring anyone to their knees."

"You've always been there for me," Victoria said. "You held me together when my engagement fell apart. That was like a skinned knee compared to this."

"You have a strong faith to draw on now."

"Which I also owe to you."

"Faith gives purpose," Angie said. "With purpose you can find your way through grief.

They both sat quietly for a few moments. "It's my fault," Victoria said. "Maybe I would have picked up on some danger signal if I hadn't been so wrapped up in work. I should have spent more time with him."

"Nonsense," Angie said. "No one could have been more attentive, more devoted than you—the number of times you rearranged your own plans to be with him, the weekends you spent helping your father redo his garden or clean out his garage, or when you took him to the play he wanted to see at the Orpheum. How about the time you rescued him from the clutches of a suspicious salesman trying to sell him a time-share condo?"

"But it wasn't enou—"

"For heaven's sake, you're entitled to feel enormous grief, but not guilt. He was so *proud* of you. How many fathers have a daughter who's a neuroscientist seeking a cure for cancer! Or with your desire to help others? You volunteer at the Animal Rescue Foundation. You tutor students in math at the library. You're not only smart; you're kind and generous."

"But, I always nagged him about church. I don't know if he knew . . . how much I loved him."

"Listen, when I saw your father at your New Year's Eve party, I asked him if he got what he wanted for Christmas. He flashed his big smile and said, 'Santa brought me the greatest gift in the world thirty-two years ago: my daughter.' " Angie reached over and turned Victoria's chin toward her. "Believe me, he knew."

"And *I* got a precious father," Victoria said. She wiped her eyes. "I also have an incredible friend."

"Well, this friend will cause incredible trouble if I'm not home when the carpool drops my girls off from soccer practice. I have to run." Angie gave Victoria a hug. "Don't turn inward. Stay engaged. Text me if there is *anything* I can do."

26

Victoria Johnson
Pleasant Hill
Day 4, 8:00 AM

The next morning Victoria jogged two miles. She'd never felt more in need of this mind-focusing ritual to combat lack of sleep, loss of appetite, and the tears at the back of her eyes. She showered, dressed, sniffed the milk in her refrigerator, judged it borderline, poured it on a bowl of granola anyway, and began on a list of phone calls she had to make: to the Garden Chapel for funeral arrangements, her church office for an appointment with her pastor, her boss to negotiate when she would return to work, and Bill Miner to confirm a time to meet at her Papa's house.

After the calls, she sat a few minutes at the kitchen table, gazing out at the serenity of the dogwood trees and redwoods in her backyard. The past seventy-two hours had been anything but tranquil. It was reassuring that she'd see Bill later. His involvement offered hope of finding the person responsible. He was a supportive, stabilizing connection, and despite their religious differences, she appreciated his intelligence and sincerity. She grabbed her car keys and headed out the door.

Victoria drove down Gregory Lane past Christ the King Church. She stopped at the signal at Cleaveland Road next to the Pleasant Hill City Hall, a striking facility designed by renowned architect Charles Moore. A message on the digital billboard in front caught her eye: a meeting of the Planning Commission to hear citizen comments on a proposed small housing development on one of the last available parcels in the city. It reminded her to be thankful she had a home in a Bay Area market that was frightfully tight and expensive.

She took Contra Costa Boulevard, then Willow Pass Road into Concord. The Todos Santos Farmers' Market would soon open. However, fresh produce was the last thing on her mind. She turned onto Concord Boulevard and, a brief time later, pulled into her church parking lot. She entered the double front doors and walked with reverence down a long, wide corridor, past the sanctuary, and entered her pastor's office on the right.

Pastor Roy Milford, gray haired, straight as a sentinel, looked out his window to a side courtyard. He turned, touched his fingertips together in the form of a steeple, and waved her into a seat. "You wanted to see me urgently, Victoria?"

She glanced at the wooden cross on the wall behind him and fell into a familiar state of comfort and trust. "Pastor Roy, your counsel has guided me, reassured me, through many anxious times. But I've never been more in need of your prayers."

"What is it?" he asked, a grim twist to his mouth.

"My father was murdered." She swallowed, her chest ached as she said those words, and she drew her arms close to her body.

"Oh no. Do the police have any leads?"

"They are investigating." Her words were fraught with emotion. "I want to ask if you would officiate at a memorial service for him."

Her pastor answered with a stare. "I cannot pray for your father, Victoria," he said after a moment.

She sank back in her chair, stunned. Her breath felt sucked out.

"The unrighteous cannot inherit the kingdom of God." His eyes turned gunmetal. "I am sorry, but he chose his path and must suffer the consequences."

She stiffened. "But, Pastor Roy—"

"However," he interrupted, "I offer my sincere sympathies to you for your loss and my condolences for your grief."

She looked away, rubbing an eyelid.

"Our church tries to teach the good news of salvation through Jesus Christ. Some people accept the Bible's plain and clear message." His thin finger stabbed at the gilded leather volume on his desk. "Those who choose to ignore his word do so at their own peril."

"Pastor Roy, you think this was *justice*?" She shook her head, rejecting his pronouncement.

Deep lines appeared on his forehead. "Tell me," he said. "Why do the police think your father was murdered?"

"I know my father. He would *not* take his own life!"

Pastor Roy paused as if to process her assessment.

"Victoria, you know that the power of Satan to deceive is enormous. Satan himself masquerades as an angel of light. *That* was the light your father saw!" he scoffed. "Your father fell under the control of Satan. It was the ultimate lawless one who laid a snare for him."

The pastor's vehemence struck her like ice water.

"Pastor Roy, *I* was the one who insisted Papa come with me to see you after his surgery. He didn't want to. He did it for *me*. You used strong words when the three of us met. You wanted to shake Papa from his illusions. I wanted his illusions shaken too. You gave a sound argument. You pointed to Scripture and told him what he must do."

Her pastor looked away.

"But Papa's gone now. . . . Despite his rejection of the church, he was a *good* man, a *loving* man. Your condemnation of him now . . . It's cruel."

Pastor Roy leaned forward in his chair, his mouth wrinkled. There was a hardness in his gaze. "Victoria, it is not *I* who denounces your father. He stands condemned by the testimony of the Word of God."

The emotion in his words felt like something gripping her throat. There was a pulse of silence. Her body tensed. Her face flushed with anger. She rose from her chair.

"That's enough!" she said. "Stop right there!" She turned and walked briskly from the room.

As she reached the parking lot, numb, she heard footsteps from behind her and turned to see the assistant pastor rushing to catch up.

"Victoria, just a moment, please," he said, out of breath. "I overheard your conversation in there. Look. Pastor Roy . . . you know how he can be. . . . He's a formidable old watchdog . . . a staunch guardian. When the church is under attack, he's one you want on your side."

"But he was heartless, Pastor Marc."

"Please recognize. Underneath that craggy, stern exterior, there's a man devoted to God." Marc's voice was warm, soothing. "He knows your father's story in the papers is nonsense, but it upset him. Pastor Roy sees no other explanation than Satan at his most deceptive." He paused, his eyes pensive. "Victoria, you cannot know whether your father's visions were from God or whether it was all a mirage induced by drugs and surgical trauma. If it was the latter, I hope you will dismiss them and not let them linger. If they were from God, then he will enable you, when he is ready, to know the visions' meaning."

She nodded and took a deep breath. "Thank you, Pastor Marc."

"And if you would like me to say a few words at your father's service, let me know when and where."

"I would appreciate that. Thank you."

"Don't mention it." He gestured toward the church. "To him, I mean."

She nodded. "I should have arrangements completed in a day or two."

When she reached her car, she sat quietly, then bowed her head. *Dear Lord, I'm so confused. I understand my pastor's accusations. But such savage judgment. Is it me? Do I have a blind spot? Yes, Papa was wrong . . . but please don't turn your back on such a dear man.*

Victoria, her hands trembling, her cheeks wet, drove out of the parking lot and headed toward San Francisco, to the house where she grew up.

27

Bill Miner
San Francisco, CA
10:30 AM

I pulled up to the white Spanish stucco house in the Outer Richmond District and parked in the narrow driveway. The front door was ajar, and I called out Victoria's name.

"Come on in," I heard from a rear room. Victoria emerged from the hallway, reached out, and clasped my hand with a light squeeze. "I'm a bit overwhelmed as this all sinks in," she said. "Thanks for coming."

"Sorry I'm late," I said. "You must've been ahead of the slowdown on the Bay Bridge." She looked nice in a blue sweatshirt decorated with monarch butterflies and a pair of jeans. "Haven't been out this way in some time. Nice location."

"If you don't mind the perpetual fog," Victoria said with a slight smile. "I considered myself disadvantaged to grow up here. My friends in Pleasant Hill didn't have to wear sweaters and jackets all summer long."

The home on Balboa was in an older middle-class residential neighborhood, just up the street from Sutro Heights Park. Ocean Beach and the Cliff House were probably within a short walk. Most of the houses had been built in the thirties, and some were still owned by older-generation, working-class San Franciscans like Victoria's father.

I looked around the living room. The place had a warm, comfortable feel. A Persian rug, centered in front of a fireplace, covered a portion of an attractive hardwood floor.

"Everything's the same," she said. "Except now nothing is the same because . . ." Her words trailed off.

I felt uncertain what to say.

Victoria led me into the den and gestured toward an old rolltop desk. "That's where he spent a lot of time . . . on the phone, emailing friends. He read a lot, wrote letters. He loved this room. The sliding glass door let in the sun, on those occasional days when there was any, and provided a view of his flowers. Papa did fine with cineraria, camellias, azaleas, even tried rose bushes after he saw mine in Pleasant Hill."

"What's with the piece of cardboard taped on the glass door?" I asked.

"Hmm. He was supposed to have that fixed. It covers the hole the burglar made. The police said some just break the glass. But this entry was silent, probably while Papa was sound asleep. Someone used a rubber suction cup with a small glass cutter on a string. Cut a circle like they'd used a drafting compass. A small squeak of the cutter, a tap to break out the circle, and a reach through to open the latch."

I eyed a laptop on the left side of the desk. "Is that where your father kept his computer?"

Victoria looked over and nodded.

"It looks new. The burglar didn't take it?"

"Papa said the burglar just grabbed some odds and ends of little value."

Victoria's eyes panned across the room. "Well, I guess we should get started," she said. "Papa knew everyone in the neighborhood, but there are two he might have told about his trip—the Brewers across the street and Mr. Gillespie next door. They're retired longtime friends who always kept an eye on each other's place when someone was away."

We picked up the mail on the way out—bills, a bank statement, some advertisements—and crossed the street to the Brewer home.

The woman who answered the door released a swell of emotions and embraced Victoria. "Oh, my dear, I am so sorry about your father. We heard about the accident on Channel 5. A complete shock. I thought I had your phone number but must've misplaced it. Is there anything we can do?"

"Thank you. I don't think so right now." Victoria said. "This is Professor Miner. He's been a great help."

"Your father was such a sweet man," Mrs. Brewer said. "Life is so unpredictable." She rested her fingertips on her cheek. "We were all concerned when your father went in for his surgery, but he came through with flying colors, even became a newspaper celebrity. Then the loss of his brother. Now this."

"Did Papa tell you about his trip?"

"No details. Just that he'd be gone for a couple of days but not long enough to bother with his mail. I think he mentioned a hike."

"Did Papa tell you where?"

"No. We wouldn't know those places anyway." Her eyes were cheerless. "We're just so grieved. You were just a baby when we moved here." She extended her hand to Victoria. "Please let me know if there's anything we can do."

"Thank you," Victoria said. "I'll let you know when there will be a memorial service."

We returned to the sidewalk.

"I met with my pastor this morning about that," Victoria said. "It did not go well. I'll tell you later." She pointed to a man across the street. "There's Mr. Gillespie now."

She signaled to the man as he came down his front steps.

Gillespie waited for us on the sidewalk, his expression somber. "Victoria, I'm so sorry. I heard the terrible news about Oscar."

Victoria thanked him for his sentiments, asked the same questions, and got similar answers.

We walked back toward the house as a car pulled up in front and a man stepped out. "Ms. Johnson!" he shouted. "Alex Browne with the *Chronicle*."

"Uh-oh," Victoria said. "That's the reporter who interviewed Papa at the hospital." She drew in a breath. "There's never a parking space around here. Why'd there have to be one now?"

Browne jogged over and planted himself on the sidewalk to block our way. "Sorry for your loss," he said. "After your father's heavenly experience, I'd hoped to have further conversations with him. Please accept my condolences."

Victoria nodded. "This is Bill Miner, professor of religion at Berkeley."

I extended my hand.

Browne looked at me, then back at Victoria. "Brought in the academic guns, huh? Your father certainly rang some chimes on religion's Richter scale. I wanted to ask if he learned whether Jesus was married."

Victoria glared. "My father already told you more than I wish he had. I don't want to contribute to any more sensationalism."

The reporter persisted. "He said you're a scientist *and* an Evangelical," Browne said. "In terms of public perception, I'm sure you're aware the word 'Evangelical' ranks somewhere between 'Klan member' and 'radical Islamist.' How do you reconcile your beliefs with your profession? Aren't the scientific and spiritual worlds contradictory?"

Victoria's right eyebrow lifted a notch as color rose from her cheeks to her forehead. "Mr. Browne, forty percent of scientists believe in God," she said. "The battle between science and religion is not as polarized as you imply. It's the extremists on both sides of the debate that lob the grenades and garner the headlines. I have no problem living in peace with science *and* God. Now please excuse us."

"You seem to enjoy tossing a match into flammable materials," I said to Browne.

"It's what a reporter has to do sometimes," he replied.

Victoria and I stepped around him, went into the house, and sat down on a couch in her father's den.

"That guy sure knew how to throw out some red meat to get a reaction," I said.

"You're right. He baited me." She paused. "Browne isn't wrong about the bickering between science and religion. That issue galls me, but I shouldn't have let him get my goat."

A quiet minute passed. I liked her grit and the way she defended herself.

I noticed some old cameras displayed on the shelf of a curio cabinet: a Yashica Mat Twin-Lens Reflex, a Honeywell Pentax, a couple of others. "I like your father's collection," I said, to change the subject. "Was he a serious photographer?"

"He was enthusiastic about taking family pictures. As a little girl, I learned to have a ready smile, because Papa loved to capture everyday life. There were times when you couldn't turn around without finding a lens pointed at you." She turned her head toward me.

"And there it is," I said.

Her smile spread.

"Browne hit a pet peeve. Any others I should know about?" I asked. "Anything I should make sure not to step into?"

"People who never shut up and talk over you."

I flinched.

"Not you," she said with a surprised chuckle. Her eyes became warm. "You're a good listener," she said. "And one who's full of penetrating questions."

"That's supposed to be in my job description, but it's much nicer to hear from you."

We looked at each other for another lingering minute.

"What's a favorite memory of your father?" I asked.

"Hmm. Fishing trips to Virginia Lakes. The first trip was when I was about six or seven. He'd wake me in our campsite at the crack of dawn, and I'd follow behind him through the woods. I wasn't a morning person. The air was chilly, and my eyes were half-closed, but I wanted to be with my papa. He loved to fish for salmon, and I wanted to like whatever he liked."

"I'll bet it was reciprocal."

She nodded. "He knew I loved butterflies, so he used to take me to Pacific Grove where the monarchs would spend winter." Her hand brushed one of the butterflies on her sweatshirt. "The gentle current of one small winged creature after another, each drawn there by an unseen force, for many their final journey. I remember Rachel Carson's words that we should admire the beauty of the moment, that when any living thing fulfills its purpose, we should accept that as nature's cycle of life." She paused as if she were back on one of those trips with her father. "I loved those brilliant, fluttering snippets of orange, black, and white. I think they awakened in me an appreciation of our existence. Did an invisible force also guide us toward our *own* purpose like it guided the monarchs?"

As she spoke, a ray of sunlight penetrated through the San Francisco fog, beamed through her father's patio door, and lit up the room. Victoria's head turned toward the light, and she became still.

A few seconds later the sunbeam vanished in the rolling fogbank and returned the room to a soft, diffuse illumination. I was touched by the significance she had given to that instant—the change in light as she reflected on her father, on butterflies—the kind of spiritual import I would sometimes see in a coincidence . . . back when I was a man of faith.

"Did he tell you he was proud of you?" I asked.

"He wasn't effusive in his praise. That wasn't his style as a parent, but I never doubted that his love was unconditional. He guided me, always looked out for me, alert to who was in my circle of friends, the activities I got involved in. Protective, yet he encouraged me to reach. I think he was proud of my pursuit of science, my work at Genentech, even though he didn't say it in so many words."

"Do you have any close friends to lean on at a time like this?" I asked.

"I have a wonderful girlfriend. Lots of acquaintances." Her forehead creased. "I haven't made much time to expand friendships. Most of my energy has gone into career."

"No boyfriend or anything?" I asked. She tipped her head down with a glance that told me she was quite aware that I was the one fishing now.

"No. Too much a workaholic. To a fault, I'm afraid."

"So, if that's your entire world—work and church—the reporter did pose an interesting question. How *do* you balance science and faith? Some scientists predict the demise of religion, while most fundamentalists predict the end of the world."

"Balance isn't hard at all," she said. "I see science and faith in harmony, and I can walk in both worlds. Not all Evangelicals are strict fundamentalists. I know some people, even in my own church, who believe the earth is less than ten thousand years old. They argue that evolution is a lie, that science wants to drive God out of existence. Some of that fear, I think, comes from their desire to feel less inconsequential."

She had fervor in her rationale but also a balanced view.

"If you buy the idea," she continued, "that humans are just a few hundred generations old, descended from Adam and Eve in a comprehendible time frame, you'll feel a lot more connected. Who knows? Your auto mechanic could be a seventh cousin. On the other hand, the thought that we are products of random mutations over billions of years is guaranteed to make you feel insignificant."

"And there's the fear that the power of Scripture would be diluted," I said.

She nodded. "The slippery slope. So some dig in their heels against a world that has adopted an anything-goes morality. Evangelicals want to recover the values that humanize—justice, compassion, forgiveness."

Memories replayed as I listened—a glimmer of my former self, once equally enraptured, similarly convinced.

"I'm drawn to my church because it understands the ills of American society but remains loyal to the core values of the Gospel. I'm not comfortable with the liberal churches that find any form of theology acceptable—that's too superficial. I want sermons that provide a rigorous exposition of God's word."

"Sounds like your church embraces a spectrum of evangelical beliefs."

"It does. My regular pastor, Pastor Roy, is conservative, while Pastor Marc seems more moderate. He's new. Marc does the evening service that I've heard is freewheeling and more expository and appeals to a younger crowd. I may switch."

"You haven't said how you balance all this with science."

"It's simple—science tells us *how* God's creation works. Adam and Eve may have come through evolution, but it all started with God." Passion danced in her eyes. "When Genesis says, 'In the beginning, God created the heavens and the earth'—that's one hundred percent compatible with the big bang. Nature didn't create itself. Biotechnology, with its understanding of molecular mechanisms and genetic pathways, gives us an inkling of God's design plan. Darwin was correct—it's through gene mutation that natural selection takes place."

"But technically, evolution is still a theory," I said—half statement, half question.

"The word 'theory' is not intended to convey uncertainty. Scientists use 'hypothesis' for that. 'Theory' means fundamental principles that underlie science. But any time science is seen to conflict with Scripture . . . boom . . . you unleash intense emotion. Look at how unglued the church became when Galileo discovered the Earth revolved around the sun. The church had a knee-jerk reaction: insisted that geometry was of the devil, forced Galileo to disclaim his work, and held him under house arrest for the rest of his life. Today, everyone is comfortable with heliocentrism, and I hope the same will happen with evolution before any more damage is done to the credibility of faith."

"Evolution is a hot button," I said.

"But some scientists and academicians can be just as bad as fundamentalists—those who turn away from religion because they think it's irrelevant drivel."

I leaned back on the couch. "You're not bad on the soapbox," I said. "While you're on the stump, how do you feel about another explosive topic: abortion?"

"You know, it kind of bugs me that it's the males who like to be the most vocal on that subject."

"Hey, I'm keeping quiet. Just curious what you think."

She paused a moment. "I can't imagine I would choose to have an abortion myself."

"What about others?"

"Who am I to judge another woman's decision?"

I sat back. "Whoa, I did not see that coming."

"Seventy-five percent of Evangelicals want to overturn Roe v. Wade," she said. "I'm in the small minority. That said, I don't want to give you the wrong impression. I still think that abortion for reasons of personal or social convenience is wrong."

"How did you come to be pro-choice?"

"Before ultrasounds, before Roe, from the time of Aristotle, it was obvious when life began—the first time a woman felt her baby's kick, the 'quickening'—*that* was the moment the baby came alive, the moment it got its soul. Along came in vitro fertilization, and the question grew complicated—scientists observed the process of sperm entering the egg for the first time. It can take hours, even days, and a series of biochemical changes before the sperm can enter. One colleague likes to say that fertilization doesn't take place in a moment of passion. It takes place the next day in the grocery store or on the bus to work. But even fertilization isn't a clear indicator of anything. The next step is implantation, when the fertilized egg travels down the fallopian tube and attaches to the woman's uterus. There's a high rate of fertilized eggs that don't implant, maybe fifty to eighty percent, and even some implanted embryos spontaneously abort. A woman might never know she was pregnant. The bottom line: since fertilization and implantation don't occur in a single moment but in a series of moments, none more important than the next, reasonable scientists can disagree about when life begins."

"And you?"

"I'm not sure anyone can say. The biologist in me tends to believe life is continuous."

"That's an interesting take," I said.

"It has brought me to the conclusion that the pregnant woman gets to decide when it's a person."

"Abortion. Evolution. You're a bit of an evangelical maverick."

Her forehead creased. "Well, just because I believe in evolution doesn't mean I'm not horrified by the way it can be used to justify behavior. Germany's militarism in both world wars grew from its belief that survival of the fittest also applied to nations—its rationale for exterminating Jews."

"Oh? You think Germany used Darwin to justify the Holocaust?"

She gave a crisp nod. "In part."

"Nah," I said. "The Germans didn't need *On the Origin of Species* for that. They had their own religious authorities that gave them all the rationalization they needed."

She crossed her arms. "Like what?"

"Like describing the Jews as venomous, accursed people who were possessed by the devil."

She drew back and dropped her arms.

I leaned toward her. "Oh yes. Christians were urged to burn down their synagogues. Drive them out like mad dogs. Show no mercy."

Victoria gave me a dismissive glance. "Every country has a few wacko extremists," she said. "The German people wouldn't have taken that seriously."

"Yeah?" I looked at her squarely. "I'm not talking about a few skinheads. I'm referring to the founder of the Protestant Reformation."

"Huh?"

28

Bill Miner
San Francisco
11:30 AM

Victoria stared at me. A line appeared between her brows.

"That's right," I said. "Martin Luther published a ferocious tirade: burn down their synagogues; destroy their homes; deny all safe-conduct; treat the Jews the way a physician eradicates gangrene."

Victoria covered her mouth with her palm.

"It's a bit of Protestant dirty laundry from which the Lutheran Church ultimately distanced itself. But the Nazis embraced every word."

"What drew a professor of religion to study Nazi justifications?"

"Because Luther went through a change in attitude that mirrors a transition that occurred in the Gospels." My pulse rate quickened as I recalled when I gained that insight. "Luther didn't *start out* hating Jews," I said. "He wanted to *convert* them. He figured the reason Jews hadn't come over to Christianity any sooner was because of the impurity of the Catholic Church. Once Protestants had broken away, Luther was sure the Jews would embrace Christianity."

"And of course, that didn't happen," Victoria said.

I nodded. "So Luther turned on them."

"But Luther died *centuries* before World War II."

"Not his writings. His malicious quotations appeared in just about everything printed by the Third Reich."

Victoria stared over my shoulder in silence.

"Few things generate as much ire as when someone rejects your fervent beliefs," I said. "Exasperation turns to bitterness, then anger, then condemnation and worse."

"True in politics as well as religion," she said.

"You can see it in the Bible—frustration and irritation build as each successive Gospel is written. You can feel tempers on the rise against those who refused to sign on to the new fledgling religion. Anger so livid that some stories became exaggerated, even contrived."

"Now you're pushing it," Victoria said, her tone stiffened. "Matthew, Mark, Luke, and John didn't *contrive* stories."

"They weren't above recording slanted memories that reinforced the view that Jews were to blame for Jesus's death. The story of Barabbas, for example, when Pilate asks the Jewish crowd if he should release Jesus or Barabbas. You know the story. Does it seem reasonable to you?"

"Why wouldn't it be? It was Pilate's custom to release a prisoner every year to honor the Passover. A token of kindness and goodwill."

"Sweet-natured, compassionate Pontius Pilate? Does it trouble you that there's no record, outside of the Gospels, of any such concession *ever* granted by *any* Roman governor in *any* province at *any* time in history? Or that this thoughtful gesture was made by a notorious, ruthless, and brutal ruler?"

"It's in all four Gospels," she said. "That's impeccable testimony."

"And when the crowd insists he release Barabbas in place of Jesus, you don't find it questionable that Pilate would allow the liberation of a criminal arrested for violent insurrection against Roman rule? Charges that likely meant Barabbas had killed Roman soldiers? And Pilate is willing to set him *free*?"

"Why would I question something indisputably stated in the Bible?" she asked.

"As a professor of religion, it's my job to do just that, and I don't think that story is the least bit plausible." I searched for a comparable example. "It's the equivalent of our president offering to release an imprisoned Islamic terrorist leader as a goodwill gesture to ISIS in honor of Ramadan."

Victoria gave a deep frown. "So you think that the writers of the Gospels added Barabbas to heighten the drama?"

"Absolutely—a theatrical flourish out of frustration and disgust with the Jewish people. Pure fake news. Their outrage—that Jews wouldn't see the obvious *truth*—was off the charts. The writers invented a story to portray the Jews as so evil intentioned that they would prefer to save a killer rather than the Son of God. A powerful story. Never mind that Barabbas never existed."

Tears welled up in her eyes, and she swallowed. "I know what it feels like to be unable to convince someone you love," she said.

I wanted to put my arms around her but held back. I had done a poor job of offering comfort to someone in despair.

"He was very fortunate to have a daughter like you," I said.

"And I'm very lucky to have had the father I did. Unfortunately, that's not the perception of my pastor."

"I gathered your meeting was unpleasant."

"I asked him to officiate at the memorial service. He refused. Even worse, he condemned Papa."

I reached over and put my hand on hers. "I'm sorry."

"Pastor Marc told me in confidence he would do a service."

We sat in silence for a few moments. The stillness in the room was broken by the soft chimes of a mantle clock. As if drawing on the inner fortitude I'd seen before, Victoria said, "OK, I'll start through Papa's paper mail if you'll look through his emails."

I smiled in a way I hoped conveyed both sympathy and admiration. We got up. Victoria took a wicker basket of mail from his desk to the dining room table. I sat down at his Dell.

"What's his password?" I called out.

"Eight characters beginning with capital *V*."

I typed "Victoria." As the laptop booted, I thought how feeble we make our passwords. The current college-freshman favorite is "Password1."

I opened the inbox and scanned the subject column through several pages of fishing newsletters, Sierra Club bulletins, TripAdvisor and AARP notices, etc., with several dozen personal emails scattered among them.

"This is interesting," I said. "Did you know he received several emails from that near-death organization?"

"He mentioned it. I told him not to expose himself to any more publicity."

I continued my search for personal communications and found an email about his motel reservation dated three weeks prior to his fateful trip. A note in the confirmation mentioned improvements to the Devil's Fall trail. Apparently, the motel manager had known that hike was his favorite. I focused on her father's emails that were sent after the date of the motel confirmation. There were several. None, however, made any mention of the trip.

"Except to the motel manager, your father didn't say anything about the trip in his emails," I said. "How did you learn about it yourself?"

"He told me on the phone."

We had worked for fifteen or twenty minutes when I heard her say, "Well, I've come up with zero." Victoria came back into the den. "Want some coffee?"

"Sure." I stared at the computer screen. *Where to turn next?* For lack of any other ideas, I clicked on the START icon and scrolled through the names of installed programs.

"Hey," I said, loud enough for Victoria to hear in the kitchen. "I thought you said your father was a novice user. What's he doing with pcAnywhere?"

"What are you talking about?"

"I just poked around and discovered he's got software for remote access. Is that so you could give him computer help when he got stuck?"

"Nope. Papa liked to figure things out for himself."

"Well, why would he need software that would let him access his computer from a remote location?"

"He wouldn't," she said, returning with coffee. "That is peculiar."

"Look at this." I pointed to an entry in the Properties box. "It was installed just a month ago. On the date shown here—and that's interesting—at two thirty in the morning?"

Victoria reached for the calendar on her father's desk. "Papa circled that date. That was the date of the burglary!"

We looked at each other as the realization struck. "The burglar didn't come to take something," Victoria said. "He came to *leave* something."

"And took a few things to give the appearance of a simple burglary," I said.

She pulled a chair up next to me, and her fingers flew over the keyboard to view System settings. "Look here. The IP address is configured to allow connections automatically." She ran a hand through her hair. "Someone could access Papa's laptop from a remote computer without his knowledge. They could read his emails as though they were at his desk. They would see the email from the motel manager. They would know about his trip, the exact date, the very trail he planned to take." Victoria came to her feet. "The person who killed him!"

29

Tim Lane
Kansas City, MO
12:00 PM

Tim Lane's white Ford Focus headed south from his motel near the Kansas City airport and crossed a bridge that spanned the wide Missouri River. He was now in Kansas and would soon approach Overland Park, an upscale suburb, twelve miles southwest of downtown Kansas City. His GPS indicated he was fifteen minutes from his destination, 1461 Belcroft Terrace.

Expansive lawns fronted homes with three-car garages on tree-lined avenues. Artistic fountains with stone-fence backdrops announced neighborhoods and gated communities. Names such as Windsor Hills, Wellington Green, and Fontainebleau suggested the residents' desire for a touch of European sophistication in a state portrayed in *The Wizard of Oz*. The serenity of the sedate residential community was disturbed only by an occasional lawn mower or leaf blower. Lane had read that Overland Park ranked in the top ten places in the US to raise a family, but the focus of his homework had been on one Florence Smith.

Facebook provided a wealth of information about her, complete with photos of her husband, two grade-school children, and an Alaskan malamute. He reflected on principles from his military-intelligence days: Draw on all sources of available information. Learn the adversary's vulnerabilities and patterns of behavior.

Lane's initial impression was that this job could be straightforward, but everything depended on the setting. He located the address halfway down Belcroft where the street curved sharply. The neighborhood was quiet—negligible traffic, no pedestrians. He studied the area and reviewed his plan.

Satisfied, he drove to the nearby Oak Park Mall and scanned the shopping center lot for a large vehicle. He pulled into an open space next to a late-model GMC Yukon. Using a small inflatable air wedge to jimmy the door, he slipped a rod through the opening and flipped the latch. The rest was easy. Lane, his rifle in hand, slipped into the full-size SUV and twenty minutes later sat parked around the corner from the Smith home. He didn't have to wait long. A few minutes past two o'clock he watched Florence Smith walk down her driveway, tugged toward the street by an eager malamute.

The dog may have distracted her from the sound of the Yukon's acceleration. Lane saw that she never turned to see the huge vehicle bearing down on her. He felt the impact, heard the wham. The left headlight shattered as the dog flew into the air, landing twenty feet up the street. The Yukon's bumper caught the woman's hip. The impact whirled her up onto the sidewalk.

Lane's heart raced. He braked to a stop, two hundred feet up the street, and checked his rearview mirror. What he saw horrified him. He had misjudged his trajectory and failed to account for the effect the sharp curvature of the road had on the large speeding vehicle. He had aimed for the woman, but it was the dog that had received the direct hit. Florence Smith had crawled to the grass by the sidewalk, injured but now with a phone in her hand.

Lane's chest pounded. By instinct he grabbed his rifle and leaped from the car. He steadied the weapon on the large side-view mirror, drew a careful bead on her, and fired one round. The woman's body slumped. The phone dropped to the grass. Lane glanced around the neighborhood. No one. He grabbed his shell casing, jumped back into the vehicle, and tore down Belcroft. Tires squealed as he swung wide at the first cross street and disappeared from the area.

Lane returned to the shopping center and parked. His pulse was still throbbing. He closed his eyes and inhaled deeply. One hand in his pocket, the other holding the rifle close to his side, he walked nonchalantly to his rental car. He slid into the driver's seat and sat motionless. He scanned the area for any signs he'd been noticed.

Satisfied he had not drawn attention, Lane pulled out of the lot and headed in a southeast direction, out of Kansas and into Missouri.

***

It was late afternoon by the time Tim Lane reached the town of Clinton. He had not been able to sleep the night before. His 2:00 AM mission in Ballard, the three-and-a-half-hour flight from Seattle, and now the worry about his miscalculation had left him physically and mentally exhausted. He took the main exit from Route 7 and drove toward the center of town. He spotted a motel, the Westbridge Inn, and turned into the parking lot.

Neither Lane's radio nor his cell phone had given him any news about Overland Park. His first question to the desk clerk—which TV station had metro Kansas City news coverage? Channel 5 at five o'clock, the clerk told him. Lane checked in, showered, and was in front of the TV as the lead news story described a budget showdown between the Kansas City mayor and the city council. Then:

> In Overland Park, a hit-and-run took the life of a mother of two this afternoon. The accident occurred in the fourteen hundred block of Belcroft, where she was hit while walking her dog. A neighbor heard a backfire but did not see the vehicle that struck and killed the woman and her dog. A cell phone next to the body caused police to suspect she was distracted by looking at her phone and failed to notice the oncoming car.

The station turned to another story, and Lane switched off the TV. He was filled with mixed emotions. He knew he had left the scene unable to confirm Smith was dead. Now that question was settled. But another issue troubled him: How soon would a coroner find the bullet? While a bullet wound in a mangled body might not be apparent at first, the slug itself would not go undetected on close examination. Unless he was lucky, and the bullet had passed completely through her body. He paced the room. His fumble weighed on him. The necessity of using his rifle.

Had he—Dragon of God—had a choice? No. The Messenger had been clear: Florence Smith was an agent of Satan, and the devil's business is to undermine faith. His rifle had allowed him to redeem himself. For that he was thankful.

Two more to go. Two more enemies of God. And time was of the essence.

30

Victoria Johnson
Pleasant Hill
Day 5, 8:45 AM

Victoria had completed her morning workout, showered, and breakfasted when her cell phone rang with the words "Mono County Sheriff" on the screen. She set her cup down sharply, spilling some coffee on the kitchen table, and picked up.

"Inspector Shreve," she said, "did you get my message about the spyware on my father's computer?"

"Yes," Peter Shreve replied, "but that's not why I'm calling. There's been a development. Police in Overland Park, Kansas, notified me of a woman killed there yesterday."

"Go on."

"Initially, they thought she was killed in a hit-and-run accident, but when the coroner examined the body, he found a bullet in the woman's neck. They ran it through NIBIN and got a match to the bullet I recovered from the tree at Devil's Fall."

Victoria's pulse jumped. "Are you telling me that the person who killed my father has shot someone in Kansas?" The hairs on the back of her neck stood up.

"All we can say is that both bullets were fired from the same gun."

Victoria rose to her feet as her mind searched for any kind of connection. "What could possibly link them, Inspector?"

"I don't know, not yet. Ms. Johnson, you said your only relatives were in the East. Did your father have any acquaintances in the Midwest?"

"He grew up in Saint Louis, so it's possible."

"The woman killed was Florence Smith. Does that name mean anything to you?"

"No. I don't know anyone by that name. Who was she?"

"A forty-year-old homemaker with a husband and two children."

"Heavens." Victoria sat back down.

"I just wanted to let you know about this development," Shreve said.

"Did they find a metal bracelet?"

"No, nothing like the one we recovered at Devil's Fall, but the police will conduct a full investigation. I'll contact you when I hear anything further."

"I can postpone my father's service a few days if there's something I or maybe Professor Miner can do."

"I know this is difficult, but be patient. I'll keep you informed."

Victoria thanked him for his call, and within moments after she hung up, she checked flights to Kansas City. Then she phoned Bill Miner.

"Bill, the person who killed Papa just murdered a woman in Kansas." She had rushed her words. She took a moment to regain her breath, then described the conversation with Shreve. "There's a Southwest flight to Kansas City from Oakland at eleven ten AM. I plan to be on it." She hesitated. "Do you think you could come? Is there any way?"

"Jeez, that's in two hours."

"Do you see the implications?" she said. "Two deaths, the same weapon, both times the cause made to look like something it wasn't—first a suicide, then a fatal traffic accident?"

A moment of silence.

"I know it's a stretch," she said, "but I can't ignore this." She paused. "We do make a good team."

"I like the way you said 'we.' OK, I'll meet you at the gate."

"Thank you." She felt a pleasant warmth as she disconnected the call.

Victoria scheduled an Uber pickup, then phoned the mortuary to say her father's service would be delayed. She threw some clothes and a toothbrush in an overnight bag and with cautious optimism was on her way to the airport.

31

Tim Lane
Missouri Route 7
11:00 AM

Tim Lane passed through a late-morning thunderstorm as he drove southeast through the rolling hills of south-central Missouri. A profusion of billboards beckoned vacationers to the Lake of the Ozarks: 54,000 ACRES OF WATERWAYS—BASS FISHING—WATER-SKIING—CAMPING. Lane imagined the oak and hickory forests provided abundant opportunities to hunt quail, wild turkeys, and deer. He would be hunting all right, but he wouldn't search for his quarry in the woodlands. His mind was on the small town of Waynesville and a rendezvous with a certain preacher. Lane was not seeking spiritual advice, of course. His sights were on a man who was no longer of the spirit of God, but of the evil one.

32

Bill Miner
Oakland International Airport
11:10 AM

I met Victoria at Southwest gate twenty-three at the last possible moment, with the aircraft doors closing seconds after we had reached our seats.

We had attained cruise altitude and were headed eastward across California's Central Valley when Victoria looked over and touched my arm. "Thanks for dropping everything for me." The words were nice, her closeness even better.

"You're very welcome," I said. Her hand lingered a moment. Her nail polish was a soft pink, not too rosy. I don't ordinarily notice such things.

"I hope you realize I haven't a clue where to start when we get to Kansas," she said.

"Neither did Dorothy. They've got yellow brick roads there, don't they?"

She smiled. "That would be helpful, except Dorothy discovered she wasn't in 'Kansas anymore.' " Her expression became serious. "I can't imagine what connection there could be between Papa and a woman who lived eighteen hundred miles away."

I figured there was a slim chance we would spot something that eluded police. But a wild-goose chase across the country with an intelligent, attractive woman? Things could have been worse. And if I was out of a job soon, they would be.

Across the aisle a young teen got up, set her book on the seat, and headed to the restroom.

"Now there's someone on the right track," Victoria said, as she eyed *The Lion, the Witch and the Wardrobe*. "C. S. Lewis proved Jesus is divine, you know." She tilted her head back as if savoring the thought, then looked at me for a reaction.

"I'm well acquainted with the interpretations of the famous Oxford scholar," I said. "A fine novelist."

"Well?" Victoria said. She had the gleam in her eyes of a chess player who had just conceived of a brilliant move. "Since Jesus called himself God, he was either a liar, a lunatic, or, indeed, the Lord. There's no other possibility, Professor Bible Expert."

Here we go again, I thought. "You're relentless," I said to her grinning face. "I admit there's nothing in the Bible to suggest Jesus deceived humankind by lying, nor that he deluded himself and was crazy."

"Um-hum," Victoria said. "That leaves just one possibility, doesn't it?" She looked like the cat who had frozen a mouse in its tracks. "That Jesus told the truth when he said he was the Lord." She tapped her fingertips together. "I'd like to see you get around *that*." The sparkle in her eyes shouted, *Checkmate!*

"And Lewis's argument almost works," I said.

She cocked her head, and an eyebrow shot up.

"In my early years, I bought that logic too," I said. "Then one day it hit me. His case all hinged on one big assumption: that Jesus actually called himself God."

Victoria leaned toward me and drummed her fingers on the armrest. "And he *did*. So, what's the hang-up?"

"I don't think he did . . . claim to be God."

She squinted and folded her arms.

"Jesus calls himself God, all right," I said, "but only in the Gospel of John, the last of the four Gospels, written some sixty years after Jesus's death when emotions had heated up in the struggle to win converts to the new religion."

"That's sure good enough for me," she said. "John is my favorite, a beautiful Gospel."

"I understand why," I said. "It's more sophisticated. And more political."

"So?" She lowered her voice. "What's your problem?"

"What strikes me as curious is that the other Gospels say nothing about Jesus's claim to be God. Why wouldn't Matthew, Mark, and Luke mention that? Wouldn't you think that's the lead story?"

"What are you talking about?" she said and stared at me. "You *know* that the Gospels are peppered with references to Jesus as the Son of God."

"Yes. But to the Jews of the time, calling someone the Son of God didn't make the person *God*. It meant a human being through whom God did his will. It meant a messiah. Like a King David. Someone who would rule Israel. That's how the first three Gospel authors used the term, not to mean that Jesus *was* God. John says that because that was John's interpretation, encouraged by overzealous supporters, not anything that Jesus himself said."

Victoria leaned back in her seat and scratched her head.

"Look," I said. "Can you imagine Jesus saying he was God and nobody, except John, reporting it?"

I looked for a response. I saw tenacity. She was like a sparring partner exhausted after a boxing round but by no means finished. I felt uneasy. We kept hitting issues that pushed her buttons. I wanted to get closer to, not farther from, this woman.

The flight attendant brought us drink refills, and I munched on some peanuts. After a while Victoria leaned toward me with renewed energy.

"Surely it's occurred to you," she said, "that Jesus may have been very careful about what he said publicly. He couldn't very well have said, *Hi, everyone. I'm God. You can call me Christ.*"

I chuckled and wiped my mouth.

"His followers wouldn't have been able to make any sense of that," she said. "They had no concept of the Trinity. They *would* have thought he was a lunatic, which would have been counterproductive to his efforts to deliver his message."

"Yes," I said, "and he did say, 'I and the Father are one.' "

"Bingo!" She flipped her hair back. "Thank you. You just fortified my case."

"Wait a moment before you cash in your chips," I said. "Two points to consider: Once again, it's only in John that he says that.

And second, what did Jesus mean by 'one'?" I paused. "Are you going to eat your peanuts?"

"You don't think it's obvious?" she said.

"What Jesus meant by 'one,' or that you're going to eat your peanuts?"

She tightened her lips in a playful grin and flicked her bag of peanuts at me.

"I think what Jesus meant," I said, "is that his followers should be united in agreement with one another as he, Jesus, was united in agreement with God." She frowned. "Where'd you come up with that?"

"Because that's what Jesus talks about a few chapters later, although probably not with his mouth full." I swallowed. "Jesus wasn't saying that he and God are of one essence. He was talking about agreement."

Victoria looked at me with a concentrated gaze. I could see wheels spinning as she searched for a counterargument. "But if Jesus saw himself in agreement with God," she said, "wouldn't that indicate he had direct knowledge of God?"

I leaned closer. "Can you name a pastor, priest, rabbi, or imam who *doesn't* think that?"

We stared at each other. Neither yielded. She sighed. We both folded back into our seats.

After a few minutes, I looked over. "So, back to the original question," I said. "Liar, lunatic, or Lord? My answer is 'none of the above.' I don't think Jesus ever made that claim."

Victoria tilted her head toward me. "There's a lunatic in this discussion all right." She slanted her mouth, but the annoyed look was betrayed by the wisp of a smile in her eyes. "Your problem, the reason you resist all this—it's because you don't understand how there could be a God who would allow so much suffering, isn't it?"

I nodded. "The Bible doesn't give a very satisfactory answer. Your pastor thinks it's God's punishment for sin—the favorite explanation of the Hebrew prophets. Do you know how many *other* explanations for suffering there are in the Bible?"

"I think I'm about to hear."

"The most popular explanation is that suffering is caused by people who use their free will to hurt others—very prolific throughout the Bible, from Cain and Abel to Judas and Pilate. Then there's the reason that suffering is good for you, ultimately redemptive—a silver lining in the hardships we encounter. How about suffering as a test of faith? Or that it's caused by evil forces, not for disobeying God's laws but for *keeping* them—Jesus himself believed that one. Recall, Jesus promised God would soon intervene and overthrow those evil forces."

"Are you finished?" she asked.

"There's more. The book of Job says suffering is a mystery and to even *ask* is an affront to God. Finally, Ecclesiastes says there's just a lot in the world that doesn't make sense. Often no justice. Bad things happen, but life also brings good things."

Victoria contorted her face. "And you call *me* relentless?"

"Sorry," I said. "Maybe a bit much. It's a pet peeve."

"And you *still* left out one," she said. "Being stuck on a long flight with a professor of religion." Then her lips curled in a cute smile as she settled back in her seat.

33

Tim Lane
Waynesville, MO
11:50 AM

Shortly before noon Tim Lane slowed for the turnoff. A road segment proclaiming itself "Historic 66" led from the highway to the Waynesville town square. He circled the perimeter slowly, and passed by a cafe, post office, and several small retail shops. Traffic was light, and the few people on the sidewalk seemed to be in no hurry. A mailman in blue shorts ambled down the sidewalk. "Howdy, Burt," a man called to the letter carrier. Lane thought it looked like the kind of town where everyone knew everyone. And everyone else's business.

The center of the square was dominated by a large redbrick courthouse. Across the street Lane spotted the first of two addresses on his list—a church. His other address was a residence on Hospital Road.

Lane drove on around the square to Lynn Street and up a hill to Hospital Road. After a couple of curves on the narrow residential street, he reached the crest of a hill with an attractive vista overlooking an expansive valley to the north. He parked a hundred feet down the road from a large two-story home, white with green awnings. King of the hill with a pastoral view. Not bad for a pastor.

Lane waited. He rolled down the window. The only sound was the soft bleating of goats that browsed in a nearby field. The clean, moist air from the morning's rain reminded him of Pennsylvania. He missed that in California.

Twenty minutes later a blue Chevy pulled up the hill and turned into the driveway. Lane recognized the driver from the photo on the church's web page. Perhaps home for lunch. Perfect timing.

Lane drove back down the hill to the town square. He parked, walked across the street, and stood solemn before the large gray-stone church. A bronze plaque stated it had been built by hand in 1918. He saw a sign with plastic letters planted near a bush:

BAPTIST FELLOWSHIP CHURCH
REV. CHESTER PARKS
SERVICES - 9:30 AND 11:00
A DIAMOND IS A PIECE OF COAL
THAT STUCK TO ITS GOAL.

Lane eyed the proverb. Too bad the pastor didn't follow his own advice, he thought.

He entered the church grounds through an old-fashioned wrought-iron picket fence and surveyed the outside of the building. He noticed dense shrubbery around the foundation interspersed with several window wells to admit light into the basement. In the rear of the church, a stairway descended to a basement door. He checked the door and was surprised to discover it unlocked. He moved back up the stairs and continued around the church before returning to his car for a flashlight.

As he opened the trunk, his phone vibrated.

"What's your status?" the caller asked.

"Everything is proceeding as planned," Lane said.

"Good. There's a development you should know about. Two new opponents have entered the theater."

"What opponents?"

Lane listened. "I see," he said. "I'll do whatever is necessary." Lane disconnected the call. He took a deep breath. He was a warrior in the spiritual warfare for souls. Nothing would prevent him from completing his mission.

Lane returned to the basement door of the church and cautiously pulled it open. Inside, his flashlight illuminated a large room, approximately thirty-five feet from front to back and extending more than halfway across the width of the church. A furnace was located at one end. Next to it, a hot water heater. A table with a lamp occupied the center of the room. Stacks of cartons filled with church literature stood at the other end. He inspected two closets. The first contained cleaning supplies. The second stored banners, framed artwork, and various religious paraphernalia. A door led upstairs. He steadied his phone on the table and took several pictures.

Back at his car, Lane began to formulate his plan. The military had taught him to look for the enemy's least defended or most fragile resource. He had found it.

He would need to locate a hardware store.

34

Bill Miner
Kansas City
4:50 PM

"You know, Inspector Shreve wasn't too happy about our going on this little jaunt," Victoria said.

I looked out the window as our aircraft began its descent, the serpentine course of the Missouri River visible in the distance. "Happy or not, we're here."

"I called him on the way to the airport because I didn't want him to think we were doing this behind his back. He cautioned we should use finesse in our conversations with their police department."

"Concerned we might ruffle feathers?"

She nodded. "Shreve said that homicide investigators can possess healthy egos and might not welcome outsiders, especially a professor from a place like Berkeley." She gave me a nudge with her elbow.

"Thanks for sharing," I said.

"I called Overland Park on the way to the airport and spoke with the head of their Investigations Division, a woman by the name of Sherry Bowers. She sounded receptive—at least I didn't pick up on any negative vibes. She said she'd be in the office until seven thirty PM."

I checked my watch and set it forward two hours. "It's a few minutes to five o'clock local time. We should be fine."

The plane was on the ground twenty minutes later. A sign in the terminal read:

RANKED IN THE TOP FIVE AIRPORTS IN NORTH AMERICA

We zipped through the modern, small, and uncrowded airport and over to the rental car agencies.

By six thirty we'd reached Overland Park. We turned down Foster Street and parked in front of a large building that housed the municipal court and police department. At the counter, we gave our names and asked to see Captain Bowers.

"Tell her it's about the Smith shooting," I said.

The police clerk punched digits on a phone and spoke in a whisper.

He pointed to a hallway to the left. As we started in that direction, a woman in a smart navy pantsuit came forward and introduced herself.

She looked to be in her late thirties and had an easy smile on her face.

"Welcome to Overland Park," Bowers said. "Sorry it's under these circumstances."

We followed Bowers into her office—a plain room, a few plaques on the wall, a tall steel file cabinet in one corner. A man was seated in front of her desk—muscular build, shaved and polished scalp, gray eyebrows, white shirt and tie, a shoulder holster under his arm. He could have passed for Mr. Clean except there was no smile and no earring.

"This is Detective Dale Kent," Bowers said. "He's handling the case."

Kent stood and extended his hand, but his eyes projected a coolness.

"First, I'd like to express my sympathies for the loss of your father," Bowers said.

Victoria nodded. "Thank you."

"We've little to go on," Bowers said. "There were no witnesses to Mrs. Smith's death, and we have no suspects, let alone a motive."

She motioned for us to sit. "Detective Kent, you want to tell them what we know so far?"

"At first we thought we were dealing with an accident," Kent said, his hands in a "fish-was-this-big" position. "A woman walks her dog, looks at her phone, is struck and killed by a hit-and-run driver. Later in the afternoon the vehicle, a GMC Yukon, was found in a nearby shopping center parking lot. Front grill smashed, broken headlight, blood."

"So that should make it easy to find the owner," I said. My comment drew an annoyed look from Kent.

"A shopper," he said, "reported she had seen a man park the Yukon, walk to another car a few spaces away, get in, and drive off. She noticed him because it looked like he had a rifle. She didn't see his face and didn't pay attention to the car's license plate. Prints found on the Yukon were those of the owner, a store manager in the shopping center. The guy who stole it probably wore gloves. The car's owner was at the store where he works the entire day, never left. It was a pretty slick job—the entry, the hot-wire, the works."

"So, the car was taken to use as a murder weapon," I said.

"Let me finish," Kent said. His voice conveyed an inflexible will. "We know what we're doing here." The visible tension in his neck emphasized his hard jawline. I could hear his tongue click and his toes tap out his disdain. "Tests of the blood on the bumper match the victim and the victim's dog. Then the twist. Our coroner discovered a bullet lodged in the victim's neck. *That*, not the vehicle impact, is what killed her. When we submitted the bullet for ballistics, we got a hit from your California crime scene."

"If we can understand that link," I said, "we may learn the motive."

Kent didn't even glance at me, as if the statement were insanely obvious. "I see why you're at Berkeley." He gave a derisive sniff and angled his body away from me.

Captain Bowers flashed him a look but didn't say anything. I let the impertinent remark slide. Victoria didn't.

"Smart people often verbalize their understanding to ensure they're on the same page, to avoid misinterpretation," she said. "It often ends up getting more things done."

Kent shifted in his seat. "Professor Miner," he said, "we understand you're an expert on cults and that a cult may have been involved in your fatality in California. Is that right?"

I nodded.

"Well, your expertise is wasted here," he said. Exuding a complacent smugness, he crossed his arms. "We're on top of this, and nothing we've seen so far suggests a cult. There are a variety of religious groups in the rural Ozarks, but they don't usually make trouble as far away as Overland Park. They may be outspoken about the civil liberties of certain minority groups here and there, but nothing close to shooting a mother of two in a peaceful, family-oriented suburb."

Kent leaned back and cocked his head as if to say, *Any last questions? Because this is a waste of our time.*

"We're here on the gamble that we might see some other tie-in," Victoria said. "Honestly, at this point, we don't have a clue what that might be. But it might help if we talked with the family."

Kent rolled his eyes and gave his boss a look of protest.

Bowers tapped her fingers on the desk as she studied the pained look on her detective's face, then the earnest expression from Victoria.

"How could that hurt?" Bowers said finally.

Kent pressed his lips into a thin white line.

"All right," Bowers said. "The husband's name is Larry Smith. Kent, give him a call and ask if the three of you can come over."

Kent shrugged but made little effort to conceal his exasperation. He dialed a number and spoke with the party. He disconnected the call, released a breath slowly, and said, "OK, you can follow me over."

We thanked Captain Bowers and walked out to the parking lot. Kent pulled around, and we followed his car as he turned out onto the street, kicking up gravel as he went.

"I wonder if he'll try to lose us," Victoria said, only half joking. "I should've asked her for the address."

"I wouldn't put it past Detective Permafrost. Hang on in case we have to run some lights."

35

Bill Miner
Overland Park, KS
7:15 PM

A few minutes later we pulled up to the home of a family certain to be in shock and mourning. The song of cicadas permeated the evening air in a neighborhood that bore no sign of the previous day's violence. A man, eyes filled with exhaustion and sadness, opened the front door.

"I apologize for this intrusion," Detective Kent said. He introduced us to Larry Smith, the victim's husband, a man in his midforties with thinning dark hair.

Smith led us into the living room, stepping ahead to clear a path through an assortment of dolls, Dr. Seuss books, and soccer balls. An older woman rose from a wing-back chair. "This is Virginia Baldwin, Florence's mother," Smith said. Her face looked smudged with tears. "My daughters, six and eight, are upstairs with a sitter. I didn't want them exposed to police questioning."

The room showed a woman's influence. A Chippendale-style secretary against one wall displayed wooden spools, some fashioned into candlesticks. A tall glass vase filled with balls of colored yarn sat on an end table. A feminine touch that would now be absent.

"Our hearts go out to you," Victoria said as we sat down. "I too am grieving. Five days ago, my father was killed while hiking in California. We're here because there may be a connection with your wife's death."

"What kind of connection?" Smith asked.

"The same person may be responsible," Victoria said. "We think he may have associations with a religious cult."

"Religious cult?" asked Mrs. Baldwin. "What kind of cult would attack a beautiful, loving mother in the prime of her life? Are you talking about terrorists?"

"This is a quiet community," Smith said. "We don't have any of that."

Kent crossed his arms and flicked me a self-satisfied smile. I glanced back. *This guy would bring a lot of joy if he would just leave the room.*

"Were you and your wife ever associated with any nontraditional religious group?" I asked.

"We're cradle-to-grave Catholics," Smith said. "That's as traditional as you get."

"Florence was raised with a strong faith," Mrs. Baldwin said. "Florence and Larry met through the local church. They married there. She would never associate with anything else." Her small head bobbed up and down as if to drum the point home. "A friend from her work once invited Florence to go with her to a Christmas program with bell ringers and all. She wouldn't hear of it—not at First Presbyterian. God would frown if a good Catholic girl were ever to step inside another church."

"That's true," Smith said. "But that changed a couple of months ago."

"How so?" I asked.

"She was in a horrible car accident. A pickup truck smashed into her head on. It was a miracle she survived." He paused. His eyes became misty. "Now this." His voice cracked.

"We've put you through enough," Kent said. He rose to his feet. "We appreciate your time."

Smith raised his hand. "No. It's OK, if there's anything that might help identify some connection."

Detective Kent shot a look toward the ceiling, sighed, and sat back down.

"After her accident," Smith continued, "her attitude changed about everything, even church."

"How was church different?" I asked.

"It might be better if you heard her own words," he said. "Florence had just finished a write-up for the TV people." He pushed himself out of his chair and moved toward a desk. "I don't think you've seen it, Mother B."

"TV people? They did a news story on her accident?" I asked.

"A *60 Minutes* producer came from New York. It wasn't the accident they were interested in. It was her near-death experience."

Victoria's head spun toward mine, her eyebrows raised.

"The girls were so excited Mommy was going to be on TV," Smith said. He searched through a stack of papers and returned with several pages. "Shall I read it out loud?"

"That'd be fine," I said.

Larry Smith sat down and began.

> I was driving to Whole Foods to get groceries before the girls got home from school. I was in the left-turn lane waiting for the light to change when it happened. Suddenly, I was surrounded by a dark emptiness. Strangely, I wasn't frightened. It was very peaceful, quiet. I wasn't alarmed. I wasn't cold. I wasn't in pain. I was just comfortable and extremely curious. The darkness changed into pinpoints of light, and I felt completely at peace among what appeared to be stars. Stars everywhere, like I was floating in the universe.

"Her near-death experience was right there?" Victoria asked. "At the accident scene?"

Smith nodded and continued.

> I felt a soft tug and sensed movement, gradual at first, then with increased speed. The stars flew past me, around me. I was in awe of the beauty everywhere. One star seemed particularly bright, and I realized I was accelerating toward it. The light from that star grew brighter and brighter as though it was drawing me in like a beacon. I flew closer and closer to it, and suddenly I emerged out of the darkness into an incredibly beautiful garden-like setting. Trees and bushes more gorgeous than I'd ever seen. Birds and butterflies in colors indescribable. A sparkling stream ran

> along a pathway paved with rugged stepping-stones, flowers tumbling around them.

Well, that's a stunning picture, I thought. I *don't get fantastical dreams like that.*

> I didn't know where in the world I was. Then I saw a man walking down the path. He stopped and motioned for me to come toward him. "Do you know me?" he asked. I was overcome with emotion. I just knew. It was my father! My father who had died thirty-five years ago, when I was little. I felt such joy at seeing him, but then I thought, *Does this mean I'm dead?* I became confused and distressed. "No, please," I said. "I *can't* die. I have a husband. I have two daughters—"

Smith stopped. He put his head in his hands.

Victoria rose, went to his side, and gave him a gentle hug. "I pray she's back in that garden right now," she said.

The faint tick of a grandfather clock seemed ponderous in the utterly still room. Virginia Baldwin's chin trembled. Detective Kent appeared to stare at the floor vacantly. I felt hearts aching around me, but my mind was absorbed by this inexplicable account.

After a minute, I broke the silence with the only words I could think to say. "Your wife's description is as beautiful as it is poignant. *60 Minutes* knew they would have a deeply moving story that would touch and inspire viewers."

Smith wiped his cheek. "It was what followed that got their attention."

"Are you OK to continue?" I asked.

He nodded.

Victoria took a seat next to him as he resumed.

> The light enveloped me, calmed me. Its radiance was more comfort than a fireplace on a Kansas winter's night. I felt a sense of complete security, of unconditional love, of total acceptance. At the same time, I felt the light focus on just me, Florence Smith. Not as the wife of my husband, not as

> the mother of our children, not as the daughter of my parents, but as totally and completely me.
>
> I thought I must be in heaven, in the presence of Jesus. That he had suffered and died for us.
>
> The light never spoke to me in words that I could hear with my ears, yet in an instant the light understood my thoughts and responded: "Jesus didn't die for your sins, because he didn't have to. You are already loved unconditionally, more than you understand."

Victoria interrupted. "Didn't die for your sins?" Her eyes strained toward his pages. "That's what it said?"

Smith nodded. "Yes, I was astonished when Florence told me." He hesitated. "Should I continue?"

"Absolutely," Victoria said.

> "Then why did Jesus die?" I asked.
>
> "Not for the sins of humankind," the light said. "Jesus died practicing what he preached—turning the other cheek, not resisting evil by violence, loving everyone, including his enemies, even in the face of torture. He chose to demonstrate how to face one's death with courage, trust, and faith."

Smith dropped the papers to his lap.

Utter dismay filled Victoria's face. "My father had a near-death experience and was told Jesus was simply the human founder of a religion." She placed her hands to her forehead as if to contain an ache. "Now Florence hears *this*?"

Victoria stood, despair in her face. She stepped behind her chair and gripped the back as though trying to wring out an explanation.

Something clicked in my brain. "*That's* the connection!" I said.

Victoria glanced at me. Her eyes widened as she came to the same realization.

Detective Kent looked perplexed. "The victims are connected because they both had a near-death experience?" he asked.

"Not that alone," Victoria said. "It's *what* my father and Florence claimed they learned."

"And these assertions," I interjected, "are *packed* with more religious controversy than a Salman Rushdie novel."

I was positively intrigued.

36

Bill Miner
Overland Park
7:50 PM

I sat stunned as the implications caromed inside my head like billiard balls. "Mr. Smith, do you have some more?" I asked. He nodded. "Go ahead and finish. We'll restrain ourselves."

He picked up the papers and resumed reading.

> I didn't know what to think. Was I being *judged*? Then I began to see images appear before me. Pictures of my life flashed in front of my eyes. Images of people I'd hurt. Some I barely knew. It seemed there would be no end to the number of small injuries I'd inflicted with my words, sometimes with just a look, sometimes with what I hadn't said.
>
> There were also occasions in which my actions had had a positive effect—people I'd inspired, sometimes without realizing it. The light didn't play the role of judge. Instead, it provided me with a perspective from which to judge for myself how my conduct had affected others.
>
> After the final image, the light spoke again. It told me I had two choices: I could walk down the path to my father and stay, or I could go back. It warned me, though. While I didn't feel any pain then, if I chose to return, I would experience more suffering and heartache.
>
> I knew I had to return, and my father smiled at my decision.
>
> "What about my sins?" I asked.

The light said, "You are expected to make mistakes. There is only one thing you can bring with you when you die: what you've learned, in your heart and by your actions."

Since I was going back, I asked if it could tell me how all this works. And the light did tell me, and it all made such logical, perfect sense. So I asked if I could share this with people at home. The light told me I could take back the answers to my earlier questions, but the answer to the last one—how it all worked—I would not be able to remember.

Before leaving I asked my father if he would give me something to prove that I'd seen him. "Ask your mother about a small red mark on my arm," he said. "If no one else believes you, she will."

When I opened my eyes, I was back in the street, trapped beneath the mangled steering wheel of my car. A man was about to cover me with a white sheet. I moved, and he yelled, "She's alive!" He turned to me and said, "Ma'am, you've been lying there dead as a doornail for half an hour. We'd called the medical examiner."

I learned later the other driver had raced to make a left turn before the light changed, then reached for his phone when it started to slide off the seat. His car had swerved into my lane and hit me head on.

As soon as I was able, I asked Mother if Dad had had a red mark on his arm. Her reply heartened me. "Many years ago," she said, "when you were just a toddler, a child's baseball hit our barbecue grill at a Memorial Day picnic. A hot briquette hit your dad's arm and left a red mark."

None of the photos I had seen of my father showed the mark, nor had anyone, including Mother, ever thought to mention it.

Smith set the pages down.

"That red mark," Mrs. Baldwin said, her head bobbing up and down as she reflected, "it was the first thing Florence asked me about at the hospital." The petite grandmother's shoes dangled a few inches short of the floor. She seemed adrift in her winged high-back chair.

"Florence was hesitant to talk about any of this," Smith said, "afraid our friends would think she was a nutcase. When CBS contacted us, she was apprehensive and wary until a producer gained her trust."

Mrs. Baldwin wiped her nose. "What does all this have to do with my daughter getting shot?" she asked.

Detective Kent's hands flew outward in appeal. "That's what I want to get to!" he said.

"Theologically, this is pyrotechnic," I said. "Florence Smith and Oscar Johnson have taken a sledgehammer to fundamentalist Christian doctrine."

Mrs. Baldwin gasped. Her hand flew to her chest. Victoria wrapped a protective arm around her. Detective Kent gazed blankly. The living room fell still, save for the faint voices of the young daughters from upstairs.

After a few moments, Victoria spoke. "Mr. Smith, you said your wife was to appear on *60 Minutes*."

"Yes, with the other people on the list."

"A list?" she asked. "What kind of list?"

"In the emails from CBS. There were five names."

Victoria leaned forward. "Can we see the emails?" she asked, her voice calm but assertive.

"Certainly." He got up, and we followed him into his wife's hobby room. Shelves overflowed with bolts of fabric. Spools of thread in a rainbow of colors decorated another wall. Smith moved some quilting rulers from a worktable, and we crowded around Florence's computer.

He pulled up an email from CBS and leaned back so we had a clearer view. We all squinted at the screen. There they were: five names—Mandy Frankel, Oscar Johnson, Chester Parks, Janie Hughes, and Florence Smith.

"Your father had emails from CBS," I said to Victoria. "I failed to look at them because I thought they were TV promos."

Our eyes scanned the text—details about travel to New York and hotel accommodations. Another email referenced CBS's collaboration with an international organization for near-death studies.

Victoria stood back and inhaled a deep breath. Her eyes searched mine as the gravity of the situation became clearer.

Kent ran a hand across the top of his head, a pinched, tension-filled expression spread across his face. "When's somebody going to explain to me how this all got started?" he asked.

Smith swiveled his chair toward the detective. "Soon as Florence got out of the hospital, she wanted to learn all she could about near-death experiences. We had both seen interviews on *Oprah* and *Dr. Oz*, but Florence wanted to know more. She learned about IANDS, the International Association for Near-Death Studies, and contacted them. They asked her to document her experience to benefit their research."

Kent raised a bushy eyebrow. "How did CBS get involved in this?"

"I think from the news story in San Francisco. CBS said they contacted IANDS about Mr. Johnson and through them learned about Florence and the others. A short time later, CBS asked my wife to be on the program."

"So, who could've known about this?" Kent asked. A slight flush appeared in his cheeks, and he rushed to answer his own question. "I guess anybody, since Johnson's story made the newspaper."

Kent came to his feet. "I want the information you have on those five people," he said to Smith.

"Please make a copy for Victoria and me," I said.

We returned to the living room. A few minutes later, Smith joined us with copies of the emails, and Victoria and I began to look through them. Kent stepped away and dialed a phone number. I heard him leave a voice message for Mandy Frankel.

Victoria took out her phone.

"Are you calling one of the others?" I asked.

"I'm not calling," she said. "I'm following an uneasy hunch."

"I'm glad someone has a hunch."

Her eyes darted around the screen of her phone and then narrowed after a few swipes.

"Oh!" she said.

"What?"

Color left her face. She held her phone up for me to see. It was an article from the *Seattle Times.*

A twenty-three-year-old Ballard woman was found stabbed to death yesterday morning in her front yard in the twenty-nine hundred block of NW 69th Street, the victim of an apparent mugging. Seattle police sergeant Mike Lacey said Mandy Frankel was found by a neighbor. A thin purse strap was still clutched in her fingers. The purse had been cut off. "Young woman, dead—for a lousy purse. Makes you sick," the sergeant said. Victoria swallowed. "Detective Kent!" she called to the next room. "We're too late."

37

Bill Miner
Overland Park
8:20 PM

A short time later, Detective Kent, mouth in a grim twist, put down his phone and turned to us. "That was Seattle Homicide. They treated Frankel as a mugging gone bad until I told them about the connection here." He squinted at the notes he'd just made. "We may want to call in the FBI." He drew his gray eyebrows together and stepped away.

"Why don't *we* try to reach someone in the Frankel home?" I said to Victoria. "If someone picks up, your voice may elicit more trust than an unknown male's." I punched in the number we had for Mandy and handed Victoria my cell.

I could hear someone answer. Victoria gave a thumbs-up gesture and moved into an adjacent room.

Virginia Baldwin sat slumped in the chair across from me, her small round shoulders hunched forward. She blew her nose softly. "I pray this all makes sense to the Lord," she said. "It sure doesn't to me."

In an earlier time, I would have had a repertoire of prayers to offer comfort. They had all since slipped away. I went over to her chair, bent down, and put my hand on hers. "I can't imagine what a profound loss this is for you," I said. Tears welled up in her soft eyes. "Victoria and I will do what we can."

She mouthed a "thank you."

Victoria returned to the room, nodding. "Yes, as soon as you can. . . . I'll keep in touch."

She handed my phone back and said, "That was her housemate. They were like sisters. Mandy had a near-death experience and did a write-up like Florence. She'll email it to me."

I closed my eyes and rubbed the middle of my forehead. "The five names—it's a hit list." My throat tightened. "We're dealing with a serial killer."

Kent returned to the living room. "Janie Hughes didn't answer, but I left a message on her machine. I talked to Chester Parks, a minister in a small town two hundred miles southeast of here. I told him of a potential threat on his life."

"And?" Victoria asked.

Kent shrugged. "He said God would provide all the protection he needed—wasn't the least concerned."

Victoria shuddered and drew a deep breath.

"What about the FBI?" I asked.

"That request must come from Captain Bowers."

"How long will that take?"

"I assure you it'll receive the appropriate priority." His patronizing smile conveyed it was none of my business. We were gnats he would have liked to brush away, all the way back to California.

"OK," Kent said, "I think we're finished here." He gathered his notes and Smith's printouts.

I accompanied him to the door. "Give us a call the moment you learn anything," I said.

He gave me a look of condescension. "Leave this to us, Miner."

I'd just about had it with this guy and stared him in the eye. "Oh, *please*," I said, "call me by my first name—*Professor*."

He turned, a flush to his face, gave the doorknob a hard twist, and exited. I went back to the group in the living room. Lips were taut, faces solemn.

Victoria glanced at me. "We should go too," she said.

"Thank you for allowing us to come," I said to Smith. "May I order some pizza for your family before we go?"

"The girls would like that," Smith said, "but only if you stay and have some with us."

D'Bronx pizzeria was at the door half an hour later. Afterward, I phoned a motel while Smith put his young daughters to bed. He came back downstairs and joined us in the living room. "The girls are handling this better than I am," he said. "In their prayers they told God they missed Mommy and asked him to take good care of her."

"They will internalize a lot of their feelings," Victoria said. "I was seven when I lost my mother."

"All this . . . over a TV program," Smith said, his face drawn.

"A *powerful* TV program," I said. "Imagine a CBS correspondent like Scott Pelley interviewing Oscar Johnson and Mandy Frankel and your wife as they described what they learned while unconscious, things they couldn't have known beforehand. Audiences would have been riveted."

Mrs. Baldwin had been quiet, but now she leaned forward. "I'm still in awe that Florence talked to her father."

"That's what makes this so sensational," I said. "Viewers would recognize the implications—that the contradictions to religious doctrine were also true."

Smith looked down with a mournful expression.

"Someone feared they would be persuasive," I said. "The story in the paper must have triggered the break-in at Mr. Johnson's home, and that gave the intruder access to his computer and emails."

The clock chimed nine o'clock. We sat quietly for a few moments.

"Here's my hunch," I said. "The reason someone was so threatened they wanted to prevent the broadcast at any cost was not because Florence was told by her light that Jesus didn't die for our sins. The church has heard that doubt expressed before." I turned to Victoria. "It's something else your father said that I think hit a nerve with conservative believers."

She wrinkled her brow.

"The part about evolution," I said, "that it's God's design plan."

Smith looked quizzical. "Evolution?" he asked.

"*On the Origin of Species* created a firestorm from the day it was published. Darwin knew it would—if we evolved from lower animals, gone was humankind's special place in creation. Victoria and I discussed that yesterday, and she reminded me just what a flash point evolution is."

"My goodness gracious!" Mrs. Baldwin said. She lifted her frail hands up. "Someone committed murder over Darwin?"

I stood to leave. "Someonc may have feared the program on *60 Minutes* would be a treacherous assault on the biblical story of creation. If that's the case, the FBI will be up against a resolute and determined adversary.

"One who believes he's fighting *for* God."

38

Bill Miner
Overland Park
Day 6, 8:30 AM

Victoria joined me in the motel's small dining room as I finished my second cup of coffee. "Good morning, sunshine," I said.

"Morning," she said.

The sadness in her eyes corresponded to my own internal gloom. I pulled a chair out for her.

"I didn't sleep well thinking about his daughters," Victoria said. "On a normal day, their household would be abuzz right now as they scurried to get ready for school. Did you see all the family photos on the refrigerator?"

I nodded.

"Happy moments of a family . . . now in pieces," she said.

I reached for a box of Cheerios on the self-serve counter next to us. "As a kid, my grandfather convinced me this was what the Lone Ranger ate for breakfast." *Anything to lighten the mood.*

Victoria opened a container of strawberry Yoplait. "OK, kemosabe, then where do we go from here?"

"I suppose it's in the hands of Kent, but I don't have abundant confidence in our great and powerful Oz."

"We're in 'red' America," Victoria said. "People have a very different world view and resent Bay Area and East Coast liberals who push for European-style socialism." She dropped her hands to her lap and stared at her yogurt. "A woman in the restroom referred to Republicans as her 'army of brave hearts,' as though Democrats had taken their country from them."

"When some hear 'Make America great again,' they yearn for the Christian nation they believe the founding fathers intended." I poured some more coffee as I recalled Thomas Jefferson's campaign to *separate* church and state, his personal disbelief in the divinity of Christ, and his own search for religious truth.

We had finished breakfast, and Victoria called Detective Kent. She hung up after a brief conversation, disappointment across her face. "He spoke in generalities," she said, "as if from a PR manual. I don't think he's even briefed the chief yet."

"It's a few minutes after nine o'clock," I said. "Maybe—"

"He wouldn't say whether he'd reached the woman in Idaho." Victoria crossed her arms and glanced at her watch, checking the time even though I'd given it to her ten seconds earlier.

"Kent made it plain how he feels about our involvement," I said.

"And we're losing precious hours. By the time they get approval for the FBI? By the time they mobilize?" Victoria's questions were more like statements. She wasn't asking for answers as she drummed her fingernails on the table.

"What are you thinking?" I asked. "That we extend our little field trip to Waynesville? Try to talk some sense into a headstrong pastor? He wouldn't listen to a homicide detective," I said. "You think he'll listen to us?"

Victoria gave me a steady gaze, a look of determination.

I put my napkin on the table. "Well then, let's go," I said.

I felt good despite what I knew were ridiculous odds. Within minutes we'd checked out and began our drive eastward from Overland Park, across the state line into Missouri.

The lush green of the landscape was in stark contrast to the dry, golden hills of the Bay Area. Cotton-like cumulus clouds towered, another disparity from the horizon-to-horizon deep sky blue of Northern California.

Traffic had thinned out by the time I turned onto Route 7. The Kansas-Missouri border was thirty minutes behind us when Victoria pointed to a bumper sticker on the car ahead of us that read: THE BIBLE SAYS IT. I BELIEVE IT. THAT SETTLES IT.

"Looks like your views may be in the minority around here," she said with the first grin of the day.

"Mmm, and Missouri's not even ground zero of the Bible Belt," I said. We hadn't had much to chuckle about that morning.

Victoria still seemed to be savoring the bumper sticker when her phone chirped. She retrieved it from her purse and studied the screen. "Mandy Frankel's housemate in Ballard. She emailed the write-up she promised."

She read to herself for a few minutes. "This is interesting," she said. "You need to hear it." She began to read:

> My grandparents emigrated from Poland to the Brownsville section of Brooklyn in the late 1930s. So my parents were the first generation born in America. Many people in the neighborhoods of New York came from villages outside of Kraków and had little formal education. Grandfather died when I was little, and Grandmother moved in with us. The house always smelled of horseradish. She took pride in making her own.
>
> Growing up in the 1990s, I'd always heard about the Holocaust. We learned about it in elementary school, but I'd never given it much thought until one day when our Hebrew teacher was out sick, and the principal had Rabbi Braverman come in to teach our class.
>
> He was old, in his seventies. "Now, *yeladim* (children)," he said, "I am going to talk to you about something important." He looked at us with such solemn eyes. Then he rolled back his sleeve to reveal a number on his arm. "Soldiers held me down and tattooed this. I was your age."
>
> I sat utterly still as Rabbi Braverman told the story of his years during the Holocaust.
>
> "They took our whole family," he said. "My parents; my older brother, who was eleven; two younger sisters; and I were forced to leave our home for a concentration camp. Auschwitz." His eyes became bleary. "Our identity and our worth were reduced to a serial number on our arms. Like cattle."
>
> He told us that children were put to work tending crops. He and the others would hide small potatoes in their pockets, often the only thing they would have to eat.

> One day the soldiers rounded them all up in the middle of the field they had just finished harvesting. He was the last one to come running out. He hurried to the end of the line and gave a salute. He said he still doesn't know why he did it, because you weren't even allowed to address a German. The man in charge pointed at him, directing him to go back to the building. He was halfway back when he heard machine gun fire. The other children were shot to death.

"Oh . . ." Victoria said. Her hand with the phone in it dropped to her lap. "God must . . . just weep." After a moment she looked again at her phone and continued.

> I was just a kid, but I was affected by his story. How could God exist and permit such a thing to occur? That doubt made me cynical, and I decided there was no such thing as a loving God. I muddled through high school. I was in a sad state after graduation, too despondent to think about college—chronic back pain, fatigue, loss of appetite, gaunt appearance. When I thought things couldn't get worse, my father, the primary male figure in my life, died from a heart attack. He had been my strength.

Victoria paused and stared out the window as if reminded of the new emptiness in her own life. My mind drifted to Pastor Parks. Our task—to convince him he was in imminent danger—loomed as large as an oncoming cattle truck that appeared over the crest ahead. A Subaru started to pass us, ignoring the solid lines on the pavement, then pulled back into our lane as the trucker leaned on his horn. Some tragedies are preventable with common sense. I hoped the pastor would have some of that.

Victoria returned to her phone and resumed reading Mandy's email.

> At nineteen I left home, escaped to the Pacific Northwest on a quest for a new life. I found a job in Seattle and a place with cheap rent—a communal house with a bunch of

unrestrained and rebellious people my age. I scarcely made it from paycheck to paycheck, but I liked the freedom. For the first time, I began to have fun. My housemates knew how to do the whole party scene. I followed their lead, following the pleasure principle. If it pleased me, I did it. It wasn't long before I got into drugs. I might have gone on to heroin, but I was always scared of needles. I lived moment to moment, and frankly, I was having a ball. My philosophy was, well, if there's no God, no afterlife, I might as well cram in all the fun I can now.

In July, I had my first ride on a motorcycle on the back of a friend's bike, part of my new devil-may-care attitude. We were on our way home from a rock concert at CenturyLink Field when out of the blue, at the foot of Queen Anne Hill, a drunk driver hit us. We were thrown to the ground headfirst. My friend had a helmet, but I did not.

I remember looking down at the accident scene, at my own body, perfectly still on the pavement. I'd barely had time to realize the weirdness of it all when I soared into the night sky like Peter Pan. Amazingly it felt quite natural. Beneath me lay beautiful Elliott Bay. I could see ferryboats ply the waters between Seattle, Bainbridge Island, and Bremerton. Below me, the lights of Pike Place Market and the Space Needle sparkled in the foggy mist. I accelerated to dazzling speeds and must have covered enormous distances before I reached a destination.

I felt a presence, and there, before me, were two beings. I knew the first was my dad. He embraced me. I was overwhelmed with love.

He introduced me to my grandfather who had died when I was too young to remember him. Grandfather told me he had bequeathed to me his prized silver Hanukkah menorah. I hadn't known that.

Then I felt the presence of the light. I struggle when I try to describe the sense of compassion, of love.

Emotions that I'd buried rose to the surface. Why did I receive so much love and acceptance now? I wondered.

Now that I'd died? Where was God during Auschwitz? Why were there centuries of persecution of Jews as Christ killers?

The light's response to these thoughts surprised me: "Jewish responsibility for the crucifixion of Jesus was greatly exaggerated to deflect attention from the betrayal by Judas. What Judas betrayed was not what everyone thinks."

39

Bill Miner
Missouri Route 7
10:00 AM

"Not what everyone *thinks*?" Victoria looked at me askance. "The Gospels are clear. Judas did it for the money."

A faint whinny—from a horse trailer we were passing—punctuated her comment. "Does Mandy elaborate?" I asked.

Victoria returned to her phone.

> The light said Jesus expected he would be king in the future kingdom on earth and, in private, told his disciples he would appoint them rulers of the twelve tribes of Israel.

"Oh, come on," Victoria said. She sat back, her expression dismissive.

"No, actually, that's plausible," I said. "Judas may have been first dismayed and then angered when it became obvious Jesus wasn't going to raise an army and drive the Romans out of Judea. If Jesus had told his disciples in secret he was the messiah and promised they would share in his power, imagine how they would have felt when he dashed those hopes at the Last Supper?"

"Wait a second. You argued on the plane that Jesus never said he was God."

"God, no, messiah, yes. But what Jesus *meant* by 'messiah' was that he would be the king in God's kingdom on *earth*—the kingdom that was imminent. Not that he *was* God."

Victoria gave me a dissatisfied glance.

"Look, what if you're one of his chosen," I said, "psyched up to be one of his rulers, then hear Jesus talk about his own death? Messiahs aren't supposed to die. What a crushing letdown. Maybe Judas went ballistic. . . . I know one thing: the Romans didn't need Judas to lead them to Jesus. They could have found him on their own—all they had to do was tail him."

"It wasn't a secret Jesus was the messiah," she said, her face flustered. "The crowds knew that. He received rock-star acclaim when he rode a donkey into Jerusalem for the celebration of Passover."

"That's an idyllic Sunday school portrayal, but I don't think it happened that way," I said.

She crossed her arms.

"The Roman army would've had Super Bowl–tight security during the Passover season," I said. "Pontius Pilate had left the comforts of his home on the Mediterranean coast to come to Jerusalem with additional troops to guard against possible riots. Why? Because the festival revived angry emotions and stirred rumors of rebellion. Moses may have led the Jews out of slavery in Egypt, but here were God's chosen, *still* under Roman rule and occupation. If Jesus had paraded into the city having claimed he was king of the Jews, he would've been arrested on the spot."

Victoria tipped her head from one side to the other as if weighing the idea.

"Jesus never said he was the future king in public," I said. "But if that's what he told his disciples in private, then Judas had all the evidence the Roman governor needed to find Jesus guilty of treason—a man who dared declare himself to be king."

"This is like total catnip for you, isn't it?"

"I don't have a problem with the responses Mandy heard." I pulled at my ear. "I'm still trying to grasp that her conversation was with a *light*! What else does she say?"

Victoria resumed reading.

> The light asked me what I had done to repair the world.
>
> I acknowledged I didn't have much to show for myself, that deep down I felt empty. The light told me life was intended to be difficult. I could complain about problems

> or confront them and grow. I became frustrated. What good was any of this advice now?
>
> The light said I was not dead, that I had to return.
>
> "To what?" I asked. "To a meaningless life?"
>
> It suggested I find a passion, a passion that contributes, that fills a need.
>
> Then it told me to be a good Jew and aspire to the words from the book of Micah—"Act justly, love mercy, and walk humbly."
>
> I was dumbfounded. The light quoted from a book of the Hebrew Bible?
>
> I'd felt overwhelmed with complete acceptance. No way was I going to leave. Then I felt my dad's presence, and he told me I had to go back.
>
> I thought, *OK, I'll return, but I know how I can get right back up here.*
>
> Dad read my thoughts and told me I must not take my own life. Suicide wasn't the answer. I had to live my life's purpose. He said it would all make sense in the end.

Victoria stopped. Her hand touched her neck as if to soothe the ache from the loss of her own father.

"There's a little more," she said after a moment.

> I felt myself returning, dropping downward. In an instant, I'd slammed into my body, back with the pain from the accident.
>
> In the days that followed, the wonder of the experience flowed through me—and I felt hope. I realized everybody struggles. That was good to know. The light had told me to recognize the benefits of setbacks. That if I learned I could rebound from failure, I might overcome my fear of defeat and take risks that would prove rewarding.
>
> As soon as I got out of the hospital, I began to make changes. I discovered I loved to bake and landed a job at a Macrina Bakery. A girlfriend and I rented a home in Ballard, and I plan to enroll in culinary school.

> Finally, I want to say what my mother found last month in her attic. She was sorting through boxes and uncovered my grandfather's will, long given up as lost. Just as he'd said, he had willed his menorah to me.
>
> I feel that writing this is part of my purpose in life—not merely as a recipient of this experience, but as one of its messengers.

We drove the next few miles in silence, past the umpteenth field with brown and white Guernsey cows leisurely, efficiently processing grass into milk at midday.

"You know, I like what Mandy wrote," I said.

Victoria shook her head—the way you do when you feel a situation is hopeless. "She's told to be a good Jew? That makes *sense* to you?" She searched my face. "It's like my religious arguments with colleagues at work—almost always unproductive."

"At least your colleagues discuss topics of consequence rather than bantering idly in the break room."

"Seriously, Bill, listen. I care about you." Her eyes brimmed with sincerity. "What if you're wrong about Jesus? Eternity's a long time to be wrong about that."

Her words hung in the air a few moments as I felt an emotion I hadn't experienced in ages. *Did she just say she cared?* I found myself self-conscious and shy and retreated to safer territory. "I admire the beautiful faith I see in you," I said.

The car was quiet, and then I heard a soft sigh of exasperation.

"Yes, but," she said.

"No, I do," I said and glanced toward her. "Just don't forget that the what-if-you're-wrong argument is a two-edged sword."

Victoria sat back, attentive but guarded.

"I appreciate and respect your decision to follow Jesus," I said. "I don't suggest for an instant you change it. But it was a *choice* you made, a choice among rival claims."

"Easy choice," she said. "Christ or eternal damnation. What's difficult about that?"

"Nothing, unless *you're* wrong."

40

Bill Miner
Missouri Route 7
10:25 AM

"Bill, I'm not wrong," Victoria said, her voice soft but resolute.

"It's not about who's right and who's wrong," I said. "It's the presumption that there is only one choice."

"You know," she said, confidence in her voice, "the Gospels tell a story so compelling that the followers of Jesus were willing to suffer death rather than renounce him."

"So what is Judaism? Chopped liver? Don't overlook that the Jews are God's chosen people."

"Christ changed all that," she said under her breath.

"But Jesus never departed from the truths of Judaism," I said. "If you want guaranteed salvation, why not be Jewish? Mandy's light didn't have a problem with it."

Victoria's eyes rolled to the ceiling.

"I can see you're not wild about that choice. How about Islam?"

"Oh, come on," she said. "Muslims relegate Jesus to the status of a prophet."

"But the Koran was transmitted directly from God's lips."

"Surely you don't rate the integrity of the Koran above the Bible," she said, her voice tight.

"The Koran is more recent," I said with a shrug, "delivered six centuries after Jesus and guaranteed authoritative. Instead of asking, 'What would Jesus do?' maybe the question should be 'What would Muhammad do?' "

"There is only one truth," she said in a matter-of-fact tone.

"I take it from that reaction that you'll stick with your evangelical beliefs."

"You know perfectly well the Bible assures us of its accuracy."

"Of course," I said, "and the Koran assures us of *its* accuracy. So, there you are. You must choose. But the choices don't end there. You decided to be Protestant as opposed to Catholic. You're aware that when Jesus said Peter was the 'rock' on which he would build his church, Jesus was referring to the *Catholic Church.* Yet you made a different choice, and according to the Vatican, you chose poorly."

Victoria crossed her arms, and I saw irritation fill her face. I should have stopped there—probably earlier—but I blathered on.

"And don't overlook the opinion of Seventh-day Adventists," I said. "They believe Evangelicals are possessed by Satan."

She rolled her head toward me and lifted an eyebrow.

"And all this assumes," I said, "that you've asked the right question in the first place—that the most important human problem is how to achieve salvation. What if it's *not* the most important human problem? Buddhists don't think it is."

She shifted away from me in her seat.

"Choices," I said. "You had to make them all along the way. Even the decision *not* to choose is a choice. Victoria, I'm not saying you didn't make a good one. It's just that you hit one of *my* pet peeves. I bristle whenever I hear the church play the fear card. 'What if you're wrong?' is used to intimidate, and the church is not above bullying."

We drove for the next mile without a word, as though the lush growth of elm and maple that bordered the highway had enveloped us in a curtain of silence.

I drew a deep breath. What in the world had I just said? Did I think I was in my lecture hall with students? She'd just told me she cared. Cared for *me.* And I had launched into an analysis of her choice of evangelical Christianity? A choice that had guided her heart, given her life focus and meaning. Jeez, a lot more than *I* had right then: A career that teetered on the precipice. A mercenary preoccupation with my book.

"Did I hear you say you cared?" I blurted out.

"Of course I care. It goes with being a patron saint of desperate cases and lost causes."

"Oh." I swallowed hard. *It's "saving" me she cares about.*

She gave me a quick, searching glance. "I mean—well, it's important." She looked out her side window.

"Understood," I said. I felt a sinking heaviness in my body.

"Sure . . . naturally . . . important as it gets," she said. She rubbed her arm and winced.

We rounded a curve and noticed a church billboard that read:

HONK IF YOU LOVE JESUS.
TEXT WHILE DRIVING IF YOU WANT TO MEET HIM.

It offered a welcome chuckle in the nick of time, as I was desperate to change the subject.

"How much credibility do you put in these near-death experiences?" I asked as nonchalantly as I could with my stomach still on the floorboards.

"How much do you know about NDEs?" she asked.

"Everyone's heard of people with heart attacks who found themselves transported through a tunnel to celestial realms."

"They're in the news more because hospitals now save more people," Victoria said. "The boundary between life and death used to be a sharp line—ten minutes without a heartbeat, and you were a goner. Now state-of-the-art resuscitation teams have extraordinary ways to revive patients even hours after their hearts have stopped."

"Before this week, I hadn't given them much notice," I said. "I pay more attention to the condiments I put on my cheeseburger. Near-death experiences have always struck me as part of a spirituality of the seventies—the 'Age of Aquarius' kind of thing. Wishful thinking, but fantasyland, nevertheless."

"In my opinion, there's far too much evidence not to take them seriously." Her face bloomed the way parents' faces glow with pride over their children. "For hundreds of years, individuals who were brought back from death's door have said they glimpsed the afterlife. From every country, every culture, all educational backgrounds and faiths. Some physicians give these experiences credence in books that became best sellers. That attests to people's high level of fascination."

"Are all your fellow scientists on board with this?" I asked.

"Many are. But some think NDEs are simply the body's reaction to unbearable stress." She glanced out the window as we passed a pasture full of Black Angus. "Skeptics think that, just as it's inevitable those cattle will end up as your cheeseburger, it's just a matter of time before near-death experiences are shown to be the product of spasms in a dying brain. An eruption of activity as the mind tries to figure out what's happening.

"Critics say there's a simple explanation for why people see the tunnel and the light. Electrical brain scans show that in our last moments, as the brain is deprived of oxygen, cells fire in frantic, random fashion in the part of the brain that governs vision. If you've got lots of cells that fire in the center and a smaller number that fire at the edge, you might see it as a light at the end of a tunnel."

"That sounds plausible," I said as I sped up to pass a UPS truck that was blocking *my* vision.

"Some think a primitive software app in our brainstem is triggered to ease pain when the brain thinks it's dying, and the life review is just a distorted recall of the memories you've always had."

"So, there's a lot of doubt," I said.

"And I haven't even mentioned that some believe the whole business is caused by anesthesia, drugs like ketamine."

"Wait. That's one argument that wouldn't make sense for all cases," I said. "Anesthesia couldn't be a factor for Florence Smith—not at the scene of a car accident."

Victoria nodded. "That's right."

"And if the body goes through a preprogrammed shutdown when it thinks it's dying," I asked, "wouldn't everyone who's had a close brush with death see those tunnels, lights, etc.?"

"That's a good rebuttal," she said. "The doubters don't have an answer for that. And how do you explain the ability of the brain to process *anything* when the patient is flatlined?"

"Like your father was."

"Yes. But, while we see various features of NDEs that *might* be caused by drugs or surgical trauma, why do those features occur in a specific, consistent order? The out-of-body experience, the tunnel, the light, the inexpressible love, the life review. That can't be coincidence, and it's one more reason I'd believed NDEs were real."

Victoria seemed grounded in the pro and con arguments of a controversial subject.

"And who wouldn't want them to be bona fide?" she said. "Think what it would mean to have evidence. Proof of the divine. Churches would overflow. If we could show that a person saw or heard things . . . things they could not have known beforehand . . . that would be huge."

"But isn't that what the IANDS organization is doing?" I asked. "Gathering evidence?"

"Yes, but it's been tough. Many people who've had NDEs aren't that interested in the science. They want to support one another, not collect data."

"The goal, then, for those who believe the mind does leave the body, is to find cases you can verify."

"Yes, that's the Holy Grail for an NDE researcher."

"Well, haven't you just found such cases? Your father saw a traffic accident while he was in surgery. He spotted a baseball cap on the hospital roof. He met a brother he didn't know had died. Mandy Frankel learned about her Hanukkah menorah. Florence Smith met her father and learned about his red mark. Wouldn't those things clinch the case?"

"But don't you see the quandary that has put me in? At last a breakthrough with genuine, verifiable evidence"—she put a hand to her forehead—"but it's contrary to everything I've put my faith in."

"So, you're questioning this because it contradicts your religious beliefs."

"Wouldn't you?"

"I suppose. Funny, though. It's the inverse for me. I'm fine with the biblical issues, but the idea there is some heavenly 'light' that *communicates* with people . . . What does your company think?"

"Genentech stays clear of the religious ramifications. They're interested in near-death experiences because they want to understand consciousness. Research has encouraged us. We've shown that medical factors cannot account for the occurrence of NDEs." She paused, and her tone became despondent. "I was so euphoric when Papa told me he went to the light. At last, I thought he might accept Jesus and that the experience might turn him into a confirmed believer."

"You carry enormous guilt that you couldn't convince him," I said.

"I *do*." She curled her hands inward and pinned them against herself. "Neuroscience is my field! My company has contributed to the research. Now NDEs are the focus of a national TV special that poses such a threat that someone killed three people and threatens two more."

Victoria became quiet. A moment later tears welled up in her eyes, and one broke free.

"I'm *so* sorry," I said. I fumbled for words. "I didn't—"

"I *miss* him."

The mournful ache in her voice sent a pain to my stomach.

"He instilled in me that the future is always uncertain," she said, "that we must always persevere, regardless . . ."

She reached in her purse for a tissue.

"When Papa and I would argue about religion, he would listen, then smile gently, as if to say, *You'll understand my view someday*."

Words deserted me. I just listened.

"I cherish the memories with him. I remember on my seventh birthday, he took me to Fentons on Piedmont Avenue. I ordered one of those giant sundaes served in a glass big enough to hold a flower arrangement, piled high with vanilla ice cream, layers of hot fudge and caramel sauce, covered in whipped cream and nuts. I was stuffed after a few heavenly bites, but Papa didn't scold me that I should have ordered something smaller. His daughter got just what she wanted. He was fine with that."

Victoria squeezed her eyes shut. I reached over and touched her hand.

"If he came home tired from work, he never showed it. He still found time to battle the store lines with a million other parents to get his hands on a Cabbage Patch Kid, the doll of every little girl's dream, or to take my Care Bear to the animal hospital when a dog chewed an arm off."

I felt a lump in my throat. "What a special man," I said. "I would love to have known him."

Victoria dabbed at her cheek. "I was incredibly blessed," she said. "Thank you for listening, for understanding."

I drove for another minute, then slowed, pulled over onto the shoulder, and stopped.

"Your faithfulness to him is a greater tribute than love alone," I said. "Don't think for a moment he wouldn't have felt that devotion."

She turned, her eyes still glistening. "Thank you," she said. She paused a few moments. "I *do*, you know."

"What?"

"Care for you."

She leaned over and kissed my cheek.

My heart leaped. I eased the car back onto the highway. Had my pulse been in some way connected to the drive shaft, we would have burned rubber for twenty yards.

41

Bill Miner
Waynesville
2:10 PM

The clock in the town square showed 2:10 PM as we arrived in Waynesville. The small midwestern town appeared bent on revitalization. Two workers were replacing an area of cracked sidewalk with colored paving stones. Vintage light posts rimmed the square. A freshly painted, white clapboard building with a two-story porch stood on the east side. A plaque in front read:

OLD STAGECOACH STOP

I could picture the scene in *The Music Man* where the Wells Fargo wagon arrives with Harold Hill's band instruments.

We located Chester Parks's church and found the recalcitrant reverend in a small office-study at the rear of the sanctuary. White-haired, late sixties, iron-grip handshake—it was no stretch to imagine this man's persona booming out Sunday inspiration to his flock. He pointed to two chairs by his desk, and we sat down.

"Pastor Parks, you're in danger," Victoria said.

"Y'all, listen," he said. "I 'preciate your trouble. But you needn't a bothered comin'. Who's gonna harm this old coot?" His eyes flashed the sparkle of a rascal. "Maybe a while back. I'm not so ornery now."

I handed him a piece of paper. "Do you recognize these names, Pastor?"

He reached for his glasses and squinted at the list.

"The first three have been killed," I said. "You're next on the list, the next target. Does that get your attention?"

"That's not worryin' me a-tall." He adjusted his glasses and scratched an ear.

I looked over at Victoria. Her lips were pinched together, her face a reflection of my own frustration. We hadn't made a dent. He was too damn cavalier for his own good.

"What can we say to make you recognize the seriousness of this?" Victoria said. Her eyes narrowed with an intense focus.

"Simmer down. I'll tell you why," he said. "But you've got to hear me out, and maybe you'll understand. You see, I'm not the least concerned, because I know what dying's all about."

I closed my eyes, shook my head, and thought of a sign we'd passed in the square that proclaimed the town was named for the Revolutionary War general "Mad Anthony" Wayne. I decided this pastor must be a descendant.

"I used to tell my congregation on Sunday mornings I wasn't the smartest man around. Didn't know much. But I do have a book. And if what I needed to know wasn't in that book, then I just didn't need to know it. You see, what I—"

"Pastor Parks!" Victoria interrupted. "I *know*. I *believe* in the Bible. But a serial killer has sent my father off a cliff, knifed a young woman in the night, shot a mother in Kansas . . . all made to look like unrelated accidents. We don't know who this person is. We don't know why. We just know that with every hour that passes, you're at greater risk."

The pastor held up his hand. "Now, now, don't let your mind run on it." He paused. "See, I used to stand on a conviction that the Bible's the absolute Word of God. Felt it to the depth of my soul. God's book of truth. And I used to tell my congregation I was gonna drag every one of them over to the Way of the Lord."

I felt dragged all right. My eyes shifted to the wall behind him as he droned on. ASK ME WHY YOU DESERVE HELL, read a caption beneath a likeness of Jonathan Edwards. A Spartan bookcase contained copies of *Preacher's Source Book: Bringing the Sinner into Your Church* and *Ten Pitfalls to Avoid in Your Sermon*. I wondered if Parks was a student of the latter . . . or a source of examples.

"Homosexuality? How clear can Leviticus be?" he said. "Whenever a nation gets into homosexuality, the earth vomits that nation out. It's gonna destroy us 'less we do somethin' about it."

My fingernails bit into my palms.

"And I never had been a major fan of women's lib," he said.

Victoria cringed. I thought of the bumper sticker we'd seen. His church probably printed them. *Now we're hearing the unabridged podcast.*

"The role of women is spelled out plain in the Bible—First Timothy," he said. "Women must not teach men because they're created inferior."

Victoria's posture turned stiff, her stare pained.

The old bull continued. "It's in the Law. God created Eve second, for the sake of man. When a woman *does* assume the role of teacher, she's hoodwinked by the devil." He tightened his lips. "Motherhood! That's the noble callin' for women. And that's what I used to tell 'em."

Victoria came to her feet. "Pastor, please stop!" She bent toward him, her hands on his desk. "We don't have time for this."

"Well, I'm getting to the part that's real interestin'. Because, you see, then I had my surgery." He took a sip of water and leaned back with a mischievous grin. "And that changed everything."

Victoria looked over to me, released an exasperated sigh, and sat back down.

"I was fixing to get an operation on my ticker but delayed it because the doc said they'd have to stop my heart. Didn't take much to that idea. The day came, though, and my wife checks me in. They put me under and start work. Next thing I know I feel something turn foul in my body, and I holler, 'Hey, Doc, don't lose me!' Course, they don't hear, because my body's down there on the table unconscious. But me, I'm floating up on the ceiling looking down at them. And I can hear 'em. They're all in a panic."

I wondered if this was the part where the Grinch tells us his heart grew three sizes. *His heart better be bulletproof too.*

"But I'm not panicked," Parks said. "I'm surrounded by peace and a sense of well-being. I'm comfortable. Feel no pain. Then abruptly, I'm flying through a tunnel and picking up speed. Away off in the distance, I see light and what looks like the end. I come out into all this brilliance. Sensation's wonderful."

Parks wet his lips, delighted by our rapt attention.

"A figure comes toward me with this powerful radiance, and I'm thinking, *Oh Lord! The light of the world. I'm standing before Christ Almighty!*"

I shifted in my chair, uneasy. This was now the fourth time in just over that many days that I was hearing about one of these near-death celestial trips. Were they *all* imaginary figments? Victoria appeared to concentrate, as though logging each feature of the experience on a mental checklist.

"I'm wonderstruck," Parks said. "Then nervous. Surely, he must be pleased with me, being as I'm so devoted to preaching his word. Loyal servant . . . spreading the Gospel. Then I hear, *Calm yourself. It's all right.* This luminous figure seems to communicate by thought. It asks what I've done to improve humankind. So, I muster up a burst of passion from a favorite sermon. . . . I compare myself to Saint Paul with his vision of Jesus on the road to Damascus. 'Me and Paul,' I say, 'inspired to Christ's service.' Well, I think I'm off to a real fine start."

I leaned forward. *This should be interesting.*

"Instead of a positive impression," the pastor said, "it's just the opposite. The light tells me Paul suffered from a medical condition that caused his vision."

Victoria blinked and drew back. I did a double take.

The pastor twisted his mouth into a faint smile at our reactions. "The light tells me that Paul got it wrong . . . drew the wrong conclusion."

What! I felt my pulse rate double. The light had said the vision Paul experienced on the road to Damascus was due to an illness? The vision that inspired his mission?

Victoria slumped in her chair.

Pastor Parks looked at us with amusement. "I see you're a little taken aback," he said, "and I hadn't even reached the bottom of the hole I was digging for myself."

42

Tim Lane
Waynesville
2:30 PM

From his car parked in the town square, Tim Lane had watched the two visitors enter Baptist Fellowship Church. He reviewed his plan. One uncertainty was the timing. He waited a few minutes, then drove to a street behind the church and parked. Just as he opened his door, a Pulaski County Sheriff's cruiser turned the corner. Lane closed the door and slid down in his seat.

The cruiser crawled by as the officer scanned the area before he continued to the next street and disappeared out of sight. Lane's heart raced. He bowed his head in a brief prayer, then looked for any passersby. When he saw no one else, he stepped from his car, opened the trunk, and retrieved the brown paper sack with supplies he'd purchased from the hardware store. His motions were smooth as he made straight for the stairway to the basement.

"Hey, mister!" The voice from behind froze Lane. His hands clenched. He turned to see a young teenager approach him. "Have you seen a dog?"

"What's he look like?" Lane asked, his pulse still rapid.

"He's a hound, tan and white. His name's Cowboy."

"Nope, partner. Sorry."

The boy continued out the front gate. Lane let out a huge breath. The moment the youth was out of sight Lane headed to the rear stairwell. Prepared to force his entry, he found it unnecessary. The basement door had remained unlocked. He slipped inside.

Lane could hear voices above him. He listened for a few minutes, but the words were indistinct. He checked around the room—lamp on the table in the middle of the room, plugged in and in working order, water heater off. Everything was as it had been the day before. Just as he needed it now. He glanced at his watch: 2:40 PM. He opened the paper sack and placed the contents on the table—a twelve-inch crescent wrench and a light-switch timer. The hardware clerk had suggested a newer solid-state design, but Lane had selected an older model, an electromechanical type, one that would generate a spark when the contacts closed.

He connected the lamp to the timer, checked to make sure it functioned properly, and rotated the dial to three o'clock. Lane went to the water heater and blew out the pilot light. With the crescent wrench, he disconnected the flexible gas supply line. He twisted the tube so that it pointed toward the center of the room. An unrestrained flow of natural gas poured into the basement. He closed the basement door behind him, hurried up the outside steps, and moved briskly to his car.

43

Bill Miner
Waynesville
2:45 PM

"I begin to realize maybe it isn't Jesus I'm talking to," Pastor Chester Parks said as he scratched his jaw. His wry grin returned.

I glanced at my watch—it had been thirty minutes since we arrived, and this grizzled codger hadn't come up for air. Victoria looked restless. Did this man intend to preach his way out of danger? I admit his story was beginning to pique my curiosity. I was familiar with speculations that Paul was epileptic, but how in the world would an old-school midwestern pastor conceive that idea? And our eccentric reverend looked like he was just building steam.

"I don't know who I'm talking to," he said, "but I'm still defiant because I'm trying to hide my complete and utter shock at all this. But this light sees right through my bluff and posturing."

A perceptive fifth grader would see through this bluster, I thought. Victoria looked down and shook her head.

"The light's voice comes right back at me: *I yearn for humbleness and receptivity from you. Your attitude denies you the opportunity of learning.*"

Victoria turned her head toward me, and we exchanged knowing looks.

"This ole boy persists, feisty-like," Parks said. "I tell the light that I'm a humble servant who's dependent on Jesus's sacrifice for salvation." The pastor raised his palms upward with a flair. "I worship him, love him.

"*Good. Then follow his teachings,* it says, and I recoil. *The world benefits from the message of Jesus, as it does from those of Moses and Muhammad. Look for where religions complement one another. Share wisdom rather than claim exclusive truth.*

"Then the light clobbers me: *Telling people there is no salvation for them except through Christianity is misguided and harmful.*"

Parks leaned back and seemed to savor our reactions. Victoria had crossed her arms.

"Pastor," I said, "it's hard to concentrate when all Victoria and I can think about is the imminent danger—"

"Give me ten minutes," he interrupted. "Then we'll talk about that other business."

I blew out a breath in frustration. My watch read twelve minutes to three o'clock. "I'm going to hold you to that," I said.

The pastor swept his arm upward as if to cue his next recitation.

"I tell the light I *do* tolerate other religions," Parks said. "But the light replies: *Not enough. It's not enough to have gratuitous awareness. You must respect other religions the way you respect your own. All faiths are windows of the same great sanctuary. Light that passes through the panels of stained glass will refract in diverse ways and will be interpreted differently. You are not to block the light that comes through another person's window.*"

I thought that if there was a more magnificent metaphor for the merit of interfaith dialogue, I hadn't heard it.

"My grilling isn't over," Parks said. "The light asks me what I think was Jesus's most important lesson. I don't hesitate. 'The Golden Rule,' I say.

"*Yes, and Hinduism teaches the same great truth, and Islam and Judaism,* it says. *All great religions do.*

"I snap back: 'There's *differences.*'

"But the light doesn't buy any of it. *Each religion has its own interpretation of human nature,* it says. *Each views the problem differently. Christianity sees humankind's problem as sin. Buddhism sees it as suffering. Islam as pride. Respect for other religions allows for collective wisdom.*

" 'But,' I say, 'some religions are half-baked.'

"The light tells me, *There are three tests: Reject any religion that conflicts with the Golden Rule. Refuse any doctrine which advocates violence. Spurn any faith that violates reason.*"

Nice criteria, I thought, *good guidelines to mention in next quarter's comparative religion class. That is, if I* have *a next term.*

"I react right there," Pastor Parks said. "I tell the light I have a problem with two out of the three."

I couldn't believe this guy's chutzpah.

"So, I ask the light, 'Why *wouldn't* you resort to violence? In the face of sin and evil? Even God Almighty had to do it—Noah's flood.' " The pastor grinned. "I think I've got this round," he said.

"The light answers: *God did no such thing. Rising ocean levels were due to natural causes, not an act of punishment. Some people perished, but most dispersed. Genesis used hyperbole. Open your mind.*

" 'Wait a minute,' I say. 'God intervened to prevent the Israelites from destruction by the evil army of Pharaoh—he parted the Red Sea!'

"*God did nothing of the kind*, the light says. *It was a windstorm that allowed Moses to pass. Violence is not the answer to evil. Brutality may be effective in the short term, but not the long term. Defeating an enemy still leaves you with an enemy. Nonviolence may convert him into a friend.*

"I *still* balk. Spurn any faith that violates reason? You can't *reason* out the Bible!

"*Yes, you can!* the light tells me. *Faith has nothing to fear from reason. Jesus did not suffer death as punishment for a fallen humanity. Only an ogre would require the blood sacrifice of an innocent person as payment for the guilty.*"

I glanced at Victoria. Her eyebrows were off the chart.

Parks gave a sheepish smile. "The light doesn't stop there," he said. "It rips into the way I've conducted my ministry. Tells me I shouldn't frighten folks with threats of hell the way I've done. Turns me on my ear . . . says that the ability to write, to teach, to lead, are found in both sexes . . . says that the most eloquent book of the New Testament was *written* by a woman."

Parks was a one-man gasbag, but I started not to mind. Woman author? Intriguing.

"At that point," Parks continued, "I begin to see pictures of my life . . . every aspect, naked and raw. Included is the real reason I wanted to be a pastor: My motive wasn't to lead people to Christ. My motive was to hold a position of unquestioned respect in the community. Everyone looked up to the pastor. I wanted that kind of *clout*. But now I see what I did to the people around me—like the twelve-year-old homosexual I said was an abomination to God. He later committed suicide. Some of the townspeople saw through me, saw my sermons as evidence of a cruel streak, saw the humiliation I inflicted masked with God's authority."

I shifted my attention to Victoria, who looked queasy.

"Do you smell gas?" she asked. "I feel nauseous."

"My apologies for that," Pastor Parks said. "We've had skunk problems. They get in the basement. I'll get animal control to come out again."

I noticed the smell, but it didn't bother me as much as it did Victoria. She retrieved a plastic bottle of water from her purse. Parks paused a moment while she took a few sips. Then, hell-bent, he continued his story.

"Well, by the end of all this, I'm terrified," he said. "My worst nightmare! Then the light tells me that I'll have to return. I'm in shambles, and I ask what I'm to do. It tells me to be a good Christian. I stare at the light and ask how I'm supposed to do that, because it just blew my theology to smithereens.

"It tells me to focus on the religion *of* Jesus, not the religion *about* Jesus. It tells me to become worthy of the Sermon on the Mount. And that's it! I feel myself slam back into my body in the hospital. Back to the world I knew, but with a whale of a different understanding."

Pastor Parks sat back in his chair, drained, as if the whole experience had just been rechanneled through him. I glanced at the time—a couple of minutes to three o'clock.

"Hardest part to accept?" Parks said ruefully. "God wasn't the least bit interested in my theology."

I sat back, amazed. Victoria looked faint.

"Been a life changer," Parks said. "My wife tells me I've become a better listener, more tolerant. I've started a community program for victims of domestic violence. The women it draws are more appreciative than I could've imagined." He gestured to the wall behind his desk. "I still keep that poster to remind me of my old self. That's why I'm not too worried about all this talk of a threat on my life. If I survived *that* ordeal, I can survive anything. You see what I mean?"

44

Tim Lane
Waynesville
2:58 PM

Tim Lane stood on a hilltop a quarter mile east of the town square. The spot, which he had reconnoitered the previous day, gave him a clear view of Baptist Fellowship. He saw a few passersby on West Street, but no one had come in or out of the church. It was dead quiet save for a blue jay squawking in a nearby shrub. He checked his watch. Three o'clock . . . 3:01 . . . nothing. Only the noisy jay. The silence throbbed in his ears.

Until 3:02.

A shock wave reverberated across the valley. A breathtaking fireball ascended. The eruption sent debris skyward. Lane's vision of the church shimmered like a mirage on the horizon of a highway in July. Gloomy shadows unfurled as black smoke closed over the area.

Lane observed the scene with great solemnity. He thought of the book of Daniel and the book of Revelation with their vision that nonbelievers would be cast into torment and outer darkness.

He watched fire trucks stream past within a hundred feet of his parked car. A few minutes later he could just make out, through enormous dark clouds, the arrival of police, who joined the fire crews. Lane stayed until his view became too obscured.

He turned and walked back to his car. He drove half a mile to an interchange, waited for an ambulance to pass, then merged onto I-44 and headed back toward Kansas City.

45

Fire Dispatcher
Waynesville
3:04 PM

Nine-one-one calls flooded in to the fire dispatcher, who radioed the alarm: "Firecon to 1C Charlie. Explosion and structure fire. Baptist church on West. Flames showing. Assignments are Engine 67, Ladder 51, Engine 43."

Another call came a few minutes later.

"Is this 911?" the caller said.

"Yes. What's your emergency?"

"The church blew up! Looks like a volcano went off."

"Yes. We have that. Fire and police are on the way."

"Smoke is sky high. I'm right down the street from the church, you know."

"Who is this?"

"It's Mrs. Miller, Doc Miller's wife."

Now the dispatcher recognized the voice. "Are you OK, Mrs. Miller?"

"I think so. The whole house shook. I've got broken glass. And I was just at the window minutes before. It sounded like a jet broke the sound barrier. . . . I hear sirens now."

"What can you see?"

"Flames. Above the roof. I don't think there is a roof anymore. . . . We got married in that church. Our children were baptized there. It's horrible to see this."

"Mrs. Miller, do you know if anyone is in the building?"

"I don't know, but I did see a person leave twenty minutes ago. I was watering plants on my porch when I looked over and saw a young man come up the back stairs of the church. I thought that was peculiar. I know all the people in our church. I know everybody in town. But I never saw him before, so I got suspicious and wrote down his license plate. He got in his car and drove off in a big hurry."

"What's the license?"

The dispatcher made a note. "Thank you, Mrs. Miller. I'll make sure the police get this. You're sure you're OK? I can send someone."

"Goodness gracious, no. You've got enough to worry about. I just hope nobody was in there."

46

Bill Miner
Waynesville
3:10 PM

I would later learn that crews from the Waynesville Rural Fire Protection District had arrived on the scene within three minutes of the alarm and hiked a waterline down the street to the church engulfed in fire and heavy smoke. Two crew members who'd entered the church's front door said they almost tripped over my crumpled body. They carried me, semiconscious, to a grassy area across the street and yelled for the EMTs who had just pulled up in an ambulance.

"He's got a pulse," I heard a voice say.

A moment later I began coughing. I struggled to sit up. Frantic, I looked around. "Victoria! Where's Victoria!"

"Chief!" a medic shouted. "There's a woman inside." He turned back to me. "Anyone else?"

"And the pastor," I said. I rolled to my knees, forced myself up, and with all the strength and determination I could summon, bolted toward the front door of the church.

A firefighter grabbed me, spun me around, and brought me to the ground.

"Let go of me!" I screamed. "She's inside!"

"You won't last a minute in there," he said, his face inches from mine. "Tell me exactly where."

"Restroom." I wheezed and gasped for air. "Left, just inside front door." I coughed. Sputum oozed from my mouth. I wiped my chin. The mucus was thick and gray. My chest heaved. "Pastor is in back room."

There was a popping noise and then a rumble as the church bell tower collapsed into the sanctuary. The firefighter motioned to another. The two rushed toward the church, adjusted their oxygen masks, and entered the front door.

The firemen later said they'd found the foyer so thick with black smoke their flashlights were of limited use. A wall of flame had blocked the main aisle of the sanctuary. They had to feel their way along the front wall. Visibility was restricted to inches. They edged toward the restroom door through the interior choked with noxious gases and located her body in front of the bathroom sink. As they carried Victoria toward the front door, a ceiling beam in flames crashed down behind them, turning the vestibule into a crucible.

They emerged from the building with a lifeless body in their arms and moved on the double to the ambulance. I strained to look. "Victoria!" I hollered.

A fireman turned and nodded.

Victoria gagged and vomited. I'd never thought I'd be so thankful to hear a woman throw up.

One of the firefighters shouted, "Chief, we can't get through the sanctuary from the front! We'll try to reach the pastor from the back."

A medic examined Victoria. She continued to gag. I was put on a stretcher and brought to the ambulance. "You both are headed to the hospital," the medic said. "We'll get treatment started for smoke inhalation on the way." He nodded toward Victoria. "You saved her life. Those seconds made the difference."

"No, they're the ones." I coughed. "They got her out."

"Yes, but a building on fire is almost always unfamiliar to a firefighter, with obstacles and unknown hazards. Knowing a specific location can make the difference between a rescue and a body recovery. Let's hope they do as well with the pastor."

The two firefighters had disappeared around the corner of the church. The engine crew was directing heavy streams from their hoses into the flames from the front. As the medics eased my stretcher into the ambulance, I heard the chief's radio crackle.

"We broke through a side door," a voice said. "What's left of the first floor just fell into the basement. The back half of the church, the pastor's study—they're gone."

The chief directed his engine crews to prevent the fire's spread to nearby buildings. It no longer appeared realistic to save Baptist Fellowship. The pastor and his church were lost.

47

Bill Miner
Waynesville
3:20 PM

For a vehicle designed to carry injured, sick people, the ambulance that transported us felt a lot like an armored car in a stock car race. Sirens blazed, cabinets vibrated, medical equipment bobbed, and oxygen tanks rattled in every niche. One of the medical technicians told me we were headed to the Phelps County Regional Medical Center in Rolla, twenty-eight miles away.

I had burns, a sore shoulder, and several lacerations. Victoria looked pale. She rolled her soot-crusted face to the side, then coughed up saliva and mucus. A second technician tended to her.

"There're particles of soot in her sputum," he said. "You both may have smoke damage to your lungs."

I reached across the narrow aisle between us and clasped her hand. Victoria turned her head toward me. Too weak to speak, she still managed a faint smile.

"They weren't able to get to Pastor Parks," I said. The smile vanished, and her eyes became slack.

"Lucky you two were near the front entrance," the EMT said.

"The smell of gas made her nauseous," I said. "Pastor Parks thought it was a skunk. She headed to the restroom. I followed and had reached the foyer when there was a great flash. I was lifted by an explosive force and cartwheeled through the air amid glass shards, wood, and metal fragments. I hit the front door and dropped to the floor like a duffel bag. Then all went blank."

"You're lucky to be alive," the EMT said.

"How long before we get to where we're going?" I asked.

"Twenty minutes."

"I need to talk to the police as soon as we get there. Call ahead. Have them meet us."

The EMT tilted his head toward me with a look that was both sympathetic and patronizing. "Our priority is your health," he said. "Doctors will evaluate your condition. At a minimum, you'll need observation for a couple of days."

"Listen to me." I lifted my head as much as I could. "What happened at the church was not an accident. The pastor was a deliberate target of a serial killer. Others are in danger."

The EMT stared, wide-eyed. His mouth gaped like that of a stunned trout.

48

Sam Jordan
FBI Offices, Kansas City
3:45 PM

Kaitlin, the FBI switchboard operator, burst into the office of Special Agent in Charge Sam Jordan. "A gas explosion leveled a church in Waynesville," she said. "I've got Rolla police on the line. They suspect domestic terrorism."

Jordan summoned Deputy Special Agent in Charge Matt Collins into his office and put the call on speakerphone.

"Three people were inside when the explosion occurred," the police chief said. "I'm with the two who survived. We need your help." The agents listened as the chief relayed the details.

Jordan disconnected the call and glanced at a bronze plaque that hung on the wall, his jaw drawn taut. "A meritorious award for investigation of suicide bombings in Kabul, halfway around the world"—he shook his head—"and I miss a bomb threat right here in our own backyard." His chest tightened. "Captain Bowers left me a voice mail about a homicide in Overland Park and mentioned a pastor in Waynesville, but I didn't get a sense of urgency."

"She takes pride in handling things within her own department," Collins said. "We've seen that reluctance before."

"Find out what you can about the situation in Waynesville. I'm leaving right away to go down there."

Jordan swung into high gear as if he were on the trail of an anarchist. With two of his agents plus an explosives expert, he was soon on a Cessna 206 headed to Waynesville-Saint Robert Regional Airport.

On arrival, Jordan and his team drove to the town square and surveyed the area with the police chief. The block where the church had stood looked like a battlefield.

Stone walls had been reduced to a stark blackened facade. Metal pipes were twisted into tortured shapes, broken beams rendered to charcoal, scorched trees and shrubbery sucked colorless by the heat.

A small crowd of citizens stood around in the somber aftermath, eyes glazed in disbelief. Firefighters mopped up persistent embers, the air still acrid and bitter to the nostrils.

"Rumors have floated that this was deliberate," the chief said. "Folks here are pretty spooked that terrorists would strike a church in this quiet small town."

"We don't know if it's terrorists yet," Jordan said, "but you're not alone in this. We'll devote our full effort."

"You'll want to talk to the woman who lives a few houses from the church," the chief said. "In her eighties but keen as a sharp-shinned hawk. Give me a minute, and I can take you over." The chief spoke to a sergeant about streets that had been cordoned off. Jordan instructed two of his agents to gather information from citizens in coordination with police. He assigned his explosives expert to work with the fire department as they began their investigation for physical evidence of origin and cause.

The chief turned back to Jordan. "The woman lives one street over," he said. "The two survivors were taken to the hospital in Rolla."

"I know Rolla," Jordan said. "My grandfather graduated from the university there. It was called the Missouri School of Mines and Metallurgy back then."

The chief and Jordan circled the church grounds, crossed West Street, and knocked on the door of a gray Victorian with white trim. Broken flowerpots were strewn across the porch. The cushion of an old-fashioned swing was littered with fragments of window glass.

"He looked like a decent young man, white, maybe in his thirties." Jordan and the chief sat in the living room as Mrs. Miller, silver haired, lean faced, with a no-nonsense demeanor, described what she'd seen. "Tall and trim, red hair. Nobody I'd ever seen around here. Peculiar for him to be coming out of the basement. I'm a volunteer coordinator for social functions. I'm in and out of the church a lot. Nobody uses those back stairs except building maintenance, and I knew it wasn't one of them. He came in this direction in a big hurry. Got into a white car parked across the street." She handed Jordan a scrap of paper. "Didn't look right, so I wrote down the license."

Jordan added her phone number and address to his notes and thanked her.

"You need some help with this cleanup, Mrs. Miller?" the chief asked.

"Heaven sakes, you got bigger fish to worry about. I'll get my handyman to deal with this."

Back outside, Jordan phoned Matt Collins at headquarters with the vehicle information and description he'd just received. Twenty minutes later, while Jordan was en route to Rolla, Collins was on the line again.

"The vehicle is a Ford Focus," Collins said, "owned by Hertz at Kansas City International. The car was rented by Tim Lane three days ago and is scheduled to be returned tomorrow."

"Get an agent over there," Jordan said. "Pick up Lane when he returns that car. In the meantime, I want a statewide all-points bulletin issued to be on the lookout for his vehicle in case he's not headed back to the airport."

"Too bad Hertz has no tracking device on the vehicle," Collins said.

"Yeah, I know. All the rental car companies stopped after customers started feeling they spied on their driving. At this point, Lane's a person of interest. I want to know where he lives, where he works, who his friends and relatives are, and especially, where he's traveled recently."

49

Bill Miner
Regional Medical Center, Rolla, MO
4:30 PM

"Anything broken?" I asked.

The X-ray tech shook his head. "I'm not allowed to tell you what I see in that shoulder. Doctors will look at the images soon."

He eased me off the table and into my wheelchair. "Trust me," he said with a straight face. "They won't miss anything. Last spring, we had a guy with a lightbulb up his rear. The radiologist looked at the X-ray and said, 'Well, it's either *that* . . . or his colon has a great idea.'"

I discovered it hurt to laugh. He'd probably added the levity to ease my tension. There had been little to smile about at the hospital. I was worried about Victoria's injuries, her longer exposure to the toxic fumes. We'd been separated when we arrived at the hospital, so I didn't know what her condition was.

An attendant wheeled me back to the ER. The sights and sounds of the modern hospital are more ominous when you're the patient than when you're the visitor—the rumble of supply carts, the guarded conversations of nurses in the hallway, the unrelenting beep of medical equipment. We reached the ER, and I was put in one of the treatment pods. A nurse helped me onto the bed and began to attach wires and tubes. In the center of the ER, medical staff studied computer screens and charted progress notes.

"Where is the woman I came with?" I asked.

"She'll be in the next pod as soon as she's back from the work-ups," the nurse said.

"How is she?"

"We're waiting for test results."

My shoulder hurt, but it was nothing compared to the stabs of anxiety that racked me. I'd been the one to say, "Let's go." *If anything happens to her . . .*

I heard sounds, then voices in the next pod. I tried to sit up. The nurse put her hand on my chest and said, "Give them a few minutes."

Another voice said, "It's urgent I talk with them." My curtain opened and the attending physician who had greeted our ambulance stepped into my pod and pulled back the curtain that separated my area from Victoria's. My head snapped toward Victoria. My eyes locked on her face: blotchy, red, eyebrows singed, lipstick gone, hair mussed, a nasal cannula for oxygen—she was the most beautiful sight in the world.

"Professor Miner, you've got a visitor," the physician said.

I turned to see a tall man in a dark business suit.

"Agent Sam Jordan, Kansas City FBI," he said. "Sorry I'm late to the party."

I felt a sense of deliverance.

"What's their condition?" Jordan asked the doctor.

"Both received first-degree burns. That's the good news, because it means only the outer layer of skin was affected. Like a sunburn. So, I'm not worried about any skin-tissue damage. It's the potential smoke inhalation injury I'm more concerned about. Professor Miner's carboxyhemoglobin level is fifteen percent, which indicates carbon monoxide poisoning. Victoria Johnson's is even higher."

"What does that mean?" I asked. "How serious?"

"We want to admit you both," the doctor said. "Those levels may be an underestimate of the severity since you received oxygen in the ambulance on the way here. I want to do some more tests and monitor you for a couple of days."

The physician stepped out, and Jordan grabbed a small chair and sat down.

"Tell me what happened," he said. "And your relationship with the pastor."

"We just met this afternoon. Knew he was in danger." I coughed, and a nurse gave me some tissues. My voice sounded hoarse. I mustered my strength and gave him the background.

Jordan listened. "They *all* had a near-death experience?" he asked.

"Yes. A woman in Washington State, a woman in Kansas, Victoria's father in California, and the pastor in Waynesville. It's important you understand these people did not have the garden-variety near-death experience. They didn't just see a light. They were told things that would be a monstrous affront to Christian fundamentalists." I raised myself up on my elbows and pulled against the IV tubes and wires from the cardiac monitor. "I teach religion. This stuff is seismic! And it was to be showcased on network television."

Jordan tugged at his tie and undid the top shirt button.

"Four people who were to be on that program are now dead: Oscar Johnson, Mandy Frankel, Florence Smith, and Chester Parks. And there's a fifth target in Idaho who's in danger, if it's not already too late." I could hear a dry wheeze in my chest. "Her name's in my sports jacket." I scanned the room. "Where's my jacket?"

The nurse retrieved it from a large plastic bag of belongings and handed it to me. I dug into the inside pocket, fished out the pages from Larry Smith's printer. Jordan took the sheets and studied them. He pulled out his cell and punched in the number for Janie Hughes. It seemed a long time before there was an answer.

"Mrs. Hughes?" He paused. "My name is FBI Agent Sam Jordan. Please listen to me carefully."

I released a long breath. Jordan talked for several minutes.

"She's fine," he said after he disconnected the call. "Mrs. Hughes will stay with a sister in Boise for a few days. Her husband is in northern Idaho on a fishing trip for two weeks. I told her it was imperative she leave immediately."

"What if she thinks your call is a prank?" I asked.

He gave a tight smile. "Mrs. Hughes is a savvy woman. She asked for verification. I gave her the number of the FBI switchboard operator in Kansas City and told her to speak to my assistant. She's probably doing that right now."

A monitor beeped as a blood pressure cuff inflated automatically on Victoria's arm. A nurse checked the reading, then left.

"I need to make some calls," Jordan said and excused himself.

It was the first time we'd been alone together since the explosion. "How you feel?" I asked.

"OK." The corners of her mouth edged up slightly. "If for no other reason than it's not just you and me in this fight alone. The FBI. A glimmer of hope." She spoke slowly, her voice raspy. "Your summary of events to Jordan. It made me realize how much you've done. We began without a clue. Now a pattern, a motive." She mouthed the words "thank you."

We looked at each other a long time. I turned my head away. A fear lingered within me. I gazed back at Victoria.

Her expression changed to a frown. "What's that concern in your eyes?" she asked.

"I was terrified they wouldn't reach you in time."

Her face softened, her pupils larger. "That is so sweet," she said. She reached out her hand as if to transmit a touch across the space that separated us. "Did that bump on your head make you forget that if you hadn't directed the firefighters—"

"They were undaunted."

"Thanks to your direction," she said. "The list of things for which I'm indebted to you seems to be growing."

"You make me want to raise my game," I said.

Her eyes became warm, and I wanted to drink in the moment, but the curtains parted, and Agent Jordan stepped back in.

"Does the name 'Tim Lane' mean anything to you?" he asked. His voice was flat, matter-of-fact.

I looked over at Victoria. We both shook our heads.

"A man who left the church just before the explosion drove off in a car rented to a person with that name. The credit card used for the car is the same one used to purchase an airline ticket from Oakland to Seattle five days ago. Southwest confirmed Tim Lane was the passenger. That would place him in Seattle at the time Mandy Frankel was killed."

I felt a rush. All this time we had moved at a crawl. Now breakneck acceleration.

"There's more," Jordan said. "The same credit card was used to pay for a flight from Seattle to Kansas City the next day. And that would have placed Lane within thirty miles of Overland Park at the time Florence Smith was killed. His credit card billing address is in Martinez, California."

"*What?*" Victoria tried to sit up. "That's near where I live."

"This is our guy," Jordan said. "Agents from the San Francisco bureau are on their way to his Martinez residence. I've issued an all-points bulletin for his rental car. Air, train, and bus terminals in the state have been alerted. This man is not leaving Missouri, for Idaho or anywhere else."

50

Tim Lane
Harrisonville, MO
7:30 PM

It was near dusk when Tim Lane pulled into the parking lot of a motel in the small town of Harrisonville, Missouri. Ebert's Lodge was an ordinary U-shaped, two-story motel, just off Route 7. Lane nosed his car up to the white brick office, stepped out, and surveyed the area. He was still an hour from the Kansas City airport. However, this looked like a good place to stop for the night. The earliest flight to Twin Falls was not until eleven o'clock the next morning. At least he would get a full night's rest. He glanced around the property, which was lined by a high wooden fence and thick shrubbery. It seemed peaceful and quiet.

His phone buzzed. Another text from his wife. He didn't read it. Barbara had left several phone messages. He had not listened to them for fear her voice might weaken his resolve. He missed her, wanted to talk with her, but didn't dare. He missed his son, the games of catch they played, the hide-and-go-seek game they had named "Kato." He opened a photo of his wife and son at a recent birthday party. "I will make this world a better place for you," he said softly. "I promise."

Throughout the afternoon, radio stations had peppered the airways with news of the event he had generated:

> And an update on breaking news you'll hear only on KTTR News Radio. Investigators say early indications point to a gas leak as the cause of the church explosion and fire in

> Waynesville that claimed the life of the church's pastor, Chester Parks.

There had been no mention of the other two. Perhaps their bodies had not yet been discovered. Lane didn't feel a need to see TV coverage. Instead, after he checked in and took his overnight bag and rifle up to his room, he walked down the street to the King Tsin restaurant.

An hour later he returned to the motel, paused on the outside stairs, and reflected on the message in his fortune cookie: "You will soon be honored by someone of great authority." Lane never took such things seriously, but it was interesting that this message happened to come at such an auspicious time. True, he had been successful. One person remained. But he reminded himself that these adversaries were defeated because he came against them in the name of Jesus. *I am proud to have been chosen a Dragon of God*, he thought. *But I should not think of being honored, nor do I seek to be honored.*

Deo Gloria. *All credit to God, for his glory.*

51

Sam Jordan
Waynesville
Day 7, 1:10 AM

Sam Jordan had not been asleep long when he was awakened by his phone. He squinted at the red numerals on the clock on his motel nightstand, then at the caller's name on the phone's screen.

"Yeah, Collins, whatcha got?" The words he heard from his deputy special agent in charge brought him wide awake. "Where?" Jordan asked. He listened. "What's the nearest airport?" Another few moments. "OK, I want to have SWAT teams, from our office and from St. Louis, in Harrisonville by five o'clock. Have St. Louis fly in. Our guys can get there faster on the road. Tell them to meet me at the airport, and we'll figure out our operations plan. Let Harrisonville's police chief know his people did a heads-up job."

Jordan had been a police officer earlier in his career and knew that most of the time local police departments appreciated the FBI's resources, if they received their own appropriate share of recognition. He knew their cooperation was crucial. In this case, an alert Harrisonville patrolman had spotted Lane's car parked at a motel and alerted the FBI—the very essence of teamwork.

Jordan called the airport to have them ready his plane. He threw some water on his face, dressed, and was out of his motel room by 1:30 AM. He had no qualms about a full-force effort to nab Lane. San Francisco agents had gone to Lane's home in Martinez. His wife had no idea where he was. Had told them he'd become obsessed with a mission. They argued. He'd left her in tears.

Jordan had shown several photos to Mrs. Miller. "That's him," she'd said, pointing to Lane.

52

Sam Jordan
Harrisonville
5:30 AM

SWAT teams from Kansas City and St. Louis assembled in a meeting room at Lawrence Smith Memorial Airport on the southern edge of Harrisonville, three miles from Lane's location. Jordan briefed the teams and outlined the operation plan. They did not want Lane to slip away. One of the agents had already been dispatched to the motel for surveillance.

Wet pavement from an overnight rain reflected the neon motel sign in the predawn hour as Sam Jordan rang the bell of the manager's office. Jordan showed his badge to a startled night manager and asked which room was occupied by Tim Lane.

The manager, her fingers jittery, checked her computer. "Room 207, upstairs. What's this all about?"

"I'll fill you in," Jordan said, "but right now I need you to wake all your guests except the occupant of 207. Have everyone come, as quietly as possible, here to your office before seven o'clock."

Within the hour all guests had been assembled and accounted for in the breakfast lounge because there was insufficient space in the office. There were not enough chairs, so with apologies, the night manager asked younger guests to sit on the floor. Agents began moving into positions on the motel grounds while Jordan chose a vantage point in the manager's office with a view of 207.

Just after 8:00 AM, Tim Lane came out of his room, shutting the door behind him. In one hand, he carried an overnight bag, in the other, a rifle.

"Subject has left his room," Jordan radioed to his team. "He's carrying a weapon."

Lane proceeded along the second-floor walkway toward the front of the motel. As he approached the stairs, Jordan saw him glance over the railing toward one of his men crouched in the shrubbery. Jordan saw Lane hesitate, then abruptly bolt down the stairway to the parking lot.

"Damn! He's spotted us," Jordan said.

Lane ran toward the street just as a large Super Suds laundry service truck pulled into the parking lot. Jordan stepped from the office and shouted, "Lane! FBI! Stop!"

Jordan aimed his Glock 22 at the sprinting figure but held his fire when Lane collided with the driver who had stepped from the truck. Lane spun the startled man out of his way and sped to the street and down the sidewalk.

Jordan took up chase. Lane hadn't gone twenty yards before FBI Agent George Toscone, armed with a shotgun, came from the opposite direction, blocking his path. Jordan closed in from behind.

Lane pivoted, changed direction ninety degrees, and darted across four lanes of moving traffic. Cars screeched, drivers wide-eyed as the man with a rifle zipped between vehicles.

The agents were more prudent in negotiating their way through the traffic even though they knew it would buy the fleeing man a few extra seconds. Jordan and Toscone reached the other side of the street in time to see Lane dash around a post office building and disappear down a narrow path behind a church. The agents edged down the path cautiously. Jordan saw a fence, one section wooden, one section cinder block, that lined the church property.

Concerned about the numerous possible hiding places, the various escape routes, and the possibility Lane could ambush them, Jordan directed Toscone to circle around to approach where they had last seen Lane headed from the opposite direction. As Jordan drew close to the church, he heard Toscone shout, "Look out!" Jordan turned to see the end of a rifle barrel pointed at him from the fence thirty feet away.

"The FBI trains for situations like that," Jordan would say later. Relying on that training, Jordan flipped onto his back like a high jumper clearing the bar, feet in the air, just as Lane fired. Time seemed to slow as the round came at him but high. At the same moment, Toscone fired his shotgun, sending splinters of wood fencing and chunks of cinder block flying in every direction.

Lane had ducked back behind the cinder block portion of fencing, but his left hand, which was on the barrel, was still exposed. Several of the shotgun pellets ripped into his hand. Jordan heard a cry of pain and the clatter of the rifle as it dropped onto landscape rocks. He reached the fence in time to see Lane dart across the churchyard, weaving around trees, rosebushes, and burial stones like a soldier running an obstacle course.

By the time the agents had reached the street, Lane was gone.

53

Tim Lane
Harrisonville
8:20 AM

Lane zigzagged between homes in a residential neighborhood until he was five blocks from where the shots were fired. He saw two workers installing a TV satellite dish and hurried over to them. "Can you help me?" He held up his left hand. "I banged it up pretty good." His hand and wrist were covered in blood.

"Jesus! Hop in the truck," an installer said. "I'll take you to the hospital."

"I was repairing a brick wall with a heavy electric grinder," Lane explained as the worker drove him away, unknowingly extricating him from the scene of an FBI manhunt. "The tip caught, and the damn thing nailed me."

The worker drove Lane north on State Route 7. As they passed a Phillips 66 service station, Lane saw several used cars for sale in the lot. "Whoa, stop here," he said. "I see someone I know."

"You sure?" the worker asked.

"Positive. I can make it from here." Lane jumped out of the truck and thanked the worker.

His first order of business was the restroom where he washed his mutilated hand and wrapped it in several layers of paper towels. When Lane came out, he strolled over to a beige 2003 Mercury Sable—186,000 miles, $1,400.

The gas station manager approached Lane. "That's my son's car. I've worked on it. Runs fine. May need new tires this winter. He got married, and they want to squeeze by with one car."

Lane looked in his wallet. Just over $2,600. That had to get him to his final target, then home, and through everything in between. Did he have a choice? The FBI was now involved. They knew his *name*. He didn't know how, but he would not be using his credit card or his real name from here on out. He'd already turned his phone's GPS off. It would stay that way.

"Is that your son's best price?" he asked.

"That's a fair amount, don't you think? Tell you what: you buy it and I'll fill it up."

Lane agreed to the deal and paid him. He watched as the man pulled the car up to a gas pump.

He'd just purchased his ticket to Idaho.

54

Bill Miner
Regional Medical Center, Rolla
8:40 AM

I tumbled through the air. In the dark, hot, blinded. My throat choked. Eardrums deafened. *Where is she! I must reach her!* I screamed, "Victoria!"

I awoke with a start and jerked my head in the direction of a nurse who had rushed in. I let out a deep breath and sunk back into my pillow. Morning sunlight streamed in. I glanced around the room: a couch, end tables, a swag draped across the top of the window. The furnishings belied a hospital room. The presence of the nurse and the medical equipment at the head of my bed reminded me where I was. I told her I was OK.

The nurse checked my IV and vital signs and made entries on a computer near the bedside.

"How is Ms. Johnson?" I asked.

"Her breathing's improved. Low levels of oxygen from smoke inhalation can lead to confusion, seizures, and other complications, but we don't see any signs of that. Your friend is a fighter."

"Yes, she is," I said. I felt enormous relief. We'd survived the events of a horrific day.

"Would you like some breakfast?" she asked.

"What's on the menu?"

"Anything you like."

"Is that because I'm improving or because it's my last meal?"

She laughed. "Humor's a good sign. We'll want more tests before we can tell if you and Ms. Johnson are out of the woods."

"How about an egg scramble?" I said. "And coffee, please."

"A good appetite is another positive sign," she said and turned to leave.

"Say, is there any chance Ms. Johnson and I could have breakfast together?" I asked.

"That's cute," the nurse said. "I'll tell her she has an invite and see if she feels up to it."

Thirty minutes later Victoria navigated her wheelchair next to mine at a makeshift breakfast table in the visitor's lounge down the hall.

"You look pretty good in those hot wheels," I said. "How's my wounded warrior?"

A smile appeared. "Better, thank you. How's your shoulder?"

"Just a mild sprain. Ice and ibuprofen. No surgery. The orthopedist said he'd recheck me today."

"I'm sorry you got hurt," Victoria said. "I dragged you into this."

"Are you kidding? I came of my own free will. No regrets."

"Do you think they'll get Lane?"

I nodded. "The FBI knows who he is and where he's headed. Jordan may have him in custody before we're out of here."

"Is that good or bad for your book?"

"I'm still behind the eight ball on that." I forced a smile. "Maybe I can get a jailhouse interview." I thought about our wild-goose chase. We could have ended up like the pastor. A small group of people passed. One of them sobbed.

I gestured in their direction. "I guess we're lucky," I said.

"Um-hum," Victoria said. "Larry Smith, the pain in his family, now Mrs. Parks . . ."

Here she is, I thought, *in the hospital, yet she continues to think of the feelings of others. More compassion than I've got.*

"I *am* fascinated by the pastor," I said. "The guy was about as far on the conservative Christian right as you can get without dropping off the earth." Coffee and juice arrived, and I took a needed sip of caffeine. "Yet Parks makes this incredible reversal. You don't see that very often, unless someone's in a foxhole with enemy fire whistling overhead."

"How about an explosion that levels a church?" she said. "Wouldn't that rank up there with bullets zinging above you?"

I sensed where this was headed.

"Maybe change the mind of someone who's lost his faith?" she added.

I saw a mischievous smile. *She must feel better. Well enough to bait a hook.* I chuckled but didn't bite.

"I'm just struck that Pastor Parks, Mandy Frankel, Florence Smith, were all affected in such a positive way," I said. "A new sense of purpose even if they weren't sure what that was."

"That *is* the church's message," she said.

"When I was a minister, I didn't have *that* kind of success in changing people. I don't know if these near-death experiences are a product of physical processes in the brain or not—that's your department—but the effect on people is mind-boggling."

"That's why it fascinates me," she said as she reached for her orange juice. "It was a drug dealer that first got my attention about NDEs. A hustler named Shorty almost died in a shootout with a rival gang. He told me that while he had been lying in the street, bleeding, he had had a wondrous experience—felt unconditional love. After prison, he reversed his lifestyle and began counseling gang youths. His girlfriend got disgusted and left him when she found out he didn't care about money anymore."

"No kidding?" I asked.

"Surprised by such a turnaround?"

"No. Amazed you know a drug runner named Shorty."

She gave me a lopsided grin. "It was a field study for a graduate class."

"But now you have doubts," I said, "doubts about the validity of near-death experiences, in general."

"I do *now*. This religious . . . reinterpretation . . . has got me tied up in knots."

"I have a problem too," I said. "That these conversations are with a *light*. But I was intrigued by two things our late pastor told us: that Noah's flood was due to natural causes and that a book of the Bible has a female author."

"I can see the attraction of information about Noah's flood, but why the fascination about a woman author?"

"Because for two thousand years, traditional doctrine has maintained women are unsuited to teach in church. How could one author a book of the Bible? To say a woman wrote Holy Scripture? That'd be an outrage to church fathers."

"It's a nice idea, but the last time I looked I didn't see a woman's name in the list of authors."

"Of course not. We don't *know* who wrote most of the books."

She rolled her eyes. "Please tell your orthopedist he needs to check for a head injury too."

"Who do you think wrote the four Gospels?" I asked.

Her mouth puckered. "Do you offer bonus points if I know the pope's a Catholic?"

"Listen," I said. "None of the Gospels gives the name of its author. The names we all know—Matthew, Mark, Luke, and John—were attached to the Gospels by the early church. The reality is most of the disciples were illiterate."

"You know," she said with a tease to her words, "Pascal observed that some people have contempt for the Bible but, deep down, fear it may be true."

"I *do* miss my faith," I said. "I don't think it's fear. I'm just skeptical because the people we say wrote the Gospels were all poor and uneducated. Jesus's closest disciple, Peter, was from the tiny, isolated fishing village of Capernaum where houses were made of rough stones and roofs were covered with reeds and packed dirt. If you ever wondered why, in Mark, men could *dig* through the roof of a house to get in when they couldn't use the front door, it's because it was a *mud hut*!"

"Yet look at the faith that emerged from such humble lives."

"Granted," I said, "but the issue is education. Peter lived in a time and place where virtually no one would have received any schooling. Archaeologists have searched for inscriptions on the public buildings from his time and found *none*. That tells them the literacy level was very low."

Victoria crossed her arms.

"The disciples couldn't have written Gospels in their *own* language," I said, "let alone in a sophisticated style of Greek."

"Well, I have a good friend whose Chinese mom never could read or write in her own language, yet she passed on a lot of oral wisdom and did arithmetic in her head. Utterly uneducated and unsophisticated but full of common sense and pragmatism about life." Victoria tilted her head toward me. "I have no problem believing that the disciples were fully capable with the help of editors."

"And we don't know who *they* were, either."

Victoria looked unconvinced.

"There were many books in circulation bearing Peter's name," I said, "but only First Peter and Second Peter were included in the Bible. Not the wisest choice, because Second Peter describes events that occurred after Peter died." I shifted in my wheelchair. "There's no way he could've written it, with or without assistance."

"Early church fathers said otherwise," she said confidently. "I think I'll go with them."

"Early church fathers might've had another agenda. Discrepancies become apparent when you make a careful check of historical dates."

"My historian's back again," she said with a half smile.

"Oh, excuse me? Scientists don't look for inconsistencies? Wasn't it Isaac Asimov who said the most exciting phrase to hear in science isn't 'Eureka!' but '*That's* funny'?"

"Touché," she said.

"Historical inconsistencies can go unnoticed with the passage of time. You don't have to go back thousands of years to be fooled. I ask my students what they would say about a letter found in the retirement papers of Ulysses S. Grant in which he criticized military strategy used in the Spanish-American War."

"And *military* history too?" she said, but her tone was playful.

"Anytime it helps me with an example," I said. "OK. What would you think of the letter?"

"I know Grant was a great general, and I've always admired his humanity toward Lee at Appomattox."

"Most of my students say they would study the handwriting and language to determine the letter's authenticity. Few recognized that Grant's death, thirteen years before the outbreak of the Spanish-American War, would make the letter highly suspect."

"Hmm," she said and nodded.

"But again, the most compelling reason to think Peter could not have written First Peter and Second Peter is the illiteracy issue."

"So, if that's true, the church fathers must have known. Why did they say otherwise?"

"Politics, probably. Peter and Paul were at odds about major theological issues. First Peter and Second Peter were someone's attempt to calm the waters by saying Peter and Paul were, in fact, unified in their views, shared the same goals, that there was no split in church leadership, only harmony. But it wasn't all harmony. They *did* have a falling out."

What irony, I thought. *Here I am discussing disharmony in the early church leadership, and I'm creating discord with the woman I'm attracted to.*

"What are you saying they couldn't agree on?" she asked.

"Whether converts to Christianity needed to be circumcised, for example, or whether they needed to follow Jewish dietary laws."

"But those aren't salvation issues," she said.

"The very criteria to become a *Christian*?"

"Only accepting Jesus as your savior matters for salvation, not the types of things you mention."

"But secondary issues often rose up to become primary truths," I said, "so it depended on who you asked. There were strong opinions, all claimed to be from authority figures: Peter had a Gospel, as did Philip. There was one from Nicodemus, even Mary Magdalene."

"Is she your woman author?"

"No. Pastor Parks said it was one of the books in the Bible. Mary Magdalene's book had little chance of selection."

"Authors, fake authors, pseudoauthors . . . these are unprovable suppositions," Victoria said.

"OK then, let me appeal to your sense of reason. One of the books, the Gospel of Peter, didn't make it into the Bible, but it survived. We have it." I leaned closer to her. "Why do you suppose it wasn't included?"

"I presume because it wasn't deemed authoritative."

"A Gospel written by *Peter*? The same Peter on whom Jesus will build his church? How could that not be authoritative?"

She paused, her juice glass halfway to her lips. "So, if Peter didn't write it, why would someone else use his name?"

55

Bill Miner
Regional Medical Center, Rolla
9:30 AM

"The reason to use a false name isn't hard to imagine." I held her gaze. "Sales and marketing."

"That's a little crass," she said. Her fighting spirit seemed as strong as ever.

"Excuse me? So, when Jesus said to go forth and make disciples of all nations"—I speared a piece of sausage—"that wasn't a marketing directive?"

"Churches aren't businesses," she said, then paused. Her forehead wrinkled. "At least not technically. I'm just . . . It's the way you said that, as if you lumped churches together with Walmart, Bank of America, or the sale of 49ers season tickets."

"What I'm trying to say is that there were contentious arguments about how to interpret Jesus's message. Suppose you thought the other writers had gotten the message all wrong. So, you decide to publish your own opinion—maybe you call it 'the book of Second Hesitations'—but you're an unknown author and discover no one pays any attention. Then you get smart. You repackage your essay. You title it 'the Second Epistle of Paul to Timothy.' And presto, it goes viral."

"A name everyone respected."

"Of course, and that was a common ploy. Of the thirteen letters in the New Testament that bear Paul's name, only seven are his."

Victoria eyed me attentively.

"Ask your pastor when we get home," I said. "He knows. It's been taught in seminary schools for decades."

"But the Bible's authors wouldn't lie."

"I don't think they lied either. The authors were passionate about what they wrote. They *believed* what they wrote. It was a political campaign to win hearts and souls. Different sides said things to strengthen their case. What's wrong with a little salesmanship?"

"There's just one version of Jesus's message—'No one comes to the Father except through me.' You're not going to question the Bible on that too, are you?"

I shrugged. "Well, just what *did* Jesus mean when he said that?"

The look in her eye made me glad she'd finished most of her egg, because she might have flung it at me otherwise.

"The author of John doesn't say *how* people get to God through Jesus," I said. "Early Christians couldn't agree. Some thought it meant you get to heaven if you accept Jesus as your savior. Others thought it meant you had to observe Jesus's teachings. The same argument continues today."

"It's clear to me."

"Fine," I said. "So is the Second Amendment to the National Rifle Association. But I dare say you'll get a very different interpretation from those who want gun control."

She drummed her fingers on the breakfast tray. "You are right about that," she said. "Interpretations of any document can vary, even when we have the exact words, in English, preserved under glass."

"And back to John, what material did the author have to work with?" I asked. "There were no stenographers following Jesus around. Nobody had taken notes. It was decades before anything was written down. How would the author of John know, long after Jesus had died, precisely what Jesus meant?"

"So, what are you implying? That John made it up?"

"I do know that ancient writers made stuff up when they were unsure."

"Who would admit they made stuff up?"

"The historian Thucydides said that's *exactly* what he did. When oral reports weren't enough, he made up speeches he thought would be appropriate to the speaker. It wasn't a lie. He said he just wanted to fill in the gaps and convey what likely transpired."

Victoria nibbled on her bottom lip as though processing our conversation, then ate her last strawberry.

"I don't think the authors of the New Testament made up stuff," I said, "but in a fierce war of words, there was a whole lot of sales and marketing going on. Does the church today interpret Jesus's words correctly?" I took a sip of coffee. "Not according to what we heard from Pastor Parks."

She gave a little sigh. "You don't even think the Bible is correct half the time," she said. "And it's made you a bit cynical."

My mouth became dry.

"I'm critical, not cynical." I shifted in the wheelchair. "It's got to get to the level of certain televangelists, or to priest pedophilia, before I get cynical."

"OK, maybe 'jaded' is a better word."

"As a young pastor, it troubled me that the church emphasized the passion of Christ, his suffering for our sins. I wanted to preach Jesus's ethical teachings—the lessons of the Sermon on the Mount, how to apply the Golden Rule in a dispute with a family member or your neighbor."

"But Christ's passion was what *Paul* stressed," she said. "Trust in Christ's sacrifice, and you'll be right with God." Victoria paused as she studied me. "You're totally at odds with Paul, aren't you?"

I nodded. Her expression softened.

"I entered the ministry to help people lead a Christian life," I said. "But the church had another agenda. One Sunday, a guest pastor spoke to my congregation from the pulpit: 'We don't want your money, not a dime,' he told them. 'We just want you to come to know Jesus.' When I later queried him about not asking for money, he gave me a smug look. He said: 'Don't get the cart before the horse, son. You got to hook 'em first. Get their butts in the pews. *Then* you go for their money.' I told him that made me uncomfortable. He said: 'But it works. Once you get 'em, you say that if they don't make a generous financial pledge, they're cheating God out of what's rightfully his.' "

I sat back, reliving that unpleasant memory.

"That's duplicitous," Victoria said, "but churches do have a budget to meet."

"I'm aware of that, but it left me with the acrid taste of bait and switch. The ministry began to feel disingenuous."

"You threw it all away because of one pastor?"

"That and the fact I kept running into mistakes in the Bible."

"I'm troubled that you think pastors subvert the truth," she said, "that they're in on a big charade."

"I think the early church fathers were of goodwill. But the fact is that concentrated power in the church, accrued over the ages, inevitably attracts and shapes men of a different brand."

"Something sinister has undermined your thinking."

"Evangelicals stress the omnipresence of dark forces," I said, "but I believe there's more misunderstanding in the world than there is evil."

"Well, you can't deny we've lost Christian values in this country," she said. "Values replaced with consumerism and a self-centered whatever-works-for-me attitude . . . a morality that winks and says, 'Whatever happens here, stays here.' " Her head turned as several teens passed, eyes spellbound by their phones. "Many young people have diminished respect for their parents, teachers, and community . . . and I think it's due to a loss of meaning and identity—that which the church provides. If that's not the result of evil, I don't know what is."

I felt the distress in her words. We gazed at each other for a quiet moment until the voice of our nurse broke the silence.

"Hate to interrupt this sweet visitation," the nurse said, "but you're due for some more lab tests. How was breakfast?"

"Nice, thank you," I said. "Compliments to your chef. My IV could use a little salt, though."

The nurse pivoted Victoria's wheelchair toward the hallway. "Is he always this hilarious?"

"Oh"—Victoria gave a slight grin and shook her head—"you have no idea what he comes up with."

56

Sam Jordan
FBI Offices, Kansas City
2:00 PM

Sam Jordan charged out of the elevator and to his office with a scowl that could have knocked bark off a tree. He motioned for Matt Collins to come to his office. Jordan knew he could vent to his deputy special agent in charge.

"I've served in the US Army Corps of Engineers," Jordan said. He pulled off his suit coat and slammed it onto a rack behind his desk. "I've been through extensive bureau training, succeeded in numerous, perilous assignments, all of which got me promoted to this job." He glanced at the framed photograph on the wall—his picture with the FBI director. "But never in my sixteen years with the FBI have I felt as outplayed as I do now. We were too obvious. Moved too slowly."

"Look, boss," Collins said, "no one here has lost a speck of confidence in you because Lane got away."

Jordan moved to his chair, disgusted with himself. Any explanation of the morning's events in Harrisonville felt like excuses. "It should have been a slam dunk," he said.

Collins jutted his chin. "So, he won *this* round." He leaned toward Jordan. "We'll get this guy."

Jordan reached for a piece of paper, made a list, and handed it to his deputy. "I'm calling Washington for approval to initiate a multiagency task force. Contact these departments to give them a heads-up."

Collins studied the sheet. It listed detectives and investigators from the crime lab, the intelligence unit, the Missouri Department of Public Safety, and the Bureau of Alcohol, Tobacco, Firearms and Explosives.

"Over thirty people," Collins said. "This'll be one of the largest task forces in Kansas City's history." He came to his feet. "I'll get right on it."

57

Bill Miner
Regional Medical Center, Rolla
2:30 PM

A nurse arrived in my room with a cart of needles and vials and proceeded with a by then familiar protocol: asked my name and birthdate to compare with the ID band on my wrist; reminded me the blood test was to assess carbon monoxide poisoning, that I'd feel a little stick, etc.

"Where do you live in California?" she asked as she filled a second vial.

"Bay Area," I said.

"Oh, I love San Francisco, and I hate our winters. I'd move in a heartbeat if it weren't for your earthquakes."

"We're just as apprehensive about your tornadoes."

"At least we have sirens to alert us," she said. "You guys have no warning." She wrapped a blood pressure cuff around my arm.

"California doesn't have a corner on US earthquakes," I said.

"Oh, I know. One of the most powerful ever recorded was here in Missouri—so strong it caused the Mississippi River to flow backward—back in the early 1800s."

"Given earthquake cycles, you're probably overdue for another," I said. "Don't rule out California for the wrong reason."

She pulled back and smiled. "You should work for the chamber of commerce."

The nurse left, and I leaned back in bed. The subject of earthquakes reminded me there was a top engineering university right there in Rolla—maybe I could get an opinion on one of the issues raised by Pastor Parks. I reached for my phone and looked up the Geology Department. I scanned the faculty list of two dozen names and punched a number at random.

"Hello, Professor," I said. "I'm interested to know if there's a geologic explanation for Noah's flood. Can you tell me—"

I heard the receiver slam down.

I dialed a second number. "Hi, I'm an assistant professor of religion from Berkeley, and I'd like to know what geologists think about the cause of the biblical flood."

"Sorry, we don't speculate about religion."

I persisted with a third call. This time a Professor Antle answered, and I made my pitch.

"Ah," came the reply. "We're kindred spirits," he said. "The first geologists were clergy back in the seventeenth century."

"I didn't know that, but I'm not cler—"

"They sought evidence of Noah's flood . . . wanted to explain why seashells could end up on mountaintops. In the process, they helped us understand the formation of landscapes, how to interpret fossils."

"Do modern geologists have any insights about the great flood?" I asked.

"Yes, we do. It wasn't a global flood—that couldn't have happened. There's not enough water on earth for sea levels to cover the highest mountains. But there's overwhelming geologic evidence of regional floods. In Tibet, for example, and Mesopotamia. The latter could have been Noah's flood."

"How can you tell?" I asked.

"Sediments at the bottom of the Black Sea showed that in Noah's day it was a small freshwater lake in the middle of a populated agricultural valley—a Garden of Eden in the desert."

"An ideal place to settle," I said.

"Especially if you consider the other choices. Mile-thick glaciers covered Scandinavia, the rest of northern Europe, and Canada. But there was climate change going on. The weather started to warm up. As ice melted, oceans rose."

"Wouldn't that have been gradual? Given people time to relocate?"

"There's debate over the suddenness and magnitude. Noah's valley was protected from the mounting sea by a natural dam at a narrow point in the Bosporus strait. This rocky sill may have held back the waters of the Mediterranean until the pressure became too great and it collapsed. *That* would have been your catastrophe. Water from the Mediterranean would have surged through the strait with a force that could have been of biblical proportions."

"You said there's debate."

"Some geologists think the flow from the Mediterranean to the Black Sea was gradual, noncatastrophic. Other evidence points to a major flood in Mesopotamia that swamped the lowlands between the Tigris and Euphrates. They're all plausible arguments."

"How widespread was the flood in Mesopotamia?"

"Massive," Antle said, "but confined to that region. However, if your world is small, such an inundation would seem global."

I thought of the Persian proverb "In the ants' house, the dew is a flood."

"How about Moses parting the Red Sea?" I asked. "Any scientific insights about that one?"

"Yes, I think we have an explanation. Exodus itself says a strong east wind blew all that night. A sustained wind speed of sixty-five to seventy miles per hour would be enough to push the water back sufficiently to expose a ridge below the surface."

"Wind can move that much water?"

"Yup, if it's sustained. The same phenomenon's been observed in many locations. Oceanographers call it wind tide. When it occurs on Lake Erie, it can produce a sixteen-foot difference in water level between Toledo and Buffalo."

"That'd hardly be enough for someone to walk across Lake Erie," I said.

"It wouldn't be enough for the Red Sea, either." He chuckled. "But that's not where the Israelites crossed. That likely occurred at a large freshwater lake noted for reeds in the Isthmus of Suez. It dried up when they built the Suez Canal in the 1860s. Fierce winds aren't uncommon in that area."

I reflected on the scene of Charlton Heston as Moses in the epic film, arms uplifted against walls of water.

"You probably know more about this than I do," Antle said. "The original location was written in the Old Testament as the Sea of Reeds."

"Yes, and when it was translated to Greek, 'Sea of Reeds' became 'the Red Sea' in one of the most notorious mistranslations in history, later embedded into the King James Version."

"A windstorm that lasted all night would've given the Israelites enough time to cross," he said. "Then, if the wind died abruptly, waters would have rushed back like a tsunami and swamped the pursuing Egyptian soldiers in their wheeled chariots."

"So, you're suggesting there was a miracle all right, but the miracle was in the timing."

"Exactly."

"This has been helpful," I said.

"I don't know about Californians," Antle said, "but we've got plenty of farmers and business owners around Rolla—decent, honest folks—who believe fossils on mountaintops are all the proof they need that Noah's flood inundated the entire planet. Never mind the business of tectonic plates that lifted ocean bottoms to the top of Mount Everest. Never mind oceanographic wind tides that can produce astounding effects."

"I know," I said. "People cling to their beliefs. But if Noah gathered pairs of all living things, too bad he didn't swat those two mosquitos." Antle chuckled, and I offered him an invitation to stop by on his next trip to the West Coast.

I lay back in bed and stared at the ceiling. If near-death experiences were the result of tricks played by the memory, how in the world could Pastor Parks have come up with a sophisticated geologic explanation for Noah's flood? Or wind tides to explain what the Israelites interpreted as a miracle? Unless he *was* told. I was stunned. Who or what was this light? This celestial spirit? *Victoria has begun to doubt near-death experiences. There's got to be an explanation.* I felt myself fidgeting.

I needed to know.

58

Bill Miner
Regional Medical Center, Rolla
4:00 PM

"If you guys spend much more time in here together," the nurse said, "we'll have to add social club dues to your bill." She parked Victoria's wheelchair next to mine in the visitor's lounge. "One minute you flirt with each other. The next you're in a knock-down, drag-out. The whole staff thinks it's pretty adorable." Her eyes twinkled. "You two would be fun to watch on *The Amazing Race*."

The nurse left. I pivoted my wheelchair toward Victoria. "How about *that* compliment? What do you think? What's your sense of us?"

I held still in expectation.

"Well," she said. She gave me an impish grin. "I think you're pretty *E-F-G-H-I-J-K*."

I drew back. "Huh?"

Her voice became soft, matter-of-fact. "You're exciting, focused, gorgeous, hot, and irresistible."

My eyes popped, then narrowed. "And what's the *J-K*?"

"Just kidding," she said, struggling to keep a straight face.

My laugh exploded in a muffled snort.

"Techie joke. I hear a lot at work."

"You *are* feeling better," I said.

She nodded. "All the oxygen they've given me." She scrunched her nose. "Or maybe it's because you keep getting me riled up."

"*Excusez-moi?*" I said. The assertive tone in her voice was further indication she was on the mend.

"Don't give me an innocent look," she said. "That business about not knowing the Bible's authors—you just said that to get under my skin." Her eyes sparkled with renewed fight. "Come on. The Gospels, all the books, they're based on eyewitness testimony." She crossed her arms, her face set in an expression of confident defiance.

If my badgering hastens her recuperation, maybe I should wind her up some more. Let her hate me . . . for the short term, that is.

I drew in a breath. "Since when has eyewitness testimony ever guaranteed accuracy?"

Her brows drew together. "Why would an eyewitness lie?"

"I'm not talking about dishonesty," I said. "People get things wrong. How about the man sentenced to death row based on the testimonies of five eyewitnesses, all who swore they saw him with the murder victim? After nine years in prison, awaiting execution, DNA evidenced proved him innocent."

"You know what I mean," she said. "Church fathers were much closer in time to Jesus, closer to the truth."

"You can be present and still not be certain what was said—Stanton's elegy at the foot of Lincoln's deathbed, for example, the most famous epitaph in American history."

"That's the remark where he said, 'Now he belongs to the ages,' " Victoria said.

"Yes. Or maybe not. Others heard Stanton say, 'Now he belongs to the angels.' Which was it? The room where Lincoln breathed his last was crowded. Emotions were high. Many wept. The point is, what's said may not be what's heard, and what is heard isn't the same as what gets reported. People were no different two thousand years ago." I reflected. "Maybe what Jesus actually said was 'Blessed are the pizza makers.' "

It got her to chuckle.

"And you think close in time helps?" I said. "Americans who met FDR said he rose to his feet to greet them. Yet, FDR couldn't have done that. He always had to be lifted to his feet by others because of his leg braces."

"Valid point, but I can see you're enjoying this way too much."

"More than I should be."

"Granted," Victoria said, "there's literal truth versus the spirit of truth. The Americans in that case just wanted to emphasize that FDR *rose*—that he had to have help was immaterial."

"And my point is that the 'untruths' in the Bible—in many cases—are the same. The writers wanted to get a message across. Jesus was generous and wanted to feed people, so they came up with a story that would show that: five loaves and two fish miraculously multiplied to feed a multitude."

She drummed her fingernails on the arm of her wheelchair, and I sensed her adrenalin was flowing. I was getting good at this.

"I study the Bible the same way you review a scientific paper," I said, "from a critical perspective. That's why I don't believe Paul wrote First Timothy or Second Timothy."

"What's your evidence? Specifically."

"OK, bear with me and I'll tell you why I think the church's argument for the subordination of women is based on faulty evidence, evidence that was tampered with."

"I'm listening," she said.

"The reason I believe Paul didn't write First Timothy or Second Timothy is because the vocabulary is very different from his. The author, whoever he was, used words that weren't in common usage until long after Paul had died. That's a dead giveaway, no pun intended. It's like handwriting analysis, but with the focus on the content. One-third of the vocabulary in First and Second Timothy consists of words found nowhere else in Paul's writings."

"That's all very interesting, in an NPR kind of way, but what's wrong with Paul varying his vocabulary?"

"That's more than a slight variation. That's somebody else's writing.

She nodded but said nothing.

"Other ideas in First and Second Timothy contradict Paul altogether," I said. "Paul tells people they shouldn't get married—they should stay single like he is. After all, the end is near, so people shouldn't waste precious time starting families. But the author of First and Second Timothy says the opposite. He tells church leaders go ahead, get married! That doesn't sound like Paul to me."

"You draw an interesting contrast," she said.

"And the discrepancies continue. Paul says you can be saved only through belief in Jesus, but the author of First Timothy says women will be saved by bearing children, by *motherhood*."

Victoria was silent.

"And women are not to teach men," I added.

"Some guys are fond of *that* one," she said.

"Well, it was just those kinds of passages in First and Second Timothy that made me realize the Bible was a very man-made book—replete with male chauvinism—not God-given truth."

I paused as a man on crutches struggled to navigate across the visitor's lounge, a sight that reminded me of my own journey that led me away from belief in God. There are no crutches to help you after that.

I turned back to see skepticism return to Victoria's face. "What I can't reconcile," she said, "is that while you say somebody tampered with First and Second Timothy, the Bible tells us that *all* Scripture is inspired by God."

"Uh-huh," I said and raised my eyebrows. "And just *where* does it say that?"

Victoria squinted at me for a few moments as if mentally scrolling through past Bible study sessions.

"Oh, jeez!" she said as her eyes widened. "That's in Second Timothy!"

"Written by an unknown author who wants us to think it's coming from Paul," I said. "Perhaps the author thought women had too much influence in the church and wanted to quell that."

"But, if Paul didn't feel that way, how come he said elsewhere that women should remain silent in church?"

Her tone had become less combative and more inquiring.

"You're referring to those little gems in First Corinthians?" I asked. "About women's proper place? That they should be silent, should not speak, should be subordinate, should ask their husbands if they have any questions?"

Victoria gave me a cautious nod.

"What would you think if I told you that those statements were inserted into Paul's letter by someone else?"

She settled back. "Go on. How can you tell?"

"Two reasons. The first: location, location, location. The person who inserted the passage slammed it smack in the middle of a point Paul is making about something entirely different. That's a red flag to a critical reader. It interrupts what Paul is saying, which therefore makes it very suspect."

"Um. OK," Victoria said.

"The second reason? Plain inconsistency. How can Paul say women cannot speak in church when three chapters earlier he says they *can*?"

"You're confident of all this?" she asked.

"Yes, and it should convince you too. And concern you, because those lines in First Timothy and First Corinthians form the church's rationale for keeping women in their place. Paul didn't write those words. He was egalitarian. Other church fathers, not so much." I drained my coffee cup. "Look how they smeared Mary Magdalene."

"What do you mean?"

"The church painted her as a prostitute when in fact, she played a huge role in the new religious movement. She was the primary witness to the resurrection—the very centerpiece of Christianity! She was the first to arrive at Jesus's tomb. She was a trusted, perhaps beloved, disciple."

"Are we talking about the same person? The infamous repentant sinner who washed Jesus's feet with her tears?"

"Yes, but that's not Mary Magdalene. Read again, and you'll see Jesus is talking about another, unnamed woman who washed his feet. There is no biblical evidence whatsoever that Mary Magdalene was any kind of public sinner, let alone a harlot. It's a classic case of erroneous assumptions and mistaken identity that played into the hands of those who resented a woman's influence . . . of those more comfortable with Mary Magdalene's portrayal as a redeemed sinner at the foot of the cross, a dutiful attendant who went to the tomb to anoint the body, but who was not even believed when she ran to tell of Christ's resurrection."

Victoria gave me a penetrating glance. "I hope you don't think she married Jesus and made him a daddy."

I took a deep breath as I shook my head. "Nope. There isn't one iota of evidence Jesus was married, and there is plenty to argue he wasn't."

She looked surprised, as if she hadn't been expecting that response. "I've heard the argument that all rabbis back then were married," she said.

"Not true. We know of many single men from Jesus's time—the authors of the Dead Sea Scrolls, for example. Paul was single. These adult males and other apocalyptic Jews, *especially* Jesus, had very good reason to stay single: the end of the world was at hand!"

"That stopped marriages?" Victoria asked.

"It did for those who believed the end was imminent. That was the atmosphere. Men began quitting their *jobs*! And that's the reason Jesus would have remained a bachelor. There's not a single reference, anywhere, that says otherwise—not in the New Testament, not in any of the noncanonical Gospels, not in any documents of any kind anywhere from that period. Nothing, nada, zero. If he'd been married, why wouldn't people have mentioned it? They had no problem mentioning his other relatives: his parents, his brothers, his sisters. The bottom line: Jesus didn't have a wife."

Victoria nodded. "Interesting," she said. "I appreciate your evenhandedness."

We seemed to be on the same wavelength for a change. I hoped it would last.

It didn't.

"I'm glad you said Jesus was single," Victoria said. "His marital status gets more attention these days than what's important—the resurrection. Nonbelievers ignore the fact that disciples saw his risen body, felt his wounds."

"I'll be honest," I said. "I have no doubt Jesus was seen after his death."

Victoria blinked. "That surprises me."

"Certainly," I said. "After all, the Catholic Church has officially validated a dozen sightings of the Virgin Mary! People do see things. So, I accept there were Jesus sightings too."

She emitted a soft groan as if I was a hopeless cause.

"My problem," I said, "is believing that a loving God would require Jesus be crucified in the first place. An innocent person tortured to death for the crimes of the guilty? Makes no sense to me. Not any longer."

"Here we go again," she said.

"What *does* make sense to me is the quickness with which the early church fathers discovered that audiences were mesmerized by the story. They realized they had stumbled upon something *big*."

Victoria settled back in her wheelchair and crossed her arms. "Let me see if I'm hearing you right. We don't know who wrote most of the Bible. Parts that we do know the author of may contain unauthorized additions by unknown persons. Sightings of Jesus may have been due to vivid imaginations. Furthermore, the church fathers orchestrated a marketing campaign that would make Colonel Sanders proud." She waggled her head. "No wonder you've lost your religion. I can't figure out why I'm attracted to you."

I raised my chin with a hopeful expression. "Um. Can we stay with that part? About being attracted to me?"

The exasperation in her face morphed into her puckered smile. "You're something else," she said.

"Well, I'm only *part* Neanderthal."

We were quiet for a few moments.

"I once revered the Bible the way you do," I said. "I miss having that nice, secure guarantee. I don't believe it's the word of God, but I remain absorbed by it because it's the most important book in the history of Western civilization. I guess I'm still a seeker."

"A devotion to questions of being . . . questions of faith," Victoria said. "That's an admirable pursuit."

59

Tim Lane
I-80 Rest Stop, Nebraska
5:30 PM

Tim Lane watched the slow, mesmerizing spiral of a bald eagle as it rode the receding late-afternoon thermals high above an I-80 rest stop about forty-five miles east of Grand Island, Nebraska. He paused at a bulletin board by the restrooms. Pictures showed a sky darkened by large birds—the spring migration of 80 percent of the world's population of sandhill cranes, who traveled three hundred miles in a day. *Slackers*, Lane thought.

He stretched his limbs and examined his bandaged hand. Lane had described his injury as a hunting accident to the doctor who had treated him an hour earlier at a medical clinic in Lincoln. "Change it every two days," the doctor had instructed.

The shotgun pellets had grazed his hand, tearing the skin, but had not broken any bones. A new bandage could wait until he was back home in Martinez. The completion of his mission was in sight, and despite the close call at the motel, he was thankful for the opportunity he had been given.

The Messenger knew what was right and wrong in the eyes of the Lord. With so much at stake, there had been no other way. He would not fail, he vowed. He slid into the driver's seat, pulled onto the interstate, and continued westward toward his final target.

60

Bill Miner
Regional Medical Center, Rolla
6:30 PM

Victoria and I had spent the remainder of the afternoon in separate clinics where I had received a physical therapy regimen for my shoulder, and she had been treated in respiratory therapy. We met later in the hospital café for dinner. Victoria chose bulgogi, the chef's Korean special of the night, and stir-fried eggplant and tofu. I stayed American with pork chops, mashed potatoes, and green beans, but when I caught the aroma from Victoria's dinner, I second-guessed my choice. She saw my envy.

"Have a bite," she said and passed her fork.

"Umm," I said, "this place contradicts everything I've heard about hospital food. You might convert me."

She gave me a quizzical look.

"To Korean food," I said.

She gave a half grin with an air of *you are hopeless.*

"On another subject," Victoria said between bites of eggplant, "you were intrigued that Pastor Parks said a woman wrote a book of the Bible. Figure out who she is?"

"I have a hunch," I said.

She paused, fork halfway to her mouth.

"One of the books gives no name but hints it was written by Paul—the Letter to the Hebrews. If I had to guess," I said, "that would be my pick."

Victoria leaned closer as another patient across from us appeared to eavesdrop.

"So, what's her name?" Victoria whispered.

"Priscilla."

Victoria's eyes widened with intrigue. "The Priscilla married to Aquila?"

I nodded. "They were in Paul's circle of friends."

"Hmm . . . interesting."

I paused as a family with rambunctious children passed through. "The thing is, there's always been uncertainty over the author of Hebrews, going far back into antiquity—one of the strangest facts in early Christian literature."

"Because?"

I picked up a string bean and poised it in the air like a pointer. "Why would the name of the writer be missing? Something of prime importance in a letter. The letter itself indicates the author is well-known, and yet there's a veil of silence. Either no one knew, or nobody would talk."

"So, everyone was mum because it was a woman?"

"If another major figure of the day—Barnabas, or Clement, or Apollos—had been the author, it's hard to imagine their name wouldn't have appeared. But if Priscilla was the actual author, the growing resistance to the role of women, the pullback expressed in First Timothy, could explain the absence of her name."

"Well, as much as I like the idea," Victoria said, "a missing name wouldn't imply that Hebrews was written by a woman. Can't you tell whether the writer was male or female from the gender of the Greek nouns?"

"Good point, and yes, you can. The gender of nouns in the Letter to the Hebrews is male. However, if the intent was to conceal that the author was female, it wouldn't be a stretch to think someone altered a few words to change that."

Her face brightened. "I'd love it if you were right."

"There are other aspects of the letter that point to Priscilla. For starters, she had an excellent education. Letter to the Hebrews is considered one of the finest Greek compositions in the New Testament, superior in style even to Paul's writings."

Victoria put her fork down. "That does jibe with what Pastor Parks said about the book's eloquence," she said.

"We know the letter was written by someone living in Rome, and Priscilla and her husband are the only couple in the entire New Testament referred to as 'from Italy.' "

Victoria shook her head slowly. "Tantalizing but not conclusive."

"Stay with me," I said. "Maybe this will help: Hebrews conveys delicate nuances about childhood and parental discipline that sound more like the tender voice of a mother speaking than that of a father. And the part that cements it for me: the letter has a closely connected 'we.' Without emphasizing it, the writer effortlessly flits from 'we' to 'I' and back again. An admirable characteristic for a couple that views itself as a team, don't you think?"

I saw a slight flush in her cheeks, then a soft smile. "Yes . . . I do."

Victoria paused a moment. Her eyes swept upward.

"To think a woman may have written Holy Scripture," she said, her face full of wonderment. "And I wouldn't mind if the trustworthiness of First and Second Timothy were knocked down a peg or two."

A volunteer staff member arrived to take us back to our rooms.

"Thank you for such a delectable thought to end the day," Victoria said. She moved her wheelchair to my corner of the table and kissed my cheek. "Sweet dreams, and may angels watch over you."

"Sweet dreams, Victoria," I called as she headed toward the hallway.

A few minutes later I eased into my own hospital bed. The room fell still except for the occasional footsteps of staff in the corridor. My thoughts weren't as agreeable as Victoria's had been when we parted. Doctors expected to release us the next day, and we'd fly home. She would have to adjust to the loss of her father, consoled only by the FBI's eventual apprehension of Tim Lane. I would have my own music to face—a career in peril because of a long shot that had come up empty. *What in the world will I do for my book?* Distraught is an understatement for what I was feeling—not like butterflies in my stomach, more like killer bees.

I rolled on my side and thought about Victoria, who was probably saying a prayer about then. A captivating woman who exuded spirit, confidence, and pluck—intelligence balanced with thoughtfulness and compassion. I'd never met anyone quite like her. I hadn't felt this way about *anybody* before.

I shifted in my bed, unable to get comfortable. There I was on the brink of losing my faculty position, yet my thoughts were of her, about us. How could I fall for someone with such opposite religious convictions? Was this my week for ridiculous long shots? What kind of relationship could we ever have? A day hasn't passed without fruitless arguments. A twinge went down my spine. *What chance is there anything could develop between us that wouldn't turn into combat?* We were like opponents on rival college debate teams, locked on opposite sides of a topic that could never be settled, every round a hopeless draw. No, it would never work. How could it?

I turned over and punched my pillow. Then there was this other matter that had thrown me a colossal curve—near-death experiences that suggested there *was* an afterlife.

How could her father, and Florence, and the others have known things they couldn't have known? Victoria's father had witnessed a traffic accident while in surgery, spotted a baseball cap on the hospital roof, seen a brother he didn't know had died.

Florence had learned about a red burn mark on her father's arm no one had ever mentioned.

Mandy Frankel had been told about her grandfather's menorah.

And how could a pastor, consumed with old-time religion, have gained insights that dazzled?

All of them had received spiritual wisdom imparted by a supposed loving, all-knowing, celestial, lightsome whatever. It was inexplicable.

God? I rolled over for the umpteenth time, surprised I could even entertain such an explanation. What kind of God would allow so much innocent suffering in the world? I'd already done the math on that one. We're loved? How did you reconcile a God who is supposed to care . . . with typhoons, malaria, and starvation?

There must be an explanation for these near-death experiences. I reminded myself that Victoria now had doubts about the near-death experiences . . . albeit, in my opinion, for all the wrong reasons: because they contradicted the Bible's claim to be God's holy word. I had reached the conclusion *that* wasn't true long ago.

But who or what was this light? I rolled over one more time, pulled up the covers, and forced myself to lie still. Eventually, sleep overtook me.

61

Tim Lane
Twin Falls, ID
Day 8, 9:30 AM

Tim Lane exited I-84 at Idaho Route 50, crossed the Hansen Bridge over the Snake River Canyon, and followed the highway into Twin Falls. At an elevation of almost four thousand feet and a temperature in the midsixties, the sunlight felt radiant, the air clean and invigorating. Fatigue from his thirteen-hundred-mile, nonstop drive from Missouri had not yet affected him.

He angled right onto Shoshone Street and found what he sought—the Magic Valley Trading Post. A large sign, emblazoned with a western carbine, hung above the establishment. Lane pulled into a parking space.

Luke 22:36 provided all the justification a Dragon of God needed as a warrior for Christ: "He that hath no sword, let him sell his garment, and buy one."

The building looked like it had once been an early-1900s department store. Old-fashioned display cases filled with handguns lined both sides of a wide center aisle. The walls, stretching to a fourteen-foot ceiling, were lined with hunting rifles. Large wooden barrels, brimming with US Army surplus gear, stood next to racks of hunting jackets and camouflage clothing.

Lane walked past open crates filled with equipment that would appeal to survivalists. The wooden boxes packed every square foot of an old hardwood floor. He picked up a gas mask. The shape and contour reminded him of the *Star Wars* "Sand People" costume he and his son had made for Halloween the year before.

Lane turned his attention to one of the gun cases, which displayed an assortment of used pistols. He eyed an FNX-9—a nine-millimeter semiautomatic. A clerk approached, and Lane asked to see it.

"That comes with three seventeen-round mags," the young man said. "It just came in. I've also got a brand new one if you're interested. Accurate. Zero failures. Double action is heavy but smooth as it can be. Trigger pull breaks clean. This gun's a nice soft shooter."

Lane flipped over the price tag on the trigger guard: $450. "OK, this'll be fine," he said. "I'll need some ammunition."

"I've got one-hundred-fifteen-grain in a box of two hundred for sixty-one dollars."

Lane nodded. "How far to Buhl?"

"Sixteen miles. You're twenty minutes away."

62

Bill Miner
Regional Medical Center, Rolla
9:30 AM

"You want me to do *what*?" I asked. I covered my phone's microphone and leaned toward Victoria across my plate of eggs and toast. "It's Agent Jordan. He wants me in Kansas City for an FBI briefing."

"Do they have Lane?" she asked.

"Doesn't sound like it." I put the phone back to my ear. "The doctors told us we're good to go. We'll be discharged this morning. When's your briefing?"

My jaw dropped. "One o'clock? Today? I don't see how—"

I listened as Jordan explained, then held the phone away. "He wants me to profile Lane, the religious side, anything I can tell them about his motivation." My pulse had quickened. "He's sending a helicopter!"

"Agent Jordan," I asked, "does the FBI know anything about near-death experiences? . . . Uh-huh. . . . OK, then you need Victoria too. Your people need to understand how NDEs play into the motivation."

Jordan described the logistics.

"All right," I said. I disconnected the call and turned to Victoria. "Ready for a change of scenery? We have to be ready in an hour and a half."

Her eyebrows shot up to her hairline.

63

Tim Lane
Twin Falls
10:30 AM

Tim Lane stopped at a Dairy Queen before continuing west on US 30 through the agricultural Snake River Plain. Circular fields of crops edged both sides of the highway. They called it "Magic Valley," the fast-food clerk had told him, because half of Idaho's produce and livestock revenue came from here.

Lane found the area attractive—a semiarid region made into an "Eden" by irrigation canals. As he approached Buhl, a sign announced he was entering the "Rainbow Trout Capital of the World."

One- and two-story buildings lined an unhurried business district in the century-old town of forty-three hundred. If there'd been any population growth recently, Lane mused, it must have been in trout, not people. He continued up Broadway, past a modern city hall building with a raised portico front that reminded him of the entrance to a cathedral. He slowed and nodded silently. What pleasant symbolism—a local city council viewed its building as a house of God.

Lane had no difficulty in locating Janie Hughes's home on Laburnum Lane, off Old Farm Road. The street was one block long with eight attractive single-story homes on each side. He cruised past her residence at 606.

There was no indication anyone was at home. He'd expected that. Facebook informed him this was the day she worked until midafternoon on her garden club's community beautification project.

The street was quiet—no pedestrians or traffic. On one home farther down, on the opposite side of the street, Lane saw a FOR SALE sign with a FORECLOSED placard beneath it. He pulled over to the curb.

The curtains were open, the living room appeared void of furniture, and the lawn hadn't been cut in some time. He contemplated what appeared to be a fortuitous opportunity—this house could provide an ideal location from which to observe the Hughes residence.

He formed a plan.

Lane parked his car and surveyed the area. Lawns flowed from one home to the next uninterrupted by fences. He would have easy access to the backyard. The downside was he'd also be more visible than if there had been fences, but there seemed to be no signs of activity in the sleepy neighborhood.

Lane stepped from his car and moved through the side yard to the back of the foreclosed house. A quick check told him it would be easy to gain entrance. He returned to his car, grabbed his sack from the gun store, and retrieved a tire iron from the stash of tools in the trunk.

He doubled back and was approaching a rear bedroom window when he heard a door slide open. Lane dropped hard to the ground next to a raised redwood deck. He watched, breathless, as a next-door neighbor stepped out onto her patio and shook a rug.

She would have seen Lane had she looked to her right. Instead, she turned left, went back inside, and slid the door closed.

Lane calmed himself, then examined the bandaged hand he'd landed on. He ignored the pain, stepped up to the window, and with the tire iron, jimmied it. A minute later he was inside, but the scare had drained him.

Lane checked each room of the three-bedroom, two-bath rancher. Empty. No furniture. Only a worn pair of living room curtains. The electricity had been turned off but not the water. He cupped his hand under the kitchen sink faucet and splashed water on his face.

He reviewed his plan one more time, took out his cell phone, and placed a call. When the party didn't answer, Lane left a detailed message.

The final piece had fallen into place. Calmness settled over him. It also could have been his fatigue. He reminded himself not to be overconfident.

Lane sat down on the floor with his back against a living room wall to rest for a few minutes. Overcome by exhaustion, he felt his eyelids grow heavy as he drifted into the first sleep he'd had in over twenty-four hours.

64

Bill Miner
Regional Medical Center, Rolla
11:00 AM

I watched an ominous thirty-five-foot black McDonnell Douglas 530 float down to the heliport in the medical center parking area. Caregivers, used to the arrival of critical patients by helicopter, were not accustomed to patients leaving that way.

Victoria and I strapped ourselves into an aircraft that we learned was used for hostage rescue operations. Above our heads rotor blades throbbed with a pulsating chuff-chuff-chuff. Moments later we spiraled skyward, then banked hard across Missouri woodlands.

The noise level made conversation difficult. We knew there'd be plenty of discussion when we arrived. For the moment, it was all about the view, racing beneath us at 155 miles per hour.

Our pilot landed at the FBI offices in downtown Kansas City at 12:45 PM. We were escorted to a dark-paneled second-floor room the size of an intimate theater. The seal of the Department of Justice was prominent on one wall, flanked by US and Missouri flags. Two immense flat-panel screens filled the front wall.

Thirty or more people circulated between a coffee service, arrayed on a sideboard, and groups clustered in conversation. Were it not for the fact that most were dressed in business attire, I'd have thought we'd just entered a secret military briefing room. I spotted Jordan in the corner and spoke with him while Victoria took a chair.

At one o'clock sharp, Jordan stood before the assembled officers. "Ladies, Gentlemen, we had an opportunity to apprehend our suspect at Harrisonville. I am responsible for that failure."

His voice was strong but his frustration visible. Veins bulged in his neck. I knew what he was referring to because our pilot had told us of Lane's escape.

"We will not let that happen again," Jordan said, "and we're grateful to have your participation as we go forward."

All eyes were on Jordan. I could feel adrenaline begin to rise in the audience.

"Our focus," he said, "is a serial killer responsible for the murder of four people."

Jordan gave the names of the victims and locations of the murders and described Tim Lane: a thirty-five-year-old white male resident of Martinez, California, with a wife and five-year-old son.

"Lane got a college degree in business, then served two years as an Army ROTC commissioned officer assigned to military intelligence at Fort Huachuca, Arizona. Afterward, Lane moved to Pennsylvania, where he married and took a job with an electronics manufacturer. A few years later he and his wife moved to the Bay Area."

An aide began to distribute handouts. A photo of Lane appeared on the left screen, a map of the victims' locations on the right.

"Lane's picture was obtained from his wife by San Francisco agents," Jordan said. "That's our man."

Jordan summarized the physical evidence collected—the bullet recovered at Devil's Fall, the bullet that killed Florence Smith, and the rifle that had fired both, recovered at the Harrisonville motel.

"Mr. Lane made little effort to disguise his identity. He used his real name to purchase airline tickets and rent automobiles." Jordan's eyes swept the room. "He staged each murder to look like a suicide, a mugging gone wrong, a hit-and-run, or a gas-leak explosion. He may have thought they would go unrecognized as homicides. It almost worked. We found charge receipts in his overnight bag recovered at the motel, all of which put him at the time and place of each of the four murders."

A hand went up from a woman in a dark charcoal pantsuit. "You haven't talked about motive."

"We'll speak to that in detail in a minute," Jordan said. "In fact, the killer's motive alerted us to contact and secure the safety of his fifth target in southern Idaho. That person—a Mrs. Hughes—has gone to stay with a relative in Boise as a precaution."

As he spoke I glanced around at the faces in the audience. Their concentration told me this crowd did not like to be skunked and would not settle for anything short of Lane's apprehension. Dead or alive.

"He moved quickly and methodically," Sam Jordan continued. "A risk taker. That much matches the profile of a serial killer. But other characteristics don't fit. A background investigation found no criminal history. His family moved from a small town in Pennsylvania several years ago." His eyes narrowed. "Lane's wife described him in loving terms—a churchgoing, devoted husband and father. But she said he'd come under the influence of someone he refused to talk about."

"So, he may not have acted alone?" The question came from a tall man in a uniform loaded with rank insignia.

"That is possible," Jordan said. A hint of uncertainty crossed his face. "However, it's Lane that we can place at the scenes of these crimes. We have his home under surveillance, but it's our intent to catch him before he leaves Missouri. All transportation terminals in the state have the picture and description that are in your handout."

He scanned the room. "Are there any other questions about this man's identity?"

"Do we have any video-surveillance footage?" asked a man in the back.

Jordan shook his head. "Now, you asked about motive. To address that, I'd like to introduce a man who's been in the thick of this—religion professor Bill Miner from UC Berkeley in California. He has studied radical cults and extremists and knows something about their personalities. I've asked him to give us his insights on what we might expect from Tim Lane." He gestured toward me.

I rose to my feet amid a sea of dubious looks and wished he'd skipped the mention of Berkeley. I stepped to the front of the room and began in a cautious tone.

"Some of you may view with suspicion anyone from the liberal Bay Area—a radical who's here to talk to *you* about extremists."

There was a light ripple of knowing chuckles.

"One of my academic specialties is cults. It's what drew me into this case and why Agent Jordan asked me to speak. However, I recognize that this group has far more boots-on-the-ground experience with deviant religious groups than I do."

Frowns in the audience began to dissipate.

"But these murders aren't the work of backwoods fanatics. From the evidence that Agent Jordan has described to you, this appears to be an individual who acted by himself. And the best I can do is to give you an idea of his possible motivation."

Victoria sat attentively. I could feel her confidence in me.

"All of the victims had one element in common," I said. "Each one had a remarkable near-death experience unlike others you may have read about. So extraordinary, CBS planned to air a special edition of *60 Minutes* to feature in-depth interviews with them and detailed accounts."

Sam Jordan stood off to the side. His eyes darted between me and the listeners as he gauged reaction.

"It might be helpful," I said, "to summarize the characteristics of a typical near-death experience before I describe what made these ones such a threat to the killer. I'm no expert on near-death experiences. I have but a general acquaintance with them, as perhaps do you. But we have someone here who *is* knowledgeable, a neuroscientist whose company has investigated this phenomenon. I'd like to call on Victoria Johnson to give a brief overview. She has an enormous stake in this case. Her father was the first victim."

I walked over to her seat. "You look uneasy," I whispered.

"I'm tense because I'm conflicted."

"You are strong. They'll be altogether taken by you."

All eyes swung to Victoria as she came to the front. She looked smart in a casual navy-blue dress and a tasteful necklace with a silver butterfly. Men leaned forward. Their expressions changed as though the reward centers in their brains had just been set off.

"I want to express my gratitude to you for what you're doing," she said.

Nice touch, I thought. I lifted my chin and took in a slow breath.

"Capture of the person responsible for my father's death and for the deaths of three others may help me find closure, but you put your lives on the line for citizens every day. Thank you."

I glanced around the audience—men's eyes were transfixed. With her first words, Victoria had deftly drawn in the women too.

"This subject has received a lot of hype in books and on television," she said. "It's often cited as evidence for the existence of an afterlife and the human soul. I am a follower of Jesus, so I am one of those who believed that near-death experiences could be viewed as a confirmation of my evangelical faith.

"I use past tense because I have now become somewhat distrustful of the validity of near-death experiences."

A hushed murmur circulated.

"Putting my own doubts aside, I can summarize a full near-death experience as research understands it. There is a sense you've died but, at the same time, a feeling of peace and well-being. This feeling is so exalted and glorious that one woman said it was like the ten best things that ever happened to her multiplied a millionfold.

"NDErs may separate from their bodies and rise above them, able to view their surroundings as though they were a detached observer, able to hear conversations like a fly on the wall. One man said he looked at his body as a discarded shell that he no longer needed. Some NDErs describe entering the famous 'tunnel.' Drawn, with ever-increasing speed, into the presence of a loving, all-knowing light of transcendent brilliance and beauty. They tell of a glorious realm of celestial landscapes where they may be reunited with loved ones.

"Some NDErs describe a detailed life review conducted with exceptional compassion and unconditional love. Scenes and episodes from a person's life are played back, showing what they contributed, how their actions affected others, what they might have done differently.

"At some point, NDErs decide, sometimes with great reluctance, to return to the world, and they reenter their bodies."

Victoria took a breath and surveyed her audience. She had their rapt attention.

"A big challenge for NDE researchers," she continued, "has always been the scarcity of verifiable evidence. What makes *this* case unique is that all four victims in your investigation described at least one detail in their near-death experience that was independently verified. That is of mammoth significance."

A hand shot up. "If these near-death experiences can be verified, why are you now distrustful?"

"I'm distrustful"—Victoria glanced at me and then back to the woman who had asked the question—"because while some of the statements can be validated, other assertions—religious assertions—are contrary to what I know to be true."

"We're in law enforcement," the questioner said. "We get *that* every day."

The audience chuckled. Victoria smiled in acknowledgment.

"My personal beliefs aren't important," she said. "It's what *Tim Lane* believes." Her voice was resolute, but the strain in her face remained. "To explain Lane's motivation, let me turn this back over to Professor Miner."

"You were terrific," I whispered as she returned to the seat next to mine.

I went forward again.

"The extraordinary aspect of the near-death experiences of our four victims," I said, "is not that they appear to confirm the existence of God or an afterlife. Many people with near-death experiences have claimed that.

"They are remarkable because of what was included in their conversations with the light: Is the Bible God's infallible word? Did Jesus Christ truly die in our place? Must you be born again to enter heaven? They learned that those fundamentalist beliefs were based on misinterpretation and misunderstanding."

"It's dangerous to mess with religious beliefs." The comment came from a man with an ATF badge in the front row. "Wars have broken out over less."

I nodded. "And if such claims were made to appear credible by a respected television network, that could be interpreted as a direct attack on conservative Evangelicals. We learned that Lane, in fact, is a fundamentalist. His wife told agents they belong to an evangelical church in their community, the Church of Sacred Resurrection."

I heard someone gasp. Heads turned to a woman with a hand over her mouth.

It was Victoria.

65

The Messenger
1:30 PM

In another time zone, a man listened to a phone message he had just received. He reflected. *If Lane eliminates Hughes, his job will have been exemplary. If she should survive, the testimony of one person can be dismissed as one woman's delusion.*

He leaned back, at ease and in control. Tim Lane had been adept and tenacious. It was time for God's servant to receive his well-earned reward.

The man deleted the message, then placed a phone call to a number he'd had ready for some time.

66

Bill Miner
FBI Offices, Kansas City
1:40 PM

"That's *my* church," Victoria said as I reached her seat, her face dazed, arms braced across her chest.

"I had no idea," I said. "Jordan told me just before the meeting when I asked if the FBI had learned Lane's religious affiliation."

"I've prayed in the same church as the man who . . ." Her voice was in disbelief. She shuddered, then drew in a series of breaths. "Go ahead. Finish your briefing."

I returned to the front of the room. "Some of you heard that. We didn't know that Lane attended the same church as Ms. Johnson. It's a megachurch with over four thousand members. It's unclear whether Lane knew her. She did not know him."

I glanced to Victoria, then looked back to the audience. "Let me explain why this TV program would pose such a threat."

I felt a roomful of eyes bore into me in anticipation.

"Conservative Evangelicals believe every word of the Bible is without error, that Jesus's death was atonement for sin, that his resurrection was literal, that he will come again.

"Our victims would have offered eye-popping testimony—on a nationwide broadcast—that beliefs cherished by fundamentalists are built on a foundation of misconceptions."

Murmurs floated throughout the room. Some expressions showed surprise. Some were grim, others just curious.

"Such claims, if accepted," I said, "would throw conservative theology into chaos. And if claims of misconceptions aren't enough, throw in a swipe at those who reject evolution: our victims would have declared that Darwin was right, that evolution is indeed God's very design plan."

A few faces that had not reacted before now showed concern.

"Here's the thing," I said. "A powerful and enduring church has always been resilient in the face of those who doubt."

"If that's the case," a man in a police uniform asked, "what triggered this guy?"

"What triggered him?" I repeated. I stared at the questioner. "The trigger?" I mumbled. "The spark. The spark that triggered him." I bit the inside of my cheek. After a long moment, I turned my eyes back to the police officer. "I think the trigger was Satan."

Snickers rippled around the room, then became a low rumble of voices.

"I'm not being flip," I said. "If there are Evangelicals in the audience, you understand my drift. Some believe Satan is active in the world today, at work as a hostile opponent to God's word. Tim Lane may have concluded that the evil one is behind the claims of the four victims."

"We have a complete religious nutcase," a woman remarked.

"It's not black and white," I said. "Some think society's unwillingness to recognize the presence of Satan's activity is foolish blindness to the true nature of reality.

"If Tim Lane believes that Satan is behind the lies and deception—believes that Satan has orchestrated an attack on Scripture—then from Lane's viewpoint, *any* action to combat the enemy is justified."

Some in the crowd shook their heads. Others exchanged glances with the people next to them.

"This brings me to the type of individual you seek," I said. "He won't be the kind to let up. The last potential victim, the fifth on the list, has sought safe haven. But she could still be vulnerable. Lane has shown he's a man of strong determination, willing to assume personal risks. You might corral him, but you won't take him easily."

I paused and asked if there were any questions. When there were none, Jordan returned to the podium and thanked Victoria and me. I took my seat.

Jordan instructed the officers to keep all details to themselves. "I want to cut down on conflicting stories to the reporters or any conspiracy theories," he said. "I'll conduct all media interviews myself."

He'd begun to announce assignments when an aide came into the room and interrupted him. They conferred for a moment. Jordan turned to the audience with a troubled expression.

"Stand by," he said, and left the room abruptly.

67

Sam Jordan
FBI Offices, Kansas City
1:55 PM

Agent Sam Jordan moved posthaste down the hall, past a wall of photos that depicted images from momentous engagements—Waco, the Rodney King riots, Wounded Knee, Patty Hearst. He entered his office and grabbed the phone with a secure line where his assistant had transferred a call from his boss at FBI Headquarters in Washington, DC.

"Jordan, it's Branford." Scott Branford, the unpretentious and respected deputy director of the Federal Bureau of Investigation, was as direct as a kick in the shins, a man known for getting to the point.

"We just received a phone tip you need to know about." Branford's voice was steady and unambiguous. "Lane is lying in wait across the street from the Hughes residence in Buhl, Idaho."

"*What?*" Jordan drew his head back. He felt a sudden coldness.

"Lane's holed up in a vacant house," Branford said. "He plans to make his attack look like a home-invasion robbery."

Jordan's blood drained from his face. "How did the person who called in the tip know this?"

"Lane told him," Branford said. "And the church in Waynesville—he knew Lane had rigged the explosion."

"Who the hell is this guy?"

"Our operator tried to finesse his identity. All she got was a soft chuckle. When she pressed, he hung up."

"What's your assessment of the credibility?" Jordan asked.

"He knew Hughes's name and her address on Laburnum. The media doesn't have any of that."

Jordan fought to control his frustration. Lane had again slipped through his net. "Were you able to track the call?" Jordan asked.

"To a cell tower in the East Bay near San Francisco," Branford said. "The phone's a prepaid burner, so we don't know who used it."

Jordan ignored the numbness in his mind and body. He jotted down the number of the burner and drew in a deep breath through his nose. "All right," he told his boss, "this is what I propose."

He outlined his strategy, then disconnected the call. Jordan grabbed his cell, flipped through the contacts, and punched the number for Janie Hughes. He felt a swell of relief at the sound of her voice.

"Where are you now?" he asked.

The answer he received felt like someone hitting his temple with a hammer.

"*What?* What do you mean you're at home? You're supposed to be at your sister's in Boise.

"You were scheduled to make a presentation to the *garden club*?

"Jesus Christ! Mrs. Hughes, you're in imminent *danger*!"

68

Sam Jordan
FBI Offices, Kansas City
2:05 PM

Sam Jordan gathered his wits. His heart thudded. He shouted to Kaitlin, "Get the police chief of Buhl, Idaho, on the phone!"

He put his cell back to his ear. "Mrs. Hughes, is your husband still away? . . . OK. Stay on the line. Do not put the phone down. Do you understand? . . . Good."

"Chief's on line three!" Kaitlin hollered.

Jordan explained the situation to a startled Chief Charles Mitten.

"I know the Hugheses," the chief said. "Pleasant, good-natured couple."

"Chief, can you dispatch an unmarked car to their home? . . . OK. Secure Mrs. Hughes as soon as you can have one of your people there, but don't approach her house from the front. I've got her on the other line, and I'll tell her to meet your officer at the back door. Do you have someone you can send in plain clothes? . . . Good. I'll give you the full background when we get there. Her husband is out of town—the urgency is for Mrs. Hughes. Is this all clear, Chief Mitten? . . . Good, thank you. Trust me. We're on the way."

Jordan disconnected the call and picked up his cell. "Mrs. Hughes, Buhl police will send someone in the next few minutes to pick you up at your back door. It'll be a woman, and she won't be in a police uniform. Do not go out the front. Do not answer the front door. Don't take anything. Just grab your purse, and be at your back door after we hang up. Do you understand? . . . Good, because I'm coming to Buhl, and I want to find you in one piece when I get there. . . . OK?"

Jordan phoned another number.

"FBI Salt Lake City," the operator answered.

"This is Agent Jordan in Kansas City. Please connect me with Agent in Charge Lillian Ferguson. It's urgent."

69

Bill Miner
FBI Offices, Kansas City
2:15 PM

Sam Jordan, jaw clenched, eyes tense, returned to the conference room and strode to the front.

"Let me have your attention," he said. His voice boomed. All heads turned, and the room fell silent.

"Our suspect is in Buhl, Idaho, in position to strike his fifth victim."

What? Had I misheard? Victoria gasped in astonishment. Eyes around me widened. Necks bent forward.

"We've just received a credible phone tip." Jordan spoke in an even tone, but his face showed emotional strain.

The agent on my left pulled his glasses down, looked at Jordan over the rims, and in a dry tone said, "I take it that Hughes is not in Boise?"

"Her relocation did not go as planned," Jordan said.

I tilted my head back in disbelief and stared at the ceiling.

"Oh no," Victoria whispered, and put her hand on her heart.

Jordan held up his hands to quiet a crowd that had begun to buzz. "I've initiated operations to act on this latest information," he said. His voice became steady and confident. His eyes flashed intensity. "Salt Lake City and Portland offices will dispatch SWAT teams to Buhl. They'll be airborne within minutes. I'll join them with a team from here. Since Salt Lake's the closest, they'll converge on the suspect's location and wait until the rest of us arrive."

I felt agitated. Lane had outsmarted us. Someone in a seat behind me referenced a Hail Mary pass.

"The plans and assignments we discussed earlier are still in effect." Jordan's eyes darted around the audience. "This tip could be bogus. Lane may still be in Missouri." He turned to one of the agents. "Toscone, I'll need you and four of your SWAT team members to go with me."

Jordan came over to my chair. "I'd like you to come with us, Professor. I've got an FBI negotiator, but I need someone who understands Lane's religious agenda." There was wariness in his eyes. "We could end up with a barricade situation."

"Give me a second," I said. I took Victoria's arm, and we moved a few feet away. "Are you willing?"

"We were on our own," she said. "We traveled across the country, survived an explosion, fire, and smoke. At last we're armed with the full support of the FBI." Her voice was resolute. "Try and leave without me."

"OK, Agent Jordan," I said, "but Victoria and I are a package deal at this point."

Jordan nodded. "All right," he said. "Toscone, show Miner and Johnson where they need to go, and have your guys ready to board a van to the airport."

He thanked everyone for their cooperation and the meeting ended.

Minutes later we climbed into a van with Jordan, Agent George Toscone, four members of his SWAT team, Deputy Special Agent in Charge Collins, and Agent Reynolds, who was the FBI negotiator. We peeled out of the FBI garage.

We reached the Kansas City airport, and the van whisked the ten of us to an area reserved for cargo transports and proceeded onto the tarmac. We pulled up to an enormous, gunmetal-gray plane. Jordan saw my incredulous stare. "It's an Air Force C-130 Hercules," he said. "It's the military's tactical airlifter and general workhorse. More than we need, but a smaller aircraft isn't available on this short notice."

The SWAT team loaded its equipment. The wind whipped up, and rain began to fall as we climbed inside the cavernous cargo hold, ten feet wide and forty feet long. A diesel-like smell wafted in as trucks fueled the plane.

Our pilot, Major Liz Robinson—midthirties, medium height, attractive, with a reassuring, punchy air of confidence—stepped from the cockpit. She instructed us to belt ourselves in, pointing to the seats made of aluminum tubing and red nylon webbing that lined each side of the fuselage.

Noise from the auxiliary power unit required her to shout instructions. "All weapons should be unloaded. Once we're in the air, I'll tell you when you can get up and move around, but keep it to a minimum. We anticipate some major thunderstorms en route. There's no real lavatory on board, just a urinal and a crapper." She glanced toward Victoria. "Yeah, tell me about it."

"Good thing I passed on the tea at the meeting," Victoria said.

"Any questions?" Robinson asked. She paused a moment. "All right. We'll be airborne for three hours. After takeoff, someone will be around to take your beverage orders before the movie starts."

We all chuckled but turned quiet as the massive aircraft taxied to the runway and lumbered into a darkened, foreboding sky.

70

Bill Miner
Airborne En Route to Buhl, ID
4:00 PM

"I hope you're not counting on me to talk Lane out of his religious beliefs," I said in a loud voice over the fierce interior noise. Sam Jordan was strapped into the web seat along the wall to my left, Victoria to my right.

"If you can do that," Jordan said with the projection of a military officer, "the State Department can use you in the Middle East." A droll twist formed on his lips. "We don't know what we'll face from Lane. Your own assessment was he'll put up a fight." He tipped his head toward me. "If we're lucky enough to surround Lane, we'll do our best to take him alive. The fiasco with David Koresh in Waco forever changed the way we do business—the bureau now does everything in its power to forestall violence."

I nodded my awareness. The FBI wanted to reverse its tainted reputation as the adversary, erase the notion it was an agency steeped in a warrior mentality. "I get it," I said. "But I appreciate that if you're worried you won't make it home safe to your spouse and kids, it's hard to give a damn if you offend some cornered, armed suspect."

"That's the challenge," he said, "but we have trained negotiators, psychology experts, good listeners. Reynolds, over there, is all of those things, but he doesn't have the knowledge about religion that a guy like Lane may throw at us."

Victoria appeared lost in thought. My stomach churned as the plane lunged and careened in the punishing turbulence. The aircraft seemed to battle for every air mile.

"Empathy is the key when you try to talk someone out of a crisis situation," Jordan said, his tone philosophical. "And it's hard to show empathy if you can't understand what they're talking about. It may never come to this with Lane, but if it does, that's where you come in. Even when negotiations lengthen the standoff, even if they aren't successful, at least they buy time to better prepare for a tactical assault."

The paradox of power, I thought. It might be the difference between whether they would take him alive and I would have the chance to write about Lane's motivations or whether I would be left to speculate on his attraction to martyrdom.

We had traveled for some time when I looked out the window at the darkness of a storm that blocked out the sun with thick clouds.

Without warning, there was a deafening bang. My heart jumped to my throat. I thought a bomb had gone off. "What the—" The aircraft suffered a violent, spasmodic convulsion and slid hard to the right. I felt the tail drop, and the plane began to climb. Victoria's eyes turned heavenward. I clasped her hand. Goose bumps rose on my forearms.

"This doesn't feel like an emergency," she said. "It feels like a calamity."

A somber female voice came over the loudspeaker. "We've lost an engine, but we can fly with one shut down."

A moment later the flight engineer emerged from the cockpit and came toward us, pale and drawn. His face told me the situation was far worse than the pilot's announcement had made it sound. "Stay buckled in," he said, and returned to the flight deck.

71

Liz Robinson
Airborne
4:30 PM

Major Liz Robinson lunged forward and took the control wheel. "I have the airplane!" she said to her crew. The plane yawed to the left and continued to shake violently as it dipped and climbed, porpoised and rolled as much as twenty-five degrees to the left and right. Robinson struggled with the controls. "Secure that failed engine!"

The flight engineer wrestled with the throttle. "It won't go back!"

"Jesus," Robinson said. "Shut off its fuel supply."

The flight engineer yanked the fuel lever. "It won't move either," he said. "It's jammed."

Robinson grimaced. "We must have suffered some sort of structural damage." She had no idea what had happened, but she knew she faced something more serious than the loss of an engine.

It had been less than two minutes since the explosion, and events began to unfold at a terrifying pace. "I can't control the airplane," Robinson said. "Radio Denver Center!" she shouted to her navigator. "Tell them we just lost an engine and need to descend immediately."

The C-130 had stopped its climb and had begun to descend and roll to the right. Robinson used the control wheel to try to steer, but the aircraft wouldn't respond. She tried to turn the aircraft to the left and bring its nose up. The plane did the opposite.

"Can you drop the landing gear?" Robinson asked.

The flight engineer released the up lock, which allowed gravity's force to deploy the landing gear. That helped slow and stabilize the airplane.

As the plane continued to roll, Robinson grappled with the failed steering. "What's our location?" she asked her navigator.

"Seventy-five miles due east of Cheyenne, Wyoming. But, Liz, something bizarre is happening. My gauges show the pressure and quantity of hydraulic fluid is dropping."

The aircraft reached thirty-five degrees of bank and was in danger of rolling on its back. Robinson rammed the fuel throttle to the working engine on the right wing closed. She swatted open the throttles to the two engines on the left.

After a moment, the left wing slowly came back up.

The copilot became wide-eyed. "Where'd you learn that trick? Steering with the throttles?"

Robinson knew if the aircraft had rolled all the way over, they would have gone into a spiral, plummeting with such speed that the wings would have been torn off before the plane ever hit the ground.

"Liz!" the navigator said. "The gauges just fell to zero. We've lost all hydraulics."

72

Approach Controller
Cheyenne Regional Airport
4:40 PM

Denver Center had alerted Cheyenne Regional Airport that the crippled plane was coming: "C-130 Hercules, call sign H715 . . . lost an engine . . . having a hard time controlling the aircraft right now . . . trying to slow it down and get to Cheyenne . . . wants emergency equipment standing by."

The Cheyenne approach controller could see the C-130 on his radar screen with the plane's altitude and an identifying transponder code. "All right," he said to Denver Center, "I see her. I've got her."

"Cheyenne Approach, this is H715. We're out of twenty-three . . . heading right now is two-seven-zero . . . and we've got a four-hundred rate of descent." Liz Robinson had radioed that the plane was passing through twenty-three thousand feet, traveling west, and losing four hundred feet of altitude every minute.

The approach controller gave her a compass heading to reach the airport.

Robinson responded, "Situation is, we have almost no manageability . . . no hydraulics. . . . We're controlling the turns by power. . . . I can't turn left. . . . I think we can only make right turns."

"Understand, Major," the Cheyenne approach controller said. "You can only turn right. What about your backup system?"

"That's gone too."

The Cheyenne approach controller was young, in his first year as an air-traffic controller. He reminded himself that an airplane steers with rudders, just like a ship of the sea. In the case of a large aircraft like a C-130, the control surfaces are so large and the airflow so great that hydraulic power is needed to move them.

Hydraulic fluid, not fuel, his instructors had emphasized, is what keeps a plane flying. If a plane runs out of fuel, it can fly as a glider. Without hydraulics, Liz Robinson and her crew would have no way to extend flaps for landing. Even if they managed to land the aircraft, they had no brakes.

The controller watched the radar track and radioed Robinson to adjust her heading: "H715 . . . fly heading two-seven-two and say your souls on board." He was asking how many lives were at risk.

A moment passed. "Fourteen," Robinson answered. "I have doubts we can make the airport. . . . If I can't get control of this airplane . . . we're going to have to put it down . . . wherever that happens to be."

The approach controller's face grew more taut. H715, he realized, was going to crash.

73

Tim Lane
Buhl
4:45 PM

Tim Lane awoke in a darkened house with vivid memories lingering from a dream. In the dream, his wife and young son were around him, his parents too. They were on a family vacation in Hawaii.

Lane could see them, touch them. Everything was idyllic. It was everything a man could imagine having, everything as it should be.

He came fully awake and jumped to his feet, startled by the time on his watch. He rushed to a front window.

A car was parked in the driveway of the Hughes home across the street. He suppressed his exasperation that he had fallen asleep.

Get back on track, he told himself. Lane mentally rehearsed his plan and loaded a full magazine into his pistol. With self-instilled calmness, he stepped out onto the back porch.

He was two hundred feet from completing his mission.

74

Bill Miner
Airborne
4:50 PM

The SWAT team, fastened tightly in the seats of the C-130, knew we were in serious trouble. They were take-charge, battle-hardened men who liked to be in control, now abruptly and totally without it, sealed in this massive tin can that was undeniably beyond their dominion, hurtling out of control.

"I don't know how this is going to turn out," I said to Victoria. Her eyes fell on me, and the world grew still, as if I had entered a half-conscious state.

The turbulent pitch and roll, the plane's frantic rise and fall, the ceaseless, deafening vibration, all dissipated into a muted slow-motion blur.

She touched my arm tenderly. Poise and grace shone from every inch of her.

"I want you to know something," I said. "I don't regret one moment of this week, this time with you."

She smiled softly, and I could have fallen headfirst and completely into those eyes. Her hand found mine and grasped it. I squeezed her fingers, returning the message—whatever the outcome, we were in this together.

"I love you," I said.

"I love you too," she said.

75

Cheyenne Regional Airport
5:00 PM

Cheyenne Regional Airport had been placed on Alert Two status the minute word arrived that the disabled C-130 was on its way.

That had been bumped to Alert Three when Liz Robinson announced she might not reach the runway. Alert Three meant that a plane crash was imminent and signaled for the rapid notification of all available emergency equipment.

Sirens whooped. Dogs wailed. Fire trucks and ambulances from nearby communities converged on the airport. Vehicles with specialized apparatuses for spraying foam roared across the field to designated spots in readiness to extinguish burning aviation fuel.

Since the field was the home of an Air National Guard base, its equipment and the airport fire and rescue vehicles would be the first to take up positions. Emergency medical equipment and technicians parked on a ramp with immediate access to the runways. They would be among the first to respond, if the plane made it that far.

The young approach controller felt a sense of impending disaster. His chest pounded as he radioed H715: "Do you have the airport in sight?"

"Affirmative," Robinson replied.

"You're cleared for visual approach. All traffic's diverted out of the area. I'm switching you to tower control."

H715 ballooned above the horizon like a great whale in breach, moving toward the airfield readied with emergency equipment. The tower controller radioed Robinson: "Wind west-northwest at twenty knots with turbulent conditions. Runway twenty-seven is the longest. You're cleared to maneuver to whichever runway you think you can make."

The controller saw the plane was not floating the way aircraft ordinarily do on final approach. The thirty-eight-ton plane was barreling down the glide slope, dropping altitude like a giant meteor in slow motion.

As H715 approached the airfield, the right wing dipped. Turbulence continued to play havoc with the plane. "You're too far right," the controller radioed. "Go left, left, left."

Jesus! *She* can't *turn left.* Personnel recoiled from the windows as the enormous plane screamed by the tower.

The controller's heart raced as the plane made a series of right turns and circled back to the airfield. This would be their final chance.

Altitude fifteen feet—five feet. The aircraft slammed hard onto the runway. Its propellers roared in full reverse thrust.

The plane careened down the ninety-three-hundred-foot airstrip, veered off the end of the pavement, plowed across rough ground dragging a chain-link fence, and stopped short of a small lake.

Miraculously, H715 had not crashed.

It had *landed.*

76

Bill Miner
Cheyenne, WY
5:10 PM

My arms had not let go of Victoria since the words "Brace! Brace! Brace!" Now the command was "Move! Move! Move!"

We uncoiled like springs, dashed out the crew doors of the aircraft, and navigated across an acre of white foam.

At the edge of the airfield, I swooped Victoria to me. She lifted her face, and I kissed her. Her arms encircled my neck, and she pressed her lips tight to mine. We were exhilarated.

"Hey, keep moving!" a voice from behind hollered.

We resumed brisk strides. Victoria glanced at me. "Tell me that wasn't God!" she said.

"My kiss was *that* good?"

"The landing, silly," she said with a flirtatious grin.

"You suppose next time God might just redirect the storm track in the first place?"

Her fingers slipped between mine. "Then maybe I wouldn't have learned how you felt about me," she said.

"It took *that* for you to notice?"

She squeezed my hand. "And by the way, you *are* a good kisser," she said.

I floated the rest of the way into the terminal, where medics gave us a quick check-over. Moments later the place burst into cheers and applause as Liz Robinson and her crew came into the building. I talked with the navigator, then spoke to the pilot.

"You deserve a medal," I told her. "We've already got street signs named for you in Berkeley: 'No Left Turn.' "

Agent Sam Jordan said a few words to each of his team members, then turned to us. "We're going on to Buhl. After what's happened, I understand if you want to head straight back to the Bay Area. We can get you on a plane right away."

Victoria and I conferred. "I think this is aging me in dog years," I said, "but I'm OK to continue if you are."

She gave my hand another squeeze and, without releasing it, turned to Jordan. "My papa used to say, 'The Saint Louis Cardinals never give up.' "

Jordan gazed at her with esteem and respect. "I'd better tell you the whole story," he said. "The good news is that the Air National Guard has provided us with another plane—"

"It's another C-130," Victoria interrupted.

He nodded.

"OK," she said, letting out a breath, "but not until I find a bathroom."

***

The cause of the engine failure was eventually determined. A National Transportation Safety Board investigation found that a fatigue crack from an undetected metallurgical defect had caused high-speed metal fragments to hurl from the engine. The shrapnel had knocked out all three independent hydraulic systems.

77

Bill Miner
Airborne En Route to Buhl, ID
6:15 PM

Our replacement C-130 bounced lightly through clearing skies somewhere over western Wyoming. Agent Jordan answered his phone and sat straight up. He listened with earnest and eager attention, then gave the caller our ETA.

Jordan unbuckled his seat belt, stood, and spoke loud enough for everyone to hear.

"Salt Lake's SWAT team has secured the perimeter of the subject house across the street from Janie Hughes's home. Residents on either side have been evacuated." Jordan's eyes scanned our group. "A figure opened the back door and stepped out on the patio. He had what looked like a pistol. When an agent called out Tim Lane's name, the figure uttered a startled sound and ducked back inside."

Victoria's hands were clasped. I heard her mutter, "Please be him" under her breath. Would luck at last tip our way?

"No further movement has been observed," Jordan said. "The team will maintain a tight perimeter."

His mouth curved into a smile for the first time since we had boarded. "We've either cornered our suspect or just scared the living hell out of some poor homeless guy."

78

Bill Miner
Buhl
7:30 PM

Our aircraft engulfed the tiny runway of the Buhl Municipal Airport and came to a smooth stop. Charles Mitten, the round-faced, bushy-moustached police chief, met us with the words we wanted to hear—Janie Hughes was in safe custody. Mitten seemed like a down-to-earth law enforcement guy with an affable manner. The tone in his voice, however, conveyed genuine concern about the extraordinary events that had befallen his quiet town.

The setting sun cast a gentle glow across the adjacent farmlands as Mitten directed our group to a small hangar where we found members of the Portland SWAT team waiting for us.

A police cruiser pulled up in front, and a man popped out dressed in battle gear—ballistic vest, military-style helmet, black boots, and full camouflage uniform. He introduced himself as David Oliver, team leader of Salt Lake's unit, and asked which one of us was Agent Jordan.

There were now four police vehicles on the tarmac. I figured we must've commandeered the chief's entire fleet. I hoped some crook didn't know this—it was the perfect time to rob a town bank.

Oliver briefed us on the status of the operation: There had been no further contact with the suspect. They had maintained a tight perimeter around the house, had not initiated, or received, any communication from the person inside.

Several times they had seen a man's outline appear at various windows. "Probably checking to see if he was surrounded," Oliver said. "He knows we're there."

Jordan outlined his operations plan. He assigned several Kansas City SWAT agents to Oliver to reinforce his team. "We have the strong possibility of gunplay," Jordan said, "so I want all local residents evacuated and a roadblock set up to prevent anyone from driving into the neighborhood."

He asked Mitten if he could arrange for a shelter in a local school gym for those families who didn't have nearby relatives or friends they could stay with and told Portland's SWAT team they would be held in reserve to relieve others in the event this went into the next day.

"We hope we'll have a give-up situation," Jordan said. "But we want this guy, one way or the other." He glanced around for questions. There were none. "All right, let's move."

Victoria and I packed into a police van with Jordan, Collins, Reynolds, and Toscone. I felt like one of those reporters embedded with a military unit in the Middle East.

Seven minutes later we pulled up to Janie Hughes's home on Laburnum Lane. A command post had been set up in her garage across the street from Lane's location. Oliver deployed the additional agents now at his disposal. They moved into their assigned positions.

Collins and Toscone knocked on doors and informed remaining residents. The sky had turned a dark, dusky purple by the time they had finished.

Jordan took up a position in view of Lane's location and lifted a bullhorn to his mouth. I held my breath.

79

Bill Miner
Buhl
8:15 PM

Sam Jordan's amplified voice pierced the evening stillness of the small-town neighborhood like an army bugle call. "Tim Lane, this is the FBI. You are surrounded. There is no possibility of escape. Come out peacefully. You will not be harmed. I promise you will receive fair treatment."

There was no response. Victoria's eyes were as wide as mine. I felt as if we were in a scene from a movie. We watched as Jordan's initiative was repeated over the next fifteen minutes. Words varied, but the,message did not.

Dead silence followed each bid.

So much for the come-out-with-your-hands-up approach. Never seemed to work in the movies either. Or was it possible Lane wasn't there, that he'd somehow slipped out?

Jordan handed the bullhorn to Reynolds. "Tim, my name is Daniel," Reynolds said. The negotiator's voice was soft, friendly. "I just got here with the others and want to make sure you get out of this situation safe and sound." He waited for reaction. Nothing. "Tim, I'd like to know if you can hear me. If you can, would you give us some sign?" Again, there was no response. The silence bristled.

"There!" someone said. "The living room curtains. He pulled them halfway closed, then back open."

My pulse jumped. It didn't take much at that point.

"Tim," Reynolds called over the bullhorn, "when I ask you a question, if your answer is yes, pull the curtains once. If it's no, pull twice. Do you understand?"

All eyes were on the living room window. The curtains closed and opened once.

Reynolds glanced at Jordan and drew in a deep breath. He continued. "Tim, I'm aware you might have been wounded back in Missouri. Listen, we can get you some medical attention. But you need to come out for that."

The curtains closed and opened twice.

Reynolds appeared unfazed by the negative reply. "Tim, I want to hear your side of the story." He paused. "Tell me how this all came about."

Again, the curtains moved twice.

"If you come out Tim, I'll listen. You and I can talk."

Reynolds paused again. His silences seemed calculated to draw Lane into conversation. "You might like to have your message reach a wider audience," Reynolds said. "I can help you accomplish that. Does that appeal to you?"

The curtains closed and opened once, then a second time.

"No again," Jordan said. "This won't work." He rubbed the back of his neck. "We need to establish a two-way conversation. Ask if he'll let us give him a field telephone."

Reynolds made the request. The curtains closed and opened once.

"All right, good," Reynolds said over the bullhorn. "A man will bring a phone pack to the front and set it on the doorstep. Then he'll leave. That's all he'll do. Don't harm him, OK?"

The curtains closed and opened once in agreement.

A SWAT agent took the phone pack to the front porch, set it next to the door, and dashed back to his position. A minute later the door opened a crack. A hand reached out, grabbed the phone, and shut the door.

In a few minutes, voice contact was established. Reynolds put his receiver on speaker.

"Tim, this is Daniel. I want you to know we'll take whatever time is necessary to talk this through. I will listen. I just don't want you or anyone to get hurt."

"You need not worry about harm to me," Lane said. "I'm not afraid to die."

A shiver went through me. The first words from him. My heart drummed.

Reynolds muted his handset. "I'm going to take a risk," he said.

He unmuted the phone and spoke calmly. "You say you're not afraid to die. Well, if you're willing to give up your life, at least be clear about why."

I stood close to Reynolds, intent on hearing anything Lane said. The phone remained silent. We knew he could hear, but we couldn't tell if Reynolds's words were having any effect. For the next several minutes, Reynolds continued to probe with assurances that we wanted to hear Lane's viewpoint and that the safe and sound course was for him to come out.

All overtures were unsuccessful.

Reynolds muted the phone. "People who are cornered often fall into a kind of paralysis," he said, "so no decision becomes the de facto decision."

"Any ideas, Miner?" Jordan asked.

"Maybe one," I said.

He nodded to Reynolds, who unmuted the phone and spoke: "I have a friend I'd like you to talk to." He passed me the handset.

"Tim, my name's Bill. Tell me about the Dragon of God."

My words seemed to hang in the air. I waited a beat. "Sounds a little like Psalm 18," I said. More moments of silence, then Lane's voice.

"Psalm 18:8: 'Smoke went up from his nostrils, and devouring fire from his mouth; glowing coals flamed forth from him.' "

His tone sent an uncomfortable sensation down my spine.

"Yes," I said. "That verse conveys a powerful image of God's strength and judgment. It portrays God as a sort of dragon. Is that what the bracelet means, Tim?"

"How do you know about the bracelet?"

"We found it. In the Sierra, at Devil's Fall. Tell me about it."

"A symbol of God's armor as it is written in Ephesians," he said, his voice prideful. "It was given to me by an angel of the Lord. A reminder to stay the course against God's enemies." His words became defiant and seethed contempt. "Against deceitful forces that claim to have been in heavenly places."

I muted the phone. "Well, that removes any doubt about his motive," I said to Jordan. "All our victims claimed they learned about biblical misinterpretation from a heavenly light."

I unmuted the phone. "So, you believe the people you killed were God's enemies?"

"*God* saw them as his enemies!" Lane's voice was solemn.

"And that's according to your angel of the Lord?" I tried to remain matter-of-fact.

"The Messenger didn't need to tell me that. The Bible makes that clear. The Messenger merely conveyed that God had blessed me with the opportunity to take up the gauntlet."

"And you have complete trust in this messenger? The one who entrusted you with this sacred crusade? Who gave you a bracelet adorned with runic characters to symbolize divine inspiration?"

"Just as I have total faith and trust in the Lord," Lane said, his voice calm and steady. "He will come back very soon, you know."

"You refer to the Rapture, Tim?"

"You must be oblivious," he said. Contempt was back in his voice. "You ignore that it is imminent? The faithful will be caught up in the clouds to meet the Lord in the air."

I muted the phone and stared at Jordan.

Jordan stared back. "This is why I wanted you here," he said.

"Lane would have as much luck if he looked for a black cat in a coal mine," I grumbled, "because there *is* no cat. It's that ignorant belief Jesus will return to snatch the faithful, sweep the steadfast believers off to heaven, and leave everyone else behind. It's blatant, unadulterated modern-day marketing—until very recently, *no one*, throughout the history of the church, ever believed in the Rapture."

"Fine," Jordan said, "but come up with something to keep him talking."

I took in a deep breath and unmuted the phone. "Tim, the Bible is the story of a God who *stays* with his people through tough times, *carries* them over his shoulder when necessary . . . *walks* with them through the valley of the shadow of death. Right?"

The line was silent.

"Do you agree?" I was careful to make it sound less like a challenge than an inquiry.

"The faithful also have *God's* back," Lane said.

"That's admirable loyalty and devotion: God watches out for you. You watch out for God." I paused a moment. "But how do you reconcile this, Tim? The Bible teaches that God stands with the faithful. He doesn't pluck them out of a situation and whisk them away. Those who would have you believe in the Rapture don't recognize that the very concept of it contradicts Scripture. It's right there in the Bible. Jesus changed his message. Remember, Tim? He initially warned of an imminent apocalypse but later preached that it's not about what will happen *to* the planet. It's about how you live your life *on* it."

Lane shot back in a sarcastic and dismissive tone: "You must be unfamiliar with the book of Revelation."

"No, I'm very familiar with it," I said. "That book is a source of fascination for both of us. Let's talk about Revelation."

Several moments of silence. My hopes began to sink.

"Tim, you need to come out," I said. "Your strong faith should tell you God will stand with you."

That got a response, but not the one I wanted to hear.

80

Bill Miner
Buhl
8:45 PM

"I've written something I want you to give my wife," Lane said.

I glanced at Jordan. "This doesn't sound good," I murmured.

Jordan took the phone and said, "All right, put it on the doorstep." He radioed an agent on the perimeter, who retrieved the note and brought it to him.

Jordan studied the piece of paper. "It's a receipt for a gun purchase. Today's date. Well, we know what weapon he has. Enough to give us trouble. More than enough to do himself in." He flipped over the page to see Lane's message written in a poor scrawl indicative of his injured hand.

Jordan read the message out loud.

> My Dear Wife,
>
> I realized this may be the last day of my life when I had a dream. I saw you, our son, our parents, all here with me. Our happy memories. God is telling me my job is done. I wanted a better world. I tried to fight those who deny Jesus. You have always been the love of my life. A devoted mother to Noah. Do not mourn me. I will wait for thee in Paradise.
>
> Tim

Jordan reached for the phone. "Lane, we have your message, and we'll see it gets to her. However, it does not have to end this way. I reiterate, if you surrender, you will receive fair treatment."

It seemed an eternity before Lane responded. "I'm not coming out. Do what you have to do."

There was an audible sigh from the group. Jordan's face filled with exasperation.

Victoria stepped closer. "What if we brought his wife up here to talk with him?" she asked.

Jordan shook his head. "Getting family members involved can be risky. We don't know what she's like. For all we know, she might use the opportunity to encourage her husband to become the next Christian martyr."

The group fell silent.

"Let me try to talk to him," Victoria said.

Jordan handed her the phone. I saw an intensity that could have split wood develop in her eyes.

"Tim Lane, my name is Victoria Johnson. You know that your refusal to surrender means your certain death—suicide by cop—and maybe you think that will make for a martyr's death and therefore an honorable one. I am a follower of Jesus also. Let me tell you something, Tim Lane. Jesus would be *appalled* by what you have done—"

"Don't lecture me about Jesus," Lane snapped. "You've got it backwards. It's the blasphemy by his enemies. *That* is what appalls."

"So we're back to fighting God's enemies, are we? I suppose you can't kill innocent people without some claim to virtue, but that ranks you right up there with radical terrorists. You share that same illusion, do you? That martyrdom will grant you eternal reward?"

"It demonstrates to God that I'm not just about *this* life," Lane said.

"And you think that is your entitlement? To break God's most important commandment?"

"As did the Lord command Joshua."

Victoria muted the phone and turned to me. "Joshua?"

"He's referring to the book of Joshua," I said. "When Joshua entered the Promised Land with his army, the Lord hardened the hearts of the local citizens so they would refuse to make peace, necessitating that Joshua's army destroy them. In other words, God authorizes murder—even colludes—when it results in a higher good."

Victoria unmuted the phone. "Tim! Any such comparison makes your faith absurd and ridiculous!"

My stomach was in my throat. *So much for the soft and gentle approach.* Jordan ran a hand through his hair, his face taut. Victoria waited for any kind of response. There was none. Then the phone clicked.

"Damn," Jordan said and turned away.

"We haven't lost him yet," Victoria said. "Hand me that bullhorn."

She shouted into the mouthpiece: "Tim Lane, pick up the phone! It's about your family."

Seconds ticked. I watched Jordan pace. The expression on Victoria's face was intense but inscrutable. I decided this was not a woman I would ever play poker with.

I looked in Lane's direction. No signal, no movement, no sound. Then his voice answered on speakerphone.

"What *about* my family?"

Victoria continued as though there had been no interruption, her eyes ablaze.

"The wife you say is the love of your *life*? You will make her a widow and a single parent in one cruel stroke. Is that your idea of how to make a better world? It won't be better for *her*, Tim Lane."

"What do you know about family sacrifice?"

"I've lost both my parents. Let me tell you, the pain you will inflict on your wife will never leave her. Your actions right now aren't about family sacrifice. Your actions represent selfish, deluded self-glorification. And you have the audacity to imply you're doing this in the name of Jesus? You're not fooling me, and you sure as hell aren't fooling Jesus! You've made a huge mess. You can either make it worse, or you can reverse this situation and come out. If you truly want to contribute to a better world . . . to live another day to follow Christ . . . then end this theatrical standoff!"

Silence. I glanced at Reynolds, who was pacing like a restless hound. Victoria's direct, in-your-face style was not in accordance with the FBI's new school of nonconfrontational negotiations. I don't know if Reynolds was impressed. I sure was.

Finally, Lane spoke. His response was terse. "We're done here," he said. The phone clicked.

A shudder went through me.

81

Bill Miner
Buhl
9:15 PM

Jordan drew his palm across his forehead as he glanced around at our group of dispirited faces. "Any ideas? Anyone?"

"His kid's pretty young, isn't he?" I asked.

Jordan nodded. "A five-year-old. Noah."

Victoria cocked her head. "Let me give this one last shot."

"There's not much line left on the reel," Jordan said. "Not much more we can try." He handed her the bullhorn.

"One final thing, Tim Lane." Her voice radiated across the street. "Pick up the phone. There's something you need to know about your son, Noah."

A minute passed. It seemed like ten.

"What about my boy?" Lane asked.

"Do you think your son will grow up to believe his father was a brave soldier for Christ? I want you to know there's not a chance in the universe he'll think that. Just the opposite."

She waited for her words to register.

"A five-year-old will think it was something *he* did that caused his daddy to go away. He will think it was *his* fault—that he must be a very bad boy. Because his daddy never wanted to see him again."

Victoria paused for some reaction from Lane.

No response.

"How will that deform his personality?" she asked. "Quite a guilt trip to give young Noah."

The group was quiet, as if spellbound. A minute of silence passed. Then another.

"So, you're willing to abandon the love of your little boy," Victoria said. "Then maybe it's just as well you won't be around to see his tears. To hear his voice when he cries out, 'I'm sorry, Daddy! I *promise* to be good.' " She paused. "It's just as well you won't be around to see him grow up . . . forever asking . . . 'Why, Father? . . . Why did you forsake me?' "

We all stood dead still.

Victoria's eyes met mine. My heart and soul brimmed with admiration and awe. "You took my breath away," I said softly.

Jordan paced as minutes passed with no response from Lane. He looked around the group, his face grim. "I wanted to avoid this." He turned to his SWAT team leader.

But before he could say anything, Lane's voice crackled from over speakerphone: "All right."

Jordan took the phone. "We're listening," he said.

"I'm coming out."

Jordan radioed his agents, and it was all over in a matter of moments.

Lane was directed to set his gun down on the porch and to step away from it. Agents handcuffed him and whisked him toward a police cruiser.

Victoria was pretty merciless in her conversation with Lane—yelled at him about how selfish he was being and how cruel to the people he loved. In the end, she appealed to things he cared about. I was awestruck by her determination to save the life of the man who murdered her father. I'd felt little pity for Lane, but Victoria's decision to choose virtue over vengeance—as if forgiveness was the best way to stick it to your enemies—made me second-guess my own feelings.

"Perhaps it was divine intervention," Victoria said, "or just dumb luck."

Jordan's dark eyes traveled back and forth between the two of us. "No, it's because you're a helluva tag team."

"But we still don't know who Lane's accomplice is," Victoria said.

"She's right," I said. "His 'angel of the Lord,' veiled in symbols on a mystic bracelet. What do you want to bet even Lane doesn't know his identity?"

Victoria's eyes flashed as though a bell had chimed. She faced Jordan. "We need to talk to Lane right now, before any of this gets to the media. His accomplice will learn that Lane has been arrested, and he'll vanish. We'll have no way of finding him."

Victoria started toward the police cruiser that held Lane in its back seat. "Wait!" she shouted to the driver. We followed her across the yard as she came face-to-face with the man who had killed Oscar Johnson. Had it been me, I would have gone for the guy's throat, but Victoria kept her emotions in check. "Who is your messenger of God?" she said, her voice firm but matter-of-fact.

Lane turned away, silent.

"You don't want to betray him?" She waited for a response. "Well, don't worry. He's already beat you to it." Lane looked back with a dubious expression. "If there is to be any justice for you and your family, we need to know who that person is."

"He would not betray me."

"Want to bet?"

Victoria asked Jordan if he had the phone number of the caller who gave the tip. Jordan retrieved a slip of paper and held it up for Lane to see. Lane's expression turned from confusion to disbelief.

"That's the person who told us where to find you," Victoria said. "He set you up. He planned for you to die here."

Lane turned ashen, as if those words had dealt a mortal blow.

"I know him only by the name 'Cyrus,' " he muttered. "We never met in person. Our contact was by phone."

"When was the last time you communicated?" Jordan asked.

"This morning," Lane said. "I left him a phone message."

"When does he expect to hear from you again?"

"When my mission is complete."

"All right, that's all," Jordan said. We stepped away from the cruiser.

"His 'messenger' knows how to lay it on thick," I said. "In the book of Isaiah, Cyrus is the name of the king of Persia—the only non-Jew ever considered to be a messiah sent by God."

Victoria appeared not to be listening and turned to Jordan.

"Can we suppress the news of all this," she said, "that Lane is in custody?"

"What are you thinking?" he asked.

"Our one advantage. We know there's a 'Cyrus,' but we don't know who he is or where he is. Our chances of getting him may depend on the fact that he doesn't know we've got Lane."

"Go on."

"What if we could find a way to make Cyrus come to us?"

82

Bill Miner
Buhl
9:35 PM

As Victoria outlined her plan, Agent Jordan listened, nodding as if visualizing the necessary logistical arrangements.

"Clever idea if we can pull it off," he said. "I'll get everyone together and make sure they know all media reports go through me. Lane's capture will remain secret. Let's get people back to their homes. Tell them this was a false alarm, a case of mistaken identity."

Jordan turned to Chief Mitten and asked where they could keep Lane for the night.

"The county jail is in Twin Falls, twenty-five minutes from here," he said. "I'll notify them and send one of my officers with your agent."

"Book him under a false name or whatever you have to do," Jordan said. "Just keep it confidential. And don't fingerprint him, because that will reveal his identity."

Within five minutes the police cruiser carrying a handcuffed Lane, an FBI agent, and a Buhl police officer headed east toward Twin Falls.

The expression on Lane's face when he had learned Cyrus had betrayed his whereabouts stayed with me. I might have expected anger. Instead, I'd seen a man stunned and shaken to the core. In the years that I'd studied cults, I'd encountered cases of good people so desperate to lead their lives according to God's wishes that they became easy prey for manipulation. They may have talked about committing horrific acts to show the strength of their faith, but it was rare for anyone to follow through. This was exceptional. So was Victoria's performance. Never had I seen illusions of a man like Lane's more eloquently disintegrated than by Victoria's cogent argument.

As Jordan finished debriefing his agents, a police car pulled up. A woman stepped out and stared at the front yard filled with SWAT officers. Chief Mitten brought her over to us.

"Mrs. Hughes," the chief said, "I'd like you to meet some of the people who've labored on your behalf."

The attractive woman in her late fifties smiled at Jordan. "I'm still in one piece, thanks to you. I am indebted." She turned to Victoria and me. "And to the two of you!"

Her expression was warm and radiated an inner glow. She appeared to make an instant connection with Victoria. I sensed there was something else in Mrs. Hughes's eyes, the kind of gaze that results from your memory registering a link.

"It's late," Mrs. Hughes said. "Do you have a place to stay tonight?"

"We haven't thought that far ahead," Victoria said. "It's been rather moment to moment."

"I can never repay you for saving my life, but at least let me offer you accommodations. Please stay with me. I'd appreciate not being alone after all this."

"What about you and your guys?" I asked Jordan.

"Our SWAT teams will leave tonight. We'll switch planes with them. Collins, Reynolds, Toscone, and I will stay in town. It's fine if you want to stay with Mrs. Hughes. You'll need to be at the airport at eight thirty tomorrow morning."

We exchanged thanks and said good night. Victoria and I followed Mrs. Hughes into her home. A brief time later we were seated at the dining room table with chicken sandwiches, potato salad, and coffee.

"I don't know the details," Mrs. Hughes said, "but Charlie Mitten told me the man who tried to attack me was the one who killed your father." She reached over and touched Victoria's arm. "I'm so sorry for your loss." Earnest emotion welled up in Mrs. Hughes's eyes.

"Thank you," Victoria said.

"When Agent Jordan called to warn me," Mrs. Hughes said, "it seemed surreal. To my regret, I was foolish and put people at risk. Thanks to you, it's over."

"Not entirely," I said. "There's someone else, a possible mastermind."

Mrs. Hughes sat back. "Another person may still come after me?" She pinched the skin at her throat.

"Doubtful," I said. "If he were intent on that, he wouldn't have tipped the FBI to Lane's whereabouts. He wanted Lane dead in a shootout with the FBI to erase any possible connection to him."

"Tomorrow we go home to the Bay Area and find out how good we are at setting a trap," Victoria said. "Lane is our bait."

Mrs. Hughes's eyes grew wide. "This sounds like a plot out of an Agatha Christie whodunit."

"No mystery about this potato salad," I said. "Best I've ever had."

"My mother's recipe. Just eggs, onion, mayo, salt, pepper, and our local potatoes. Glad you like it, but Buhl can't match the Bay Area when it comes to tasty food. My husband and I were there three months ago. It was to be my dream vacation. My sweetheart isn't keen on big cities, but a ride on a cable car and a walk across the Golden Gate Bridge were always on my bucket list, so he took me."

"We sometimes take those attractions for granted," Victoria said. "Hope you had a good time."

"Unfortunately, all didn't go according to plan," Mrs. Hughes said. "The first morning in San Francisco, I woke up with bad chest pains. I insisted it was nothing, anxious to see the sights. But I'd never had anything like that, and my husband said, 'Oh no, we're seeing a doctor first.' We spent our entire vacation at the hospital."

"Everything OK now?" Victoria asked.

"Yes, but the close call scared me. My San Francisco surgeon said she'd like to see me again, but I've had to settle for post-op checkups here because another trip to San Francisco isn't in our budget."

Victoria tapped her fingers on the table and shot a glance at me. I sensed wheels spinning. She excused herself, stepped into the next room, then returned three minutes later after placing a call.

"Mrs. Hughes, do you think you could arrange a drop-in appointment with your surgeon tomorrow?" Victoria asked. Our host sat back in her chair with a puzzled expression. "If so, I think we can offer you a pretty attractive travel package."

83

Bill Miner
Buhl
Day 9, 6:30 AM

I awoke to the smell of fresh coffee and bacon. Sleeping on a lump or two in a living room sofa bed had been nonetheless superior to the previous nights attached to an IV. Victoria had slept in the guest room.

At eight fifteen a neighbor drove Mrs. Hughes, Victoria, and me to the Buhl airport, where we met up with Jordan. Lane was handcuffed to Collins.

Jordan gave Victoria and me an update while the others boarded the plane. "The medical center administrator was a tough sell, but we worked it out," Jordan said. "Agents from San Francisco will be at the hospital by the time our plane arrives at Buchanan Field."

The Cessna turboprop that would take us home was as different from the C-130 as a sports car is from an eighteen-wheeler. The passenger section had three rows with two seats in the first two and three seats across the back row.

I told Jordan I wanted to talk with Lane, and Jordan suggested I take the back row where Lane would sit handcuffed to Collins. Victoria sat with Mrs. Hughes two rows up, and the two fell into comfortable conversation. I expected my exchange with Lane would be less agreeable.

The pilot stepped out of the cockpit and gave us the perfunctory instructions about the plane. First class—on this plane we had a bathroom, with a door.

"It's a three-hour flight," he said. "With the time change, we should touch down around ten thirty."

Moments later we were airborne, and my mind turned to what I wanted to find out from the man slumped in the center seat with the expression of a football player who had dropped the pass that cost his team a victory.

"We share one thing," I said to Lane. "We both spend a lot of time with the Bible."

He raised his head. "Well, there aren't enough people who do that. There isn't a single fact about God's will for mankind that can't be learned from the Bible."

"As someone so devoted to a savior who taught his followers to turn the other cheek, what brought you to this point? To the point where you had to fight?"

"This country was founded on Christianity, but you wouldn't know it from the way our government is determined to take God out of our lives. God, the *creator* of all life!"

Lane gave me a pained stare and rubbed his handcuffed wrist. "Liberals in black robes take away the rights of Christians." His face tightened, lips pressed together. "Two thousand years ago, someone died on a cross!" he blurted. "Someone needed to take a stand for him."

Collins rolled his eyes. I nodded to Lane to convey I understood his viewpoint. I didn't want to draw him into a debate about the separation of church and state. That would have been futile.

What I desired to understand was what had made a family man, with no criminal history, turn so violent. Jordan had told me Lane had been in public service, so I asked him about that.

"You were on a school board in the East, weren't you? That means we're both involved in education."

"Yeah, well, that was one of the most frustrating things I've ever done." He uttered a disgusted snort. "We worked long and hard to promote critical thinking in our classrooms, improve science education. Instead of appreciating it, the teachers resisted, and the courts fought us. It wasn't about the merits of a sound education. It was all politics."

"I can relate to being on the receiving end of politics." I tried to sound as empathetic as possible.

"We wanted to inform our children that evolution is a theory, not a fact," Lane said, "but lawyers claimed that to give students a choice was a violation of the establishment clause." He shook his head in disdain. "Incredible."

Lane's free hand made a gesture of appeal. "This country wasn't founded by Muslims," he said. "It wasn't founded on Hindu beliefs. And it sure as hell wasn't founded on evolution. No, this country was founded on Christianity, and our students deserve to be taught as such."

"What happened?" I asked.

"We went to court to prove that the school textbook in use at the time wasn't balanced. We wanted our students to know that Darwin's theory is still being tested. There're gaps in it . . . gaps that science can't explain."

His words seemed ingenuous, and I began to see where this was headed.

"We wanted to introduce a supplementary textbook," he said, "one that would give another explanation for the origin of life, another scientific theory different from Darwin's view." His expression revealed a childlike bewilderment that anyone could object to what his school board had done. "I mean, it's inexcusable to have a book that says man descended from *apes* with nothing to counterbalance it."

The realization hit me.

"Dover, Pennsylvania? You were on the school board in the *Kitzmiller* case?"

Lane's eyes turned wary, as though I'd just opened a closet door and exposed a family skeleton.

"I do know about that," I said. I bit my tongue, determined not to say anything that might add to the ridicule he had experienced in the court case. "You wanted your science classes to teach an alternative theory to evolution, but the courts ruled against you." I spoke in a nonjudgmental, matter-of-fact tone. Lane gave a cautious nod.

The *Kitzmiller v. Dover Area School District* trial had attracted national attention. The truth of the matter was that the Dover school board had forced their science classes to adopt *Of Pandas and People*, a textbook that said biological origins weren't due to evolution but were brought about by the actions of an intelligent agent—in other words, by God. Teachers objected to the pseudoscience, and parents didn't want religion brought into the classroom.

"We were dedicated public servants," Lane said, "trying to serve children's best interests. My wife and I had wanted to start a family, but what kind of education lay ahead for our future kids? I wanted to do something, now."

The verdict had been a crushing setback for the Dover school board. A federal judge had ruled that the new textbook was a ruse—intelligent design was identical to creationism and, therefore, unconstitutional to teach in American public schools.

"The courts belittled us," Lane said with bitterness. "I'll never forget that."

There had been plenty of evidence of the school board's subterfuge. The greatest embarrassment had been proof that the publisher had merely taken a textbook that the courts had previously rejected, made a superficial change, and claimed it was new.

"We tried to do the best for our community," Lane said, "but the court turned the townspeople against us."

Indeed, most of those school board members had been voted out of office.

"In the aftermath," Lane continued, "I felt so alienated. I couldn't stay in the community. We moved to the Bay Area and made a fresh start." He sucked his cheeks in. "I've learned a lot since my naïve years on the school board: You can't change the system from within. You're no match for a biased judicial system, for judges who battle Christianity. It's one of the most unjust wars ever fought in the history of our country."

"Did things get better after you and your wife moved to California?" I asked.

"For a while." His eyes shifted past me to the view out the aircraft window. "Especially when our son was born. But I began to worry about the kind of faithless world our son would inherit. A day didn't pass that I didn't imagine the horrible judgment God was making on America."

"So, when did you perceive that God reached out to you with a messenger?"

"Our church teaches us to recognize God's voice. There were several days in a row when I sensed that God was urging me to action. I prayed to him, asked what I could do. A few weeks later, his answer came to me—a phone call—from an angel of the Lord, a messenger named Cyrus."

I reflected on Mitch Albom's best seller about phone calls from heaven—*How easy it is to believe what you want to believe.*

"Cyrus said God had chosen me," Lane said. "Chosen *me* to serve in a one-man holy legion—a legion to protect the faith, a defender for Christ, a Dragon of God."

"How did you get the bracelet?"

"The Messenger said a silver amulet would materialize to me. The next morning, it appeared."

Lane's eyes widened as though he was reliving the experience. "I found it glittering in the sunlight on a branch of a dogwood tree in our front yard." His voice became reverent. "The symbolism left me in awe because the Cross of Jesus was made of dogwood. Did you know that?"

I nodded in acknowledgment. I didn't want to dispute this popular legend, though it's implausible when you consider the typical size of a dogwood tree.

"Cyrus told me I could help take back this nation for Jesus, for whoever stands with the Savior will rule with him."

"So, you were directed by Cyrus to commit murder?"

He looked down. "I prayed over that, but Cyrus left no doubt. God identified those people as Satan's ministers of light who would obstruct Christ's work of salvation."

"So, you felt you were doing God's work even though it meant violating God's commandments."

"Wouldn't you?" he said. He stared at me as though the answer should have been plain. "If God had asked me to sacrifice my own son . . ." He leaned back and squeezed the armrest. "I pray that, like Abraham, I would have had the courage to do so."

"Did you ever question if you had crossed the line?" I asked.

"Well, if people aren't willing to cross the line to defend God, it'll be the end of Christianity in America."

84

Bill Miner
Concord, CA
10:30 AM

Mount Diablo, a 3,848-foot peak visible from many parts of the Bay Area, loomed under an azure, white-streaked sky as our turboprop approached Concord's Buchanan Field. Now rather quiet, Buchanan once logged more takeoffs and landings than San Francisco or LaGuardia, until noise became a concern, and restrictions were placed on aircraft operation.

Two FBI vans from the San Francisco office whizzed out to the tarmac. Jordan and three agents took Lane in the first vehicle. Janie Hughes, Victoria, and I climbed into the second, and our caravan headed to John Muir Health in Walnut Creek, the area's designated trauma center hospital.

"I feel the weight of this plan on my shoulders," Victoria said.

I put my arm around her. "You came up with a great idea," I said.

Victoria's plan was ingenious: Tim Lane would be staged as a hospital patient after a "near-fatal highway accident" that occurred as he returned from Buhl. Lane would be "expected to make a full recovery." If Cyrus wanted Lane dead, we hoped this setup would lure him out to finish the job. Of course, Cyrus would need to be alerted. That little piece of finesse would fall to Victoria. She had a plan for that too.

We followed the first van along Oak Grove Road. A school bus pulled out from Ygnacio Valley High School and stopped, blocking us. My imagination leaped into overdrive. Was this like a movie scene where a vehicle blocks police, and the prisoner breaks free from his captors?

A moment later the bus pulled forward, and we caught up. I slumped back in my seat. I needed some sleep.

Victoria turned cheerful. "Mrs. Hughes and I had a wonderful conversation on the flight."

I felt a pang of discontent about this new rival for Victoria's attention—Mrs. Hughes had slid into the spotlight with ease and success.

"She called her surgeon during the flight and arranged to see her later today," Victoria said. "Mrs. Hughes wants me to come with her to the appointment to hear firsthand about her experience. She thinks it'll help me."

I frowned. "Help you with what?" I fidgeted and tapped my foot. Was our relationship eroding?

"To find resolution . . . about Papa."

"Professor, why don't you come along too?" Mrs. Hughes said. "I think you'll be astonished. That's how the CBS producer described it."

I started to feel like the third wheel.

"Please, come with us," Victoria said.

I didn't want to sound eager, but I didn't want to be left out.

"I guess once the stage is set, the rest will be up to the FBI," I said. "I'll tell Jordan that the three of us will drive into San Francisco and return to John Muir afterward."

Victoria planted a kiss on my cheek. My irritation eased.

A moment later our vans arrived at the medical center and circled behind the large facility to a service entrance in the rear. Tim Lane, under tight escort, was ushered into the hospital and to a sixth-floor room isolated from other patients, a location the FBI had negotiated with the administrator.

Lane, so far, had been cooperative. However, Jordan had told me at the Buhl airport that the FBI would take no chances. They'd assured the hospital staff that Lane would be incapable of any physical movement whatsoever. He would appear to be an immobile patient connected to medical monitors and IV, but dressings, bandages, and bed linens would conceal that Lane would be tied and bound to the bed. Traction braces would keep even his arms stationary, and he would be under continual surveillance.

It took an hour or so to stage the room. Sam Jordan, Daniel Reynolds, and George Toscone, dressed in scrubs, would be posted at a nearby nurse's station. From there they would observe Lane via a video monitor. Matt Collins would be stationed at the visitor reception desk in the lobby, dressed as a volunteer.

The final touch was entering Tim Lane's name in the hospital's patient census.

When all arrangements for the trap were complete, it was time for Victoria's performance. We went with Jordan to the administrator's office to use a hospital phone for the call that would cock the trigger.

Victoria studied notes she had made, lifted the phone, and dialed the number of the person we knew as Cyrus. No one breathed as a recorded voice directed the caller to leave a message.

"This is a nurse at John Muir Health in Walnut Creek." Victoria spoke in a low, taut voice to give the impression she didn't want her call to be overheard. "Tim Lane begged me to call this number for him. I could get in a lot of trouble for telling you this, but he's been badly injured in an automobile accident. He muttered something about a messenger and a dragon, but he has drifted in and out of consciousness, and I didn't understand. I'm not supposed to divulge patient information, but he seems so kind and sincere. We expect him to make a full recovery. Sorry, that's as much as I can tell you. I have to go now."

Victoria hung up the phone and let out a breath.

"I'd sure bite on that," I said.

Jordan glanced at his watch. "It is twelve thirty. Visiting hours end at nine. That gives us just eight and a half hours to find out if *he* does." He faced the administrator. "You've bent over backwards to cooperate with us. We'll honor our agreement. I promise we'll wrap this up tonight, Cyrus or no Cyrus."

85

Bill Miner
Pleasant Hill
1:00 PM

"How many gardeners do you have?" I asked as I stared at Victoria's front yard, which overflowed with roses.

"Just one—and you're looking at her," Victoria said.

An FBI agent had just driven Mrs. Hughes and us to Pleasant Hill. "I didn't notice all this when I dropped you off after Bridgeport," I said.

"I love the pink climber on the porch," Mrs. Hughes said. "Is that 'Eden'?" Victoria nodded. "And your azaleas, maples, and dogwoods!"

"My therapy," Victoria said.

Mrs. Hughes bent to smell a rose. "Mine too, but we don't have a growing season like yours. And look at your zauschneria. I'll bet you draw a ton of hummingbirds." Victoria beamed.

Just great, I thought as I grabbed Mrs. Hughes's suitcase out of the car and put it on the porch. *One* more *thing these two have in common about which I know zip.*

"I want to check inside to make sure everything is OK," Victoria said. "Then we'll be off." A minute later, car keys in hand, she asked Mrs. Hughes, "Are you hungry? You can't come to California without a stop at In-N-Out."

Thirty minutes later, munching burgers and fries, we headed westbound on Route 24 toward San Francisco on our way to the UCSF Medical Center.

"I can give you the background," Mrs. Hughes said, "but there's a reason I want you to hear the technical details from my surgeon, in person."

"It must have been pretty serious," Victoria said.

"Enough to eclipse my dream vacation—I woke up with chest pain on our first morning! Thank goodness my husband insisted I get medical attention. Hotel Nikko sent me to the ER at Saint Francis Memorial Hospital, eight blocks away. An EKG showed it wasn't a heart attack. I was relieved. 'See!' I told my husband. 'Come on. Let's go to Chinatown.' "

"Then what was it?" Victoria asked.

"The doctor didn't know, but something concerned him, and he wanted to do further evaluation. I thought, *I'm fine, no heart attack. I don't want any more tests.* But my husband was adamant."

"A smart precaution," Victoria said.

"They gave me a CT scan, and I *did* have a problem—a tear in a large artery from my heart. The diagnosis was aortic dissection."

"What does one do to tear an artery?" I asked. "Gardening, no doubt."

Mrs. Hughes chuckled. "I have high blood pressure, and they think that may have precipitated it. The next shock came when the doctor told me I could die if I didn't have immediate surgery. They notified UCSF, and within minutes I was headed there. I had looked forward to touring your beautiful city by cable car. Instead, it was by ambulance—" Mrs. Hughes stopped abruptly. "Is this your normal traffic?" she asked, staring ahead. We had just entered the MacArthur Maze near the east end of the Bay Bridge.

"This is a good day," Victoria said. She pulled past a pickup and navigated into a FasTrak lane. "You must have been terrified by that diagnosis."

"I was shaking, but it all happened so fast I had little time to think about it. I later learned that forty percent of patients with my condition die before they ever reach the hospital. Bless my dear husband for insisting on those tests. That saved my life.

"But what happened in surgery forever changed it."

86

Bill Miner
UCSF Medical Center, San Francisco
3:00 PM

I admit—I was jealous Victoria's attention was now absorbed by this woman. And I'd seen enough of hospitals to last me a good long time.

We pulled into the UCSF parking garage and walked up Parnassus Avenue to the cardiothoracic surgery clinic. We waited but a few minutes before a petite woman in a white coat greeted us.

Mrs. Hughes gave her surgeon a hug and introduced us to Dr. Ginette Ojha. I'd expected a heart surgeon, who often held life in his or her hands, to be a solemn, humorless individual, not an attractive woman with smooth autumn-russet skin, dimpled cheeks, and a radiant smile that lit up the waiting room.

"Mrs. Hughes is a very remarkable patient," the doctor said. "I want to examine her, and then you can join us in my office."

Fifteen minutes later a clinic assistant called us, and we followed her down a hall, past the exam rooms, to the surgeon's office.

"It's great to see her look so good," Dr. Ojha said as we sat down in front of her desk. "Mrs. Hughes asked me to share the details of her procedure. The operation was complex, but Mrs. Hughes's case is extraordinary."

Dr. Ojha's face glowed. The mutual trust and admiration between doctor and patient was obvious.

"She was very ill when she came to us—and, I might add, just in the nick of time. Her condition required a radical surgical procedure that involved deep hypothermic circulatory arrest. It was her best hope of survival."

"I was terrified," Mrs. Hughes said, "but sooner or later you have to get ahold of yourself and do what's necessary."

"Hypothermic . . . that means you stopped her heart and cooled her blood," Victoria said.

"Yes. We lowered her body temperature to sixty-four degrees and halted her respiration and heartbeat."

"Like forced hibernation?" I asked.

Dr. Ojha nodded. "It's similar. If blood flow were stopped at normal body temperature, permanent brain damage would occur in three to four minutes. But we had to stop the heart because it's difficult to operate on an aorta while the heart is beating."

Dr. Ojha smiled at her patient, then glanced back to Victoria and me. "Mrs. Hughes remained in that condition for a full hour while I repaired the tear."

"I had just one thought when they prepared me for the surgery," Mrs. Hughes said. "Please don't let this be the only time I visit San Francisco."

Victoria seemed absorbed. I wasn't. The specifics seemed a blur of medical jargon concerning the walls of the aorta, achieving just the right level of oxygen consumption, and the number of special instruments involved. I heard something about her eyes being taped shut.

"You're a little pale," Dr. Ojha said to me.

The sparkle in her eyes and easygoing manner belied the drastic nature and high danger of what she was describing to us in excruciating detail. The outcome had plainly been successful—I sat next to the recovered patient. Why did I feel a shiver?

"If this sounds like an incredible procedure," Dr. Ojha said, "it's because it was pioneered by the renowned cardiovascular surgeon, Dr. Michael DeBakey."

"The last thing I remember," Mrs. Hughes said, "is the pre-op room. After that, nothing . . . until I felt a tingling in my chest, and I just sort of popped out of myself.

"I stared down at my body. I knew it was me, but I felt sort of indifferent. I floated above Dr. Ojha and the others. I saw a scalpel in Dr. Ojha's hand and could hear her conversation with another doctor about albumin and Dacron, and I wondered if they were using egg whites and fishing line."

"At that stage of the operation," Dr. Ojha said, "a patient is under deep anesthesia, unable to see, feel, or hear anything. It's inconceivable that Mrs. Hughes could have exhibited any normal senses whatsoever. Inexplicably, what she heard was correct. I did discuss the grafts we used to repair her aorta. The material is albumin coated and is made of knitted Dacron."

Victoria had an expression of wonder. In contrast, my breath was about to stall.

"I felt a presence," Mrs. Hughes said, "and turned around to look. That's when I saw a tiny pinpoint of light, and it started to pull me." She paused. Her face tightened. "I know what you're thinking, but it's true."

"Oh no, we're with you," I said. "We've heard enough near-death accounts this week to qualify for continuing education credits for becoming a paranormal investigator."

"Good," Mrs. Hughes said, "because after you hear this, you'll have earned your certificate." She gave a soft smile, then became serious. "There was a physical sensation, sort of like going over a hill real fast, and I went toward the light. As I got closer, I began to discern different figures, different people. Some were headed in the same direction I went. Others traveled the opposite way."

Mrs. Hughes's description was familiar all right. What I felt nervous about was whether we'd hear anything else that would assault Victoria's religious faith.

"I heard my Aunt Pearl call out to me," Mrs. Hughes said. "Her distinctive voice—clear, light, and pleasant—was full of the same love she had always shown to me in life. I went to her, breathless, overwhelmed with emotion. I asked if the light was God. The question amused her. 'No,' she said, 'but you could think of it as the breath of God.' And I thought, *Oh! . . . I'm breathing God's air.*"

Victoria reached over and intertwined her fingers with mine.

"An absolute sensation of awe swept over me," Mrs. Hughes said. "Everything was beyond what I could have imagined . . . yet at the same time, familiar, as if I'd always known of its existence, as if I'd been there before . . . as if I'd come home.

"The light itself was a being, and it spoke to me: What had I gained in self-knowledge?

"My life was projected before me on a vast canvas. Oh, the range of emotions that swept over me, from childhood to the present: fear, pain, joy, shame, anger. And how others, whose lives I'd touched, had been affected.

"The being of light had shown me my entire life, yet it loved me still. 'I've made so many mistakes,' I said.

" 'But you were walking in the right direction,' the light answered.

"I didn't feel a sword of judgment over my head. Never once did the light condemn me. Instead, it helped me understand what I'd learned in life, assessed my strengths and weaknesses.

"Then, a realization struck me with a jolt: lessons learned . . . lessons I hadn't learned . . . the sense I'd been here before . . . those figures traveling in the reverse direction . . . Did that mean . . . ?

"The light knew my thoughts almost before they formed. 'Yes,' it said. 'Before you were Janie Hughes, you were Kathy Christen of Wabash, Indiana, a young girl who died in 1955.' "

Mrs. Hughes's words struck me like the snap of a wet bath towel. "What?" I blurted out. Had I heard her correctly? *Is she talking about reincarnation?*

Victoria's mouth dropped open, incredulous. "You were told of a previous *life*?"

Mrs. Hughes held up a hand. "I know this makes it sound like I've gone around the bend," she said. Her voice was calm, her words straightforward, unembellished. "Please hear me out."

She continued: "I asked the light if this meant I have a soul.

"It said, 'You *are* a soul. You *have* a body.'

"Then, I saw a seven-year-old, at play in her backyard on a spring day. Fuzzy memories came into focus. It was *me.* I could hear sparrows and cardinals singing in the woods behind our house. I lay in the grass and imagined the clouds were giant puffs of cotton candy. A dragonfly zipped back and forth like Tinker Bell."

Mrs. Hughes's loquacious, childlike tone was beguiling as she spoke of herself in the first person, in the voice of a little girl.

"I knew I wasn't supposed to leave the yard, but the train whistle called to me. Wild flowers would be blooming in the field on the other side of our fence. A cardinal might have left me a feather. I hated that dumb old rickety fence. It made me a prisoner like Rapunzel.

"If I climbed over, Mother would give me a spanking. . . . I decided it would be worth it. I scooted a picnic bench next to the fence, stood on it, and pulled myself up. I was halfway over. Then my pant leg got caught. I twisted hard to get loose. That's when the whole fence crashed down on me. I landed in all the rotten boards and jaggy nails. One went through my hand, and I screamed."

Victoria winced. I expected Mrs. Hughes would say it was all a nightmare. Nevertheless, I felt a chill between my shoulder blades.

"Neighbors heard me crying. They pulled me from the pile and said Mother needed to take me to the hospital. Mother told them we didn't believe in doctors. Prayer would heal. God would make my hand better if I prayed really hard.

"But I didn't get better. Mother said my fever would go away, but my jaw hurt so much I couldn't talk. My arms and legs got stiff, and I had trouble breathing. Other women from the church came to our house to pray for me, but all I wanted was Daddy to come back from his business trip."

Mrs. Hughes paused. The recollection of tragedy was obvious in her eyes.

"The last thing I remember," she said, "was my mother on her knees at my bed and Daddy very scared as he came home just minutes before I died."

Victoria swallowed. "Tetanus vaccine," she murmured more to herself than to me, "available since the 1940s."

I crossed my arms to constrain a shudder in my chest. You would think that if a person were to fantasize they were someone in another life, they would pick Cleopatra or Joan of Arc or Jane Austen, not an ordinary little girl in a small, everyday town suffering an unglamorous fate.

Mrs. Hughes nodded at our solemn expressions and was silent for several moments.

"The light comforted me for a time," she said. "But then it told me I couldn't stay. I would have to return. Before I went back, however, the light spoke of the future. I'd already gotten a powerful sense that ordinary time boundaries didn't exist there, and as the light conveyed that notion, a figure of a man appeared. I didn't know him but perceived he was someone special.

"With a gentle kindness in his eyes, he asked if I might do him a favor: Would I purchase something as a gift for someone? He gave me a description of the item and where to find it. He said I would know, when the time came, for whom it was intended.

"In a blink, I was back in the hospital—thankful but overwhelmed. I had to find out about Kathy. I thought the gift was somehow associated with her.

"As soon as I could talk, I gave my husband the directions I'd received and asked him to go to the designated place, which was an antique store. He had no trouble. It was close to the medical center."

Mrs. Hughes's story had my attention all right, but I scratched my jaw. To stumble across an antique store in San Francisco is about as difficult as it is to find a crab cocktail in Fisherman's Wharf. So what was this mystical quest about?

"As it turned out," she said, "the gift had nothing to do with Kathy, and in the weeks that followed, I put it out of my mind"—she turned toward Victoria—"until I saw you last night." Mrs. Hughes reached into her purse for a small jewelry box and handed it to Victoria.

"*Me?*" Victoria straightened in utter surprise.

"It's the reason I wanted you to hear the whole story."

Victoria opened the lid and froze. Her chin began to tremble, and a tear rolled down her cheek. Her eyes, in disbelief, rose to Mrs. Hughes, then went back to the box. Victoria's fingers lifted an elegant vintage brooch, decorated with a blue, green, and gold enamel butterfly.

Mrs. Hughes put her hand on Victoria's. "He said . . . it was so you wouldn't forget him."

"*Papa?*"

Victoria dissolved into a chandelier of tears. I dug for a tissue, but Mrs. Hughes encircled Victoria in her arms before I could come up with one.

The two separated enough to peer into each other's eyes. "That's why I know," Mrs. Hughes said, "you will see him again."

Total strangers less than twenty-four hours ago, they were now like mother and daughter. I felt chagrin I had resented their quick bond.

She had just given Victoria a priceless gift—hope.

87

Bill Miner
UCSF Medical Center, San Francisco
3:45 PM

"I didn't know about the brooch," Dr. Ojha said as she handed Victoria more tissues. "Your story had already topped the charts."

"My husband and I are forever indebted to this hospital," Mrs. Hughes said, "and to the dear doctor who saved my life."

"I can't take all the credit," Dr. Ojha said. "We have a slogan for difficult cases like this: better lucky than good. We're thankful you got here in time."

Victoria's face glistened, part, I think, from tears, part as if a light shone within. How I missed that power of belief. Miracle surgery, granted. But reincarnation? How could anyone be OK with *that* concept? I knew a scientist like Victoria wouldn't be—once she came down from cloud nine.

"Dr. Ojha," I said, "what's your take on this? Mrs. Hughes's recollection of a prior life."

"The remarkable feature," the surgeon replied, "is that our medical instrumentation recorded in detail just how close to death, perhaps even into death, she had come. For her to come back and to report what she's described?" Dr. Ojha gave a cute little head bobble. "My heritage does not make reincarnation the great stretch it is here, in the West."

I glanced at the others uneasily.

"Mrs. Hughes, perhaps you want to tell them the rest of the story while I see my next patient." Dr. Ojha rose. "If you like, you can all remain right here. You will always have special visiting privileges."

Mrs. Hughes twisted her chair toward us. We must have appeared quite the contrast: I was skeptical. Victoria was elated.

"You don't think I had doubts?" Mrs. Hughes said. "All I could think about, night and day, while I recuperated back home, was Kathy Christen. I knew I had to find out."

Good, I thought. *She'll discover there is some rational explanation.*

"As soon as we got back home to Buhl, I was on the computer. Several Christens were listed in the Wabash white pages, and I phoned them. Two were related, but none knew a family that once had a little girl named Kathy. Of course, more than a half century had passed.

"I tried the online obituaries, but they didn't go back that far. My husband suggested I contact the Mormons—maybe their genealogy records would show something. I talked with a volunteer in one of their family history centers who said she would do some checking. The next day she called back with information that made my pulse leap. She'd found an entry for a Kathy Christen, born in 1948, died in 1955, the only child of a John and Emily Christen."

I folded my arms, doubtful this would lead anywhere.

"The records showed Emily was deceased, but there was no date-of-death entry for John. Was he still living? He'd be in his eighties, maybe nineties. And if he wasn't in Wabash, where?"

"How about property records?" Victoria asked.

Mrs. Hughes nodded. "I phoned the Wabash Assessor's Office. They told me their online records go back to 1988. Earlier records were still paper and had to be searched manually, in person."

I said nothing. At least she'd begun a systematic investigation. How long before we would hear how it all unraveled?

My eyes drifted to an intricate diagram of a heart on the wall behind Dr. Ojha's desk, peppered with Latin names of all the things that could go wrong. It didn't do much to calm me.

"As soon as I was well enough to travel," Mrs. Hughes said, "we took our savings—a bit low after all the medical expenses—and bought plane tickets to Indiana. I remember the morning my husband and I walked up the steps of the stately two-story Wabash

County Courthouse. I was anxious and jittery. Would we find records of property once owned by the Christen family? Records that might establish my existence in a prior life? Dark storm clouds had gathered. My husband asked if I'd noticed the thunder in the distance. I told him that was my heart pounding."

I noticed my own heart rate had quickened. Victoria seemed calm and attentive. I glanced at a corkboard by Dr. Ojha's desk filled with photos from patients. In one, a happy youth tottered upside down in a handstand. *My* world would be turned on its head if property records confirmed the existence of such a family. I turned my attention back to Mrs. Hughes.

"A young clerk with a pleasant manner retrieved a large bound volume for the decade of the 1950s and showed us how to proceed. It was organized by street and parcel number. We had neither. So, we began a meticulous page-by-page search for the name. The time wore on, and I grew discouraged. Then, when I was halfway down a page, my breath caught. There it was: John Christen, 538 Fillmore Street. My husband smiled and shook his head.

"I showed the clerk what we'd found. Could he tell us who the current owner was? I held my breath while he checked some records. 'It's under the same ownership,' he said. 'Property taxes were paid last year.' "

"But how do you know if that's *your* John Christen?" I asked.

"I was prepared to camp on the man's doorstep, if necessary, to find out."

Dr. Ojha returned, but before she'd sat down, another doctor poked his head in. "Ginette," he said, "if you've got a sec, can you come listen to this guy's arrhythmia? I don't like what I hear."

One of the advantages of group practice, I thought. *Second opinions are a mere door away.*

"I'm on the edge of my seat," Victoria said. "Was it him?"

"We drove right over there," Mrs. Hughes said. "A block from Fillmore we crossed old railroad tracks. I grabbed my husband's arm. 'Honey!' I said. 'Kathy heard a train whistle from her house!' A moment later we pulled up to a small cottage. My hand was trembling so much, my knock on the front door was more like a vibration. No answer. I knocked louder. Moments passed.

"My husband said he'd check the house next door, in case a neighbor might know something. He was halfway to the sidewalk when the front door squeaked open a few inches and an older man peered out.

" 'Mr. Christen?' I asked.

"His eyes shifted from me out to my husband and back.

"His voice, scratchy, almost inaudible, answered, 'Yes?'

"I took a deep breath, then just spit out the words: 'Mr. Christen, did you have a daughter named Kathy?'

"He gave no response, only a melancholy stare. I searched his vacant face, and my heart began to sink. I thought, *No, this can't be him. He has no idea what I'm talking about.* Then his chin began to quiver, and I saw dismay and sadness in his eyes. He started to close the door. 'Please,' I said. I put my hand up. 'If you're Kathy's father . . . she is very special to me too. May I talk with you?' "

Victoria leaned toward Mrs. Hughes as if that could help nudge her through the door.

"It was him," Mrs. Hughes said.

Victoria smiled. My head rolled back.

"John Christen led us into a living room furnished in the manner a man in his late eighties might find comfortable—dark wall panels, a braided rug in front of a brick fireplace, an RCA television in a console cabinet opposite a dated davenport sofa. A dim table lamp provided scant illumination.

"He shuffled to the mantle and retrieved a framed picture of a sparkling seven-year-old in a blue polka dot dress. Soft yellow curls framed a sweet face—a ringer for the little girl you might see on a jar of peanut butter or the wrapper on a loaf of bread. He spoke with great tenderness about his daughter, his regrets about the birthdays he'd missed, not being home for her first-grade performance in *Goldilocks and the Three Bears*.

"As a Federal Reserve bank examiner, he had traveled throughout the Midwest, often on trips of two to three weeks. He couldn't talk about the accident, other than to blame himself for having been away. His heartache must have continued all these years. 'God took my angel,' he said, 'April 28, 1955.' His anguish had been made worse by town gossip. He didn't belong to the church, but people were fierce in their criticism of his wife.

"I hesitated to mention how I knew of Kathy. Finally, I told him that I believed I had once lived there. He drew back surprised and grew cautious. Perhaps he thought I had been one of the neighbors who had condemned the family. But when I spoke about Kathy's death with care and nonjudgment, he seemed moved."

Victoria's eyes were moist. My brain insisted there had to be an explanation. "Isn't it possible," I said, "that this is an extraordinary coincidence? 'Kathy' is a common name. And what if you misheard the light? Or even got the town's name wrong?"

Mrs. Hughes gave me a thoughtful look but didn't answer.

Dr. Ojha swept back into her office and glanced at my befuddled face. "Mrs. Hughes, have you told them about the birthmarks?"

"Not yet."

88

Bill Miner
UCSF Medical Center, San Francisco
4:10 PM

"I have two birthmarks on my right hand," Mrs. Hughes said. "Look." She held out her palm and pointed to a circular coloration.

Victoria and I bent closer. The spot measured about three-eighths of an inch in diameter and was depressed below the skin around it.

"It's the place where the rusty nail entered Kathy's palm," Mrs. Hughes said. She turned her hand over and pointed to a smaller birthmark on the back of the hand. "This one is less prominent."

The second mark was roundish, about an eighth of an inch wide, and darker than the skin around it.

"The nail went all the way through Kathy's hand and poked out here," Mrs. Hughes said.

I stared in disbelief as I listened to her logic. *Those spots on her hand are supposed to be Kathy's wounds? Many people have spots.* I cleared my throat. "Isn't that a stretch?" I said. "What makes you think those birthmarks aren't a chance coincidence?"

"Let me answer that," Dr. Ojha said. She removed the stethoscope from her neck and settled down behind her desk. "Mrs. Hughes contacted me after her trip and asked if there was any way to substantiate that this was her Kathy. So, I requested the coroner's autopsy report from Wabash County. The cause of death was unequivocal. Kathy Christen of Wabash, Indiana, died at age seven from respiratory failure from severe, tetanus-induced muscle spasms."

Victoria's eyes filled with empathy. I inhaled and tried to think.

"Kathy's father did not say what caused his daughter's death," Mrs. Hughes said, then paused as if to allow us to follow the implication. "The only way I knew how Kathy died was from my near-death experience."

My chest tightened as I struggled with Mrs. Hughes's uncanny details. My brain scrambled for any alternative to the unthinkable concept of reincarnation.

"OK," I said. I knew I was grasping at straws. "*That* Kathy died—horrible, unnecessary, tragic in every way. But, couldn't you have *read* about it? Seen it on the news?" My eyes scanned Mrs. Hughes's face as I tried to coax some plausible, alternative explanation.

Mrs. Hughes responded to my questions with a half smile. "But *I* wasn't born yet," she said.

I drooped back, tilted my head toward the ceiling, and grimaced. Me, the one who had lectured Victoria about mindfulness of historical dates. My face felt flush.

"The coroner's report included another significant detail," Dr. Ojha said. "A sketch of Kathy's right hand." She paused like a prosecutor about to make a final summary argument to a jury.

"Mrs. Hughes's birthmarks are in the precise location where the nail pierced Kathy's palm and emerged on the back," Dr. Ojha said. "The exact spots."

Victoria and I sat motionless.

Dr. Ojha gave a slow nod. "We've had a little time to digest this," she said. "Don't think I wasn't just as dumbfounded. I asked our chief of pediatrics about Mrs. Hughes's birthmarks. He told me a fact I didn't know: the cause of most birthmarks is a complete mystery. Most of us have a birthmark. Yet, medical science doesn't know why a person has them . . . no idea why they are at one location instead of another."

I didn't feel comfortable. What kind of conclusion was I expected to draw? Christianity has always repudiated the doctrine of reincarnation for the simple reason that it undermined its basic tenets. The very concept is repugnant. Why look to Christ's redemptive sacrifice for our sins? A gradual evolution of the human soul over multiple lives would render Christ's sacrifice unneeded! But, I was no longer a believer, so . . . why were my insides tied in a square knot?

"Are you OK?" Victoria asked. She seemed to have regained her own composure.

I wasn't OK. Reincarnation? Was anyone serious about that stuff? We joke about it. Johnny Carson once quipped, after an opening had flopped: 'I now believe in reincarnation. Tonight's monologue is going to come back as a dog.'

I wanted to change the subject that had me so uncomfortable. I checked my watch and rose to my feet. "Maybe we should call Jordan, see if there are any developments."

We thanked Dr. Ojha and left her office. We took a few steps down the hall. Then I remembered. I *did* know someone who took reincarnation seriously! Someone I'd met at a conference the year before who had a practice right *there* at the medical school!

"You call Jordan," I said to Victoria as we came to the front desk. "I need to reach someone." I spoke to the receptionist. She wrote down a phone number and pointed to a building down the street.

"Nothing yet at John Muir," Victoria said. She eyed the time and slipped her phone into her purse. "That leaves four and a half hours. Jordan said the evening visitor surge was our last hope."

Victoria didn't have my attention. "I need to see someone before we start back," I said as I dialed a number. The man I was trying to reach answered, and we spoke briefly.

"Is that a scowl?" Victoria asked. "That doesn't seem like you. Are you angry?"

"All of the above," I said. A vein in my forehead was pulsing. "There's a man I *have* to talk to." She and Mrs. Hughes rushed to keep up as I darted across Parnassus.

"Where're we going?" Victoria asked.

"Psychiatry."

"You *are* upset!"

89

Bill Miner
UCSF Medical Center, San Francisco
4:30 PM

"Do people *research* this?" Victoria asked. "Reincarnation?"

"Felix Kingsley does." I maintained a brisk stride down the sidewalk. Colleagues saw him as an intelligent man who wasted his time in an unintelligible field. Most, like me, had ignored his investigations—work that was now of acute relevance.

A placard on the clinic read: PERCEPTUAL RESEARCH. I swung the door wide.

Victoria later told me she had expected to meet Carnac the Magnificent, not a kindly, well-dressed, gray-haired professor who could have been the grandfather in one of Norman Rockwell's paintings.

No stranger to the clutter of faculty offices, I helped Kingsley move some journals and books from chairs. Victoria, Mrs. Hughes, and I sat down in front of his desk.

I took a deep breath, more to calm my emotions than to recover from the rapid walk. "We've just heard an incredible story, Felix." There was a sheen of sweat on my palms. I cleared my throat. "No offense to this fine lady here, but her account is out of my comfort zone . . . and it's right in your bailiwick."

"I want to hear it," Kingsley said. "Most of my research is with children, so you had me the moment you said she'd had her recollection as an adult." He gave Mrs. Hughes a warm smile.

"How in the world do you do that?" Victoria asked, her tone more curious than combative. "Research something like reincarnation?"

Kingsley tapped his fingers together, a gleam in his eye. "My research doesn't involve a lot of work in a lab. You can't see reincarnation happen or measure it when it does. My techniques are a closer match to the skills of a genealogist and a police detective. A lot of legwork. I talk to families. Look for what I can independently verify."

It was a toss-up who was more fascinated—Kingsley with us or us with him.

"Are your subjects all from India?" Mrs. Hughes asked.

"Many are, and there's a good reason for that," Kingsley said. "If a young child in New Delhi begins to talk about a name that's unfamiliar to the family, the child is not automatically discredited or rebuked."

"So, it's cultural," Victoria said. "Part of Hinduism."

"Yes and no," Kingsley said. "It's not just India, by the way. I've found cases all over the world. Brazil, Lebanon, and here in the United States. And it *is* cultural, because when a kid from Texas speaks about having been another person, the parents assume it's just their child's imagination."

"And adults?" I asked.

"If someone talks about a previous life, it's nearly always a young child. By the time children reach five or six, those memories have faded. That's why I'm so intrigued by Mrs. Hughes."

His kind eyes turned to her with an expectant look.

Mrs. Hughes spilled her whole story: the near-death experience, the revelation of a previous life, the trip to Indiana, the telltale birthmarks, the coroner's report.

I fidgeted, as if movement would flush out an inconsistency, would help Kingsley spot a detail we'd overlooked, anything. Instead, when he heard the final piece of evidence, his eyes lit up, and a satisfied smile spread across his face.

"Fascinating," he said.

My shoulders dropped.

Kingsley became animated. "In the cases I've documented," he said, "most of the children speak about a previous life with considerable emotion. Their description often includes an account of their death, especially if that death was violent."

"Kathy's death had an element of violence," Mrs. Hughes said. "The situation was charged with emotion and guilt. Her mother put the whole blame on Kathy—the injury was the fault of her daughter's disobedience."

Kingsley lowered his head and closed his eyes a moment as though searching for a comparison.

"But what would explain birthmarks on my hand?" Mrs. Hughes asked.

Kingsley stood and went to a bookcase behind him. "This isn't physical science," he said, "and we don't know how such a thing would work." He peered over the rims of his glasses and reached for a book. "But we do know of cases in which mental images that are highly emotional have produced changes in that person's body." He pulled out a volume and thumbed through it for a page. "Let me show you a notable example. Bill knows this one." He set the book on his desk, opened it to a painting of Saint Francis of Assisi, and turned it toward us.

"Notice the wounds on his hands and feet," Kingsley said. Victoria and Mrs. Hughes leaned forward and studied the image. "He was one of the first people recorded to have developed stigmata, a term that refers to body marks that appear in locations that correspond to the wounds inflicted on Jesus during his crucifixion."

I crossed my arms. I was familiar with the phenomena.

Mrs. Hughes's mouth became slack.

Kingsley tilted his head forward. "Saint Francis became so wrought with emotion about the crucifixion of Jesus that his *own* wrists and feet looked as though they had been pierced by nails," he said.

Victoria glanced to Mrs. Hughes. "You're in pretty rarefied company," Victoria said.

"There've been some three hundred fifty cases of stigmata recorded that I think are authentic," Kingsley said. "The marks vary in size and appearance, which, to me, suggests they were produced by the mental images of the person."

"But how in the world!" Victoria said.

"It's my hypothesis that the connection occurs through the concentration of the mind on particular parts of the body as might occur in a violent, emotion-filled situation."

Victoria looked puzzled.

"Your field is neuroscience," Kingsley said. "Maybe you'll help answer that question one day."

"Excuse me," I said. "Before we stamp this signed, sealed, and delivered, I'd like to keep another possibility on the table—that her birthmarks are a coincidence."

Kingsley shook his head. "I don't think so, Bill. Even in the case of a single birthmark corresponding to a single wound . . . the odds would be small. Do the math."

Felix adjusted his glasses, which seemed to accentuate the sparkle in his eyes. He was loving this. I was not.

"The skin of a normal-size female adult is about twenty-seven hundred square inches," he said. "If you assume, for simplicity, that Mrs. Hughes's birthmarks are each one-half square inch in area, the odds of a random birthmark matching the wound on her palm would be one chance in fifty-four hundred." He leaned toward me. "But now, if you consider the odds of having two birthmarks matching the two wounds Mrs. Hughes described, the probability diminishes to one fifty-four hundredth times one fifty-four hundredth." He reached for a calculator, punched the keys, then glanced up.

"One in twenty-nine million," he said with a self-satisfied smile.

Kingsley paused a long moment for us to digest how remote the probability would be that her birthmarks were a coincidence.

"OK," I said, "but isn't there still another, bigger arithmetic problem here? The population explosion."

Kingsley gave me a dry smile as if he already knew where I was going.

"If we're all reincarnated from previous lives," I said, "where do all the souls come from? The world's population is now near eight billion people. In the beginning, it grew slowly through endless centuries of war, famine, and disease, but a significant percentage of all the people who have ever lived are alive today. It's not even mathematically possible for there to have been enough people who have lived in centuries past to come back today as all the people alive today."

"Astute observation," Kingsley replied. "In other words, if that were true, how would all the new souls get added to the world? Where would they come from?"

"Exactly," I said.

"But your numbers are off, Bill. The Population Reference Bureau in Washington, DC, has calculated the number of people who have ever lived on earth to be more than you think: one hundred eight billion. But you raise a valid point. How does it all work? And I don't know. I don't know if reincarnation is limited to just this world. Some have reported that it may not be confined to Earth."

I sighed. Kingsley seemed disgustingly evenhanded about all this.

"Getting back to why you stopped by," he said, "I can tell you there are common factors in passion-induced marks that appear on the body. Violence and strong emotion are foremost. If Mrs. Hughes remembered her fatal wound as Kathy Christen, even in the womb, then it's conceivable this could have precipitated her birthmarks."

"In the womb?" Mrs. Hughes said. She pressed a hand to her cheek.

"I'm not saying what happened with you proves this," Kingsley said. His words were gentle. "Maybe there is some genetic or environmental influence that explains those birthmarks." He gazed toward the window as if weighing those alternatives. "But I've worked in this field for thirty-five years." He turned his head back to the three of us.

"The evidence I've accumulated convinces me that reincarnation, as implausible as it might sound, explains unsolved problems of psychology and medicine which otherwise have no answer," he said.

Victoria hadn't blinked for a minute, maybe two.

"In my work," Kingsley said, "I've just focused on verification and documentation of cases that I've heard about or that've been reported to me. I have over seven hundred cases, all of which I've examined critically, rigorously, scientifically. Researchers at the University of Virginia have gathered far more."

"But you said yourself, you couldn't see it or measure it," Victoria said. "How can you claim to examine reincarnation scientifically?"

"That's a fair question," he said with a nod. "One can't make blanket statements that reincarnation occurs. And I don't. Instead, I'm careful to collect observations in a way that can be tested. I look for those cases where reincarnation is the best explanation *for the data.* Approaching my research this way, I can formulate a reincarnation hypothesis scientifically."

Victoria leaned forward like an English pointer, as if on guard to catch a flaw in his logic.

"Any case can be disproved," he said, "if it fails to meet either of two criteria: first, if the details about a previous life do not turn out to be accurate and, second, if the details are accurate but could have been known by some other means."

"But how can you claim to test in a scientific way a phenomenon so baffling that nobody understands how it could work?" Victoria asked.

"You're the neuroscientist," Kingsley said. "How much do we understand about how the brain interacts with the mind?"

Victoria sat back. "Good point," she said.

Kingsley turned his head to Mrs. Hughes. "I would like to stay in touch," he said. "From what you've told me about Kathy—that you had no prior knowledge of this young girl, a girl who died in Indiana five years before you were born"—his eyes twinkled—"I've got to think that's pretty robust evidence that reincarnation is the best explanation for the data."

90

Bill Miner
UCSF Medical Center, San Francisco
5:40 PM

That was not the way I'd anticipated that conversation going. We'd left Kingsley's office, and I quickened my pace to the parking garage as if distance would provide relief. His words flogged my brain: "reincarnation . . . the best explanation for the data." It was *an* explanation all right. It was also a Roman cavalry charge on everything I'd concluded about God's existence.

"Slow up!" Victoria called. "Mrs. Hughes is not a marathoner."

I pivoted and waited. Victoria must have sensed how unsettled I was. Her expression changed from annoyance to concern.

"Bill, do you want to stop somewhere for a cup of coffee?" Victoria asked as she slipped into the driver's seat.

I held the passenger-side door for Mrs. Hughes, then climbed in the back. "No," I said, "let's head on back." Truth was, I needed something a lot stiffer than what they serve at Starbucks. How was Victoria able to cope so well with a phenomenon that had rendered me numb? We pulled up to the garage exit, waited for an ambulance to pass, then edged into the late-afternoon traffic.

"Bill, could you call Jordan for an update?" Victoria asked.

She's right back on point, I thought. *Resilient as a willow in a windstorm.* I punched Jordan's number and exchanged a few words with him. I put the phone down and shook my head. "Nothing," I said. The distraction had done little to ease my mental plight. "Visiting hours end at nine." I checked my watch. "With this traffic, we'll be lucky to get back by seven thirty. Maybe they'll have

Cyrus in custody." My tone was halfhearted. "If not, at least we've got Lane."

"But that would leave the kingpin still out there," Victoria said.

It was difficult for me to think about kingpins or anyone else. I was in a mental stew. My gut tried to tell me that the rationale I'd reached long ago—the reason I no longer believed in God—was now in question. But my brain was unable—or refused—to comprehend.

Victoria's eyes continued to dart at me in the mirror. "Mrs. Hughes, I didn't see Bill this dazed when a church blew up around us. . . . I think we're both flabbergasted by what you've told us." She hesitated, as if reluctant to dispute Mrs. Hughes. "If reincarnation does happen to a person," Victoria said, "doesn't it seem peculiar that they wouldn't remember *something* about a past life?"

Eureka, I thought. Victoria has come to her senses! Her scientific mind has begun to question the idea of multiple lifetimes.

Mrs. Hughes responded with a modest shake of her head. "I don't know why we don't remember," she said. "Maybe we're not intended to. Maybe we'd be overwhelmed. When I'm indecisive about something, I try to mull over similar situations . . . from last month, last year. What if you could remember all the choices you had made in previous lives, innumerable lives?" She lifted her eyebrows. "How many regrets would *that* total? It might render you too paralyzed to figure out an original approach to a problem you face in this life."

Victoria continued: "But, if we can't remember, we're free to repeat the same mistakes."

"You don't have to wait for another life for that," Mrs. Hughes said.

"Doesn't that seem inefficient?"

"Is *evolution* inefficient?"

Victoria wrinkled her forehead. "No, I suppose not," she said. "Evolution is genius . . . a grand progression that has culminated in *Homo sapiens*."

Mrs. Hughes became wistful. "Perhaps the assimilation of life experiences is likewise a grand progression," she said, "where what we learn in each life is woven into something greater."

"I do think human progress is advancing," Victoria said, "but some days I wonder whether we've become wiser."

"Two steps forward and one step back is still one step forward," Mrs. Hughes said. "The notion of human rights, of toleration, of justice—those concepts haven't always existed. There was a time when we burned witches."

The car was silent as we waited for the light to change. My mind wobbled like an unbalanced top. Thoughts I'd buried long ago—when I lost my faith—reared up to badger me: What *are* we here for? What is our purpose? What is the meaning of our existence? If there *was* a soul, why was it so undetectable? Why could I not feel even a smidgen, one iota, the faintest tinge of it, let alone catch a miniscule whiff of a previous life?

"If we're supposed to forget, I think there's sometimes a glitch," Mrs. Hughes said, "and maybe memories of past lives peek through. You know what I mean? Those moments of déjà vu when you look in the eyes of a total stranger and feel a connection, as though you've known them before."

We crept through the Haight-Ashbury neighborhood, passed Dreams of Kathmandu, a store with Hindu tapestries and incense sticks in the window. The customers there would have been a lot more comfortable in this conversation than I was.

"Go back to the part you described in Dr. Ojha's office," Victoria said, "about how there was no judgment."

Mrs. Hughes didn't answer right away but seemed to look inward. "You're not judged," she said finally. "That's a wrong notion. It never felt like a courtroom where I stood before a judge to be tried for my deeds. On the contrary, the light offered me suggestions for improvement, helped me identify the various choices I'd made in life, what I might've done differently." She turned toward Victoria with an animated expression as though she'd just thought of the perfect metaphor. "Think of the guidance you receive from a loving parent, the inspiration from the best teacher you ever had in school, the motivation from a great coach who knows your strengths and weaknesses—then multiply that a bazillion times. That's what I experienced."

Victoria drew back in her seat, contemplative.

"However," Mrs. Hughes added, "I was told that all souls are held accountable for their conduct."

"How can you be accountable if there's no judgment?"

"Accountability comes into play when you recognize there are important lessons you could have learned but didn't."

"So, there *is* a judgment," Victoria said.

"No. You are not punished. You are *shown*," Mrs. Hughes said.

"What about someone who has inflicted extreme harm on others?" Victoria asked.

"My Aunt Pearl told me during my near-death experience of a cardinal who had been at the center of a Catholic sexual abuse scandal. When he came into the light, he received much stricter treatment."

"What does 'stricter' mean?"

"He was returned to earth again, to be born into an environment that would prove sexually abusive."

"As punishment?" Victoria asked.

"Not as punishment, but that he might gain understanding."

"What if the cardinal had insisted he was innocent?"

"Let me tell you," Mrs. Hughes said. "When you stand in front of that light, your soul is laid bare. The 'real you' comes out quickly. You can't hide a thing. No amount of chutzpah—or ecclesiastic rank—will enable you to pretend you're something you're not."

"This is *so* different from . . ." Victoria said, her voice trailing off.

"Yes and no," Mrs. Hughes said. "Don't think of it as a contradiction, but rather as an evolution of your thinking. The church has emphasized judgment in the past, but it too is evolving: 'Who am I to judge gays?' and 'The death penalty is *always* wrong'—those statements have come from the *pope*, no less!" Her eyes gave a generous smile. "The light told me they don't give up on you no matter how dreadfully you may have messed up."

Victoria glanced at me in the rearview mirror. "I miss hearing from you in this conversation," she said.

"Don't think I haven't taken it all in," I said.

Mrs. Hughes turned toward me, reducing the distance between us. "I've come to understand our purpose is to further develop our souls," she said. "And if that's the goal, what makes us think it could be accomplished in a single lifetime?" Her eyes checked mine as if to gauge acceptance of the idea. "Each life," she said, "presents another opportunity, another chance to gain the abilities and experiences we need for growth. And while I sensed that we receive superb coaching between lives, when we're ushered out of the locker room and back onto the gridiron of life, it's up to us to execute the plays."

She paused and shook her head. "I can't believe I just said that. I scarcely know the difference between a blitz and a block in football."

That made me chuckle.

"All right, Mr. Quiet," Victoria said, "can you top that sports metaphor? What would the Lone Ranger say?"

My gut continued to scream. My thoughts were a muddle. I could feel Victoria's concern about me, her persistent effort to draw me into the conversation and ease my discomfort. I reflected a moment, then piped up: "God put the firewood there, but the individual must gather and light it himself." They both laughed. I felt better.

Mrs. Hughes turned in her seat. "In Buhl last year, the mayor's four-year-old son died of a rare lung disease," she said. "Half the town was at the memorial to hear the minister do his best to console: 'How could God allow an innocent child to die?' he said. 'It was part of God's plan. We cannot understand his purposes.' The little boy's uncle came to the podium: 'My nephew was here to teach us about love,' he said. 'Now he's gone to be with Jesus.' Those words didn't instill in me a sense of God's mercy and justice. But reincarnation does." Her voice softened. "The idea of reincarnation also made the difficult act of forgiveness easier for me when I realized that any pain I received from another person was temporary compared to the injury they may have inflicted on their *own* soul." She cracked a smile. "Seems consistent with those famous words: 'Forgive them, for they know not what they do.' "

We were quiet for several minutes as we limped, stop and go, along the Central Skyway toward I-80.

"I have a question for you," I said. Mrs. Hughes twisted her head toward me, attentive. "If people started to believe in reincarnation, what would prevent them from thinking they shouldn't trouble themselves about a homeless man asleep in a bus shelter, because he chose that life to develop his character?"

Victoria shot me a glance of surprise. I wasn't sure if it was because of the nature of my question or because I'd at last spoken up.

"Or what if," I continued, "people were to view a girl born with some horrible deformity and think the deformity is a result of a choice the girl made in order to gain a new perspective?"

"Yikes!" Mrs. Hughes said. "I'm not ready to draw conclusions about those kinds of things." She gave me a characteristic considered look. "You ask good questions, and you point out some sticky implications. I don't know all the answers. I'm afraid a near-death experience didn't make me the Dalai Lama."

Her manner didn't strike me as disingenuous or dishonest. Nor did she seem deluded, but her fantastic story made my hair stand on end. Would it all fall apart on closer examination? I'd been burned before when I'd bought into religion, lured by the promise of eternal salvation. I'd put my entire trust in the Bible, a career devoted to faith. Then had come the crush of disillusionment when after careful study I found Holy Scripture riddled with inconsistencies and errors. I could no longer accept that there was a loving God—one who would allow untold millions of innocent people, throughout countless centuries, to suffer. So, I'd unfriended my faith, said good-bye to the powerful urge to believe. I'd raised my defenses, on guard not to be deceived that way again. Was *that* the reason every fiber of me was fighting this? I didn't know what I thought, and I hated not knowing what I thought. I was half listening to the conversation as Mrs. Hughes said something about the light.

"It told me that's the way it works," she said. "Life's *meant* to be hard here. However, I didn't hear a single word to suggest you shouldn't try to help your fellow human being, to practice the Golden Rule."

Victoria edged around a FedEx truck midway through the Yerba Buena Tunnel as she tried to advance around a clot of unholy gridlock.

"And, by the way, that's one hard rule to follow," Mrs. Hughes said. "Anyone who says the Golden Rule is simplistic has never tried to apply it. I mean, all day, every day, you have to think of the other person." She rubbed the back of her neck. "So, I don't know. Maybe the people who are apathetic about the suffering of others will have that deficiency to work on in their next life."

"*What* did you say?" I said. I pulled myself forward. "About suffering?"

Mrs. Hughes glanced over her shoulder. "It changes the perspective, doesn't it?" she said.

As we emerged from the darkness of the tunnel, I was dazzled by sudden illumination. *Reincarnation solves suffering!* It was as if a lightning bolt had been hurled directly to the inside of my brain. I felt a rush through my whole body as my brain let the pieces come together:

That death isn't an arbitrary, one-time fate levied by an indifferent, uncaring universe.

That an intrinsic essence within us *continues.*

That each of our lives—each existence—is a mere chapter in our personal evolution.

I sunk back, stupefied. *Did my problem with God just evaporate?*

I looked out as we passed beneath the five-hundred-foot suspension tower of the Bay Bridge that soared, shimmering white, against the sapphire sky of late afternoon, a monumental exclamation point to my epiphany. I turned back to the conversation in the front seat.

"What you've told us," Victoria said to Mrs. Hughes, "flies in the face of everything I've believed." She put a hand to her blouse and touched the butterfly brooch. "But I want it to be true."

Mrs. Hughes gazed at Victoria with tenderness. "It's straight from the highest authority," she said. "I've breathed his very air."

91

John Muir Health, Walnut Creek Medical Center
7:30 PM

FBI Agent Matt Collins eyed the four people in line at the visitors' desk in the hospital lobby. The number of visitors had been light, and with less than two hours to go, Collins had heightened his vigilance. The first two people, a gentle, gray-haired couple, didn't raise any red flags, nor did the third, a pastor. Those three were about as suspicious as flowers at a funeral. Collins's attention turned to the fourth person. A man, muscular, forties, dressed in work clothes, he had a somewhat menacing expression, the kind of demeanor one wouldn't expect from a visitor intent on consoling someone sick. Collins noticed the man carried a metal box.

The older couple identified themselves, showed their photo IDs, and said they were there to see their daughter. The receptionist, Velda, checked her patient census, printed their name tags, and directed them to their daughter's room.

"Hello, Pastor," Velda said. She reached into a drawer, found his badge among those preprinted for the regulars, and handed it to him. "How have you been?"

"Better than our dear Mr. Ambling, I'm afraid. His wife called me to say that he had taken quite a fall."

Velda checked the printed list that was provided to the scheduled chaplains when they arrived. "Yes, he's in room 208."

The pastor thanked her, turned toward the elevator, but then paused. "Velda, some days my mind's a blank. I can't remember if there was another parishioner I was supposed to see."

Velda showed him the list. The pastor made a quick visual scan, then said, "No. No one else. Thank you. You're an angel." He headed for the elevator.

"He's here almost every week," she said to Collins. "Always tends to the sick in his flock."

The fourth person seemed annoyed by the check-in process as he stepped to the desk. Collins observed him closely. He identified himself as a maintenance worker who had been called in to make a repair. Velda asked to see an ID, which she checked and logged before she printed a name tag.

The man placed the name tag on his shirt and walked to a nearby stairwell.

"Are outside maintenance workers brought in very often?" Collins asked.

"Rarely. Our own maintenance staff handles most everything."

"Where does that stairwell go?" Collins asked.

"To all the floors."

Collins punched a number on his phone. Jordan picked up on the first ring. "A suspicious white male, about five-eight, dressed as a maintenance worker, just signed in and is headed up on the south stairs," Collins said.

"OK. We're ready here."

***

Jordan had just alerted agents Reynolds and Toscone when his phone rang again.

"Agent, this is hospital security. We just received word that a patient saw a man with a gun in the stairwell."

"What's the exact location?"

"South stairs. End of your hall on the left."

"We're moving. Lock down the hospital."

Jordan hung up. "Our suspect's armed and coming up the stairwell," he said. He headed toward the stairwell and motioned Reynolds and Toscone to follow. "We're not waiting for him to reach this floor."

As the three hurried down the hall, Jordan dialed Collins and directed him to position himself inside the stairwell on the ground floor. "Don't let him back into the lobby."

Jordan, Toscone, and Reynolds, guns drawn, entered the stairwell and began a cautious descent.

***

The sixth floor had fallen silent. Tim Lane's eyes darted in a restless circle—to the ceiling, around the room, past the tubes and wires, across the bed in which he was confined, and back to the ceiling. He could hear his own heartbeat. Then the soft chime of the elevator. *The FBI's back*, he thought.

A solitary man stepped into the room. "Hello, Tim," he said softly. "I came to see you off."

The man approached the bedside. Lane relaxed as he recognized him. "You have been a faithful servant of the Lord," the man said. "There is one final sacrifice you must make."

***

Victoria, Mrs. Hughes, and I had arrived and entered the hospital lobby. We showed our badges at the visitors' desk.

"You'll have to stay here," the receptionist said. "Security has just placed the hospital on lockdown."

I jerked my head toward Victoria. "He must be here!" I bolted toward the elevator with Victoria and Mrs. Hughes at my heels.

"Wait!" the receptionist shouted. "You can't go up there!"

***

Tim Lane's eyes grew wide with disbelief as a strip of adhesive tape was placed over his mouth. The visitor removed a syringe and small bottle from his jacket. Lane struggled against his restraints. Panic consumed him.

***

Jordan and the two agents had reached the fourth-floor level when they heard a grinding, mechanical sound from below. The FBI agents dashed down two more flights and came face-to-face with the maintenance worker. He saw their weapons, let out a shriek, dropped his electric drill, and threw his hands in the air.

***

The words Tim Lane heard were anything but comforting. "God's reward will be great," the man said as he inserted the filled syringe into the injection port of the IV line. He pressed the plunger all the way down. "This works quickly. You will soon be in the arms of Jesus." He turned, gave Lane a final glance, and left the room. Lane twisted in agony.

***

The elevator opened on the sixth floor. Victoria, Mrs. Hughes, and I rushed to exit and collided with a man at the door. Victoria's eyes locked on the person in front of her. The man's expression went from surprise to alarm. In a mysterious way she'd later describe as intuitive, Victoria knew.

"*Pastor Marc! It's you!*"

The man, jolted by Victoria's instant and decisive perception, turned and sprinted down the hall. He opened the stairwell door and disappeared. I punched Jordan's number. "We're on the sixth floor!" I shouted. "We saw Cyrus! He's headed down the stairwell!"

"We're *in* the stairwell," Jordan said. "Jesus! . . . Here he comes."

I heard Jordan's words over the phone: "FBI! Stop!"

Victoria and I looked at each other with the same thought: *Lane!*

We rushed to the room and found him in a frenzy, horror in his eyes.

I grabbed his head to steady the terrified man and shouted, "What did he do!" Fearful we were too late and realizing he couldn't speak, I grabbed corners of the tape that sealed his mouth and ripped hard.

Lane squealed, gestured toward his IV, and hollered, "Poison!"

"The IV?" Victoria said. She turned to me. "Is it even connected?"

I grabbed the line of tubing from the bottle of saline, reeled it in from under the bedsheets, and held up a loose end. "No," I said. "The IV was clamped off. He was covered with a sheet, so the staff saw no need to insert it into his arm."

Lane sunk into the mattress.

"I guess no one explained that little detail," Victoria said. "He looks like he just aged ten years."

92

Bill Miner
John Muir Health, Walnut Creek Medical Center
8:30 PM

Victoria, Mrs. Hughes, and I gathered in the administrator's office with Jordan and Collins to debrief. Tim Lane and Pastor Marc Drexel had been secured, each in a separate FBI van, under the close watch of Toscone and Reynolds. With the lockdown lifted, the hospital was moving toward a resumption of normal operations.

"Got it done with a half hour to spare," Jordan said with a tight smile. "Your cooperation is appreciated and reflects highly on your entire staff. We'll be out of your hair as soon as we finish the collection of evidence in Lane's room. We expect to find digoxin in his IV. A syringe and empty bottle were in Pastor Drexel's pocket."

The administrator shook her head in disbelief.

"Together with the phone records of his contacts with Lane, prosecutors will have conclusive evidence to bring charges of attempted murder and accessory to the four interstate murders. We'll be on a plane by ten o'clock tonight. I'm sure that will be not a moment too soon for a certain maintenance man whose gun turned out to be a three-eighth-inch Black & Decker."

"Pastor Drexel is here so often we almost think of him as a member of the staff," the administrator said. "Digoxin! A dose above twenty-five milligrams is fatal. All drugs are kept in locked cabinets under very tight control."

"He got it somewhere else," Jordan said. "Clergy are assumed to be trustworthy. When we put him in cuffs, he ranted about doing God's work, denounced liberal interpretations of the Bible, and expressed his great frustration with the senior pastor, who Drexel said was too old and naïve to combat fierce enemies of the church."

"Agent Jordan?" Victoria said. "Is it possible Lane's wife could see him for a couple of minutes before you take him back with you?"

"If you want to try and reach her and have her meet us at Buchanan, go ahead," Jordan said. "But it must be brief."

I took Victoria's arm as we left the administrator's office. "Your compassion never ceases to amaze me," I said. "After what Lane has done, you still think about his emotional well-being."

"Not his," Victoria said.

Jordan and Collins joined us in the lobby and thanked us. "We'll see each other again when this case goes to trial," Jordan said. "Lane's cooperation and the apparent manipulation by Drexel may allow him to avoid the death penalty."

Jordan dug through his records on his cell, scribbled a phone number on a slip of paper, and handed it to Victoria. He shook hands with both of us, and he and Collins headed to the FBI vans.

Victoria, Mrs. Hughes, and I stepped outside the medical center. The sky had transitioned to dark navy. The air was crisp and fresh.

"I promised to take Mrs. Hughes on San Francisco's 49-Mile Drive," Victoria said. "That'll be tomorrow. Tonight, we need to unwind. How about we go to my house?"

"I don't mind a drink with two lovely women," I said.

"Would you drive?" Victoria asked me as she glanced at the slip of paper. "I have a phone call to make."

93

Bill Miner
Pleasant Hill
9:15 PM

Mrs. Hughes and I got settled in Victoria's living room while she went to the kitchen and returned moments later with champagne.

I popped the cork on the bottle of Gloria Ferrer and poured three glasses.

"To the memory of four special people," I said and lifted my glass. "To Mandy Frankel, Florence Smith, Chester Parks . . . and to Oscar Johnson, one very remarkable father." I gazed into Victoria's eyes. "When you are sorrowful, look again in your heart, and you shall see that in truth you are weeping for that which has been your delight."

Victoria brought her hand to her lips.

"Kahlil Gibran had a way with words," I said.

"I don't know how to tell you how grateful I am," Mrs. Hughes said. "Without your courage, grit, and determination, I wouldn't be alive." She rose and gave Victoria a long hug, then stretched out her arms and embraced me. "Thank you."

"The esteem and affection extend in both directions," I said.

Victoria let out a long breath. "Anyone else famished?" she asked.

"If you have a good Chinese restaurant nearby, I'll go pick up," I said.

Victoria reached for her phone and placed an order. "It'll be ready in twenty minutes. Ming's, at the corner of Pleasant Hill Road and Taylor." She handed me her keys.

94

Victoria Johnson
Pleasant Hill
9:45 PM

Victoria sank into her sofa across from Mrs. Hughes with a weighty sigh.

"You look defeated, not like someone who just caught the murderer," Mrs. Hughes said.

Victoria stared at the ceiling and wiped a trace of moisture from her eyes. "Nine days ago, the worst I could imagine was not having Papa around. Now I'm reeling with shock that my own pastor was behind Papa's murder. Pastor Marc's deception . . . his pretended sympathy . . . his offer to hold a memorial service . . . All he wanted was for me to stay in touch, so he could monitor my involvement. I told the mortuary that Pastor Marc would officiate but that I had to go to Kansas. They must have notified him."

A lump formed in her throat as her eyes fell to Mrs. Hughes. "I feel I can talk to you like you're my surrogate mom."

"I'm flattered," Mrs. Hughes said and bent closer.

"Lane's wife told me her husband had experienced despair, isolation, and disconnection. Pastor Marc, instead of guiding Lane toward spiritual renewal, preyed on a vulnerable parishioner . . . callous manipulation to convince him God had selected him for a mission to stop evil."

"At the bottom of those words, I hear guilt," Mrs. Hughes said. "Guilt that his horrific deeds sprang from your church."

Victoria closed her eyes. Humiliation and self-condemnation tugged at her conscience.

"Faith can be a conundrum," Mrs. Hughes said. "We want our religion to express the deep, intimate relationship that gives meaning to life. But pastors that preach the constant need to defeat satanic enemies—*that's* when your alarm system should go off. The lesson from Tim Lane is to be vigilant that faith doesn't become so blind that it hinders you from thinking."

"I need to tell you something in confidence," Victoria said, "something I'm not ready to confess to Bill yet." Victoria brought her hands to her lap. "My beliefs have been turned upside down. I trusted that salvation came through Jesus Christ and that the most important thing in life was to glorify God."

"You know, dear," Mrs. Hughes said, "God isn't that needy. Lots of people love God—they fight and kill one another over who glorifies him more. God would prefer we strive to bring out the best in ourselves and the best in others. That's what *I* came away with."

"But how do I come to terms with losing Jesus?"

"Oh, for heaven's sake, you don't have to give up Jesus! It's the fundamentalist dogma you can dial down." Mrs. Hughes locked her eyes on Victoria. "You do not have to *purchase* salvation." She reached over and took Victoria's hand. "Draw on Jesus to become that better person—the Sermon on the Mount is one of the greatest contributions to humanity ever made."

"All along, Bill has had good arguments," Victoria said. "I couldn't admit to him, even to myself, how taken I was by his logic. I argued with everything he said. I protested every step of the way, unwilling to let anything he said go unchallenged. I felt as if God would hear every word and note whether or not I defended the faith."

"There may be some pride mixed in with all that resistance."

Victoria felt a flush in her cheeks. "Maybe," she said. "Bill recognizes that the way to win an argument is by persuasion instead of polemic rhetoric."

"There is a tension between you two all right, but I also see a beautiful, complementary chemistry."

"I feel balanced with him," Victoria said. Her thoughts became introspective. "He listens. He sees other aspects, points out my weaknesses—not to ridicule, but to strengthen me. We were in some tough spots, and he never lost his cool, his dignity, his commitment."

"Qualities of a good partner," Mrs. Hughes said. "And it's obvious he cares for you."

Victoria looked up as she heard the front door and saw Bill come in. Her hands, clasped together, touched her upper lip. "I know," Victoria said, "and I for him."

95

Bill Miner
Pleasant Hill
10:00 PM

I had that uncomfortable feeling you get when a conversation goes silent as you come within earshot. "I didn't mean to interrupt some serious female bonding," I said. I saw a glow in Victoria's face.

She rose, took the restaurant sack, and kissed me quick on the lips.

"Hmm," I said. "That's way better than the tip I left at Ming's."

She gave me a flirty grin, said, "I need to get some dishes and set the table," and disappeared into the kitchen.

Mrs. Hughes called after her, "Let me help," and started to rise.

I reached for her arm. "Stay a moment," I said. "I need to tell you something while Victoria's out of the room."

I sat down next to her. "Mrs. Hughes, you feel indebted to us, but it's the other way around." I saw a puzzled look on her face. "You see, I had lost my faith, and you opened my eyes to an aspect I'd never imagined." I felt a release of tension as I verbalized those thoughts, a reawakening within me.

"Tell me more," she said.

"You rescued me from my dilemma about how a caring God could allow so much suffering, tolerate such injustice, permit blatant unfairness." I swallowed. "The anguish, the hardship, the loss—you enabled me to see that it is all temporary: lessons to be absorbed, while something inside of us continues on."

"It redefines the circle of life, doesn't it?" she said, her voice quiet and reflective. "We worry about the world that we will leave for our children. In fact, that's the world we leave for ourselves." She paused. "I take it Victoria doesn't know how you feel about this?"

"That's right, and please don't say anything to her, because I'm still working this out. She and I have argued over more religious topics than a convention of Baptists. I have to admit it's bruised my ego a bit that I haven't been the least bit persuasive with anything I've said to her."

She tilted her head, a curious little smile on her face. "You're certain of that, are you?"

"Yes, and that's OK," I said, "because I admire her strong convictions. I see the heartfelt acts that flow from her faith in Jesus. A belief that guides her. Has her so well anchored against adversity."

Mrs. Hughes's expression softened as if in agreement.

"I love how she's compassionate," I said, "faithful to her convictions, fights for what she believes. I wouldn't want to change one thing. The world's in need of such counterweights to the analytical tendencies of people like me."

"A teacher *and* a philosopher, I see." She nodded with a smile. "My lips are sealed, but let me say how much I appreciate that you shared this with me. Now, I better see if there is anything I can do to help in the kitchen."

***

A brief time later we sat down to crispy ginger chicken, honey walnut prawns, mu shu pork, plenty of wine, and the most relaxed conversation we'd had.

"I still can't believe I was taken in by Marc Drexel," Victoria said toward the end of the evening. "It makes me question whether I can trust my own judgment."

"Don't think that for one moment," I said. "I'd trust it for you anytime."

"I second that," Mrs. Hughes said. She gazed at the two of us. "You're both treasures to me. You make a sterling team . . . and who knows what surprising things you have yet to learn about one another."

"Surprising things?" Victoria asked. She glanced at me with a cute smile. "Is one of them, given the late hour and the excess of wine, that this dear man is destined to spend another night on a sofa bed?"

Two of the three of us laughed.

96

Bill Miner
Pleasant Hill
Three Weeks Later

Victoria and I watched our story air on *60 Minutes*. The program dramatized the extraordinary near-death experiences of Oscar Johnson, Mandy Frankel, Florence Smith, Chester Parks, and Janie Hughes, amplified by the clandestine effort of Tim Lane and Pastor Marc Drexel to prevent the program's broadcast. Social media exploded with a barrage of positive and negative reactions to the remarkable revelations, and the show received one of the highest Nielsen ratings in recent years.

I completed my book with Tim Lane as an exceptional case study and concluded:

- Religion is at its worst when religious leaders preach that their truth is the only truth, when they label other beliefs as blasphemous, when they discourage critical appraisal and independent thought, and when they teach that to question is a sin. Such dogma breeds spiritual divisiveness that impedes world peace and human progress.
- Religion is at its worst when religious leaders characterize the perceived threats from science as part of an epic battle against forces of darkness—fearful that science will crush all that is good in their country. The emotion in such appeals shuts down the consciences of individuals, gives adherents the implied permission to engage in acts of violence, and fuels the passion of

terrorists who are driven by the same vision of a world that must be cleansed by force.

- Religion is at its best when it relies on the strength of reason, when it allies with science, and when it adheres to the Golden Rule and to the principle of nonviolence.

Despite my previous presumption to the contrary, I conceded that there is solid evidence for belief in reincarnation.

The university was satisfied with my work and granted me tenure and promotion to associate professor.

An outcome I had not anticipated was that the long shot I took to complete my book would lead me to the woman I'd fall in love with.

Plus another little revelation.

I had been convinced there was no God, just as Victoria had been convinced there was no salvation apart from Jesus.

It seems we were *both* wrong.

ACKNOWLEDGMENTS

ON A JULY EVENING SOME YEARS AGO, I accompanied my wife to a talk by Annie Barrows on her new book *The Guernsey Literary and Potato Peel Pie Society*. I anticipated boredom. Instead, I was riveted and inspired. Thank you, Annie Barrows. You were the catalyst to germinate a seed.

That seed had lain dormant from the time our young son asked: "Dad, what happens when we die?" Thank you, Son, and thank you, Daughter, for the inspiration and insights you've provided over the years. It is a privilege to be your father.

In the years it took to write this book, no writer could have had a wife more supportive with patience, understanding, and encouragement. Darling, it is the joy of my life to be married to you.

This story would crumble if I didn't get details correct in many complex subject areas, most importantly, the Bible. But also current research on near-death experiences and on reincarnation. That didn't come lightly. I am beholden to the scholars whose work made it easier for me.

After an initial introduction through the writings of John Shelby Spong, I based the foundation of biblical textual criticism on the work of Bart D. Ehrman, PhD, at the University of North Carolina. To say I am enormously grateful seems inadequate.

Likewise, my debt to world authorities in near-death studies is immense: Raymond Moody, MD; Bruce Greyson, MD; Kenneth Ring, PhD; P. M. H. Atwater; and the International Association for Near-Death Studies. And to pioneers in reincarnation research: Ian Stevenson, MD, and Jim B. Tucker, MD, at the University of Virginia.

I am appreciative of the many individuals who provided their professional expertise: Manisha Ojha, MD, for her critique of my description of complex medical and surgical procedures; Police Chief Howard Jordan and terrorism expert Jonathan R. White,

PhD, for authentication of police and FBI protocols; commercial pilots Scott and Lisa Robinson and pilot Derek Mims for verification of aircraft flight procedures and control-tower communications; and Zoe-Ann Mazur for information on hospital administration. Any mistakes in these pages are my own.

To Jerry Kong, thank you for your invaluable literary perspective, and Leah Retherford for guarding me from the pitfalls of subtle sexism. My heartfelt gratitude to you both for astute suggestions to improve character and story development.

I am forever indebted to a writing critique group that cheered me on throughout the game and got me over the goal line: Lyn Roberts; Nancy Hurwitz Kors, PhD; David Flower; Jo Mele; Ann Damaschino; Judith Overmier, PhD; and Chuck McFadden. Nancy chose my novel as the selection for her monthly Wild Women Book Club, and Lyn circulated my novel to readers in her network: Don Chaffee, PhD; John Marvin; and Ellen Barrons. Don further distributed my work to friends and colleagues: Harwood Hoover Jr., PhD; Henry Post, PhD; and Mary Moran Barr. You're the best.

To Chicago journalist Michael Miner—a friend since high school days—thank you for encouraging me to 'go for it.' To Barry Stewart, thank you for pointing me to a superb writing class.

To my past writing group, my sincere appreciation—Jim Brennan; Donna Darling; Virginia Estabrook; Deirdre Johnson; Brian Shea; and to friends who read drafts of this book—Dave Bourdon; Shirley Cahill; Joan Countryman; Tom and Karen Jefferson; Diane de Pisa; Robyn Sekel; and Barbara Timmons.

I reserve enormous thanks for Camille Minichino—you are a mentor and writing teacher extraordinaire. You put me on the right track and kept me there.

And to Katie Herman—you are the greatest copyeditor I could imagine. Your exquisite attention to detail, the striking improvements you made to wording and sentence structure, your rigorous fact checking and thoughtful questioning of my reasoning—all resulted in a story better told.

ENDNOTES

EVERY EFFORT HAS BEEN MADE to acknowledge the author's sources and his inspirations for this novel. If any references were overlooked, this was unintentional. Please notify me of any omission at Earl.Thor@yahoo.com, and it will be rectified in future editions.

***

Quotations from the Bible are drawn from *The New Oxford Annotated Bible: New Revised Standard Edition* (New York: Oxford University Press, 1991).

Chapter 1

"Devil's Fall" [Devil's Fall is a fictitious location. This opening chapter was inspired by Dan Brown, *Deception Point* (New York: Washington Square Press, 2001), 1–2.]

Chapter 2

"we saw something brown and blue fall from the top." [Adapted from a description in Michael P. Ghiglieri and Charles R. Farabee, *Off the Wall: Death in Yosemite* (Flagstaff: Puma Press, 2007), 536.]

Chapter 4

"like trying to push a wheelbarrow full of frogs" [A Dutch metaphor used by Professor Niels Röling to describe the unpredictable nature of the social learning process. Cees Leeuwis and Rhiannon Pyburn, eds., *Wheelbarrows Full of Frogs* (Assen, Netherlands: Koninklijke Van Gorcum, 2002).]

Chapter 6

"I stared at the symbols between two crosses on the bracelet." [The idea of mystic symbols as a plot device was inspired by Dan Brown, *Angels and Demons*, Special Illustrated Edition (New York: Atria Books, 2005).]

Chapter 7

"Noah held out Dr. Seuss's *The Lorax*." [Theodor Geisel, *The Lorax* (New York: Random House, 1971).]

"a vast emptiness, a frightening loneliness and loss of control." [Chris Hedges, *American Fascists: The Christian Right and the War on America* (New York: Free Press, 2006), 38.]

"Education and social welfare should be handed over to the churches." [Ibid., 13.]

"He told us all that's necessary for evil to triumph is for good men to do nothing" [Lane's pastor had quoted British philosopher Edmund Burke.]

"My soul hung on every word." [Adapted from an evangelical expression in T. M. Luhrmann, *When God Talks Back: Understanding the American Evangelical Relationship with God* (New York: Alfred A. Knopf, 2012), 103.]

"Jesus also says: 'Bring my enemies before me and slay them.' " [Luke 19:27.]

"I have not come to bring peace, but a sword." [Matthew 10:34.]

"Remember what Mordecai told Esther" [Esther 4:14.]

Chapter 9

"My leaf blower had more horsepower" [Adapted from a similar comparison in an excellent religious thriller: Ian Caldwell, *The Fifth Gospel* (New York: Simon and Schuster, 2015), 20.]

Chapter 10

"[Cults] start out passionate about their religious views built around a single charismatic figure." [For an in-depth look at an infamous cult, see Marc Breault and Martin King, *Inside the Cult* (New York: Signet Penguin Books, 1993).]

Chapter 12

"He rubbed some of the film away and took another look across the street." [Description inspired by a San Francisco stakeout scene in Bill Pronzini, *Scenarios: A "Nameless Detective" Casebook* (Waterville, ME: Five Star, 2003), 181.]

Chapter 14

"I bought a treadmill" [Adapted from a quote by Daniel Lin, *Reader's Digest*, December 2017/January 2018, 99.]

"God blocked free will *then*." [Bart D. Ehrman, *God's Problem: How the Bible Fails to Answer Our Most Important Question—Why We Suffer*, (New York: HarperCollins, 2008), 12–13.]

"So does meningitis." [Paraphrased from dialogue in *Doc Martin*, Season 2, episode 6, British television medical comedy-drama series created by Dominic Minghella and starring Martin Clunes in the title role.]

"Science tells us how, but not why. . . . Who am I? Why am I here?" [Rabbi Jonathan Sacks, *Not in God's Name: Confronting Religious Violence* (New York: Schocken Books, 2015), 13.]

Chapter 15

"Papa didn't believe in heaven but was scared to death of hell." [Inspired by one of the remarkable interviews in Phillip L. Berman, *The Search for Meaning: Americans Talk about What They Believe* (New York: Ballantine Books, 1990), 75.]

"Papa's squad was on patrol along the banks of the Mekong Delta" [Ibid., 77.]

"Sometimes I tell myself the calories printed on the menu are points" [Adapted from *The Late Show* host Stephen Colbert, "Confessions."]

Chapter 17

"Manners may be more important than laws!" [Adapted from Edmund Burke, *Select Works of Edmund Burke*, vol. 3, *Letters on a Regicide Peace*, 1795, http://oll.libertyfund.org/titles/burke-select-works-of-edmund-burke-vol-3.]

"Papa! That's Jesus's message too—just as you treated the least of my brothers, you treated me." [Victoria is referring to Matthew 25:40, although she paraphrases it according to her understanding.]

"the Gospels were written in a mood of euphoria and acclamation." [The religious components of Oscar Johnson's near-death experience are fictional. This one was inspired by Mahatma Gandhi, *Gandhi on Christianity*, ed. Robert Ellsberg (Maryknoll, NY: Orbis Books, 1991), 24.]

"the writers of Genesis wanted to assert their faith in God, not give a literal account of how the world was formed." [This aspect of Oscar Johnson's near-death experience was inspired by Darrel R. Falk, *Coming to Peace with Science: Bridging the Worlds Between Faith and Biology* (Downers Grove, IL: InterVarsity Press, 2004), 32.]

" 'Even terrorists?' It said yes." [Adapted from near-death experiences reported by renowned researcher Kenneth Ring, *Lessons from the Light: What We Can Learn from the Near-Death Experience* (Needham, MA: Moment Point Press, 2006), 163–64.]

"Like when you're in traffic, and the driver ahead of you doesn't notice the signal's changed, and you get annoyed and lay on the horn." [Ibid., 156.]

Chapter 19

"is able to see a baseball cap, out of sight of his physical location, and identify its specific features?" [Adapted from a near-death experience that described a tennis shoe, Ibid., 65–66.]

Chapter 21

"We entered the bullet into NIBIN" [https://www.atf.gov/firearms/national-integrated-ballistic-information-network-nibin.]

Chapter 22

"Whoever is not with me is against me." [Matthew 12:30.]

"Whoever is not against you is for you." [Luke 9:50. Mark 9:40 says, "Whoever is not against us is for us."]

"if you don't think Satan exists, then you won't engage seriously in the fight." [A central theme in C. S. Lewis, *The Screwtape Letters* (New York: Bantam Books, 1982).]

"Only seven percent of all conflicts throughout recorded history have been due to religion." [See Rabbi Alan Lurie, "Is Religion the Cause of Most Wars?" *The Blog* (blog), *Huffington Post*, April 10, 2012, accessed March 23, 2017, https://www.huffingtonpost.com/rabbi-alan-lurie/is-religion-the-cause-of_b_1400766.html.]

"But there *is* a connection." [Beautifully argued in Sacks, *Not in God's Name*, 18, 23, 41, 101].

" 'You have heard that it was said . . . but *I* say to you . . .'?" [Matthew 5:38.]

Chapter 23

"one who was willing to step over the line and out of his comfort zone. One who showed himself by his actions to be a true disciple of Christ." [Adapted from Hedges, *American Fascists*, 33.]

"Murder may be wrong" [Ibid., 87.]

"Scientists found evidence of cancer in the bones of dinosaurs." [https://www.theguardian.com/science/2003/oct/23/dinosaurs.science.]

Chapter 26

"Satan himself masquerades as an angel of light" [2 Corinthians 11:14.]

"If they were from God, then he will enable you, when he is ready, to know the visions' meaning." [Paraphrased from Morris L. West, *The Clowns of God* (New York: William Morrow and Company, 1981), 22.]

Chapter 27

"Mr. Browne, forty percent of scientists believe in God." [This statistic is from Francis S. Collins, *The Language of God: A Scientist Presents Evidence for Belief* (New York: Free Press, 2006), 4.]

"Rachel Carson's words that we should admire the beauty of the moment, that when any living thing fulfills its purpose, we should accept that as nature's cycle of life." [From Rachel Carson, *Lost Woods: The Discovered Writing of Rachel Carson*, ed. Linda Lear (Boston: Beacon Press, 1998).]

"the kind of spiritual import I would sometimes see in a coincidence." [For an insightful discussion of the perception of God, see Luhrmann, *When God Talks Back*, chap. 2.]

"Some scientists predict the demise of religion, while most fundamentalists predict the end of the world." [An observation by George M. Marsden, *Fundamentalism and American Culture* (New York: Oxford University Press, 2006), 231.]

"their desire to feel less inconsequential." [Adapted from A. J. Jacobs, *The Year of Living Biblically: One Man's Humble Quest to Follow the Bible as Literally as Possible* (New York: Simon and Schuster, 2007), 107.]

"I'm drawn to my church because it understands the ills of American society" [Hedges, *American Fascists*, 38.]

"liberal churches that find any form of theology acceptable" [Ibid., 37.]

"When Genesis says, 'In the beginning, God created the heavens and the earth' " [Adapted from Collins, *The Language of God*, 67.]

"molecular mechanisms and genetic pathways" [Ibid., 106.]

" 'theory' is not intended to convey uncertainty" [Ibid., 142.]

"when Galileo discovered the Earth revolved around the sun" [Ibid., 153–56.]

Chapter 28

"Martin Luther published a ferocious tirade" [Martin Luther, "On the Jews and Their Lies," in *Martin Luther's Basic Theological Writings*, ed. Timothy F. Lull and William R. Russell, 3rd ed. (Minneapolis: Augsburg Fortress Press, 2012), 497.]

"when Pilate asks the Jewish crowd if he should release Jesus or Barabbas." [Bart D. Ehrman, *Jesus Before the Gospels: How the Earliest*

Christians Remembered, Changed, and Invented Their Stories of the Savior (New York: HarperCollins, 2016), 171–73.]

Chapter 29

"The Yukon's bumper caught the woman's hip. The impact whirled her up onto the sidewalk." [Inspired from a similar deliberate hit-and-run in Mickey Spillane and Max Allan Collins, *Kiss Her Goodbye* (New York: Houghton Mifflin Harcourt Brace Publishing, 2011), 99–101.]

Chapter 32

"he was either a liar, a lunatic, or, indeed, the Lord." [C. S. Lewis, *Mere Christianity* (New York: HarperCollins, 2001), 52.]

"His case all hinged on one big assumption: that Jesus actually called himself God." [This insight adapted from Bart D. Ehrman, *Jesus, Interrupted: Revealing the Hidden Contradictions in the Bible* (New York: HarperCollins, 2009), 141.]

"I and the Father are one." [John 10:30.]

"Because that's what Jesus talks about a few chapters later" [John 17:22.]

"Jesus wasn't saying that he and God are of one essence. He was talking about agreement." [John 12:49–50, 14:10–11.]

"Do you know how many *other* explanations for suffering there are in the Bible?" [Seven reasons for suffering adapted from Ehrman, *God's Problem*. For sins: p. 39. For free will: p. 120. For redemptive: p. 131. For test of faith: 164–68. For forces opposed to God: p. 204. For a mystery: p. 188. For Ecclesiastes: p. 189].

Chapter 33

Waynesville's Baptist Fellowship Church is fictitious.

Chapter 34

"his hands in a 'fish-was-this-big' position." [Credit to A. J. Jacobs, *The Year of Living Biblically*, 74.]

Chapter 35

"You are already loved unconditionally, more than you understand." [This aspect of Florence Smith's experience was inspired by religious scholar Elaine Pagels, "Finding My Religion," *San Francisco Chronicle*, April 2, 2007, https://www.sfgate.com/cgi-bin/article.cgi?f=/g/a/2007/04/02/findrelig.DTL.]

"He chose to demonstrate how to face one's death with courage, trust, and faith." [Ibid. See Matthew 5:39.]

"I began to see images appear before me. Pictures of my life flashed in front of my eyes." [Religious components of Florence Smith's experience are fictional. Other aspects were adapted from near-death experiences described in Ring, *Lessons from the Light*, 146, 173, 296. Also Kenneth Ring, *Heading Toward Omega: In Search of the Meaning of the Near-Death Experience* (New York: William Morrow, 1985), 63.]

Chapter 36

" 'Young woman, dead—for a lousy purse. Makes you sick,' the sergeant said." [Adapted from a similar murder in Spillane and Collins, *Kiss Her Goodbye*, 35.]

Chapter 38

"A woman in the restroom referred to Republicans as her 'army of brave hearts' " [Adapted from Arlie Russell Hochschild, *Strangers in Their Own Land: Anger and Mourning on the American Right* (New York: New Press, 2016, a superb examination of our nation's political divide.]

"My grandparents emigrated from Poland to the Brownsville section of Brooklyn in the late 1930s." [The fictional Mandy Frankel's childhood background was adapted from Myrna Katz Frommer and Harvey Frommer, *Growing Up Jewish in America: An Oral History* (New York: Harcourt Brace & Company, 1995), 83, 108.]

"Growing up in the 1990s, I'd always heard about the Holocaust." [Ibid., 131–132, David Landau's account.]

"Thomas Jefferson's campaign to *separate* church and state." [See https://www.monticello.org/site/research-and-collections/jeffersons-religious-beliefs.]

"I felt a presence, and there, before me, were two beings." [The religious components of Mandy Frankel's near-death experience are fictional. Other aspects were adapted from near-death experiences described in Ring, *Lessons from the Light*, 29, 147–48, 156, 237. Also from P. M. H. Atwater, *The Big Book of Near-Death Experiences: The Ultimate Guide to What Happens When We Die* (Charlottesville: Hampton Roads Publishing, 2007), 261.]

Chapter 39

"God, no, messiah, yes. But what Jesus *meant* by 'messiah' was that he would be the king in God's kingdom on *earth*" [Bart D. Ehrman, *How Jesus Became God: The Exaltation of a Jewish Preacher from Galilee* (New York: HarperCollins, 2014), 118–22.]

"Jesus never said he was the future king in public" [For an excellent reconstruction of Judas's betrayal, see Bart D. Ehrman, *The Lost Gospel of Judas Iscariot: A New Look at Betrayer and Betrayed* (New York: Oxford University Press, 2006), 164–69.]

"I could complain about problems or confront them and grow." [Adapted from M. Scott Peck, *The Road Less Traveled: A New Psychology of Love, Traditional Values and Spiritual Growth* (New York: Touchstone, 1985), 16.]

"find a passion, a passion that contributes, that fills a need." ["Find a need and fill it" was a slogan of industrialist Henry Kaiser. This advice was cited in print in 1935: "Presbyterians Hold Review," *Evening World Herald* (Omaha), February 7, 1935, 10.]

"Act justly, love mercy, and walk humbly." [Micah 6:8.]

"if I learned I could rebound from failure, I might overcome my fear of defeat" [Inspired by Emily DeRuy, "UC Berkeley Wants Students to Know It's OK to Fail," *East Bay Times* (Walnut Creek, CA), August 20, 2017, sec. B.]

Chapter 40

"What would Muhammad do?" [Stephen Prothero, *God Is Not One: The Eight Rival Religions That Run the World* (New York: HarperOne, 2010), 38.]

"On my seventh birthday, he took me to Fentons on Piedmont Avenue." [For Victoria's memories of her father in this scene, the author drew inspiration from women writers remembering their fathers in Margaret McMullan, *Every Father's Daughter: Twenty-four Women Writers Remember Their Fathers* (Kingston, NY: McPherson & Company, 2015). For Mako Yoshikawa: p. 64. For Susan Perabo: p. 219–21.]

Chapter 41

"And I used to tell my congregation I was gonna drag every one of them over to the Way of the Lord." [The fictional Pastor Parks was inspired by an interview described in Berman, *The Search for Meaning*, 393.]

"When a woman *does* assume the role of teacher, she's hoodwinked by the devil." [Bart D. Ehrman, *The New Testament: A Historical Introduction to the Early Christian Writings*, 4th ed. (New York: Oxford University Press, 2008).]

"Motherhood! That's the noble callin' for women. And that's what I used to tell 'em." [From an interview in Berman, *The Search for Meaning*, 396.]

"I'm floating up on the ceiling looking down at them. And I can hear 'em. They're all in a panic." [Adapted from a near-death experience described in Ring, *Lessons from the Light*, 61.]

"A figure comes toward me with this powerful radiance" [Ibid., 37.]

"This luminous figure seems to communicate by thought." [Ibid., 16.]

Chapter 43

"I was familiar with speculations that Paul was epileptic, but how in the world would an old-school midwestern pastor conjure up that idea?" [Miner reflects on Paul's vision described in Acts 9:4, which bears close resemblance to the symptoms of a temporal lobe seizure. See D. Landsborough, "St. Paul and Temporal Lobe Epilepsy," *Journal of Neurology, Neurosurgery & Psychiatry* 50, no. 6 (June 1987): 659–64. Paul acknowledges he has an illness (2 Corinthians 12:7), which he describes as "a thorn in the flesh."]

"Your attitude denies you the opportunity of learning." [This aspect of the pastor's near-death experience was inspired by Gandhi, *Gandhi on Christianity*, 37.]

"Telling people there is no salvation for them" [Ibid., 40.]

"You must respect other religions the way you respect your own." [Ibid., 14.]

"All faiths are windows of the same great sanctuary." [Adapted from Berman, *The Search for Meaning*, 390.]

"Hinduism teaches the same great truth, and Islam and Judaism. . . . All great religions do." [Gandhi, *Gandhi on Christianity*, 12.]

"There are three tests" [Gandhi, *Gandhi on Christianity*, 66.]

"Only an ogre" [See John Shelby Spong, *Jesus for the Non-Religious* (New York: HarperCollins, 2007), 236, and John Shelby Spong, *Rescuing the Bible from Fundamentalism: A Bishop Rethinks the Meaning of Scripture* (New York: HarperCollins, 1991), 69.]

Chapter 51

"local police departments appreciated the FBI's resources" [James Botting, *Bullets, Bombs and Fast Talk: Twenty-five Years of FBI War Stories* (Washington, DC: Potomac Books, 2008), 89.]

Chapter 52

"I need you to wake all your guests except the occupant of 207. Have everyone come, as quietly as possible, here to your office before seven o'clock." [The Ebert's Lodge motel scene—the FBI's confrontation with Tim Lane, the gun battle, Lane's wound to the hand, and his escape—is based on a similar situation that occurred when the FBI confronted Bob

Mathews. I have heavily drawn on the description in: Kevin Flynn and Gary Gerhardt, *The Silent Brotherhood: The Chilling Inside Story of America's Violent Anti-government Militia Movement* (New York: Free Press, 1989), 341–45.]

Chapter 54

"It was a drug dealer that first got my attention about NDEs." [Based on a similar case described in an interview with Bruce Greyson in Lee Graves, "Altered States: Scientists Analyze the Near-Death Experience," *University of Virginia Magazine*, Summer 2007, http://uvamagazine.org/articles/altered_states.]

"The reality is most of the disciples were illiterate." [Acts 4:13 describes Peter and his companion John, also a fisherman, with a Greek word that literally means "unlettered"—that is, "illiterate."]

"If you ever wondered why, in Mark, men could *dig* through the roof of a house" [Mark 2:4.]

"Well, I have a good friend whose Chinese mom never could read or write in her own language" [Jerry Kong, personal correspondence with the author, 2018.]

"Not the wisest choice, because Second Peter describes events that occurred after Peter died." [A major portion of 2 Peter is from the book of Jude, written after Peter's death. See Ehrman, *The New Testament*, 465. See also Wikipedia, s.v. "Second Epistle of Peter," last modified August 23, 2018, https://en.wikipedia.org/wiki/ Second_Epistle_of_Peter.]

"So, if Peter didn't write it, why would someone else use his name?" [A definitive book on this subject is Bart D. Ehrman, *Forged: Writing in the Name of God—Why the Bible's Authors Are Not Who We Think They Are* (New York: HarperOne, 2011).]

Chapter 55

" 'The author of John doesn't say *how* people get to God through Jesus,' I said." [Adapted from Rob Bell, *Love Wins: A Book About Heaven, Hell, and the Fate of Every Person Who Ever Lived* (New York: HarperOne, 2011), 154–55.]

"I think the early church fathers were of goodwill." [Adapted from a Milton Friedman comment about the effects of power in government in "Milton Friedman's Critique of JFK's 'Ask Not What Your Country Can Do for You—Ask What You Can Do for Your Country," *Christian Perspectives & Free Market Economics*, December 25, 2012, https://churchlayman.wordpress.com/2012/12/25/milton-friedmanscritique-of-jfks-ask-not-what-your-country-can-do-for-you-ask-what-you-can-do-for-your-country/.]

"but I believe there's more misunderstanding in the world than there is evil." [Adapted from Berman, *The Search for Meaning*, 279.]

"Many young people have diminished respect for their parents, teachers, and community . . ." [Adapted from Sacks, *Not in God's Name*, 256.]

Chapter 57

"The first geologists were clergy back in the seventeenth century." [Bill's conversation with Professor Antle draws on hypotheses presented in David R. Montgomery, *The Rocks Don't Lie: A Geologist Investigates Noah's Flood* (New York: Simon & Schuster, 2012), xiii, 150, 218–20, and William Ryan and Walter Pitman, *Noah's Flood: The New Scientific Discoveries about the Event That Changed the Earth* (New York: Simon & Schuster, 1998).]

"Exodus itself says a strong east wind blew all that night." [Exodus 14:21.]

" 'Sea of Reeds' became 'the Red Sea' in one of the most notorious mistranslations in history" [Antle's explanation is adapted from Colin J. Humphreys, *The Miracles of Exodus: A Scientist's Discovery and the Extraordinary Natural Causes of the Biblical Stories* (New York: HarperCollins Publishers, 2003), 186–87, 244–60.]

Chapter 58

"How about the man sentenced to death row based on the testimonies of five eyewitnesses" [Bill Miner is referring to Kirk Bloodsworth, sentenced to life imprisonment and subsequently exonerated by DNA. See Wikipedia, s.v. "Kirk Bloodsworth," last modified September 9, 2018, https://en.wikipedia.org/wiki/Kirk_Bloodsworth.]

"Stanton's elegy at the foot of Lincoln's deathbed" [For an in-depth discussion, see Adam Gopnik, "Angels and Ages," *New Yorker*, May 28, 2007.]

"Maybe what Jesus actually said was 'Blessed are the pizza makers.' " [Referring to Matthew 5:9. Inspired by the line "Blessed are the cheese makers" from *Monty Python's Life of Brian*, directed by Terry Jones, written by Graham Chapman et al. (1979).]

"He always had to be lifted to his feet by others because of his leg braces." [*The Roosevelts: An Intimate History*, directed by Ken Burns, premiered September 14, 2014, on PBS, http://www.pbs.org/kenburns/the-roosevelts/.]

"The reason I believe Paul didn't write First Timothy or Second Timothy is because the vocabulary is very different from his." [See Ehrman, *The New Testament*, 396–97.]

"in an NPR kind of way" [Quip from *Elementary*, Season 1, episode 23, "The Woman," written by Robert Doherty, aired May 16, 2013, on CBS.]

"Paul tells people they shouldn't get married—they should stay single like he is." [1 Corinthians 7:28.]

"But the author of First and Second Timothy says the opposite. He tells church leaders go ahead, get married!" [1 Timothy 5:14.]

"First Timothy says women will be saved by bearing children, by *motherhood*." [1 Timothy 2:15.]

"And women are not to teach men" [1 Timothy 2:12.]

"the Bible tells us that *all* Scripture is inspired by God." [Victoria is referring to 2 Timothy 3:16.]

"You're referring to those little gems in First Corinthians?" [1 Corinthians 14:34].

"How can Paul say women cannot speak in church when three chapters earlier he says they *can*?" [1 Corinthians 11:4–6. See Ehrman, *Forged*, (New York: Oxford University Press, 2011), 93–103. Also see Gregory A. Boyd and Paul R. Eddy, *Across the Spectrum: Understanding Issues in Evangelical Theology*, 2nd ed. (Grand Rapids: Baker Academic, 2009), 256.]

"She was a trusted, perhaps beloved, disciple." [Adapted from Rev. Kathleen C. Rolenz, "Was Jesus Married?" (sermon, West Shore Unitarian Universalist Church, Rocky River, OH, April 4, 2004), http://www.wsuuc.org/documents/sermons/04archives/SER%20Was%20Jesus%20Married.htm. In the noncanonical Gospel of Mary, Mary Magdalene is known as the savior's beloved, possessing knowledge and teachings that are superior to those of the other disciples.]

"Are we talking about the same person? The infamous repentant sinner who washed Jesus's feet with her tears?" [Luke 7:37–50.]

"There is no biblical evidence whatsoever that Mary Magdalene was any kind of public sinner, let alone a harlot." [Adapted from Heidi Schlumpf, "Who Framed Mary Magdalene?" *U.S. Catholic*, April 2000, 12–16. In the Gospel of Mary, Peter admits to Mary that he knows Jesus loved her more. Later, Peter complains to the other disciples that Jesus spoke with a woman without their knowledge: "Are we to turn about and listen to her?" For the text of the Gospel of Mary, see: http://www.maryofmagdala.com/GMary_Text/gmary_text.html.]

"Men began quitting their *jobs*!" [2 Thessalonians 3:6–15.]

"They had no problem mentioning his other relatives: his parents, his brothers, his sisters." [Adapted from Ehrman, *The New Testament*, 271.]

Chapter 60

"There are other aspects of the letter that point to Priscilla." [Bill bases his hunch on the research of Ruth Hoppin, *Priscilla's Letter: Finding the Author of the Epistle to the Hebrews* (Fort Bragg, CA: Lost Coast Press, 2009) and the research of Adolf von Harnack, "Probability about the Address and Author of the Epistle to the Hebrews," in Lee Anna Starr, *The Bible Status of Woman* (Zarephath, NJ: Pillar of Fire, 1955), 392–415. For examples of nuances about childhood and parental disciple, see Hebrews 5:13, 12:7–11. For an example of "we" to "I" and back, see Hebrews 13:18–19.]

Chapter 64

The Church of Sacred Resurrection is fictitious.

Chapter 70

"But I appreciate that if you're worried you won't make it home safe to your spouse and kids, it's hard to give a damn if you offend some cornered, armed suspect." [Adapted from an article by Jamil Zaki, "When Cops Choose Empathy," *New Yorker*, September 25, 2015, http://www.newyorker.com/tech/elements/when-cops-choose-empathy.]

"The paradox of power." [Descriptions are adapted from the FBI hostage negotiation strategy described by Gary Noesner, *Stalling for Time: My Life as an FBI Hostage Negotiator* (New York: Random House, 2010), 154, and, Botting, *Bullets, Bombs and Fast Talk*, 41.]

Chapter 71

"Robinson struggled with the controls. 'Secure that failed engine!' " [These scenes draw heavily from the vivid descriptions of a crippled McDonnell Douglas DC-10 jumbo jet in the excellent book: Laurence Gonzales, *Flight 232: A Story of Disaster and Survival* (New York: W.W. Norton, 2014), 8–10.]

Chapter 72

"C-130 Hercules, call sign H715 . . . lost an engine . . . having a hard time controlling the aircraft right now . . ." [Pilot and air traffic controller dialogue is adapted from Ibid., 17–23, and the author's conversations with airline pilots.]

Chapter 76

"a fatigue crack from an undetected metallurgical defect" [Adapted from the cause of the crash of United 232. Igor Korovin, ed., *Air Crash Investigations: Drama in Sioux City; The Crash of United Airlines Flight 232* (Lulu.com, 2011), 160. A complete loss of hydraulic flight-control systems also occurred in 2003 in Iraq when an Airbus A300 cargo plane was struck on the left wing tip by a surface-to-air missile. The crew successfully landed the crippled aircraft using differential engine thrust. See Wikipedia, s.v., "2003 Baghdad DHL attempted shootdown incident," last modified September 20, 2018, https://en.wikipedia.org/wiki/2003_Baghdad_DHL_attempted_shootdown_incident.]

Chapter 79

"All eyes were on the living room window. The curtains closed and opened once." [The signals and communication methods were adapted from the account of the FBI standoff with Robert Mathews in Flynn and Gerhardt, *The Silent Brotherhood*, 377.]

" 'People who are cornered often fall into a kind of paralysis,' he said" [Noesner, *Stalling for Time*, 170.]

"It's right there in the Bible. Jesus changed his message. Remember, Tim? He initially warned of an imminent apocalypse" [Ehrman, *Jesus Before the Gospels*, 208–210].

Chapter 80

"He's referring to the book of Joshua" [Joshua 11:19–20.]

Chapter 81

" 'There's not much line left on the reel,' Jordan said." [Paraphrased from a line in Caldwell, *The Fifth Gospel*, 30.]

"as if forgiveness was the best way to stick it to your enemies" [Inspired by commentary on Shakespeare's *The Tempest* by the Shmoop Editorial Team: "The Tempest Compassion and Forgiveness Quotes," Shmoop, last modified November 11, 2008, http://www.shmoop.com/tempest/compassion-forgiveness-quotes-3.html.]

Chapter 83

"Kitzmiller v. Dover Area School District trial had attracted national attention." [Tim Lane is a fictitious school board member. The case was real. Complete trial documents for the *Kitzmiller, et al. v. Dover Area School*

District federal court case can be found at http://www.talkorigins.org/faqs/dover/kitzmiller_v_dover.html. PBS produced a two-hour feature on the case: *Nova*, "Intelligent Design on Trial," directed by Gary Johnstone and Joseph McMaster, written by Joseph McMaster, aired November 13, 2007, on PBS, http://www.pbs.org/wgbh/nova/evolution/intelligent-design-trial.html.]

"Our church teaches us to recognize God's voice." [For an excellent understanding of the evangelical relationship with God, see Luhrmann, *When God Talks Back*].

Chapter 86

[Janie Hughes's surgery and resulting near-death experience were inspired by the case of Pam Reynolds, documented in: Michael Sabom, *Light and Death* (Grand Rapids: Zondervan Publishing House, 1998), 37–47.

"Some were headed in the same direction I went. Others traveled the opposite way." [From a near-death account described in Pim van Lommel, *Consciousness Beyond Life: The Science of Near-Death Experience* (New York: HarperOne, 2010), 28.]

"And I thought, *Oh! . . . I'm breathing God's air.*" [Paraphrased from a documentary on the near-death experience of Pam Reynolds: *The Day I Died* (BBC, 2002), http://youtube.com/watch?v=WNbdUEqDB-k.]

"My life was projected before me on a vast canvas." [Adapted from a near-death experience described in Ring, *Lessons from the Light*, 165].

"Never once did the light condemn me. Instead, it helped me understand what I'd learned in life, assessed my strengths and weaknesses." [Adapted from a near-death experience described in ibid.]

"Before you were Janie Hughes, you were Kathy Christen" [This case of reincarnation was inspired by Ian Stevenson's report of a Walter Wilson from British Columbia who suffered a shotgun wound to the hand. He died from his wound because timely medical care was not available. See Ian Stevenson, *Where Reincarnation and Biology Intersect* (Westport, CT: Praeger Publishers, 1997), 45.]

"It said, 'You *are* a soul. You *have* a body.'" [This quote is often attributed to C. S. Lewis, but the exact phrasing can be found in multiple earlier sources, including from George MacDonald and Walter M. Miller. "Never tell a child you have a soul," George Macdonald wrote. "Teach him, you are a soul; you have a body." And earlier, in 1881, Rev. Dr. R. Thornton wrote: "We should have taught more carefully than we have done, not that men are bodies and have souls, but that they are souls and have bodies."]

"I'd already gotten a powerful sense that ordinary time boundaries didn't exist there" [Adapted from a near-death experience described in Ring, *Lessons from the Light*, 151.]

Chapter 89

"It's not just India, by the way. I've found cases all over the world." [Edward F. Kelly et. al., *Irreducible Mind: Toward a Psychology for the 21st Century* (Lanham, MD: Rowman & Littlefield, 2007), 233.]

"If someone talks about a previous life, it's nearly always as a young child." [Stevenson, *Where Reincarnation and Biology Intersect*, 5–6.]

"the number of people who have ever lived on earth to be more than you think: one hundred eight billion." ["How Many People Have Ever Lived on Earth?" Population Reference Bureau, last modified March 9, 2018, http://www.prb.org/Publications/Articles/2002/HowManyPeopleHaveEverLivedonEarth.aspx. Also see "The Birth of Religion," *National Geographic*, June 2011, 33.]

"Researchers at the University of Virginia have gathered far more." [Felix Kingsley is fictitious. However, the work he describes is real and is based on the research currently being conducted at the University of Virginia's Division of Perceptual Studies. See Jim B. Tucker, *Life Before Life*, with a forward by Ian Stevenson (New York: St. Martin's Griffin, 2005). Also see Ian Stevenson, *Twenty Cases Suggestive of Reincarnation*, 2nd ed. (Charlottesville: University of Virginia Press, 1974).]

Chapter 90

"You are not punished. You are *shown*." [Ring, *Lessons from the Light*, 164.]

"When he came into the light, he received much stricter treatment." [Adapted from Michael Newton, *Journey of Souls: Case Studies of Life between Lives*, 5th rev. ed. (Woodbury, MN: Llewellyn Publications, 2008), 50.]

"The church has emphasized judgment in the past, but it too is evolving" [Joshua J. McElwee, "Francis Explains 'Who Am I to Judge?' " *National Catholic Reporter*, January 10, 2016, https://www.ncronline.org/news/vatican/francis-explains-who-am-i-judge and Elisabetta Povoledo and Laurie Goodstein, "Pope Francis Declares Death Penalty Unacceptable in All Cases," *New York Times*, August 2, 2018, https://www.nytimes.com/2018/08/02/world/europe/pope-death-penalty.html.]

"It was as if a lightning bolt had been hurled directly to the inside of my brain." [Adapted from Sanford Meisner and Dennis Longwell,

Sanford Meisner on Acting, Introduction by Sydney Pollack. (New York: Random House, 1987), xiv.]

Chapter 94
"God isn't that needy." [Spong, *Jesus for the Non-Religious*, 269.]
Chapter 96
"Religion is at its worst" [I have drawn heavily from the superb works of Sacks, *Not in God's Name*, 234, and Hedges, *American Fascists*, 26, 34-36, 57, 87.]
"there is solid evidence for belief in reincarnation." [Tom Shroder, *Old Souls: Compelling Evidence from Children Who Remember Past Lives* (New York: Simon & Schuster, 1999), 33.]

Front Cover
"The timeless tale…" The style of this tagline was inspired by a tagline of the film: *The African Queen.* Directed by John Huston. Produced by Sam Spiegel. Los Angeles: United Artists, 1951.

ABOUT THE AUTHOR

BORN AND RAISED IN MISSOURI, I've lived most of my life in Northern California with my wife of fifty-five years. My educational background in math and computer science enabled a career in clinical systems software development at Kaiser Permanente.

While many parents worry about their wayward children, my wife and I have experienced the opposite: a grown son who worries because his parents don't share the same religious beliefs.

My response took me on a spiritual journey to understand both myself and our son – I wrote this novel.

This was my first book. I spent five years in research, then another five years in writing, an endeavor that would not have been possible without a devoted wife and the inspiration of a loving son and daughter. I've had the time of my life, and a new perspective.

Made in the USA
San Bernardino, CA
05 December 2019